The Horses of Instruction is an extraordinary novel about life on a university faculty. The unique thing about Mr. Adams' novel is that it is both an "in" novel and an "out" novel. It is "in" because no one who has ever worked as a member of a university faculty can fail to find counterparts to his own experience—counterparts that arouse ribald laughter and releasing indignation. But it is also "out" in the sense that there is nothing that happens in it that will puzzle someone who has never lived faculty life. It makes it abundantly clear that the same drives for power, the same emotional and sexual entanglements, pertain to gown as to town.

The setting is Walton University, which has in Henry Hastings "the Fastest Dean in

Hazard Adams was born in Cleveland, Ohio, received his B.A. from Princeton University and his M.A. and Ph.D. degrees from the University of Washington. He has been a college teacher since he left the U.S. Marine Corps in 1951, and is at present Professor and Chairman of the Department of English at the University of California, Irvine. Mr. Adams has published several books, most recently *Fiction as Process* and *Poetry: An Introductory Anthology*. This is his first novel. He lives with his wife and children in Newport Beach, California.

The
Horses
of
Instruction

Hazard Adams

The
Horses
of
Instruction

HARCOURT, BRACE

& WORLD, INC.

NEW YORK

for

Mary and Jim

for

Fred

"We'll tak a cup o' kindness yet"

Contents

My master, after some expressions of great indignation, wondered how we dared to venture upon a Houyhnhnm's back, for he was sure that the weakest servant in his house would be able to shake off the strongest Yahoo, or by lying down and rolling on his back squeeze the brute to death. I answered that our horses were trained up from three or four years old to the several uses we intended them for; that if any of them proved intolerably vicious, they were employed for carriages; that they were severely beaten while they were young, for any mischievous tricks; that the males, designed for common riding or draught, were generally castrated about two years after their birth, to take down their spirits, and make them more tame and gentle; that they were indeed sensible of rewards and punishments; but his Honour would please to consider, that they had not the least tincture of reason any more than the Yahoos in this country.

—SWIFT

The tygers of wrath are wiser than the horses of instruction.

—BLAKE

► 1

*"Come
join
the
band"*

With Jack Emory

WHY HE DID IT   For years and with a choice of season utterly outrageous to the sensibility—December 27, 28, and 29 to be exact—The Modern Language Association of America has held its convention in Chicago or New York. On any of these three days the casual visitor to the Palmer House or the Statler Hilton will find himself caught up in vast throngs of college professors displaying name tags from Sul Ross State, UCLA, Alaska Methodist, Tulsa, Texas, Bowdoin, and practically any other college across the country that one would care to name. They come in vast migrations by air, bus, train, and car. They are Czechs, Croats, Danes, nineteenth-century specialists, linguists, phonologists, philologists, teaching nuns, critics (bearded and otherwise), Shakespeareans, Miltonists, bibliographers, and experts on everything from prose style to printers' errors. In common they profess the modern languages and literatures in American universities.

They come to read scholarly papers before large lackadaisical audiences, to sit in those audiences, to confer with peers on recondite subjects, to see, to be seen, to wander through the exhibits of textbooks, to freeload whiskey at publishers' parties, to get out on the big city,

perhaps to escape their wives, to live it up with old gradu-
ate-school buddies and colleagues from years past; but
most of all to seek new employees for their respective departments or to land jobs from the seekers. It is, finally,
not a meeting of minds but of slave traders, of academic
politicians, of men and women who have made a profession of professing and who would not, incidentally, be
caught dead among the Rotarians, the Kiwanians, the
Elks, or the Legionnaires.

To the academic who somewhere along in his career
has discovered in himself a penchant for wheeling and
dealing and cannot suppress it, the convention offers
shining opportunities. His floor of the Palmer House be-
comes a corridor of power. In the tumult and crush—for
the convention draws more than ten thousand souls—he
may, like anyone else, be annoyed trying to get down to
the lobby by elevator; but it will be worth it if, once there,
he is constantly accosted by old friends, scholars who
know him by repute, and young Ph.D.'s seeking an audience with his chairman, who is no doubt interviewing in a
room somewhere above.

December 27th of 1955 was generally no different
from those that have since come and gone; but for one
young man, four years into his profession, a reasonably
obscure instructor in English at Middleton University, it
was a first convention. His name was Jack Emory. He
was thirty, pushing six feet, slim, and B.A. Princeton.
The Ph.D., well, it was not Princeton; or Yale, or Harvard, for that matter. It was a West Coast degree: Washington. He was in Chicago, anyone would suppose, because he was energetic, on the rise, and perhaps ready to
be plucked from the ivy at a better salary. He was in Chicago, perhaps, to mingle, to assess his own position in the
profession, to see who might offer him a job.

The truth was really a lot harder to get at. Emory had
not actually spent a lot of time thinking about "getting

ahead" or securing position. He had been too thankful
for and surprised at his luck in landing the Middleton job
in a bad year. Since he had come there four years before,
however, Middleton hadn't actively ingratiated itself with
him. Recently he had allowed the suspicion to grow that
in those greatly revered and ivied halls reality was
dimmed. He had never felt at home there. When he decided to forgo a pleasant, nearly snowbound holiday in
Middleton for sleeting Chicago, he had tacitly acknowledged some uneasiness about his professional life—uneasiness that had been intensified by recent events.

But he had foreseen no drastic act on his part; he had
wished only to test the world a bit, skeptical of his own
feelings. Acceptance of the interview with the Dean of
Arts and Sciences at Walton followed out of a sort of disinterested curiosity. He had heard, of course, of Walton
in the way one hears of Kansas or Nebraska or Colorado,
but not of its Dean. It was a growing mid-American institution in that area where the flat lands begin to slope up
toward the Rockies. It had built up a certain notoriety for
seeking out the papers and libraries of almost anyone involved in modern letters. Indiscriminately it had landed
some interesting research materials; but the University itself was not well known for the excellence of its faculty.
There had been troubles in the past—something about
speakers on the campus or loyalty oaths or legislative in-
vestigators. Faculty members had resigned. There had
been action by the AAUP. But that was some years ago.
Now, as enlightened 1955 ebbed out, all was apparently
quiet.

For a day at the convention, Jack Emory had wandered aimlessly through the exhibits, mainly to glance
furtively and with secret pride at the display of which his
own new book was a part. A study of the poets of the
nineties, it represented the salvageable matter from what
he now saw was a verbose, huge, disorganized doctoral

dissertation. Out of idle curiosity on the first evening he had attended a meeting or two. He had heard the distinguished medieval scholar Kemp Malone speak on "Chaucer's Double Consonants and the Final *e*," sticking it out mainly because he had studied under a man who was always mentioning Kemp Malone. The lady professor from Vassar who followed with a fifteen-minute talk about some aspect of Chaucer sent him, however, in flight to another room. There Northrop Frye, definitely an *in* figure, was discoursing on *Finnegans Wake*. Following this, his head full of quests and cycles, of mythic patterns and archetypes, and it being about 11:30, he went to bed, only to dream a conversation with William Blake on the subject of Charles II.

The telephone rang at 8:00 in the morning, dragging him up from a vision of his own head as a hollow planet which turned itself inside out without breaking its shell. His mind had momentarily contained the world, but not the man on the phone, who said through the fog of his awakening, "Hello, this Emory? Hastings, Dean at Walton, here. Heard you're attending. We've admired your work. Now, say, how'd you like to drop down this morning to talk?"

Emory's answer was brief: "Well, Mr. ah . . ."

"Look here now, the point is we want you to come visit with us in term time, study the collections, maybe speak to our graduate students on the nineties. Ten-thirty all right? I'm in 1004."

No more than that.

Dean Hastings' accent was a strange mixture of professional precision and midland nose. He spoke rapidly in a clipped way and gave the impression of doing something else of great importance while he was talking. The inevitable vision was that of a man at the head of a shiny table holding an executive meeting of the board with a phone at his ear.

After a leisurely breakfast and accurate allowance for time to get up to the tenth floor in the press of the convention crowd, Emory presented himself at 1004. The door was ajar. Inside, Dean Hastings and three elderly professors were interviewing a young man. The candidate was asserting in a somewhat high-pitched, querulous voice that in his present job there was no time for research. He wanted to work in a place that gave him the opportunity to exploit his special talents. He was first of all a *research scholar*. The candidate was probably talking himself out of a job.

At his knock Emory could see a man he presumed to be Hastings spring up and advance with hand outstretched—a small, thin, wiry man of perhaps forty-five with a mane of carefully combed silver hair, prematurely turned. He was dressed in a light-gray flannel suit; his shirt collar had a collar bar, his striped quiet tie a pin. He wore black-horn-rimmed glasses. His face was not deeply lined, his complexion fair. There was a vague air of the effete about him. He apologized that the interview was still going on, they had expected to run them through every twenty minutes, but things had bogged down a bit, that boy in there just wouldn't shut his mouth. He smiled a curious set grin. He took off his glasses, dangled them from his fingers, twirled them. Instead of ushering Emory into the room, he suddenly took his elbow and propelled him rapidly down the hall to a long divan facing the elevators.

"Now son," he began as they seated themselves (while masses of people were entering and exiting from the cars), "what strikes me about you is your interdisciplinary interests and your work on modern poetry." Emory wondered from where his information came; Hastings was treating him as an applicant. "You may know of us at Walton. Well, we're advancing on the departments, trying to get across them. And we've just firmed up mod-

7

ern poetry for the library; we mean to have the best darned collection of manuscripts in the country in that field. Maybe in the world. We have the money to do it, and I mean to see it's done." He glared—smugly, firmly, or both—glasses on, and followed himself with various brief descriptions of certain collections. Thomas, Millay, Stevens, Williams, Auden, Binyon, Wylie, Hodgson—the names flowed indiscriminately on. "Well now, we're anxious for you to visit us as a consultant and maybe give us a talk about Auden or someone. He's coming to lecture us next year, incidentally."

There was no time for reply, only to shift one's legs, one's arms, one's seat. Hastings moved rapidly on from poetry to plans. There was a series of visiting poets coming up, a new honors program; he mentioned the young men who were already "signed up and delivered" to Walton for next fall, a new "corps of intelligence." Though talking as if he were conducting an interview, the Dean managed to say nothing at all about a job.

"You think it over and come on down and see if you like us. We'll make it worth your while. Five hundred all right?"

"Yeah, well, yes. Why, ah, yes, I'd be glad to, to . . ." The answer trailed off and was enveloped in additional effusions by the Dean.

It was a spiel, not an interview—with the substance of a carnival barker's, but transposed into an odd key, the persona being all wrong, for one thing. Emory realized he had not made adequate rejoinder.

The Dean stood up. A frown came quickly upon his face and was gone. He adjusted his glasses with one hand, waving vaguely with the other. He turned away, turned back, contrived a set grin.

"Now look here, Mr. ah, Emory, there's a good job in this for you! You understand that of course!" Clapping Emory on the back, he hurried off to his room. Over his shoulder he called, "We'll be in touch." It was a classy performance in its own terms. Emory thought of minor-league shortstops. He was intrigued. He had a failing for minor-league shortstops.

Had he by some mystical osmosis of the surrounding convention found pleasure in such politics? Or had it been in him all along? Was this the "reality" of the profession, in contrast to the settled smugness of his Middleton life? Curiously though, almost a month before—it was a windy northeastern November day and he could remember watching from his attic office in MacIntyre Hall the clouds gather for winter and rain in the offing—he had raved inside at Middleton politics. There he stood that day, vassal to all he surveyed, four years an instructor, and barely a raise to—what was it?—$3,900. And all the prestige you could inhale from the place. Well, it was a bad time to consider anything. The morning's second class of freshman English composition was behind him. He knew it had not been a success, even if the students didn't. In the hall after class an associate professor who had once belonged, on the strength of two vitriolic articles, to a renowned school of criticism, offered him a curt nod complete with lip-curled smile and passed swiftly on. For the critic it was a show of good nature. Had the department's recent munificence caused the critic to crack his face? On the strength of his new book and good behavior he would, next fall, become an assistant professor with a three-year contract, possibly renewable. The critic, a small dapper man with the expression of a crow, had not deigned to nod in the previous three years.

Sitting at his desk, he thought of lunch, and he expected Dave Eriksen, who shared the office, along soon. They would get out their brown bags and thermos bottles and, as Dave liked to say, put their feet up. He thought that in the meantime he might as well do the chores: he emptied the mouse in the wastebasket out the window onto the sloping roof. Every day a mouse investigated what was left in the paper bags from the day before. Every day a mouse trapped itself in the wastebasket. He often wondered whether it was the same one, falling each day from the window, scrambling back by who knows what secret ways only to trap itself again. First one in emptied the mouse.

Dave was a little late. Then suddenly it flashed that this was Dave's day without classes. He'd be at home working at his carpentry, polishing his car, or playing his piano right now, taking a break from the stack of papers he would have to return to later. During the lunch hour they often discussed their freshman classes. Sometimes they exchanged classroom anecdotes. ("Mr. Eriksen, I just don't understand this *case* business." "Mr. Jones, *you* are a case.") Sometimes they theorized. It was a perpetual subject. Older teachers would try not to think about freshman comp, would no longer have to teach it, or had simply decided it couldn't be done.

And so he was alone. There was little to prevent him from considering the next pedagogical problem, his next class, the afternoon creative writing group, which in September he had been asked to take on at the last minute. Despite his inexperience, he liked teaching it, but he faced each meeting with doubts and occasional annoyances. What should be done about Doris Weinstock, who could not bring her story—something about a murder, alas—to a satisfactory conclusion? What about Ruth Willow, who was bright enough but just had, as she said, "a block," and hadn't done anything except a few short sketches? Much as he detested the old student line about "blocks," he felt she might be brought along. This time he really did believe her pitiful and outrageous excuse for a word harbored some remote but definable problem. Then there were a couple of kids he had to lead by the hand up to short stories, they were so afraid of them, and finally there were the barbarians from journalism who wanted only to know how to get published in *True*. Their faces lurked, their necks craned always in the corner of his eye. "The giraffe by heck is principally neck." He remembered fondly the man who, years ago, coined such phrases for him and other children—parts of long bestiaries he had written. He smiled at himself glaring at those journalistic giraffes.

He sat facing his soup-brown, two-tone walls with the dark stripe running shoulder-high around them and the wretched nail holes where years before hunks of plaster had been gouged out. The walls had probably once been graced by brown photographs of Hadrian's Tomb and the Roman Forum. In some way he was pleased with the awfulness of it. He thought: We deal in aesthetic questions and live in this half our waking lives. He was either gleeful or disconsolate: he wanted to push the critic's face in, cram the *Writer's Guide* down some agriculture student's throat, and talk jazz or baseball with Dave. It was just one of those days his dissertation director should have warned him about.

Then at the half-open door appeared Doris Weinstock. She was a short, dark-haired, pale girl with a big bosom, nervous as a bird. Against her white blouse she held a large Manila folder. Her hair was carefully done, her lips carefully made up into an immaculate pout, and she wore a tight black skirt. But she did not cross the threshold, and she would not speak. Startled for a moment at her immobility, he merely stared. At this, her eyes, which had been fixed on him like some expectant but not giraffe-like wordless animal, turned away and down to the floor.

"Come in, Miss Weinstock. I'm eating my lunch. Do you want to see me now?" He would give her the chance to retire gracefully after making a later appointment. But obviously her courage had gathered itself together, foaming and rushing. She was going to come in on its crest if she could.

"Yes, Mr. Emory, I mean, you see it's about my story. I've finished it, and I wanted to turn it in."

Poor bird, he thought, she has been frightened of me.

"You can turn it in at class time if you wish."

"I know that, sir, but you see, I wanted to, I mean I thought I'd explain what I've done. I'd like to know what you think."

He could see she was not to be denied. Neither would she enter until he told her to. So he gave her words and, grateful, she came to his desk. He asked her to sit down please. She sat on a chair edge, legs together, hands clasped in her lap.

"You see, Mr. Emory, Dr. Emory, I've finished it, but I want to apologize for it. I had to murder you."

"Murder me?"

"Yes, I sort of put you in it." Now she seemed composed, even bold. But he began to think he had suddenly been thawed from an eon's sleep.

"You're sort of in it, and I have you—him—murdered. I thought I should explain it. The girl who does it is mad—no, angry, because the other girls come to his classes because they like him, and they don't add anything and waste his time; but he pays attention to them anyway, so she kills him. I mean it's a lot more complicated than that. I guess, well, she *is* mad. It's all psychological."

"Well, are you the murderer?" He laughed, or tried to, but there was something sad about the whole business.

"Oh no, I'm the central consciousness, or someone like me—a bit. She, well, she finds the body. I mean like—well, she solves the crime, but it's not really a mystery story. I mean I just didn't want you to get the wrong idea. I mean I didn't do it. I—she—finds you after it's all over.

Of course, I guess, you isn't really you. It's her you—or him."

"Well, thanks." He didn't hit quite the right tone—too ironic perhaps. But he smiled and she flickered.

"Yes—well, here it is, and, and I hope you can come to the house for the poetry reading." She brushed some hair back from her forehead. He could smell expensive perfume.

"Oh yes, that's your house, is it? Yes, I'm coming."

"I suggested you. I hope you'll read some Thomas. Maybe you'll have read the story by then."

"Maybe. When do you plan to do the job? After the reading? No sooner, I hope." At that she smiled fully for the first time, but she couldn't look him in the eye, and her mouth quivered a bit.

Then, "Oh no, sir." She tried mustering a smile, then flew from the room.

"Good God," he said out loud to himself. Well, now that it was over—ridiculous as it had been—perhaps they could get to her writing next time.

He had somehow entered a different world. He was well aware of the disdain for creative writing of that respectable professor on the ground floor who without doubt had labored industriously for his doctorate, learned the requisite languages, published in *PMLA* once or twice, took the romantic view of art, and consistently opposed the promotion of the creative writing people. It was easy to imagine him snorting in his office at the parade of bearded poets and gloomy, stringy-haired coeds, at the potential sweet singers of New York, and the hopeless sonneteers trooping in ragged order by his door toward their conferences. He would surely hold that the horrible moments with Miss Weinstock and those still to come were totally wasted, indeed not to be tolerated. Well, one had to admit that the simple odds did not seem

very favorable. There was too much fishing. Who was to
know for sure whether or not in the awful confusions of
Doris Weinstock there might be the embryo of a few
pages of decent prose, this year or next, or if not that
(and it would be enough) some understanding of what
writing was all about?

He cursed to himself, not a curse of disgust, but just a
good old soul-clearing oath. Should he read the story
now? How had she done him in? A crime of passion? He
hoped not. No, he would get at it in the evening after a
couple of beers.

At that moment his colleague Assistant Professor of
English Sherwood P. Morrow sauntered by, craning neck
in, passed the door, returned, entered, and flopped on a
chair.

"So you have *that* one, too? One of your creative
types, I suppose. Gawd, you must have to put up with a
lot of guff from those people. Now *that* one is in my Victorian Poets, when she comes, but I haven't taught her a
thing. She and her pals are about as arrogant a crowd as
I've had. I ask them a straightforward question about
Hardy and they sling around the texture-gesture garbage,
think they know enough to decide they do or don't like
him."

Emory didn't answer. Why hadn't Doris Weinstock
murdered Sherwood Morrow? O psychology, O patience!

But when he did read the story that evening it was only
about half bad. How much was consciously analytical he
couldn't tell. The girl certainly had astonishing perception of her classmates. But, alas, he found himself—or
whoever it was—depicted in a cloud of abstraction, and
the plot, well, it didn't wholly escape silliness. The tone
was all wrong. He wondered whether all that infatuation
could be safely converted into some intellectual advance.
The girl was improving, but she walked a tightrope all the
time. She would doubtless cut the next class, and he'd

probably have to call her up to get her to come in and discuss the story. Then he thought of Sherwood P. Morrow and the old professor on the ground floor. He'd had those two beers and stretched it a bit for a third, and decided to see how things were on the outside, if there was an outside. So he sacrificed part of the Christmas recess. Besides, he felt like finding out what Morrow would say if someone, even from the provinces, offered him a job.

Well, jobs for 1956 were not exactly hanging on trees. After Dean Hastings, the convention merely lumbered to anticlimax. Later in the same day he met a nice man from somewhere in Kentucky who really did offer him a job but ended up advising him to stay where he was. He saw a few friends from grad-school days, to one of whom he casually mentioned Walton University and a dean named Hastings. A curious, possibly ironic smile crossed the friend's face, but there were no accompanying words.

Another day and the convention was over. The publishers packed up their displays and stole off, the elevators stopped again at every floor when called upon, and Jack Emory boarded the train back east to Middleton. In the club car with a bourbon was his own chairman, who allowed he had seen his friend and former colleague Hank Hastings, a fine fellow in the old days; and he knew, with the sort of leer that develops with minor bureaucratic power, that Hastings was recruiting bright young men. So now Emory knew how it had come about. He wondered why Hastings had not mentioned his source.

But back at Middleton weeks passed, and nothing came from Walton University. Perhaps it had been only talk. Did Dean Hastings really remember him? It was embarrassing to be asked periodically by one's chairman just how nonexistent negotiations were proceeding, how he felt about his "offer." After all, he knew next to nothing about Walton and had his own reservations about the novel approach of its Dean.

By late February he willed that he should forget the whole matter. At the same time he recognized his own curious reluctance to let it slip away, because Hastings troubled his mind. He kept returning to their meeting. Something there intrigued him, and he amused himself by admitting that he must, really must, be related to that bearded grandfather he had known only in a picture who lost a good farm speculating in Arkansas mining stock.

But these were momentary thoughts, thrust back behind his present day-by-day professional life. He was coming to be pleased with his moderate success as a creative writing teacher. He'd been doing freshman English for four years and was vaguely satisfied with that, so he no longer fretted when he prepared for class. With the creative writing students it was different; he prepared diligently and at the top of his nerves read their stories, wrote criticisms, and conferred and conferred. And beyond it all he was lucky. Two students who could write fiction had somehow wandered into his class. The *Campus Lit* took a story in the first semester and one poem from the class. Doris Weinstock submitted the story of his murder, heavily revised and well disguised by an alien setting, but it was summarily rejected. He consoled her with an offhand remark that the subject matter just wasn't fashionable, though he knew a better reason was that it just didn't come off in the style. Still, she had signed up for the second term and was working on a piece of fiction and some poems she wouldn't let him see.

One day in late March she called him up for an appointment, for he had trained her finally not to come and stand expectantly at the door like some dumb beast. Her poems were finished, she said.

He arranged for a time when Dave Eriksen would be present. His meetings with Miss Weinstock had put him on his guard. He worried about a scene in which she would break down over his criticism or throw herself sobbing on the floor or, worse, on him. He realized now that if he allowed her to, she would try to make him her psychiatrist, and after that who knows what? Already he had sidestepped the theme of a story clearly about her parents and their troubles with her (written nervously from their point of view), keeping strictly to style. And he ignored her attempts to turn the discussion back on her personal life, taking the strict classical line.

This time she came quietly, her hair all up in a bun, and he realized that her cheekbones were really quite handsome. As usual she was very carefully made up, and as usual he was quite aware of her perfume, which was expensive. It was difficult for him to read poems over quickly and say anything at all intelligent. He meant only to give her some encouragement and say he'd keep them for a few days, then they could talk. He had never been able to convince her that she should submit things at class time and come around to talk later. But as he read these poems he could tell at once that they were far above what she had ever submitted before and even by a sort of sophomore standard exceptionally good. They were a sequence of six love poems, rough sonnets written in syllabic verse with considerable internal consonant play. She had overdone the sound a bit, and here and there maybe she had aped Hopkins too much. Mainly though, he was taken by their simplicity. They weren't the sentimental rubbish he had come to expect ninety-nine percent of the time from his coed poets. They were almost brutal analyses of the speaker's own emotions. And here he backed away. The speaker was herself. She had suddenly and unaccountably revealed to him a certain intellectual fiber, and yet from all his experience of her she was as sentimental as could be. Had her spoken words simply failed her, as his own had often failed him in class? He did not really consider that she was growing up in strange, abrupt leaps. He tried to say something about a few lines, suggesting she tone down the assonance and take out some Hopkins-like phrases. Then he simply said what he meant —the poems were quite good; she should submit them to the *Lit.* He returned them to her.

He knew as he did it that it was a mistake, because he almost always kept poems a few days and wrote out his critiques. And it wasn't just that this time he wanted to tell her they were, with a few changes, finished. She had intimidated him. He knew that he was frightened of her emotions and feared they were a net in which he might somehow be trapped. In that moment their roles were oddly reversed; he was without the strength to face up to the poems as a useful critic. Had she sensed his reticence or merely thought him too summary with her efforts? He forced himself to remember his role: they all needed to have your time before they sensed your sincerity. But after all, well damn it, he *had* said take them to the *Lit,* hadn't he?

Yes, and she had thanked him rather solemnly, even distantly.

Some time after she was gone, and after a long silence, Dave turned to him from his stack of papers.

"Well, that wasn't so bad, was it?"

"You should have seen the poems."

"Oh? No good?"

"They're good; that's the surprise; too good to come from what I thought she was."

With that the matter rested. He didn't want to go on, and Dave could tell. He appreciated Dave, a good man to share an office with. Golden silences.

Two days later, some time very early in the morning, Doris Weinstock killed herself by jumping from College Street Bridge one hundred feet into the river gorge. That same morning he received an unsigned message in the mail: "I'm sorry that they were the best I could do. Thanks."

For a day he was helpless, struggling between outrage and sorrow. He canceled his classes and sat looking at walls. On the second day the walls came in, and he decided to write to Hastings at Walton. He had posted the letter at seven that evening and was back trying to read through a stack of papers, but it wasn't working. There was nothing he could do. Something was finished, and he faced an unredeemable failure.

Then Dave Eriksen rang the doorbell. Jack had avoided the office, and he hadn't seen Dave since it happened.

"I've just learned something," Dave said, as he opened his own beer in Jack's little kitchen. "I just happen to know that over at the infirmary they've known for a week or two that Doris Weinstock was pregnant."

"Oh, good God," Jack said. "Well, I suppose . . ."

"Oh, they know who the boy is. He's told them himself. Some sophomore in engineering, I believe, although it's supposed to be a secret."

He felt as if he had been floored. "Look at this." He found the note and handed it to Dave.

"Well, I'll be damned. Over at the infirmary the counselors say they talked to the girl a few times, but they wouldn't tell me much beyond that. Anyway, for heaven's sake, don't get to thinking you're more involved than you are. You aren't, you know. The girl was—she was sick, as well as troubled."

"Well, okay, she was neurotic and troubled, but she was reaching for something, and she was beginning to write."

"Yes, I know that, and you knew it, and it must have meant something to her that you knew."

"No, she wanted more than that. She needed more than I was willing to give her. Those poems and her coming up with them were a plea. I thought they were just infatuation poems, but now I see they were to her lover, and she wanted me to—well, she wanted something more than criticism, some personal gesture. She got over the infatuation when she had me done in last fall, you know. The nerves were just residue." He hated his incompetence in the situation and his incompetence in expressing it. "I muffed it, Dave, I really did."

"You know, Sherwood Morrow tells me he thinks she was whoring around. He'd seen her around."

"The hell with him. He has an abstractly filthy mind, the bastard. Professorial jokes about the coeds. He's a verbal Peeping Tom. How the hell can you be that snide?"

"I don't know, but he's a good scholar. Why, Stout's turned practically the whole eighteenth-century collection over to him. Consider him a fixture."

"He could go to hell with Sam Johnson if it weren't that poor Kit Smart would have to put up with him. In fact, this whole place can go to hell. Look what goes on here. You break your ass for three years doing freshman English, and then they say, That's all, brother. Morrow comes in with his Harvard degree and a computer or something and he's set for life counting lines and words and attributing stuff. He'd just as soon dissect a student as teach one."

"Oh now, I'd say Sherwood's bark is worse than his bite. Maybe he's not the best, but he does a decent job. I can tell from his students. And anyway, you've got it made here, too, if you want it; they like you both."

"We're all guilty, Dave. Hell, I was afraid to be alone in the room with her. How can you ever meet someone that way?"

Dave finished his beer. "Don't make a federal case of it," he said.

▶

The letter to Hastings got results:

Dear Dr. Emory,

Let me apologize for not writing you sooner and missing you in New York. I have been indisposed and a New York trip had to be canceled. We shall be delighted to have you come at any point in time. Call me when you receive this, as the mails have apparently delayed my earlier letter. You may be interested to know that at this point in time we have negotiated for the Clarkson manuscripts, of which we spoke. All is firm.

He could not remember anything about either manuscripts or arrangements for a New York meeting. The letter was either strangely vague or ambiguous. Had Hastings actually been to New York or had he not? Had he let something slip, and if so, what was he hiding? But he called Hastings anyway, and they arranged for a visit. A few days before he was to go, a three-line letter came from the chairman at Walton University offering him an assistant professorship with a salary just large enough to keep him interested. So now he was looking *them* over; that was nice enough, because it took the pressure off. It must have been Hastings' doing. But what did they know about him? It was a very strange way to proceed, and he reminded himself to keep definitely on his guard.

A part of his mind, however, thumbed its nose defiantly. Striking a mood perhaps too theatrical for his own reason to tolerate, he saw himself gazing down on the rocks below College Street Bridge. The water was rushing fast in the spring thaw.

But at Walton when he made his visit nothing was rushing. One of the many people in the English Department remarked offhand that the city of Walton was one of the very few of its size in the country without a river running through it, and that was bad, no natural sewer, no principle of cleanout. Another joked that from the perspective of Walton the earth was flat, and beyond the slope of the Rockies was the ultimate edge of things. But at the time there was spring in the air; the square flat fields, with the roads fencing them at right angles, were various shades of tender green, wheat mostly, some alfalfa, occasional corn. Occasional lone trees. Oases of farmhouses. The campus itself, on the city's edge, stretched out from a quadrangle toward those fields. At the geographical or social center, amid elms, stood a gray wooden Victorian bell tower. Last year, one of his hosts remarked, there had been an attempt to fire the tower. Two students with torches, reasonably drunk, had been apprehended on the evening after the first day of classes. They objected to the bells playing "School Days" at 7:40 A.M. as they set out for chem lab. His hosts seemed in sympathy with the students. There was a generally held grudge against the bell ringer's taste and tact. There were Wesleyan hymns every Sunday noon.

On his home ground Dean Hastings proved a voluble if syntactically irresponsible host. His talk was of research in terms of grants, library acquisitions in terms of modern literature, a new journal to be published in terms of humanities, and major opportunities at this point in time generally. A mandarin smile of accompaniment, not apparent in Chicago, clashed with the verbal style. Above all, he made it clear that he was working for "cooperation beyond departmental spheres," where disciplines could meet. The Emory visit, as it seemed to be called by everyone, went well enough until the interdisciplinary emphasis faded and he was interviewed by Vanner, the chairman of English, a taciturn elderly gentleman who gave the impression of very nearly knowing who the visitor was and why he was there. Again one part of his mind took in the reality that this so obviously disclosed and saw in Vanner's noncommittal manner a certain danger.

Somehow he cared less when he got back to Middleton

and entered the routine of work again. Because Sherwood Morrow heard about his offer, flopped in his office chair, and told him he was MAD to consider it, and because in a few days he received a totally unexpected visit from Doris Weinstock's father, known to him only in one of her stories.

The Dean of the College himself brought Mr. Weinstock around—a stout little balding man with glasses and a constant cigarette hanging precisely from the center of his mouth. He was fiction come to life. Mr. Weinstock was tired and didn't try to hide it, and he was embarrassed. The Dean introduced him and departed. Mr. Weinstock took a seat. It seemed that he was just barely suppressing a long eye-rolling sigh. Emory waited for him to speak.

"Mr., er, Dr. Emory, we've been trying to figure out how this has happened to us, but it's like, well, like being born, I guess. A few days ago I read through, er, ah, Doris's journal, and after that, well, I thought maybe I could come to you."

Emory waited, heart poised. But it was not what he thought, no, thank God, not what he thought at all. The journal, it turned out, was devoted almost wholly to her writing. In it she remembered remarks he had made in class, copied out quotations from books, wrote down lines from poems that had struck her, and things other students had said or written. Also, Mr. Weinstock explained, there were a good many poems.

What he wanted to do—maybe it seemed silly—was to have some of Doris's best poems privately printed, just for a few friends and relatives, as, well, a sort of memorial. It was what she thought she did best, and they would like to remember her by it. Could Emory choose the things to go in—the last six poems she had submitted to him, he knew about those, and anything more he thought suitable? Maybe, well, if it wouldn't be too much trouble, could he—as her teacher—write a brief foreword, only a paragraph or two, just to explain that this was a student's work—and because she thought a lot of him? Then Mr. Weinstock did sigh, because he was very tired and because he wasn't quite sure how to act in a college professor's office, and he felt a little foolish, for poetry wasn't his line.

Emory thought he had done very well. He could hardly bear to look at him, sitting there edgy and sighing. He accepted at once, and Mr. Weinstock left, greatly pleased and sad. Emory congratulated himself. He had thought for only a fleeting moment about what some of his colleagues would say. The journal lay thinly on his desk. Poor dear, he thought,

> I, with no rights in this matter,
> Neither father nor lover.

In an evening he chose the poems. Then he read the journal through and decided to include also a page of prose written apparently not long before Doris skittered away. It was entitled "What the teacher cannot do":

> He cannot tell me what to say.
> He cannot give me my subject.
> He cannot live my life.
> He probably doesn't fail me if I do poorly, only if I do
>   nothing or too little.
> I fail myself.
> He can make me write a sonnet, but not a good one, and
>   he cannot ask me a second time.
> He cannot make his mind mine even if I should want it.
>   I do not want it.
> What can he do? He can speak and listen.
> P.S. For cannot read should not.

It didn't quite make it, he thought, but it was a good try.

In the page and a half of introduction he said the usual

things about her promise, her inexperience, and quoted a few lines from Roethke's elegy. Not very inspired, but the occasion called for ritual. He got everything together and mailed it off to Mr. Weinstock in New York City, and then he sat down and typed off a letter of acceptance to Vanner at Walton, and another with appropriate greetings to Henry Hastings, the Fastest Dean in the West.

William Person

BACK IN OHIO IT'S THIS WAY   Well, spring begins to show a bit, a crocus here and there, a few birds. The snow doesn't fly much any more, the season changeth, the bus sloppeth us no longer. It's the end of a season, beginning of a new. The departmental chairman —old manic Kit Jensen (how has this happened to me?) —tuneth his soul to the throats of returning birds. Only yesterday there he was, cap and wand, down behind the power plant along the canal protecting the ducks from vandalous sophomores. Kit's a nature lover; he'll pull you out of the chow line to tell you he saw a hawk soaring or a bobwhite in a field. That's a far cry from taciturn Pappy Vanner at Walton, or from devious Hasty Hank Hastings, for that matter.

But though spring reneweth, death doth undo so many year by year. What is my return to Ohio? Can I say I face renewal this spring, or was my mythic round played out when I staggered back from Walton last fall? For, yes, here in the flat, stalk-brown fields of home, stretching off and somehow down to the horizon, yes, here indubitably I am. It was hardly a return up the beaches in triumph; there was hardly an old gorgon's head slung casually underarm, hardly sword in hand to slit the suitors' gullets.

No, it was, I'll admit, more like an Okie who in that last suspenseful moment before the cap blew realized the old A wouldn't cross the desert, wouldn't make Bakersfield, and just gave it up, retired, crapped out. It's pure and simple, my Aunt Nell would say. If you want to know the truth (she'd say), I'm back on my ass (I'd say) in Ohio, and spring brings me only, like winter and fall in their turns, a couple hundred goddamned freshman themes to grade—grist for the mill of the mind, Old Willie the First would say (He lives!).

Have I dropped back into the womb? Pretty close, because old Sciota's only what? A few miles from London, O., where I used to hang around the drugstore watching the girls. But hell, you never really leave; you take Ohio with you when you go—a little humus between the toes, straw in the hair; and when you come back with all that experience the I-want-you posters talk about (wars of intellect, mind you), even when you come back from descent into the bowges of Walton University itself, a minuscule grain of sand, maybe more, remains. And the straw, the straw would be there, too, if it weren't for that awful retreat of the hair. Flowing into the sink, the drain, the pipes, and away.

So I'm back where I started. Not much to show for— what is it?—my God, fifteen years' devotion to the aims of education, starting with that Indiana teacher's certificate I posted over a rathole in Bloomington (I went abroad to college). What is there? Two wives, one worn and traded, oh; children scattered about; a '55 Chevy. Hell, neither the car nor the age to make me a campus character, ever. Leaks around the window will be worse this spring; mildew in the floorboards will flourish like my athlete's foot. Then there are those three surviving suits, Chicago gangster stuff, Mighty Mouse lapels. [Yes, robin, you idiot, I see you on my sill while I try, those themes fouling my desk, to compose a line or two. While

I give in to brooding the Walton *roman* I shall *not,* hear this, *not, never, no never* put on paper.] Also, I acknowledge, for sanity's sake, about a hundred poems showing from under the pile of those two years. Without that accumulation, it would be a perfect round. But that's the poet for you, always messing with perfection. Perhaps I should tear them up for the sake of symmetry. Besides, I'm a better poet now. If I were really strong I'd destroy my juvenilia, food for editors and collators hunched shrewlike in their dens.

The other accumulation is what I've learned this year. I have learned that I work at a plant. It's from the plant my money comes, and I'm not to forget it. The big hawk-eyed, red-necked desert birds (see Willie II) who drop criticism on us five days of the week always say to watch the images. Notice, then, that I said "plant" [didn't I, robin?]. But set aside for later examination the ambiguity which the word contains (romantic organicism and all that). I have learned it is a plant, I mean a real-type factory. The shift change at Boeing has nothing on old Sciota's south campus between classes! Chrome-domed traffic police culled from the honors class in theory of the billy club! It's authentic modern life; the education building—the Kiva, it's called, because it's *round,* man— where they perform those tribal rituals, is the best General Motors Gothic I've seen outside Michigan.

And I have learned more. I have learned to go over there in my, shall we say, car, every day, to enter the classroom striding with my studied air of poetic detachment, the very social form of negative capability [robin, you will drive me nuts; go fetch up a worm or something, make like it really *is* spring]. The students will watch in awe, for—who knows?—the great man may be composing. By this simple ruse I postpone those dreary preclass questions, which, when the whole thing gets the best of me and I let them be asked, force me to be some kindly late Whittier. A colleague who is Twayning it (the biggest gang rape of the muse in history) tells me old Whit *did* have a youth. Well, enter I do, shove words at them—the hayseeds, barefoot boys, cross-thighed and leg-kicking mouse-mouthed coeds—and they write words back. Read and return. Those words go where the straw goes. It gets so you can practically do it without thinking. It's the acting between that bugs you.

Come to consider it, I didn't really have to go way out to Walton and stagger back here to learn all this—unless I've finally become one of those well-Fryed and Blooming necessary-descent-and-dark-night-of-the-soul boys. At IU they taught me to expect it all. [Why do you irritate me so, robin? You goddamned optimist. Go blunt your beak on the cold, cold ground. It isn't right yet; it's obscene. There, fly away, persistent one. You remind me of fauns from my past. The same expectancy. Soon the bears themselves will come lumbering out of hibernation. I have walked on the squares all my life, alas. I do not like to think of it at all. Well, Ann will come with the coffee soon.]

Only for minutes then, damn it:

Walton, 1956—a hot September. [Robin, you are responsible for this.] J. Brendan Berrigan holding out the cup of his paw at our office doors. Jason Talbot, Jack Emory, novice trainers we. But now we are old campaigners. We have allowed our fires to decay.

The comic-book figure called Brendan Bear was drawn from life, from the exploits of J. Brendan Berrigan, B.A., M.A., Ph.D. The day this dawned on us must have been about with the first snow, year of the beasts; and the abominable Brendan, there he came, red bear hair askew, shuffling through our halls begging candy from our pockets. Should have dredged up the old Ex-Lax trick. No, the problem was to plug him.

I'll now proceed to remember having coffee one evening with the Talbots later on in that first Walton winter. Jason's boy Charley (about eleven then? Chuck to everybody now) enters shouting with pleasure, prancing a gawky caper, his little sister toddling after. On one of those ridiculous comic books, he's found the real thing. "Mr. Berrigan! Why he's Brendan Bear!" Who says there's nothing to pop art? Sometime somewhere that boy had heard us talking. Was he embarrassed when he saw me there? Perhaps, but who could have given him a better audience? Then there was the time he discovered a real Alfred E. Neuman, officer in MLA. That kind of thing would make my day at Walton. Simple pleasures of the poor (James I).

[So even here Berrigan walks in, as I try putting and taking in this damned poem. If it's not a bird at the window, it's a beast pounding the past's door. Give in and brood, damn it. Make it a dream, then force it into some shape. Walton, after all, really was.] Okay. All right, all right. Laura and I had been in town about a week. It was hotter than hell. And finally we found this crumbly damned house with two bedrooms and almost a john to rent from one of those old lady hares who somehow among them own the town and make a career of faculty fleecing. The kids were started to school; there was just enough money to stash a few cans of beer in our $1.98 refrigerator. Why not go up to the hallowed halls and stare at my beautiful new desk and fancy paneled bookshelves in my air-conditioned grand office? Yes, we were all kings then! I suppose the grandeur was an enticement to get out of our dreadful rent houses and THIMK. The provost or someone even sent around a directive the spring before when the building was opened. Subject: Advice—file under "Advantages of private offices, the." Old horse trader, he confidently expected a real triple-layered birdhouse of literary activity in the English Department from now on. Or *was* it the provost? Because no one ever really understood what the hell his directives said: stuff on matching funds, computation of time for nonacademic employees, overhead, policy on deferral of sabbatical accumulation. Verbal trots the only gait he had, but constipation of meaning. [Ha, old redbreast hasn't come back. Scared him off, I did. Probably struggling with a ground-stuck beak. It can only mean my gruff routine still works: I now see my only mistake was that I didn't use it sooner at Walton, on larger beasts. Now, I Virgil myself down and away into my own dark wood and the lurking Brendan.]

I go to my office via special faculty elevator, for who says theah ain't segregation in the midlands, suh? Then down the hall comes this tall, rangy, athletic-looking fellow, face lined like a fallow Arkansas field. He fumbles for a key, making ready to open his door right next to mine. Avoiding speech, I guess. I got used to that later, most of the staff looking the other way:

"... Down back ways, avoiding mockers,
they skulk, all stricken with their sad fortune."

Finally I thought: What the hell? "I'm Person." Or something to that effect.

Slowly he turned, a man falling a long way through the sky. He held out a big hand, dropping his head, pulling in his chin like Goodman in a riff. Then a slim grin. The answer:

"I'm sure pleased to meet you. I'm Jason Talbot. I'm new here."

Texan, I thought, courtly-manner-type Texan, soft voice. (Wrong. He was pure Okie, from McAlester, except his family was sometimes on the road: Ada, Ardmore, and Denton, Texas.) But turned me inside out and watched. Whew. From that moment I could have known he was a potential bear expert. But then I didn't know any bears—yet.

He'd been in town awhile. He invites me into his office. It looked as if he'd settled in fairly well. A lot of books, including a whole edition of Bret Harte on the shelves. I'd learn he was the kind of guy who wouldn't bother to explain messing around with Bret Harte even if he saw you staring. I keep remembering that visiting Yale hotshot, I think it was, tearing around Emory's office pulling books from the shelves and saying, "Look, this man acknowledges my help! See? This is dedicated to me." As if we didn't already know he was king bibliomaniac of North America. And then Farrell, out from Columbia to lecture, trying to bug Jason about old Bret: "Deep into Bret Harte, I see?" said he, sitting in Jason's office enjoying, but letting us know he knew the fakery of, the hospitality Hastings had forced us to force on him. [Say nuthin', Jason, that's right.] Jason wasn't spending his time on research into Bret Harte either. The books were left over from some jerk who did a thesis on Harte and escaped, raving, the last I'd heard, toward Mexico and south. Never sent for them when he started seeing everything through a slice of lemon.

Jason hasn't forgotten those bad manners [elephant, he], but he won't ever rake Farrell over in a review. From the looks of Farrell he wouldn't care anyway. Armed to the tongue. Actually Jason was only watching Farrell just as he studied bears. When I think of Jason now I see Thurber's dog after the bug. I even remember Jason broken up, collapsed over that cartoon. Absurd old himself, he allowed. The bug? Ourselves. The world.

So we talked. With Jason you didn't have to play that damned "I'm So-and-So and I've done this and that and have these degrees and those publications" game. I knew all about it because they played it back in my Bloomington days. The few parties I was permitted to attend—I, assistant to an unknown assistant professor with tenure—

were regular stadiums for it. Old Stanley John Howell could practically force his whole bibliography into a stentorian sentence of self-introduction. Guide an errant conversation all the way from the Cincy Reds back to the galley proofs he'd worked on in Paris last summer. Who says scholarship isn't ahrt? You had to be damned good to play in Stanley John's backfield what with all the ploys to memorize, the chalk talks, the dummies to tackle. Taught a whole generation of IU graduate students to run through the open field of the departmental cocktail party. They went on to coaching jobs in all the major conferences. There he was, old Stanley John, in the hall one day telling some crew cut in the Renaissance not to buck the Spenser trust. I suppose he was talking about those Johns Hopkins people—poeticide, I charge them with. Mafia. Exterminate poets. Poor Edmund Spenser.

What is all this delay? [Get on to it, get on to the beast and then his master. Put it before yourself and CRINGE.]

So satteth we getting acquainted, when lo, out of the midst thereof suddenly there echoed rapid clip-clops and knocking of prodigious force upon our cell door. And burst upon us with equal loudness, well, this stocky, wild-haired, redheaded, well-paunched, totally freckled man in a hound's-tooth jacket. He ungathered the spoken word something like this:

"You're Talbot, aren't you? Glad t'meet ya fella I'm Berrigan just in from Kansas a few days ago had a terrific talk with Hank Hastings what a man for Dean what ideas he's gonna build our department and we're the bricks pal." Thought: Something about no dean or anybody's going to mortar me to this guy. But thought, grim or no, did not stop the likes of him.

"Lots of dead wood here going to be tossed out he's got a whole new honors program up his sleeve and we're gonna teach New Criticism didya hear that? Criticism—

Ransom, Warren, Tate! We'll revitalize the whole program he wants to get T. S. Eliot over to talk and Auden, Wimsatt, Brooks . . . !"

I gasp—mainly for him. He's still running on the lump of air he chewed up in the hall. All the time he's walking back and forth between Jason and me, his stomach swaying slightly before him in his strutting swagger, his arms swinging free on the periphery. Jason leans back in his chair, legs crossed, head slightly tilted, his turnip face a reserved quizzical stare. Not a word from us yet. What could you say that was decent? Of course I wasn't so fierce then, old Doberman pinscher me.

Finally Jason: "Mr. Berrigan, I'm Jason Talbot." Then he introduced me.

"Yeh yeh—Blackmur, Wellek, Burke," to Jason, "Hastings told me all about you fella when he was trying to get me signed up. Thinks you're a real comer. Solid type. Yeh told me all about the new young colleagues. Met Emory yet? Had drinks with him two nights ago. Swell guy. Likes Ellington and James and all that. Play the bongos myself. Two books I mean one out already and another coming good ones too! Winters, Vivas, Tate! Boy fella you're on the inside I mean really the future's bright." Brendan did nip-ups trying to break Jason's cordial detachment.

Jason smiled distantly. Me? Bugged. But now I know Jason was also entranced, watching Berrigan like that Thurber dog studies the bug. And for two years he'd watch him for hours, a long-legged fly on the water. Yeah, well *he* was a Yeats scholar.

Now Hastings was some big shot upstairs, wasn't he? I personally never expected any truck with deans. From where he sat I certainly couldn't have been any great catch. He hadn't personally looked me over at MLA the way he had Berrigan, which is a great testimony to his peerless judgment. For genuine innocent I, there was no hasty-tasty treatment, only a quaint letter of greeting after I'd accepted the offer. I'll say one thing for old Hank, though: he was sure as hell more cordial than the department. Pappy Vanner hadn't even come to MLA to interview anybody, and nobody asked me out to Walton to be looked over. Pappy sends a short note in January: The department is directing him to make me this offer. Well, I don't suppose he meant he'd been *forced* to do it. He was always fairly friendly with me, even after I was in social disgrace all around.

Then the old locomotive yell from Hastings:

> Dear Dr. Person,
> I want to tell you how delighted I am by the cognizance that you have cast your lot with us and the future. I was detained by illness in my arrival at the Modern Language meetings and at that point in time was compelled to leave early with respect to New York commitments, the unhappy result being that I was unable to interact with you there. Here, of course, you will perform significant roles in our Honors Program, which will be implemented soon. We are pushing hard to firm up the creative arts, and your talents will help complete our grand design.

Deathless prose. Talked that way, too; really an expert.

Hell, I'd never heard of Hastings. No one ever mentioned honors work to me, or anything else for that matter. In fact, I was all set to be one of those good old one-gaited freshman English workhorses every department needs a gross of. Somebody at the home stable probably wrote: Faithful, obedient, and not known to shy if provided with blinders. Now all of a sudden here I was the Pegasus of Henry Hastings' stable. Who says there's no temptation in the poetry game?

Let's see, though. By the time Berrigan had burst in on us, I'd learned a bit more about the fastest Dean in the

West, or Hasty Hank Hastings. (I would learn more from Jason, whose intense concentration on our swift leader must have seared the epidermis.) Hastings was a prewar Waltonite called to service, mainly stateside duty; in the postwar world he became bibliophile to the library rare-book room, carried a big travel chit, and was very large among rich citizens, owners of books and banks. Soon, there he was, the public face of the college. Word had it, President Cotter heard footsteps from the rear. He had helped develop the "Honors Program"—a cultuh-type curriculum in general arts and sciences for social bettuh undergraduates. It was, in truth, a den of department tea-cups. Assistant Dean, then Dean. Always an idea man. People you met at cocktail parties told you he was a real live wire. In truth, there seemed to be some sense in talks he had made about interdisciplinary study and breaking the power of the departments. I never had much in common with English professors.

That was what I knew of Hastings when I met Jason. In my ignorant bliss of a few months before, I assumed Hastings probably knew more than he did about me. Wrong again. Simple, natural egocentricity. Finally when I met him he had me confused with someone else. Man, did he scramble to pick up the pieces! I should have booted him through the uprights then when he was bend-ing over. A quick three points.

Now there is Berrigan [haunting presence yet] waving his arms, extolling the virtues of Hastings, and telling us Hastings really runs the department, Vanner is a figure-head, don't get him wrong, Vanner's a swell fella, a bit reserved, but a great guy (Ransom, Brooks!), goes to football games and really is a swell chairman, not like what you'd run into in the Big Ten (I'd always liked the chairman at my school) and the other big factories. Then off on a bow-bend to flatter Jason some more about a Yeats article (apparently he wasn't very well up on *my* bibliography—a few poems in *Cosmos, Quidnunc, Back-lash,* and *Burma Review*), wheels suddenly, shouts over his shoulder, his head disappearing out the door, then his ass, that he is off for coffee with Fred McCrea. To talk over the Honors Program—the answer to Oberlin—they want him to begin working in. He'd put in a word for us. I almost shout after him, "My name's Person," but then I think he really might put in a word.

Gone as noiselessly as come. Jason's face is momentarily impassive. Then one eyebrow flickers up; he grins broadly. "Man, we've been Berriganed," he says. Makes a friend for life.

Now there were enough warnings in that encounter, weren't there? It is simple: we were damned fools all for having anything to do with Berrigan. But really it wasn't that simple. Even Jack Emory was roped and tied, and Jack was distant as hell with someone he didn't care to take tea with at the moment. Who could we blame? Hastings? We were all in Hastings' boat, like it or not. But we were all curious, too, like cats, or even bug-watchers. Poor Jason. Sometimes I feel Jason was sorry for Berrigan, and for his wife, Wilma, the bitch. But it was Brendan who made Walton impossible for him—after all that listening, all that watching.

Anyway, make way for the great Emory. Scene: Same morning, Beaver Room. "Water Vole Room," Ralph Ware's name. His *Cold Comfort Farm* phase. It was where we all had coffee or iced tea, depending upon the weather. Blamed for Emory's supposed ulcer, which was actually a stomach full of Walton. The tea was pretty bad, mostly bag flavor. Emory in the Walton world used to go over there with me or Jason, ready for a cell meeting: plans to fire the library, mouse the secretary's wastebasket, bug out with the Shakespeare quarto. He'd work up a terrific state of nerves by discussing Hastings' latest ploy, the department nitwits, Berrigan's penultimate stupidity. Ascending order of outrage, that! And plenty of truth in his invective.

The Beaver Room was a kind of shit tan, well known to all who attended junior high in the Midwest circa '36. The tan blended with a shade of nausea green around the windows. Murals of beavers making dams, gnashing fangs at rabbits, doing whatever else beavers do, except, of course, making other beavers. It was a moral mural. No university can be without a heraldic beast-type room. Ours wasn't much compared to some I've seen, strictly utilitarian and self-service. Watch your own ass, that means. I'd say about half the student body on the upper campus and a third of the faculty tramped through the Beaver Room every day. In the winter the floor was wet and muddy, and the whole place smelled like a subway rest room. Our unfriendly colleagues or everybody or THEY thought it was where WE went to plot overthrow, to work out ways to steal poetry classes from the worthy course horses now teaching them, to make cracks at instructors with Harvard book bags. Our colleagues weren't far wrong either, but they overestimated our strength. After all, revolutions come and go but Mother Russia remains. Something about the damned place, the whole of Walton, really did make us measure out our lives, just as the Bard says, with coffee spoons. Back here south of London I stay away from such dens, keep to the corner bars, and throw real darts.

Oh yes, Emory. Jason and I, we allowed a few unspoken thoughts on the fatal subject of Berrigan to flow electrically between us. Then we betook ourselves over to the Beaver Room—Jason for what turned out to be his usual hot coffee and cream, the temperature being near 95°. Jason never turned down a cup of coffee. [I could use some now. Ann? Hey ANN! Down in the basement wrestling diapers. Big advance for her, this new marriage!] Jason, yes, well if Jason didn't have any coffee near him he was searching it out or pining away. There we were in the cafeteria line when Jason spotted Emory sitting alone at a table along the wall. Emory turned out to be a slender, tanned, dark-haired, almost crew-cut character dressed in Ivy League fatigues. Looked about twenty-six or twenty-seven, but I found out later he was thirty-one. Possible to tell after studying his face awhile. There were some slight lines around his eyes, but the voice was very youthful. He later told me people still took him for a student now and then. It didn't seem to irritate him though—the student bit—and he probably even liked it, being a bachelor and everything, because of the coeds.

All fools we.

Hell, I haven't been taken for a student since I was about fifteen.

At first I guess I didn't like Emory very much. One of those eastern snots explorers bring back stories about. But the fact was he had a touch of nasal twang in his voice. Could even put on an Ahia accent when he chose to bug people, which was enough of the time. And born in Portland, Oregon, for God's sake! With a Washington Ph.D.! Why even I could ask where those places were and make cracks about the Injuns. According to Berrigan, Emory was one of Hastings' prize catches. Wooed from some place in the East, but that's about all I knew of him at the time. Who would have thought, with a shirt and tie like his, that he had some of the old berserk in him, or that he actually knew something of literature and life, bear-baiting and love?

Sat down we did, followed by a little light glove and helmet sparring—weather, where from, how long, and all that. Thought: This fellow is a real operator and watch out. I hadn't yet learned it was the unreal operators who cause the real trouble. A good true operator doesn't mess up the turf. I could see he'd get the subject steered around to his own specialty pretty quickly, and sure enough we heard about a few of his major works. But it wasn't a really notable performance, and he didn't soar too high. No fiberglass pole in those days. All in all, well, he wasn't pushing it the way Crowder or Klaus would have, and he didn't put on a lot of airs about ahrt or what he read or hadn't deigned to read. Better still, he didn't seem to be a misplaced soap salesman or anything like that. I'd give him the benefit of the doubt and chalk up what I hadn't liked to Pavlovian easternism. Hell, who can blame an eastern pedant for salivating when they ring the bibliography bell?

Mentioned Berrigan all right. Up until then he was almost stonily serious; he could be very serious, old Jack, though he had an impudent grin. Fact is, he thought about his work most of the time—until Walton obsessed him, that is. But on this particular day, after the professional matters, there he was, suddenly trapped in a foolish smile. He'd rather have suppressed it. One of his failings as an operator: he couldn't hide his feelings for long. Then he blurted out, "Have you guys [he liked the word "guys"] met Berrigan?"

Took me by surprise, didn't even give us a chance to answer, just went right ahead to tell how he met him, assumed all the time somehow we couldn't have missed him. Well, could we?

Scene: Emory all settled into his little rent house. Saw it myself a few nights later. Even spent some time there once when Laura dashed me on the rocks. He had those few pieces of Danish modern furniture (it wasn't cliché yet) he'd brought in a U-Haul trailer, a big library for an assistant professor, piles of brick and plank for shelves, St. Vincent de Paul style, an old piano painted flat gray which Ralph Ware would come over and tune later on— every department must have a novelist who is also electrician or piano tuner—one Charles Eames chair (it *was* cliché), a big collection of old 78 records, mostly Chicago jazz and Bach, I think—at least that's what he played most—and several original paintings by Northwest artists that he'd sit and stare at for inspiration. Sea gulls. On the night he was talking about, things were in disarray—no rugs on the floor, boxes piled around, and all that. Unpacking. Bach. Bourbon. And then Berrigans.

Oh Lord save me, I knew I'd drive myself to Wilma Berrigan, and on an empty stomach. [Where is Ann?] Well, no remedy for it. I've got to warn Ralph Ware by letter he can do anyone else in his novel but Wilma is *mine,* my very own. Haunt him if he steals her, even if I won't, won't, no never, write it. Behind all those bear-claw scars where is the real Wilma? [Makes me think in corny sentences, doesn't she?] One interpretation blames Wilma completely on Berrigan, says Berrigan drives her to act like the bitch she is. I suppose it's credible. Jason leaned to it at times. Except if she didn't have some of the real stuff in her she'd never have tied herself to Brendan. A big platinum woman, on the hefty side at least, with a moon face. Brendan was in love with seeing her hair pulled back *severely*—that's the word, isn't it?—knotted in a pony tail. All wrong! All wrong! You'd think she'd just come off the farm somewhere north of St. Paul (Well, she *was* from Minneapolis), and anyway her face was too damned big for that. Like looking in the reflection of an old chrome headlight. When she broke down and hung all that fake platinum hair around her face like a spaniel or cut it short, she was fairly decent, if you could forget her neurotic spaniel soul. Brendan probably beat her when she did. And she usually wore black—to make her add up to Brendan's idea of glamor.

Boy, doesn't she live for me now? And as for glamor, Brendan's hipped on it still, I suppose. Give him a couple of drinks or even a short talk with Hastings—boy, the power of that—and add Wilma to look at across the room. He'd rave about glamor and the importance of appearance and refer to Wilma over there. Take my wife, he'll offer, she always looks slick, no faculty type she! No sir, when she goes to supermarket she's presentable! And then after Wilma comes across the room, they both begin to allude to the frightful taste of certain colleagues, such as Jason and Betty Lou. How can they live in this atmospheah and not pick up a little cultuh? Oh, that dreadful rug! For a while old sheep dog I supposed Laura and I got off because I was a poet, though Laura's taste went to ten-cent Virgin Marys and Woolworth wicker. But wrong again. In wretched alternation they marched forth their opinion of *our* decor to the Talbots. One happy group we. [Yes, coffee!]

Wilma: played it to the hilt. But Laura knew: while Brendan hooey-hooeyed at the office Wilma boohooed on the bed at home. It's true. Yes, it's true. She used to come over to Laura and let go. All the time in her tiny Minnesota nasal sneer there she was behind Laura's back calling her dowdy and hickish. How much did the terror of Brendan make her that way? Laura and I used to debate it. Did we debate it? We even screamed it after a while. It was part of our sickness. For Laura, poor Brendan was sick of soul—if she could just bring him back into the Church—and Wilma was merely nervous, poor girl.

But I buy Ralph Ware's theory. Ralph had known her longer than anyone at Walton. She went back somehow to his own Kansas days. Once when we were sitting around talking about Wilma and Brendan—substitutes conversationwise, as they say, for Walton's having no pro ball club—Ware stopped us all. Everyone had a tale to tell, like Jason's trip to Danforth when Wilma got tight and made Brendan furious kadoodling with Kit Jensen for halfway and then disappearing half the night. We all had these stories to tell. Finally there was Ralph raising his hand pontifically. "Silence! Silence! Now gentlemen, you people have no right to talk about Wilma that way. You haven't known her very long. I've known her five years, and I've known Brendan three. And after that—after you've known her that long—well, then it's possible to be fair, and you can really say with absolute honesty what a REAL BITCH SHE IS."

Laughter, through set teeth. It was true. I got to hate Wilma like an acrobat. But Ralph had more experience. He used a good old straight hatred and honed it every morning to a fine edge. He got so he couldn't stay in the same room with her, and, well, he could stand cats. Yet Brendan and Wilma tried and tried to break him down. Invitations every week. Funny in a way, Ralph never blowing up at anyone else and keeping utterly secret all his reactions to galloping Hastingsism. [I really should stop this. Wilma throws me.]

The Berrigans call on Emory. [There's no stopping, really.] Who are they, Jack wonders. That was their first deflation. I imagine Wilma didn't forget it. There is Brendan sagging like an old French ascension balloon. All year before Jack he suffers deflation after deflation. I watch Brendan roar into Jack's office only to go limp on the floor, his chins waggling and shoulders like ski slopes. Jack simply turns off his Brendan-aid, plays the solemn unspeaking judge. Down corridors Brendan skulks like Pindar's wrestler. But I imagine a different Jack that first night, pleasant, slightly formal before strangers.

Brendan and Wilma somehow get the record player on and end up jitterbugging to Ellington records. They damn near shake the house down. No rugs. Jack's neighbors the Whites say to him next morning over the fence they were afraid some New York Jews had moved in, what with his license plate and the noise.

Well, some of the parties later on must have made them think all Israel was there, and maybe a few Arabs, too. But they never complained again. Even on the night people tell me I had to be restrained from going next door and inviting them over for a little crucifixion. Laura prevailed, bless her.

Beaver Room again: Jack sitting there telling us all this. What struck him and made him bring up the whole matter was Brendan's conversation. It careened from strutting optimism to abject fear with Henry Hastings acting Pavlov. In the course of half an hour, Jack, a total stranger, finds out that Brendan is optimistic about Criticism (capital "C" please)—Ransom! Warren! Tate!—afraid Hastings will lose interest in it, ready to take over the Honors Program, worried about Hastings alienating the professors in English and leaving him in the middle, worried Hastings will get so high up in administration that he'll forget B. Berrigan Ph.D., upset that he hasn't been able to publish like Emory, insistent that he'll have a book on Faulkner or someone out by the year's end, proud that Hastings expects big things from all of us, particularly from the new magazine he is going to start, and terrified that Hastings may dump us all next year when the new bright boys show up.

Emory mentally held his head, but later he admitted it was an education: he couldn't have had a better introduction to what winds up Brendan Bear and makes him chime. The tune was "Who's Afraid of the Big Bad Wolf?"

Thank God I'm far away from it now, but it still gets me thinking like this, doesn't it? And on the really bad days, well, it jacks me up out of my chair and makes me tour the study. At this place I avoid bears. I have a genuine Riding-Hood complex about dark woods at night. Life is duller, certainly, but the old mind is not as clouded, and I drink for pleasure again. I suppose the bear-and-Hastings business helped change my life. I can see my kindly old biographer or young snot chalking up the various sources of my discontent—my dark night of the soul and a passionate adulterous love affair. You know, Willie, he may have a best seller here. It all counted, and I can't deny that Old Kindly got some of it right. But unless he has tried to write some poems himself, looked bears and administrators in the eye, and found sniveling pedants protecting their own more than he can stomach, he won't have solved the mystery of Me Willie III, Man and Poet. [Goddammit, ANN, where *is* the coffee?]

Jason Talbot

I CHRONICLE THAT FIRST AUTUMN It's a little embarrassing to try to express myself about our Walton in-group and its pathetic fate. It seems so long ago, and I've really put it quite far to the side. Betty Lou likes to sprinkle references to it in her speech now and then. But, mind you, they're only a sort of shorthand, a set of dead metaphors. The other day Louella Groat dropped by and casually got around to asking why Betty Lou hadn't been at the last meeting of the Pierpont Dames. Well, Betty Lou, when she reported, conveyed quite a bit by saying "I gave her a lion." It's simply part of our language. Jack Emory would know exactly what it meant. It goes back to an exam week at Walton before we all busted up and took off to our respective rest camps. There was Will Person pasting up a big picture of a staring lion inside the clouded glass of his office door. The typical student was supposed to come up and think, "I know he's in there, but I'll wait and hope to catch him in a better mood." What I'm trying to say is that Betty Lou's remark doesn't call up the image of Will or that door any longer. It makes its own meaning flat out.

There are a lot of others. Things like "the Céline gambit" or "braking like Jensen" or "the old firm-up." They'll come clear in time. The scholar in me insists on keeping alive their real derivations. And from those little histories emerges the story of our little culture. I trust it won't be too offensive if I remain the central consciousness of the whole as I try to turn philology into reminiscence and homemade art.

First to my tragic flaw. I have learned that I tend to stare—figuratively, I mean. But literally, too, I guess, because while I'm decorously silent people get antsy, want noise. Particularly the Berrigans. Will Person was right: people like the Berrigans got my curiosity up, and while I was watching the bears, some animal would leap. But Person was partly wrong after all: it wasn't really my abstract interest in "characters" that led me into difficulties. It was—and I guess it still is (though I control it better now)—some outrageous desire to fix the ridiculous in my memory, perhaps to find the world itself ridiculous. Lord, I find it easy enough to forget most things. I *always* have to look up W. B. Yeats's birthday. And that's my field. But that's ridiculous, too, come to think of it.

In the Walton days I got into things before realization struck. The whole direction of our two years at Walton seems to have been foreordained quite simply by the events of four days back in late October of '56. And that's where to begin. I remember in the midst of those days thinking I was climbing a tall mountain in the day, sleeping down the other side, only to face a taller one the next morning.

The first speaker in our Critique of Culture Series, as it was advertised, was to be Christian Jensen, Professor of English at the Berrigans' alma mater. How he'd figure even at a distance in the lives of some of us later on you'll have to wait to see. Jensen would swing through Walton en route to the regional MLA meetings at Danforth, where he would chair the "Later Literature" section. Brendan himself was going to read a paper there. Profes-

sor Jensen, as tradition orders, was offering his protégé a
chance to show himself off and gain an item for his bibliography. It certainly didn't seem madness at the time to
plan a togetherness trip to Danforth with the Berrigans.
Indeed, why not? I was going to go anyway. Up to that
time I—well, I was more or less amused by Wilma and
Brendan (Betty Lou warned me early on about this),
and besides I'd recently discovered that Jensen was sitting
on some photostats of Yeats manuscripts I badly wanted
to see. In my little old scheming mind togetherness was a
fair price.

Now until Brendan began singing his praises I had
never really thought much of Jensen. I'd even missed his
Yeats articles—having to do with maps of Sligo, I believe
—in the yearly bibliographies. But my lapse wasn't the
crime an astonished and chagrined Brendan implied it
was. Emory himself admitted candidly to me that he'd
never heard of Jensen, and Emory had a wide acquaintance in the profession. To hear Berrigan talk, Jensen was
a sort of local corn deity in Kansas. And that annoyed
some of us a bit.

Jensen came in on a Wednesday. With his arrival we
faced our first real test. By "we" I mean the boys from
English on the so-called Critique of Culture Series Committee—Berrigan, Emory, Person, Ware, Crowder,
Klaus, and myself. Jealous associate professors later gave
us all sorts of other names, but we weren't without invention ourselves: "Henry's Hasty Boys," "Hastings' Hooey
Boys," "The Culture Clerkes," things of that sort. Early
in the term Dean Hastings, our esteemed leader, had begun to use some of us as a "nucleus," he liked to call it, on
his various projects from proposing interdisciplinary
courses and changes in the Honors Program to discussing
in "creative informality" new library collections and a
possible new journal.

However, up until the time we converged on the air-

port, a portion of the treeless plains on the other side of
town, we had never yet actually met together in a body.
The first Critique of Culture program had been sprung
full-blown from Dean Hastings' forehead as an "engagement in cross-disciplinary liaison." Jensen had apparently
been snagged to get things moving. Our first group duty
was to greet and convey safely to his hotel the visiting
dignitary.

The strange, brief history of our committee, culled
from the junior bright young men recruited by our Dean
because of "broad cultural interests," would not be that
of an originally homogenous bunch gradually become
heterodox. Instead, it would be a heterodox one that
never reached the stage of "prolific disagreement" our
ambitious Dean so verbally valued. Picture us for a moment: young, eager, impatient. We were too mixed a bag,
each too intent upon his own ends, nefarious and otherwise, too aggressive or too passive in our attitudes toward
each other and toward the important and influential objects of our hospitality. This showed itself fairly early, in
fact at the airport that mid-October afternoon—in
Berrigan's nervous pacing and whispering to his wife as
we waited for the plane to disgorge its passengers, in the
ironic musings of Person upon "crickets of modern literature," in the amused but silent audience provided him by
Emory, in the pipe-sucking, studied, but unfortunately almost bovine nonchalance of our junior Renaissance man
Crowder, in the composed and half-smiling face of the
departmental novelist Ralph Ware. It appeared flickering
but well-stoked in the bristling expectancy of Dick Klaus,
a round, chubby little fellow from Cleveland who worked
on the American novel and whom Person in a fit of deri-
sion later was to name Dickie Mouse. All year Dick
would send Person into gray-faced scowls or private
rages. It was not Dick's celebrity-chasing alone which
drove Person to these extremes. It was his trappings, par-

ticularly his ubiquitous sidekick Paul Davis, who, in Person's words, "always toddled after him," and whom Klaus began putting up to acts he didn't quite dare to involve himself in. "Art-nannies," Person would snort. Yes, Davis was there, too, on this afternoon, looking somewhat wildly wide-eyed and Yaleish, tie and double-vented jacket flapping in the wind from the propellers. Davis wasn't officially a member of our group yet, but he was working to insinuate himself. As the door of the plane opened I watched Davis await the second coming.

I'd recently opened a discreet correspondence with Jensen about the photostats, and one often forms a picture in one's mind of the person at the other end. Well, I certainly didn't expect the big hawk-nosed man who swooped swanlike from the plane, coat flowing, into the arms of waiting Wilma. She, an expectant Leda, was hardly helpless on his breast. Obviously they had been in the Kansas days great and good friends. In the annunciation we were witnessing it would have been a question of who raped whom had not Berrigan somehow wrestled Jensen away into his own grip. For a moment the two of them seemed matched in a test of forearm strength. Then Jensen, losing his balance, broke from Wilma into a dance of welcome with Berrigan. And there all the time at Berrigan's pumping elbow, boldly braving the danger of backlash, was Klaus, and on his right, one step behind, was Klaus's ever-faithful companion, Davis. Emory, Person, and I, like the chorus, remained discreetly at stage left and to the rear. Ralph Ware, as apolitical academically as anyone I know, was off somewhere hunting a cigarette machine.

Once they were settled in the back seat of my car, Wilma and Brendan did more than flank, gangsterlike, the visitor; they surrounded him verbally, talking rapidly of people back in Kansas, most of whom seemed to be

having, to have had, or to be on the verge of having serious marital difficulties; and the unmarried ones generally,
when not homosexual (sometimes when they were), were
the cause. But after a while Jensen, preoccupied or
bored, began answering Wilma's questions mechanically,
warding off with another voice Klaus's attempts to raise
the conversation to literary heights. Poor Dick, bouncing
in the seat like the ball he was, wanted his opinion of
Céline.

I suspect that Jensen had never read Céline. He *had*
read Henry James, however; and most of his quips involved references to or quotations from the Master—
points scored mainly at the expense of absent, maritally
tortured Kansans. Each tally was met by loud guffaws
from Brendan, who had probably read far into *The Turn
of the Screw* and *The Ambassadors*. Wilma offered literate giggles. It is quite possible she had read all of James in
a fit of scholarly and/or faddish vigor, but, like as not,
she remembered little in detail. With Person and Emory,
who usually acted as restraints upon Klaus's gaucheries,
off in another car, Klaus continued to seek desperate en-
trances into the discussion, even as Jensen turned the subject in his own direction. Klaus, craning around to the
rear and grinning foolishly, still wanted Jensen for a part-
ner and was ready for any tune. He thought he could lead
by describing the Critique of Culture Series, its history
and future. A hollow discourse, I'm afraid, since the real
content of what it should have been existed embryoni-
cally only in the mind of the Dean. Jensen was not impressed. He had obviously wanted to probe us about
Hastings.

Through Klaus's discourse Brendan Berrigan, sulking,
stared out the window. He had already begun to consider
himself the champion of the committee, and here he was
ignominiously unhorsed and struggling with a stuck visor.

So he limited his remarks to a few grunts of accord and other vague noises. He might as well have curled up on his shield.

I drove. No one had yet introduced me to Jensen, and I had nothing to offer anyway, except that I'm a pretty steady driver with a twelve-year no-accident certificate. My photostat business could wait. Besides, I was listening. Slowly the conversation dwindled. Klaus was eying me furtively. Somehow I felt responsible for the silence, but what was I to do?

When we arrived at Jensen's hotel we all—Emory and Person had rejoined us—collected ourselves like cattle in a Kansas City freight car up against the bed, bureau, and chairs of Jensen's small room. When I think back on those VIP visits now, I see the celebrity surrounded by crowds, like Khrushchev in an Iowa barn. Right off, Jensen opened his big suitcase out on the bed. One side was lined with bottles of gin, and I saw tucked in among the socks several artificial lemons and a couple of boxes of tea bags. We all gaped. Jensen sensed our astonishment. "Well," he said defiantly, "I just couldn't come out here only to find a dry county now, could I? And decent tea, you know. There just has to be decent tea!" Klaus smiled foolishly. Davis giggled. We stood about. But he didn't offer us any of the gin, or even tea, and after standing some more we all seemed to decide he'd be just as happy alone.

Then oddly enough, as everyone made his farewells (Klaus tried to be last, but by a quirk of the furniture arrangement, it was I), Jensen grasped my arm and said in a new low conspiratorial voice, "Hold it a minute. You're Talbot, aren't you? Come along and we'll talk a bit about Yeats and things." I was surprised. Up to then he hadn't seemed to know me or to care who I was. So Klaus, blankly crestfallen, suffered the door to be closed in his face. I told him, as the crack narrowed, that he had better get a ride home with Emory.

But I was not to achieve my desire. Jensen wanted to talk about *things,* not Yeats manuscripts. And *things* turned out to be the *real* reasons he had come. Soon I could tell he was placing some mysterious importance on his visit. Warily enough he unwound.

"I'm glad we have this chance to talk, Talbot. You know the way things are likely to go; there may not be any more free time. Brendan said Dean Hastings wants to confer with me in the morning. Say, I really like his inter-disciplinary approach. Then let's see, a meeting with the grad students and the luncheon with the committee and the lecture and the party at—where? Warner's. In the evening. Look here. Brendan sent me the whole schedule. Very efficient." He was holding out a sheet of blue paper.

I'd seen it already. In fact, I'd written it up. My pal Brendan had snookered me into making the arrange-ments. It was a heavy day for Jensen, all right. He'd be on stage most of the time, but I couldn't see any real cause for alarm. Nevertheless, he was fidgety.

Then I got an inkling of what was working upon him. There he was straight-eying me, saying, "Tell me, Talbot, is Hastings really serious? Is he going through with this magazine idea he wrote me about?"

Well, I suppose Jensen thought I was in on the know, but, like anyone else, I only wondered what Hastings had in mind. Oh, I'd heard Hastings mention the magazine idea as he skied off the slope of some other subject; but nothing more. But I played the game. "I'm not sure how far he's gone on it." I kept wondering why Jensen had chosen me for all of this.

At that he turned quickly to his suitcase. Watching me out of the corner of his eye, he produced a folded sheet of paper, flipped it open with a flourish, and stood as if stage center. (He'll make it through the day, I thought.) "Now Hastings says right here it's practically a certainty that Walton will be publishing a journal of culture and the arts. I'm out here as a visiting consultant on it. I'm supposed to have ideas. But, Talbot, I'll be damned if I know what he has in mind. This series business is a smoke screen, isn't it? Who's going to be editor of that magazine, Talbot?" It was a great firm line. I felt like a witness in the dock, but I didn't show it one bit. That would have spoiled the scene.

Jensen stared oddly at me, then paced the room. Too willingly he had opened himself up for me to look, and I saw. I understood a measure of his anxiety. Hastings' letter, or maybe Brendan, made him think he was invited to an interview for the editorship. Well, perhaps. I wasn't yet experienced enough in the ways of Walton University to know that Hastings' letters seemed to promise more than they actually contained. When I had seen more of him it would become clearer to me that he operated on vague big ideas and used people to come up with what he called the "specifics." If they did, good for them. He wanted people to discover what he'd vaguely envisioned and the details would emerge—"finalize themselves," he called it. It made me feel at times like one of those natives who dive for pennies when the big liners come around. Ralph Ware, in the detachment he managed to maintain, used to assure us that in spite of it all some of Hastings' wildest dreams came true, even if the truth, with all of its worldly freight of confusion and frustration plainly evident, was an odd copy of the Platonic original.

But was Jensen really a possible editor? There were certainly bigger names around, and people with more editorial experience. Could it really be that Brendan had hooeyed and convinced the Dean that Jensen was the man for the job? The way Berrigan talked he had practically brought Jensen to the campus himself.

I couldn't disclose much, then, about Hastings, or about Walton. I hadn't found a Utopia there, and Jensen was in no mood to be disillusioned. Besides, the Dean's staccato assertions about "firming up plans" in the course of a couple of conversations on the library steps were not much to go on, so I chickened out.

My reticence, or whatever it was (I supposed there was method in it—I enjoyed Jensen), only drove him to greater efforts and even to verbal self-immolation. He sought clues as to how he should behave, but now his questions were punctuated with running comments on life back home. He wanted a new start. The job in Kansas was becoming intolerable. "They" were shoving him into a corner, first for his advocacy of contemporary literature in the curriculum and then because of the puritanical priggishness of his colleagues and the whole town. I could not believe that he would talk to a stranger as he did. But then, remembering Brendan Berrigan on his own sex life a few days after I first met him, I concluded, shades of Abner Dean, it must be the norm to talk that way where they all came from. Then why the complaints about persecution by prigs? During the ride from the airport, I had picked up the idea that the whole town was wide open and nobody gave a damn.

Well, it didn't work. He had tried a kind of voodoo dance before me, but with nothing to show for his efforts, he became vague and distant, as he had in the car with Wilma and Brendan. He had thrust me back into the pack. No ace I. It was a relief to get away, photostats or not; and besides, there was a full day ahead. On the way home I tried to puzzle out what the truth of the situation was, just why Jensen was visiting the campus. The conclusion I missed or avoided (old rational me) was that there was no special reason, that it just happened, that most things are snafus, not plots. If we'd all remembered that about Hastings it would have ended better. As I turned up our street I saw the Berrigans' big-finned convertible parked in the driveway. I couldn't get into the garage, and that meant dragging out to the car again when they went home. You couldn't park overnight in town. I was profoundly irritated. Later on I would have put it differently to myself: IF they went home.

Besides, I knew I was in for it, and I sighed. It had been a hard day: three classes, one of bonehead composition, the Jensen business, and, sandwiched between, a crazy conference with a neurotic blonde freshman coed, her problems in unity, emphasis, and coherence so hopelessly interwoven with her daily desire to attract the attention of a basketball player in row three that I nearly ran shouting from the room. My humor had held me back from desperation only by meeting Will Person in the hall as he returned from a four o'clock class. One could tell Person the poet had been teaching poetry. His big Roethkean body shuffled as if it were following some monstrous broom; his lined face was puffy and drawn, almost gray. He saw me and shouted, "Jason, goddammit, eighty percent of these students will *never* learn to read a poem." The door of Miss Elvira Horne's office had just opened a couple of inches. Now it discreetly closed. Later on Person assured me that his figure had been wildly optimistic; he hadn't wanted to disillusion Miss Elvira, ninety-eight percent was more like it. There were times when he even thought only he and Emory could read a poem, and he wasn't always sure about Emory.

All in all I was hardly in a mood to be Berriganed, but there was no help for it. All Brendan needed was a foot in the door, and in those days I opened a crack out of wonder. Quite by chance, I'd discovered he had once embarked on a brief but very successful career in real estate. Just after the war, it was. I imagine he still tried to sell John Crowe Ransom to students as if he were the house of joy.

Brendan and Wilma were sitting in the living room. Betty Lou was in the kitchen making coffee with all of that immense concentration and single-mindedness she has when something is going on that she doesn't like. Charley—pardon me, Chuck—and Emily were asleep in bed. Only children could have managed oblivion under the circumstances, for our bear was rattling the bars of his cage. When he saw me he leaped up and shouted, "Where ya been, for God's sake? We lost ya. Did ya stay with Kit? What'd he want with you?" His face displayed outrage and terror. He was on the edge of a sulk, but the body wouldn't stay down. The trouble was that Kit had wanted to talk with me, good old Jason, and not his old pal and student. Brendan simply could not play it cool like Wilma, who sat icily in our one good chair, not a jiggle in her pony tail, smoking rapidly and punctuating her husband's remarks with "Sit down, Brendan, sit down." In their general excitement, in the great hooey-hooey of the total event, the Berrigans had overlooked my absence until they were on the street and Emory announced that he was taking everyone home. Then they'd apparently hightailed it over to our house to wait out my return. Oh they had been very mysterious, Betty Lou sarcastically allowed, about where I was and why they had come over. I guess we didn't know the Berrigans very well yet or sense how deep Brendan's fears went. Person hadn't begun to call him "the heavy bear that goes with us."

Somewhere inside Brendan there was a demon as vigilant as Socrates'. It could smell trouble a mile away, and Brendan recognized it in the faintest hint of competition. He was, poor man, jealous and hurt. I didn't really know how much Brendan knew about Jensen's hopes or whether perhaps he had planted them himself. He didn't have much control over his anxieties, but he could sense things that passed between people. I could see that he wasn't going to leave until I told him all.

But again, as with Jensen, all wasn't very much, and suspicion and jealousy demand an outrageous satisfaction. I stupidly did tell him what I thought troubled Jensen. (There are things worse than watching.) Emory's theory of bear-handling was to be ruthlessly polite but speak only through the mail slot. I went too far in the other direction. Neither strategy was perfect self-protection even in theory, but I think mine was the more disastrous. I told Brendan I thought Jensen was hoping for the editorship of Hastings' proposed magazine and was worried about his meeting with Hastings tomorrow. At that moment I knew he had not connected Jensen with the magazine at all.

"Gee dya really think so, I mean dya think there's a chance?" Then he beared his way through. "Well, why didn't he ask me? I could tell him all about Hastings. You know, sell him! Tell him what he wants! Boy, you hardly know him. Why did he ask you?"

Now I'm not sure myself why Jensen asked me, but hearing the question put by Berrigan was annoying. He had rummaged through one garbage can too many. Wilma saw this and tried to calm him.

"Now Brendan, he understands that, but he probably wanted another opinion. You know, for objectivity's sake. I mean, he'd really want to make sure the interview's a success." Now, she'd annoyed me, too!

Brendan was still steaming, but he moped, "Yeh yeh, I guess so," and sat in his chair. Wilma could sometimes control him in public, but I know it was pure hell at home.

Then suddenly he saw possibilities. "Well whaddya think? Is Hastings really going to do it? Boy, what a coup. With Kit Jensen as modern-lit man, why we're in, man, we're in. I mean he's really got advanced ideas." I looked at Betty Lou. Betty Lou looked back at me. Her eyes rolled to the ceiling; she shrugged solemnly, made a face as if she were whistling, tapped her foot twice.

If Emory had been there he would have pricked Brendan's bubble with a dispassionate analysis of departmental politics. As usual Brendan saw only half the situation, according to his manic phase—the part he sensed immediately by nose. As he paced the floor again, extolling Jensen's tolerance, his scholarship, his liberalism, his critical perspicuity, I could see him imagining himself and Kit supported by me, Person, Emory, and Klaus raising on some academic Iwo Jima a flag with the figure of Henry Hastings rampant, bearing the shield of critical theory since Croce, gules.

Something was wrong with the picture. Where was Professor Warner, who did the modern American stuff? Where was Vanner, the chairman? Where were all the dissatisfied associate professors, resentful of any newcomer? How long before Person spat at Jensen? If in the future Berrigan extolled the virtues of Jensen, the old guard would shore up their defenses and fire away. When Berrigan said "we," the old guard would think, "Talbot, Emory, Person," too. Berrigan's big mouth, I thought.

I was very tired. I wanted Wilma to take her accordion and bear and go home. Finally she did, but only after a few remarks on her own implying that I had acted badly in staying on without them, we were all in this together weren't we, and what had they done to deserve this? Brendan Bear, I was beginning to think, was one of those friends who hug you to death. But, of course, he was not really my friend, or I wasn't his.

Betty Lou and I finished up the coffee. "Do you really think Brendan engineered an appointment for Jensen? It seems incredible," she said. "Well anyway, to coin a phrase, I thought they'd never leave." She paused and, contemplating me, drawled, "Maybe they never do leave." I thought about that. It was my good, pretty wife getting to me again, saying don't stare, little boy.

I acknowledged her sagacity with no comment, then answered the question. "It would be incredible if any of us engineered an appointment. Why, heavens, we just aren't that important, just a bunch of assistant professors. But then you haven't met the great man! I don't know, dear; if Brendan managed it, we have more to fear than fear itself. We have Hastings, too."

Part of me itched to say, no, Hastings couldn't, just couldn't, be influenced by Berrigan. When I finally achieved the bedroom, I remembered the car. Now that Brendan was gone from my driveway I could, ho hum, get into my own garage. After that, flopping into bed would be no struggle, only a graceless fall from the peak of my daily identity.

On the next morning I, as unlicensed chauffeur, took Jensen up to Hastings' office and left him there with his syndrome. The lecture wasn't until afternoon. What happened between him and Hastings no one knows to this day, though we are not without the benefit of interpretations. I for one think Jensen came away sadly disappointed. Nevertheless, when I picked him up again back at his hotel to deliver him to the lecture hall, he was quite jovial. He walked through the lobby with his big coat open and flowing, his body tilted a bit forward like a gigantic bird dog's. He was speaking on what had become his principal theme: the terrible situation in his department back home, how he was simply not appreciated, how he was carrying on a really one-man campaign for the arts there, how Hastings' emphasis on interdisciplinary programs was the only answer. Then suddenly he began a monologue about his brakes giving out on the longest hill in town and he careening at almost ninety miles per hour into and nearly through the campus. How he was ticketed by a campus policeman and threatened with prosecution for resisting arrest when he wouldn't stop.

"My God," he intoned, his eyes alive, "I thought I'd lose my MIND! And then the damned cop was mad because I didn't stop when I saw his bloody light. Did you ever hear of anything so RIDICULOUS?" His voice was a squeaking shout. Then, pleased with himself and calmer: "Of course it's like an allegory. I DON'T stop for that damned campus anyway, and they know it, and that's why they resent me. Why, I'm gadfly to the state! Do you know?" He continued, peering at me with big eyes, leaning farther forward as we teetered on a curb edge waiting for the light (and now I knew he'd been cutting into his gin supply), "Do you know that back there the President PERSONALLY refused me a new typewriter? I mean finally I had to go to the President and HE refused me! And then they made me start to pay for my own mail, just because I'm their professional scholar instead of a half-ass. I USE the mail."

Later I discovered, by getting on his mailing list, just why it was either a new tax levy or no mail privileges for Jensen. Over a period of a year or so I guess he mailed a hundred items to me, mainly squibs from the local paper about his lectures or interviews with him by student reporters. It was clear that the students there knew where they could get copy to fill up a few extra inches on a slow day. They would rout him out on every conceivable subject. In one interview he appeared to be advocating a relaxation of sexual standards for college students, retracted the statement the next week, shouting that he had been misquoted, and that, well, he had certain qualifications to make. Then he would mimeograph short articles and poems and send them around to everyone who knew him. The implication was that there was a general conspiracy of editors against him. I could see why the administration had cracked down. They should have locked the mimeo room as well.

Suddenly he was off on another tack, worrying about the lecture. He had doubts about it being the right thing for his audience. Hastings said something about wanting it for the magazine, if and when. Would he still hold the copyright? After all, it was part of a new book. I decided the gin had been to ease his fright about the lecture, which was called "The Hole in Time in Modern Poetry." Time was the thing these days: Poulet, Auerbach, Meyerhoff—everyone was discussing art and time. The hole in time, well, it was something like Eliot's still point in the turning wheel, Wyndham Lewis's vortex, Yeats's gyre.

"Spudnut aestheticism," I joked, but he ignored my trivial levity.

"What will the audience be like? Sophisticated? They'll like this time stuff, full of paradoxes—movement and stasis, linear and cyclical. It all relates back to the fortunate fall, you know!" I nodded. He looked at me quizzically, looked again. I realize now that it was a lion look I'd given him.

I suppose Brendan hadn't really told him what kind of audience to expect. He should have given Jensen the word in his letter, but we later learned you had to follow Brendan around. "With a shovel," Person said.

The lecture was, from my point of vantage, a disaster, tragicomic in its movement toward the final perception. Let me begin by observing that the department as a group was very critical of the whole idea of the series. Too many people were left out of the planning, and too many bright young new men were on the inside of it getting to meet academic celebrities. Almost all the older professors, we later learned, had been told—and not too obliquely—by Dean Hastings that the series was for the younger people and to stay in the background. He couldn't have done us a worse turn as far as our standing with our colleagues was concerned. Besides, the simple fact that it was the Dean's project was enough to call down the scorn of people like Warner, who knew Hastings when he "hadn't burst his britches trying to get around the department." Poor Jensen, in other words, had it against him from the start among the old folks at home. Being Douglas Bush might have saved him, but he wasn't.

Brendan Berrigan himself introduced the visiting dignitary. Brendan was obviously nervous and might have been incapable of duty had he noticed that Jensen was slightly in his cups. Haltingly he began, outlined Jensen's career, allowed that we were most honored to hear him, and announced the topic. Meanwhile, Jensen, sitting off the small raised platform, shuffled through his papers. Then a ridiculous thing happened. He rose to take his position, but somehow his manuscript slipped out the end of the Manila folder and spread itself on the floor. Instantly he bent to pick up the papers. Berrigan, quick to react, leaned down behind the lectern to help. There was a barely perceptible dull thwack as their foreheads met. From my front-row corner I could see around the lectern, but most of the audience was unaware of what had occurred. There were merely slight gasps and titters from a couple of coeds near me, one of whom didn't regain her usual composure until Jensen had bored her to death a half hour later. Generally the view from the hall was that of Berrigan suddenly popping bolt upright like a puppet taking the stage, then walking stiffly to the chair Jensen had vacated. Jensen, reeling momentarily, collected his papers and began.

For one thing, it was too long. For another, Jensen, whether under the pressure of gin or a healthy knock on the head, or perhaps merely speaking in his usual style, called attention to his manner of delivery. One kept forgetting the content of his words. He was so tall that he dwarfed the lectern, and it seemed that he must accommodate himself by stooping and sprawling upon it, leaning far out over his audience. Then occasionally he would move about the platform, teetering and swaying on the edges so that many of us were in great anxiety about his falling off entirely. The distance to the floor was only a foot, but Jensen's peculiar equilibrium made us feel that he was treading the edge of a great abyss. He affected also at times, under the influence of the gin perhaps, but more probably because of his own penchant for self-dramatization, a parody of an Oxonian stutter, so that his speech alternated between fuzzy mumblings and great booming expirations of sound and breath. Those directly below him braved asphyxiation.

In the first half hour he soared above his audience with a theory about time in Yeats and later English poets. Then he proceeded to quote a short poem by Herbert Mortimer, subjecting it to a long, patient, loving, solemn explication. The poem had been mimeographed and passed out to the audience along with some extracts from Yeats. About halfway through the analysis I noticed Ralph Ware, who was sitting beside me, barely suppressing a monstrous guffaw, and Person, on his other side, whispering something in his ear. In the back of the lecture room there was, here and there, a meandering restlessness. I could not understand what Jensen might have said to cause this reaction, but Ralph Ware was nevertheless nearly helpless with the giggles, turning red in the face and jiggling in his seat. Jensen himself had become vaguely aware of him.

At this point Jack Emory, who had been sitting in the front row close to the door, tiptoed up to Berrigan near the platform. He whispered something in his ear. Berrigan, startled for a moment, nodded. Jensen was reaching his conclusion: ". . . and therefore it is possible to say that time spirals through Mortimer's poem or that, and perhaps more accurately, the poem's thoughts wheel through time around that central place, which is the speaker's own visionary location, the hole in time, into which we look." I heard a giggle far back in the audience. I was still in the dark when Berrigan, rather than asking for questions, very abruptly brought the meeting to a close with thanks to the lecturer. Jensen was a bit surprised; he had been advised to expect questions and had clearly warmed to his subject, his self-confidence beating its chest. As I rose, Emory was at my arm propelling me to the hall, and Person and Ware were acting like schoolgirls behind us.

The root of the business was an acrostic in Mortimer's poem, overlooked entirely in Jensen's solemn analysis. The first letters of each line, reading downward, offered this pleasant blessing to the reader:

S
H
I
T
H
E
R
E
C
R
I
T
I
C

A perfect Italian sonnet, nicely divided between two discrete quatrains and the final sestet.

Person, who had a fantastic knowledge of modern poetry, knew of the acrostic. Emory, who analyzed things, spotted it and said later that being adviser to a campus literary magazine had made him alert for anything. It was he who saved the day. Some smart aleck would surely have popped up to say, "Dr. Jensen, there seems to be a dimension of this poem that you have ignored." It was clear, of course, that Jensen had no idea—no idea at all —that the poem contained a built-in spoof of his solemn reading. He had been defending poesy.

In the hall afterward, Person, barely controlling his giggles, pointed out that the acrostic was the poet's own fond message to "stupid crickets," and he was elated by the triumph of poetry over explication. "No matter what you say, the poem always says a little more than its paraphrase does," he chortled, mimicking the poetry textbooks he particularly disliked.

We would have to see whether Warner or some of the people in power got the message and whether they would cherish it; if they did, not even Henry Hastings would care to save Jensen for Walton. We all had a way to go, late as it was and rarefied as was the air, before we found this day's downward slope.

▶

Not only were these events putting into microcosm our world and our Walton careers; they were also introducing to us some who would contribute to denouement in another year and another place. In the evening, Betty Lou and I went out to a steak house with Jack Emory to meet his sister Ann and his brother-in-law George Brocklin, who were passing through from Seattle. George taught in a prep school there. Ann, a tall, brown-haired, striking girl, had been a fashion model for a while, Emory told me, and then married George—well-to-do and very excited (as only someone whose income doesn't depend upon it could be) about teaching. He had a Columbia master's degree in education and was traveling on some sort of grant designed to keep secondary-school teachers in touch with college curricula. I heard all about this at great length, for I sat next to him, and the steaks were slow.

When finally we did eat, Jack recounted for George and Ann the remarkable events of the lecture and how he had told Berrigan for God's sake not to allow any questions. Berrigan hadn't noticed the acrostic, so he asked an innocent "why?" Well, there wasn't time to explain it right then; Jack simply invoked the name of Hastings: Hastings didn't want questions, he said, and Brendan snapped to. We all had a good laugh over this and wondered whether Brendan had yet found out the truth about the poem.

We drank a lot of beer. Emory enjoyed himself immensely at dinner. His remarks about Jensen and Berrigan were particularly scathing as he contemplated the eventual fall of Berrigan from administrative esteem. I could tell that having Ann for an audience pleased him, and he tormented George with disclosures about the seamy side, the "real" side of the profession. Emory hated educationists with a vengeance. Ann hung on his words worshipfully, enjoying everything almost too much. Meanwhile, George interposed questions about Jensen. How could he have been so stupid? Would this dent his career? Didn't anyone care? Oh, the cruelty of man to man, I thought. George belonged to the new clergy. From time to time Ann glowered at him, as if, for heaven's sake, can't we be a bit more detached than that? I got the idea that George's attitude toward things, embodied in a sort of missionary zeal for education, embarrassed Ann, at least in this company. She mistook her brother's ironic scathing manner for cynicism and didn't really seem to understand that there was a lot of missionary in Jack, too. Ann saw the surface sophistication, and that was enough for her, or perhaps it was all the reality she could handle. Jack once told me, after everything had worked itself out at Walton, that Ann despised George's intellectual vapidity, but I doubt that Ann knew much of intellect. She saw some vague sort of glamor in the intellectual life. I wondered how much having that pretty face and body made her live on the surface of everything. In her own way she matched George in naïveté, but their surfaces were incompatible.

The talk went on.

"No wonder scholars hate poets so, with tricks like that being played on them," Emory remarked.

"But they deserve it, don't they?" said Ann. I thought, Person would like that.

"Some of them," said Betty Lou, *sotto voce.* How I adore that girl!

The dinner out was supposed to stoke us up for the party at Professor Warner's, and it did so quite adequately. We arrived about an hour after it had begun, but Mrs. Warner was ready and waiting at the door nevertheless—buxom, post-blonde, completely unintellectual, and certainly the opposite of the fictive faculty wife intent on getting her Ph.D., *too.* I supposed that Ann might be a little disappointed. In departmental circles Sylvia Warner had caused Vanner, as chairman of the department, no end of trouble by her feud with Clarissa Cassoway, wife of another departmental statesman. It was a feud both would have liked to see everyone eventually implicated in. Sylvia Warner was bold and crude in her attempts to corral visiting celebrities; Clarissa Cassoway was sly. At first public notice of an important visitor Sylvia would call and harangue Vanner about arranging entertainment, but Clarissa, who called her husband "love dove" in public and used him as a spy, often had the advantage of prior knowledge and acted to snag the celebrity before poor Sylvia had been cued in. Warner himself didn't really seem to give a damn about entertaining celebrities, and so he never brought home to his wife any inside information. Through all of this, we young men seemed to be asked to choose a side.

On this night Sylvia Warner was up on her luck. Apparently Hastings had delivered Jensen to her. Clarissa Cassoway hadn't stood a chance. Beaming in her triumphant hour, Mrs. Warner ushered us in with the usual flurry, laying a peck on Betty Lou's cheek. I must have been watching impudently, because Betty Lou gave me not just a lion look but a long lion look. Soon we were near the punch bowl, where Jensen was engaged in conversation with about a dozen people, most of whom were really only listeners, hanging on to his quips and cracks. He was answering at length the questions he had been prevented from entertaining at the lecture. He was still clearly oblivious of the acrostic, that monstrous question not having, through some miracle, arisen. He lectured and posed, his great neck stretched above the listeners and protruding slightly forward. His most rapt attendants included Wilma Berrigan, Klaus, the inevitable Davis, and several graduate students. Betty Lou retreated, whispering "See ya, pal," but I was not inclined to join the group, partly because I'd already seen quite a bit of Jensen and didn't want anyone to think I was trying to be a hog, as Klaus surely would. And I certainly didn't want another visit from the Berrigans. Betty Lou had been swept away by Clarissa, and I gravitated to a corner where Person was loitering with one of the vast number of associate professors in the department, a tall drink of water named Fred McCrea. Person, whose definition of "fairy" was pretty broad, didn't care much for McCrea. Once I met an old primary-school teacher of Fred's in St. Louis who remembered him as a rather good boy soprano. When I told Person, he merely growled, "Still is." Fred was a rich but gaunt bachelor with an apartment that looked like a brothel. He must have had a mama somewhere. He was effeminate in his manner, but Person, after his other comments, graciously decided that he didn't have the verve to go through with an affair. To me he was a fairly harmless sort, all six feet five of him, including his impeccable sport jackets and ties. Fred was an old friend of Hastings. I think maybe they had gone to college or high school or something together. Anyway, Fred McCrea wasn't with a boy friend this night. In fact, he was escorting Ellen Fraser, one of Hastings' assistants and former students. Jack Emory had also been dating her now and then, and why not? She was a doll who could talk. Ellen and I had something in common. We'd attended the same high school in Denton, Texas; several years apart, I might add. I didn't interrupt their talk, got a nod from Will, a "Jason, my boy," from Fred, and a composed smile from Ellen.

Person and McCrea were engaged in a curious banter, with Ellen listening, gravely amused. She didn't often give herself away, and didn't have to, being the sight she was. McCrea's conversation was filled with Puckish remarks about Warner's real purpose in giving the party—to poison Jensen in a large crowd. Person played straight man. No one really knew where McCrea stood vis-à-vis Hastings, whether he was one of *us,* so to speak, or one of *them,* meaning the old guard. He qualified in the eyes of some for either camp. It seemed that he was willing to affect friendship with Hastings' hobby boys—Emory, whom he seemed to like, Person, who disliked him, and even old neutral me. This was unusual enough, because it wasn't too often at Walton that we ran into a live, speaking, friendly colleague.

Soon Jensen's claque broke up and, true to his Kansas publicity, he tried to pick up one of the prettier girls at the party, and Ann filled the bill. I could see Wilma watching far across the room with Berrigan. Brendan talked rapidly and gesticulated at some helpless graduate student who to everyone's amazement had followed him from Kansas. I could imagine from the vehemence of Brendan's address and his occasional glances toward our group that he was proclaiming the imminent elevation of Jensen to professor at Walton, at which point the graduate student would have two mentors and a certain Ph.D. Berrigan, who like the rest of us in his first term at Walton was teaching nothing above the sophomore level (being Hastings' boys didn't at once make us departmental whizzes), was already throwing his weight around among some of the more impressionable graduate students, trying to indicate where possible that he alone was the modern criticism man, the man of intensity, the true disciple of John Crowe or Allen, or whomever he had been told about in that survey of criticism he must have taken.

Jensen and Ann had probably been discussing things like dogs and the weather, and I presume they were desperate to find a real subject. They wandered our way. The trouble was that we were discussing Jensen, so when they turned up there was an embarrassing silence. Even Jensen had no Henry James quips, and it was only by ridiculous chance that we turned to a discussion of the local newspaper. McCrea, who had read it for years, was something of an expert on comic misprints. The Walton *Chronicle* was evidently never proofread, but simply run off from type. Practically every night it gave cause for hilarity. This time, however, Person topped him, from having perused the paper carefully only a few nights before. A young singer had performed at the civic center: "So-and-So Gives Walton Rectal," the *Chronicle* had announced. Jensen recalled a headline in upstate New York: "Watkins Glen Holds Prix." Ellen smiled and flicked a cigarette ash. Ann laughed a little too hard, and there was a lull. Then, without realizing what I was setting in motion, I thought in my slow steady way to introduce Person to Ann.

Well, they played a little of what Will himself calls the "do-you-know bout," and finally they landed on a discussion of Northwest poets, particularly Arthur Ryerson, who was a friend of Jack's and whom Ann had met. He was one of those poets I read because Jack knew of him. In a way I got education picking up things Person, Emory, and Ware talked about. Where I am now, I'm a real avant-gardist. Ryerson was one of Person's culture heroes, second in rank only to Pound, Williams, and Rexroth. From names, Ann and Will went on to painting, which was, it turned out, Ann's art form. McCrea and Ellen disengaged themselves in the direction of the punch bowl. I looked for my wife, but she was in between Clarissa and Sylvia Warner now. I waved gaily and moved away to talk to Laura Person in another corner. As I left, Person was actually *listening* to Ann discoursing on Morris Graves, Mark Tobey, a man named Callahan, and some other painters she knew, and that was something for old pontificator Will. He wasn't even muttering "yes, ah yes," as he so often did to various colleagues who would pop into his office to bore him. Actually, Will wasn't too sure of himself with strangers. It was only after he got to know you that his invective became scathing and his metaphor hyperbolic. And with senior members of the department he was maybe a little too much good old Will. Anyway, he warmed up pretty quickly to Ann and was all personality. Jensen, meanwhile, was simply out of it and retired to his claque. I guess he appealed to fat women, but also I think Ann had decided from the dinner-table conversation that he was beyond the pale of good sense and enlightened criticism. During the whole time Person was listening, though, he'd glance at Laura now and then. The trouble with Person was a tough Lutheran demon down inside reminding him that he was a miserable sinner.

"I see lover boy is all ears," was Laura's first remark. I

wouldn't have been surprised at that combination of soap-operaeze and sarcasm a year later, when we all knew each other better, but right then and there it took me off balance. Then I realized that it had slipped out of her unawares. She was really talking to the ceiling, not to me. Even that was characteristic of her naïveté. The real Laura was seldom sarcastic and had little irony. She was a possessive wife with some rather rigid conceptions of how life should be run. All the same, she was very appreciative of Person's hyperbole, which he did manage to raise almost entirely above malice to the realm of art. I liked this appreciation in her, but the most charming of her attributes was her capacity for wide-eyed surprise and renewed astonishment, totally without malice, at the antics of Brendan Berrigan. Eventually, as the year went on, she discovered that her manner was charming to us, and after that she couldn't help cultivating it. She naturally wanted to prove that she was an interesting person in her own right, but her moral attitudes fought against her. She would conclude that Brendan and Wilma simply needed friends, and may have wanted to bring Brendan back into the Church even more than she wanted to convert Will. Later Will would talk to me a little about this, but not too seriously. I think the only thing he really disliked about her Catholicism was that it seemed to require seeing the Berrigans more often than he could stand. Laura was a small blonde girl with a turned-up nose, a face beginning to harden around the mouth and eyes.

Now that I look back on it I realize that from my first meeting with her I was aware of Laura watching her marriage the way a nervous collie watches a recalcitrant ram. Particularly she disliked young student poetesses, whom she may have suspected, not without some reason, of nefarious designs on her husband. Person was capable of giving her cause to worry, I suppose, because he frequented the taverns in town with his entourage of young people, leaving Laura home with the children. But the main thing she disliked about the poetesses was that they just weren't folks. In that way she wasn't so very different from Betty Lou, or from me, I guess.

"She's pretty, isn't she?" Laura looked grimly at me, took my arm, and actually steered me in their direction. Yes, Laura was frank. In our company that was, at least, something of a relief. When we got there, and there was even a larger crowd at the party by now, Will wasn't listening any more but entrancing Ann with a criticism of Jensen's talk, which, he said, turning to me, "begging your reverence, was horse shit." Old Warner joined us just in time to hear this and, grinning slyly, made some remark about Jensen's soon going back to Kansas, where he'd undoubtedly be more at home. I couldn't tell whether Warner knew about the acrostic or whether he sensed that the temper of things in our little group was to his liking. He would in that case play along. He didn't want Jensen around, and he also wanted to capture us as trophies in the chairmanship steeplechase when Vanner retired.

"Perhaps Mr. Hastings will be a little more careful about whom he invites for these lectures after this. Why, that old boy Jensen better stay back in the nineteenth century and leave the twentieth to you young fellows." I got the message.

"Now Harold," Alex Cassoway chimed in over his shoulder, "don't you approve of critics?" Cassoway and Warner probably didn't dislike each other as much as their wives did. In fact, they respected each other as rival chieftains do. There was a courtly formality in their professorial confrontations that was in its way splendid to see. Warner's reply was measured and without vagueness of reference: "I have always thought critics tolerable, Alex, when kept in check by stubborn fact, more tolerable than romantic biographers." He was alluding to Cassoway's studies of the Brownings.

Stubborn fact was the right phrase, for Cassoway couldn't match Warner for stubbornness. But Warner was really out of place; he should have been a smalltime politico walking the halls of a courthouse or possibly a state senate; he had a certain awkward dignity, and you could say of him that he never put on airs. He was friendly in a way to us, but he never really pretended he wasn't a loner. I think that is why he rather appealed to Emory, and it is one of the reasons I preferred him to Cassoway, though I would not trust him. Besides, Cassoway called me "Jay boy," which was annoying almost beyond endurance. He was also a patter and pincher. At the moment of his remark to Warner, he had begun his latest feeble lechery by lighting Ellen's cigarette. I gazed at her. She raised her eyes to mine—blank, as blank as to convey all. Ellen was sharp; she read Cassoway like a book (just as I guess she could read me).

Let's face it. I really disliked Cassoway, and I guess from the way things went the feeling was mutual. Cassoway's power came from sensitivity to the winds of administration above and discontent below. He thrived on a claque of older and nearly forgotten associate professors. Whenever he walked across campus or took lunch in the cafeteria, they surrounded him like pigeons looking for food. Warner, on the other hand, would often eat alone or with one or two, usually younger, men.

But in their attitude toward Jensen, Warner and Cassoway were in rare accord. They could join forces when there was a threat from outside the department to the balance of power within. Emory thought that after so many years they would be lost without each other, and Person called them Gog and Magog.

Before either could get very far on the subject of literary critics, Berrigan, with Jensen in tow, moored himself off Person, and said he was going to take Dr. Jensen back to his hotel since they all had to leave early in the morning for the meetings at Danforth, where he, Berrigan, was giving a paper on etc., etc. Of course, we'd all see Dr. Jensen again. Cassoway smiled, Warner smiled, but neither at Jensen nor at Berrigan—more or less in the general direction of Mars. The guests walked to the door, Dickie Klaus now on Jensen's elbow saying something like "Now Dr. Jensen, don't you think there's a certain irony in that poem?" Ellen Fraser, Freddy McCrea, and I stood looking quizzically at each other. I was wondering whether Klaus was about to tell him of the acrostic. But they were down the front steps and away before the conversation progressed. Ellen shrugged. McCrea toodle-ooed good-bye. Betty Lou tapped my shoulder. The second day ended with me hanging, Pauline-like, from the summit.

Apparently Klaus's question was innocuous and Jensen escaped from Walton University and its verbal environs ignorant of the awful truth. We heard not a word about it during the drive to Danforth the next day. With Betty Lou in front, I steered our middle-aged Plymouth out onto the highway, and we drove past wheat-cut brown fields and scattered farmhouses toward the state line. In the back, dressed regally in her squirrel coat, her blonde hair pulled back from her big face, sat Wilma, flanked by Kit Jensen and Brendan. It was to be Brendan's first paper, and naturally he was nervous. But Brendan never expressed any emotion with restraint. Knowing all this, Jensen took malicious delight in reminding him of his coming ordeal. He began by asking Brendan if he'd marked his paper, but Brendan had no idea what he was driving at.

"Oh come now, when I give a paper, in fact when *anyone* gives a paper, he practices it in front of a mirror, marks the pauses, underlines the words he should emphasize, tries to anticipate questions from the audience. Boy, take some advice and do that this evening. Here, give me your paper and I'll check it over."

There was considerable fumbling around in the back seat, Brendan apparently searching his jacket pockets, his overcoat, and finally the ledge behind the seat. Then in a high-pitched querulous voice, uncommon to bears: "Wilma, did you pack my paper? I thought it was in my pocket. Jason, stop the car, will ya?" Betty Lou, who had begun the trip with great solemnity, was now on the verge of laughter.

I pulled off on the shoulder and handed Brendan the keys to the trunk. In a flash the Berrigans were out hunting through their luggage for the paper. Brendan was really agitated.

"Did ya pack it, Wilma, did ya pack it? Goddammit, where is it then? I thought I had it. You must have taken it out of my coat. Damn, why did you do that?"

"Oh now, Brendan, I haven't touched your paper."

But it simply wasn't with us. Back inside, Berrigan was casting accusations at his wife. Betty Lou had recovered herself. I had turned the car around, and we had begun to retrace the thirty or forty miles back to Walton. With pedantic pomposity Jensen poured in the salt. "Well, Bren, that can happen when you're nervous. You probably put it somewhere you'd be sure to remember. Incidentally, it's a good idea to have an extra copy. I always keep two, and in separate places, so this won't happen. Anyway, you're very lucky we noticed it, aren't you?"

Berrigan only grunted, "Yeh, yeh, I guess you're right," and I could imagine him as I drove settled down inside his big topcoat and scarf, grim-faced and moping.

In the rear-view mirror the great face of Wilma filled the back window like an Easter Island statue.

Jensen would not let him off. "You know, if you're nervous it's all the more important to be well prepared. You must practice the talk tonight. That is, providing we find it."

"Kit, for heaven's sake, let's forget it," Wilma hissed, and we all sat in silence. Finally I flipped on the radio, and we heard the news. Betty Lou pointed out that I was straddling the center line. I condescended to move over for a Greyhound bus. Betty Lou looked condescendingly at me. I was deserving everything that was happening. Her look reminded me that it was I who had agreed to this trip.

The first search of the Berrigan house failed to turn up anything but a rough draft. Finally, however, Brendan himself found the paper on the bathroom floor, where, at his ease, he had last reviewed it. Jensen, pleased at this turn of events, remarked that some of the best work of mankind had probably been accomplished in the jakes, though he preferred light reading himself at stool. Which —too bad—only indicated that he probably would never have the big idea. He was delighted that Brendan used all of his time to good advantage. Brendan would go far, no doubt, if Hastings gave him time to shit. Brendan made a good imitation of Andrei Gromyko.

Back in the car, Wilma hysterically sought out new subjects for conversation, her voice rising awkwardly, her laughter stilted. Jensen proposed gin and produced a pint flask from his topcoat pocket, offering it around. Betty Lou, who doesn't do much with gin but has had it do plenty to her, graciously refused, and I as driver begged off. I'm not much of a drinker anyway, past coffee. But the three in back settled down to finishing it off, Brendan somewhat reluctantly at first, then warming to the occasion. Jensen fanned the flame of good fellowship with tales of his Kansas troubles—first with the university authorities, next with his children (now teen age), and finally, as the gin disappeared from view and took hold of his stomach, with his wife, who, thank God, would never accompany him anywhere on lecture trips. With these last revelations I could see in the mirror Wilma's face turning all soft and rosy. I noticed also, after some neat triangulation, that her head was somewhat closer to Jensen's side of the car than to Brendan's. Meanwhile, Brendan was reading over his paper.

Wilma giggled now as Jensen described possible infidelities engaged in by his wife while he was away. He assured Brendan he was lucky that Wilma was along. I could see that Jensen's arm now lay along the top of the seat, around Wilma. "You'd think my wife might want to hear one of my papers sometime, wouldn't you? You're lucky Wilma supports you, Bren. Now my wife begs off saying she'd be a nervous wretch watching me, thinking I'd lose my glasses or fall off the platform or something." I had an idea of how she felt. "And then questions afterward. You've got to think up something fast." He was after Brendan again, and if it continued he would reduce him to gibbering helplessness. But he punctuated the torture with jokes.

"You know, my first paper reminds me now of a joke I heard at MLA from a fellow named Donovan. It's about a young priest and his first sermon. Kinda like you, Bren. Of course, you're a renegade Catholic, aren't you? Pervert, they call it, ha ha, in Ireland." Brendan was silent, but Jensen went on with it. "You see, there was this young priest who was so nervous about giving his first sermon that he went to the oldest priest in the parish and confessed he could hardly face the ordeal. The old priest was very understanding. 'Son,' he said, 'you are very young and inexperienced. These things are sent to annoy us, but sometimes there are simple solutions. When I began, I used to take a small glass of gin to the pulpit, and a sip or two would steady my nerves. The congregation thought it was water for my throat. Try it. It helps.' So the young priest promised to take the advice. Then the old priest decided to hear the sermon and observe how well his advice had gone. Well, after it was all over they met, and the old priest laid his hand on the young man's shoulder. 'Son, you are very young and inexperienced, but I shall limit myself to only four criticisms of your sermon. First, follow directions—discipline, my son—always follow directions. I said to sip the gin, not to gulp it. Second, you will recall that the whale swallowed Jonah; Jonah did *not* swallow the whale. Third, as I remember Genesis, Cain *slew* Abel, he did not beat the shit out of him. Fourth, on Thursday next there will be a taffy-pulling party at St. Peter's, not a Peter-pulling party at St. Taffy's.' "

Jensen settled back proud of himself after that. Then he delivered the moral. "You know, Brendan, you're rather in the position of that young priest, and here I come with the gin!" He passed it again. Brendan even laughed a little up out of his brown study, and Wilma was giggling. Maybe Kit was pinching her, maybe she was still laughing at the joke, and maybe, just maybe, she had decided to enjoy Brendan's torment. You couldn't always tell about Wilma.

Wilma combined tenacious loyalty to Brendan with cringing fear and haughty disdain. Of course, I didn't know then that a past affair with Kit was complicating her actions. Kit had almost driven her and Brendan together in Kansas, I'm told, probably to get her off his hands. I can't imagine him quite the hearts-and-flowers matchmaker. Betty Lou and I were witnessing an off-campus reconciliation of sorts, except that now Brendan was there to be turned on the spit—old White Goddess Wilma. I doubt that Wilma had what most people call a moral sense, except a mockery of conscience inherited from her fundamentalist upbringing. This would come out only in odd pruderies. Life with a berserk bear had made necessary all sorts of compromises with her picture of herself, and yet she pretended the picture was yet the reality. Person just called her a bitch and let it go at that, but he had a tendency to take simplistic views of women anyway. I think Emory was more accurate when he said she didn't have enough moral fiber to endure the terrors of life with Brendan, that it slowly ebbed away and she was left constantly trying to make appearance pass for substance. That's a sloppy use of philosophical terms, but what I mean is that she always doted on appearance. I imagine that the glow of faculty society had impressed her when she went to college and got involved with Kit. She had an outrageously puffed-up view of the importance of the faculty wife. Betty Lou said that in no time she'd be terrorizing new departmental wives about joining the Walton Dames. She clung frantically to Brendan, even though she was often tormented by him. Then, forsaking all poses, she would run crying to Laura or Betty Lou. She hated to lose face, but in those sessions with our wives she virtually ripped off her own skin. What made it doubly pathetic was that the face she lost wasn't worth keeping. Every time she did come to our wives for comfort you could bet your life the next time we saw her she would be arrogant and grand, as if it had all never happened.

We got to Danforth before six even after the trouble about Brendan's manuscript and a few necessary stops. Berrigan recited parts of the Gettysburg Address and all of "Dan McGrew" toward the end and seemed actually to have recovered himself. He couldn't wait to get into the hotel and "on the town." I think he was reliving the anticipation of an army furlough. He talked a lot about his army exploits. Kit insisted that he be sober when they checked in. It was a nice hotel. We had rooms down the hall from the Berrigans, and Jensen was somewhere in between. In the elevator Berrigan embarrassed Wilma by making all sorts of remarks about hotels being the best place for it, and trying out the new bed, and how Wilma had a new nightgown, but he'd tear it off her if she dared wear it. He had her into their room and the bellboy out before we had opened our door. Even Jensen was non-plused—he who in the later stages of our trip had advanced from shoulder-holding to a variety of fondlings and unspoken endearments.

When we all met for dinner later, Wilma was trying to keep a slightly more sober Brendan from further remarks about how they had spent their time, but he insisted on going on about how they weren't practicing birth control, they couldn't seem to have children anyway, see, at least he hadn't caught her quite right yet, and boy was he hungry! Kit was by now furious with him and adopted a high, solemn, and most stern attitude. Betty Lou and I were just disgusted, I guess, but even more surprised; and Wilma tried for good reason to hog the conversation.

For a moment or two I thought it was Berrigan's well-plotted revenge against Jensen, showing him that he had the upper hand with Wilma now; but a little reflection makes me think it was just old berserk Brendan being advanced in his thinking. It was an example of what Emory was to call the "Bohemianism of the Plains." The Jensen-clique syndrome.

Kit was not long in launching a counterattack, because he took it personally. And he nearly ruined dinner, beginning with a long commentary on Henry Hastings, Dean of Deans. It was all to soften up Brendan, and it was terrifying how he systematically built up and crushed all Brendan's hopes for the future, built them up, and then crushed them again. He began obliquely with a few hints that his special relation to Hastings made it possible for him to do things for Berrigan. Bear sat on his haunches and waved for peanuts. He managed at one time to suggest that Hastings' eye was really on Brendan for important duties, probably in the Honors Program, maybe even as director. How did he get along with people like McCrea, Temple, Sheffer? There followed a catalog of senior departmental citizens. "Okay, okay," Brendan would grunt. At another time Hastings was a man to watch out for, a dangerous egotist, who would chew a man up and spit him out. Brendan alternately whooped and cringed, strutted in his seat, moped in his soup. Then Jensen pressed his terrors further by deciding right then and there to refuse any offers Hastings might make with a letter critical of all his plans for the magazine (it must be said that as this went on Jensen drank a prodigious amount of whiskey). Jensen was not going to allow Hastings to reject him. It would be the other way around. He had Brendan so confused by now that Brendan did not know what finally to feel.

But what about Jensen himself? Had he really fathomed Hastings' attitude? Had he foreseen his own failure with him, or was he merely feeling drunk and sorry for himself?

Betty Lou and I left Jensen and the Berrigans to the town after tagging along from restaurant, to bar, to cocktail lounge. We thought we'd walk a bit and go to bed. Besides, Betty Lou needed some air. When we were outside, she said, "Jason, I just don't, well, I can't understand these people. Are they insane? There are Brendan and Wilma scared to death of Jensen, and Jensen seems to hate Brendan, and yet they pour their hearts out to each other as if they were all magnetized or something."

What more could be said? They were drawn toward each other. Did we know what iron in us would be attracted, too, in time?

▶

The next day was mostly downhill after promise of a devastating vertical climb. About six o'clock there was a knock on our door. Wakened out of a sound sleep, I called, "Who's there?"

"It's Brendan, Jay. Jay, I can't find Wilma. She's gone; she been with you?"

Betty Lou, a lizard in the morning, half-asleep, answered, "Go ask Kit, Brendan. We haven't seen her."

I thought, My God, woman! There was no reply, and then, "Okay, thanks kids."

And that was that. Betty Lou was asleep again. I thought I might as well not bawl her out right then and there, so for about a half hour I stared at a curious bug wandering around on the big white expanse of our ceiling. There seemed to be a ridge running somewhere across it that puzzled him or her or it. I'd worked myself up into quite a state of empathy when Betty Lou woke up hungry as a beast. She didn't remember saying anything, I guess, and I decided to drop it. Years later it would be funny maybe. Brendan had passed by Jensen's door to knock and ask his question at ours. Why had he abased himself at all? He and Wilma were very pleased, we later learned, to criticize us to others—the behavior of our dog, our taste, the color of our rug (it was pretty bad), and yet they sought us out as confessors. I guess they were hunting for Daddy.

The meetings that day were not too well attended. The room was only about half full for Brendan's paper. Too early in the morning, for one thing. It was not surprising that Brendan was visibly nervous at first, but as he got going things seemed to be okay. The questions were elementary enough, and he had no trouble answering them, or at least seeming to. The paper—on the Fugitive group —was adequately received, and after it was all over he was on a manic high, proclaiming loudly that the whole thing had been fun, that he'd give lots more papers now and publish his dissertation, from which the paper came. Actually, what he had to say seemed disgracefully platitudinous to me.

The other manic upturn was in Brendan's relation to Wilma. They seemed hysterically reconciled. Jensen faded off in the distance to some meeting of MLA politicos. We never did find out what actually took place the night before, and this was probably a good thing. I've since learned that the more you know about Berrigan the more deeply he involves you in his affairs, or in this case Wilma's. He would have *wanted* us to know that Wilma had been unfaithful, if she had. The fact was, we didn't see them again until we were all back in Walton. They were staying over another day, taking the bus back; and Jensen was heading directly home. Betty Lou went shopping, and I took in some fair-to-middling Anglo-Irish literature papers. Then I ran into Person, with whom we had a hilarious joke-telling ride back to Walton. Fact was, I had to stop the car once, laughing at old Will laugh.

Ellen, Jason, Jack

PLAYING THE HASTINGS GAME   "You really ought to meet Jack Emory, Ellen." Mr. Berrigan was pacing around her office, looking at the pictures on the wall, fingering objects on her desk, inspecting the out basket. He was waiting for Mrs. Bolyard to peer around the door and usher him in to the Dean's presence. "Wilma and I were out there last night, and he's a sharp cookie. Boy, I'll tell you one thing"—he looked around, then lowered his voice—"the old guard will have to face him." She watched him scratch his head from back to front, then run his hand through his unmanageable flaming hair. It reminded her of his classroom performance. His lecturing pose always threatened to overflow into a swagger. As he walked and lectured he would occasionally run his hand through his hair. He was a flamboyant teacher. She'd signed up for his night course because they were going to do O'Neill—it appealed to her drama interest—but the class obviously wouldn't make it that far. Mr. Berrigan was spending most of the time on Dreiser and Hemingway. She had an A on the first test, and she recognized him as the type who thought of her as one of his "bright girls." Even though she already had a B.A., she could tell he would always insist on treating her as a sort of protégée, complete with mild flirtation.

"I'll arrange it," he said. Indeed, she thought of him as Dean Hastings' arranger, for he had become ubiquitous of late, conferring frequently and at some length with the Dean. He seemed to turn up everywhere. If she walked across the campus, there would be Mr. Berrigan hurrying along to somewhere or other. When he came to see the Dean he always stopped by the office with a pleasantry or an awful pun. He'd frequently be excited and nervous. He had plenty of ideas about how to publicize the Critique Series, and that was helpful. It was part of her job as a sort of general assistant and agent of information in the College to get publicity out to the newspaper and have the bulletin-board placards made when various academic celebrities came to lecture.

She got a kick out of Mr. Berrigan. All that Irish effusiveness was not her style, but it had a certain appeal if not overplayed. Of course, she imagined, he could overplay. When Mrs. Bolyard finally did admit him she watched him leave, noticing the curious sway to his gait. She heard him all the way into the Dean's inner sanctum, complimenting Mrs. Bolyard on the flower arrangement on her desk. "Roses, yes, ah roses, Mrs. Bolyard, what a lovely scent, umh umh." He sniffed them all the way. Mrs. Bolyard could be counted on to smile effusively. Of all Dean Hastings' "young men," as she called them, she clearly liked Mr. Berrigan the best. It was clear, however, to Ellen that Mr. Berrigan had never been the type to deal with in the back seat on a blind date.

Apparently this day a meeting was in the works, because the next person to pass her door was Jason Talbot. He waved and went right on. Mrs. Bolyard was beckoning him like a traffic cop. He'd had no time to stop, but he wouldn't have chosen to anyway. At least not when he was alone. So he was embarrassed, he with his great reticence, his watching eyes. All of that had been little enough back in August.

August 15th, to be exact, hot and humid, and the sea-breeze party. It was there, after tolerating for a while the amused contemplation of that husband on the loose, that she simply walked over to him and said, though she'd only seen him once or twice and never passed a word with him, "You're staring like that lion in the ads." Now why had it been necessary for her to do that? Why did she flick some lint from his shoulder and pull at his tie and joke at him until he took it off and stuffed it in his seer-sucker pocket, and why did she insist on another cup of punch and then, when he didn't introduce himself, introduce herself?

"I'm Ellen Fraser, and you're Jason Talbot. I've known you a long time. You lived in Denton. I remember seeing you playing in the band out at Frank's Castle. Did you have Mrs. Collins for math?" She really had remembered him, because he'd been something or other in the high school before her time and had fought on Okinawa and come back and gone to college at Austin, playing summers in the band. And besides that, the first night she saw him it just happened to be the night he played "The Old Rugged Cross" on top of the riff from "One O'Clock Jump" and about a hundred Baptists, sober enough to know what was being played, walked off the floor. She remembered him; he was the leader at the microphone, his trombone held way up high. He played up there, too, more in the Lawrence Brown style. And, then, a high-school girl still, she wanted as much as anything to sing with a band like his instead of the bunch of kids called the "Spotlighters" that she did sing for during the school year. Right about then she hated her time, her place, and all circumstance. Besides, that night she was with a nice crew-cut basketball player whom she'd cajoled into taking her to the Castle, and he wasn't sure "The Old Rugged Cross" à la Basie was quite the right thing. But she asked him, whispering close to his ear and running her fingers up the back of his neck, to maneuver near the bandstand, and he didn't bolt for the sidelines. As a kid singer she was not a fan of the Helen Ward or O'Connell chick type; her singers were Anderson and Holiday and Fitzgerald. But in Denton she didn't say much about that.

"Good Lord, Frank's Castle. Why, you must have been a mere baby. When was it?"

"Well, to tell the truth, I was sixteen. I wanted to be a singer with a band as good as yours. You guys were something to me."

Jason laughed. He was taken back a few years. He laughed some more.

"You're remembering something."

"Well, yes, there was one night that summer we almost got canned out of there. You see, I . . ."

"Played a hymn."

"Why, why yes. Good heavens, you were there. Isn't that wonderful. It's perhaps my one claim to fame in those parts."

The party was growing diffuse. People were wandering off through the garden down toward the lake. They were nearly alone, so they began walking for no particular reason. Except that she and he with some gin in them had discovered their whereabouts a few years before and for a moment lived back there and were partly those people. And so this time she could speak to him, and even touch him, which she did. She held his arm as they strolled, bumping against each other, and soon his arm was around her waist. They were supporting each other, and he was broken up with laughter recalling the manager and how if it happened again there was going to be a new band in the Castle, which was a decent place and not to be confused with Plubber's down the road. He could go down there and "blaspheme his ass out" if that's what he had to do, and on and on.

He had drunk somewhat more gin than he should. Parts of his face seemed numb. They were walking along a hedgerow under some maple trees. She was laughing, too, telling about the Molière she had played in on campus last fall, and then she lost her footing, and he toppled with her, their punch glasses flying up and away, she hugging him, and at the base of a tree her arms around him, and he thinking how lovely this girl was. Suddenly they were kissing as she threw her body against his.

They did not exactly think better of it right away, and the gin wasn't going to wear off. In fact, his face was numb everywhere, as if his face were not his own and he were not his own body, and so they looked for his car. It was driven the requisite mile to her flat, where no amount of coffee had any effect, and where they found themselves very disheveled on the sofa, then in the bedroom, where horizontal he, in the process of various efforts at zippers and snaps which he with some help from her was very objectively directing himself to deal efficiently with, passed vastly out.

At four he awoke ill, crawling in darkness for the bathroom, retching on all fours into the john, trying for the kitchen and failing and not knowing why he tried, flopping horribly on the sofa, his tongue thick as a giraffe's and feeling just as gray.

For her part, she had been past caring and angry that it was so, for here, she laughed to herself with her final consciousness, was the trombonist of the spotlight, the occasion for triumph, and she so far beyond it that as she felt herself hardening into statuary, her hands folded sarcophagus-like, she, jazz-singer Ellie, compelled herself to hear "The Old Rugged Cross" hummed out over Basie's saxophones. They died off into numb sleep, replaying the death of her adolescence.

►

"And miles to go before I sleep," he said.

"What?"

"That's the way I feel about the day." He was sitting on the sofa trying to make sense of the coffee cup he held. "Thanks for this," he finally managed.

She was businesslike in the kitchen with toast. She wore a striped robe, her red hair long and down her back. Even at this hour she was something to look at.

She knew he thought so. The problem was, what now? What would he say? Because it had to be over, she supposed.

But he did say, and smiling, "I'm sorry. Lord, that sea breeze grabs you and hangs on." A pause. "Ellen, I'd better get along, but . . ." He touched her tentatively on the forearm, no more. She turned to him, put her hand on his face, unshaven, tired.

"Another line of that poem says something about promises to keep. You don't have any to me, Jason."

He looked at her a long time; she turned away to the kitchen. She was a beautiful girl.

"Thanks much, ma'am," he whispered.

And so Jason had waved and walked on by into the Dean's office, as he always would have to do, because although he hadn't quite committed adultery with her while the wife and kids were gone, she knew that the spirit had willed it. And he, being what he was, couldn't forget that and was too just to blame it on the gin.

Nevertheless, it was Jason Talbot and not Brendan Berrigan who introduced Jack Emory, precisely thirty-five minutes later, when, the meeting over, Dean Hastings drove them with smiles, various shoulder-holdings and

back-pattings, jostling and neighing from his corral.
Somehow Berrigan, Jason, and Jack Emory were cut out
from the herd and headed up into her office. For Berrigan
she now was Miss Secretary: "Ellen, will you see to it
there's a reservation for Jensen, you know, Professor, er,
Dr. Jensen beginning the twenty-eighth at the Lincoln?"
In the midst of this, Jason found himself saying, "Ellen,
this is Jack Emory."

Oh, she had heard enough about him—him and another newcomer, named Crowder, whom she hadn't liked
at all. She had hoped this one would turn out better (besides, there were certain known credentials), and so she
smiled smile number two, which was cordial toward sexy,
and he responded with a straight, well-held grin—ear to
ear—which she hadn't in the least expected and which
froze (she was sure) smile number two into a silly smirk-
ing mask. Her face suddenly seemed unmanageable, but
she was talking, unintelligibly, as far as she could tell, and
her silly, unmanageable . . . beautiful face, he thought,
grinning as he watched her retreat behind it. A beautiful
cool face. So it seemed incumbent upon him to stay on
and talk, while Jason somehow wandered off, and Brendan, having issued his orders, hesitated, made various
verbal flourishes about, well, let's get back to the office,
and finally decided to cross the Quad alone.

It was coffee time, so they ended up in the Beaver
Room, and he found himself telling her about his first
days at Walton, mainly the Berrigans. How was it that the
flaming, freckled head of Brendan had insinuated itself
into conversation with this pretty girl? Brendan had accomplished it in much the same way as he and his wife
had insinuated themselves in the first few days after he
had arrived.

It was back in September, hot and stifling; the wind
blowing from the west hadn't yet turned October cool.
The land was parched, the campus grass here and there

brown and dry hard. The tan brick buildings, mostly square and new, except for a central Victorian group, faced quadrangles with few shade trees. The elm blight had come and gone, ravaging what had been a major virtue of the whole place. With time to spare before school got under way, he worked hard in his newly furnished private office at a nearly completed manuscript. Before him were a typewriter and a bottle of sherry, which against regulations he had smuggled in. There was not even a mouse for company. The evenings he spent fixing up his small rent house. There was a lot to do and not much furniture to fill even it. The Berrigans appeared on one of the first nights.

Strangely, he found himself telling her about their visit without quite knowing why. Perhaps it was the meeting just ended, where Berrigan had bristled with excitement every time the Dean's expression changed. She knew Hastings and she knew Berrigan. What, he wondered, did she think—he, a complete stranger, talking about someone she might well be friendly with?

But he recounted the unannounced visit and how he really didn't know who they were and his embarrassment at that, and their sensing his embarrassment but not retreating to a less precarious level of intimacy.

"And ever since, you know, I get the same thing from Brendan, as if Hastings is a god or something. Does the Dean really have a thunderbolt in his fist?"

She eyed him, fingering her coffee spoon, smiled. "Well," she said, "he had the good sense to hire Jack Emory. That doesn't deify him, but he can't be all bad."

"Well, I see you've learned from your boss. By God, it's infectious, isn't it? It's a whole technique."

"You'll get used to it; it's part of the folk mores here."

"Golly, I don't know. I mean, here's the sort of thing that happens. I take my suit into the neighborhood cleaner, and this beer-fed cat with a big paunch sees me

write my name on the slip and says, 'Well, I'm mighty
pleased to meet you, Jack. Call me Orville, Orville Hud-
gens. Now you just come back tomorrow and we'll have
this suit all cleaned up and pressed spick and span.' And
so on. Why, hell, I'm not Jack to him and he's not Orville
to me. And I go back in two days and Orville doesn't remember me from the guy who pumps his gas."

"He's just being friendly. That's the way the people
around here are."

"Let them save it for Rotary."

"No, it's just a matter of what meaning you put on it.
Like people thinking all New Yorkers are rude."

"Okay, okay. I brought it up because—well, Brendan
on Hastings is the same thing."

"Brendan on you isn't bad, by the way," she said.
"You're a culture hero, too."

"Aha, see, you also resent it."

"No, I didn't imply that. Maybe you *are* a heroic type.
Anyway, no damsel rejects the possibility out of hand."
She looked right at him. "Can't afford to."

"Well—well, okay, you win." And she had won, too,
because she had a very soft and pretty smile. But he had
to go on. "Now here's Brendan. We're supposed to have
this tremendous renaissance. Hastings is going to revolu-
tionize the whole program, move the young men with
him. It sounds like a basketball coach I once hated. You
know, his pep talks—we've got to moooove, and all
that."

"I suppose before you recite all the Berriganisms there
are, I'd better get back to work."

"Yes, and I'm sorry. I've been ranting. Can I make it
up? Maybe dinner tonight?" He didn't want to leave her.

"Yes, but at my place. Home cooking is the answer to
everything, suh." And over her shoulder as she hurried
away, "I think you're just warming to the subject." He

94

watched her appreciatively as she walked away, her long red hair bobbing on her shoulders.

She was right, of course. And it wasn't just Brendan. It was how everyone somehow got positioned in relation to him. It had not taken him long to understand that Berrigan was seeking an ally in him and trying simultaneously to quash the specter of competition. It was Berrigan who had come to Walton as a modern-literature specialist. He knew Jack would be working partly in his field, perhaps in his way. To make a division of the spoils seemed wildly premature. There were no spoils yet.

Jack had learned to expect every day in his office a visit from Berrigan and a repetition of exhortation to intellectual battle: he and Berrigan should influence the curriculum together, push reform through. Berrigan used a classy word for all this. Jack could not remember it. At times there was grace.

Behind his relations with Talbot and Person, from their first meeting in the Beaver Room, he sensed the specter of Berrigan. He wondered whether Berrigan had collared each of them in turn. Were they all to look suspiciously at one another for the rest of their association? There was something slightly withdrawn about them, Talbot reserved and Person carrying perhaps a bit of a chip. They talked of Berrigan all right, and it was clear that Person didn't think much of him, but Person also held something back. Was it that he couldn't league himself against a midwestern colleague if the prospective ally was from the East? If the name of Hastings came up, Person would withdraw even farther. It seemed strangely important to weigh every word carefully. He missed his old office mate at Middleton. He began to recall fondly the mouse.

The evening with Ellen was a success. She did not take his every pronouncement with total solemnity. "Very serious student, very serious," Berrigan had said of her. Jack considered that she must have played Berrigan well, uttered what Will Person called "the pieties" ("Thou shalt believe in Ransom, Warren, Tate"), or perhaps remained silent and industrious. Her face alone was, after all, enough to get her by.

But it was true that with him, at least, she let out her laughter and punctured gaily those pomposities that, as a teacher, he had inevitably picked up along the way. He liked it, he needed it, and, besides, she did it in a style that put him at ease, invited rejoinder, loved the ridiculous, yet at the expense of no one not present, only of Man in general.

So they tried it again, and he learned without too many words spoken that she didn't especially want to hear jokes at the expense of or efforts to analyze the motivations of the Dean. Fair enough, he thought; it was a subject upon which he was too solemn. It was not easy to refrain, yet he knew it was good for him to turn it off. Perhaps Ellen recognized that he needed a refuge. He had been discovering that conversations about Hastings or Berrigan were far too common, a sort of addiction, in fact, when he got together with Jason Talbot. Jason had broken the ice one day by allowing that they should go out for coffee and a little bear-baiting.

Jack took to dropping around to Ellen's office occasionally during the workweek to entice her away for coffee. For her part, his presence was interesting. She had not before met up with his quiet impertinence, for one thing. Most of the people around the University—those who came by her office—were so conscious of rank, so humorless, and so obsequious around the Dean. Emory had suddenly made her suspect that she had become humorless in that way, too—ground into the hierarchy. He seemed to take people less seriously the higher their rank. She wasn't so sure she liked this as a steady diet, particularly if it became brooding and solemn, but it was amusing to hear someone like Crowder taken down. She couldn't stand Crowder, with his pipe and his annoying offhand way of ferreting out information. He'd come by the office and make stupid small talk—just to find out where the Dean was or whom he was having lunch with.

So she appreciated Jack's remarks about Crowder on Hastings' *ad hoc* Honors Program Committee. Jack would quote Hastings' charge to the committee: Walton had to provide "a quality education for the mentally advantaged student," it had to "get across the disciplines" (oh yes, she recognized that whenever he quoted Hastings he scored a point). Then he'd describe Crowder on the committee, bumming cigarettes until the fellow from philosophy in philosophic exasperation distributed a whole carton to the group with the elaborate explanation that he hadn't been able to offer much that was specific, only general principles, and this was to be considered his major contribution to peace, harmony, and interdisciplinary liaison.

"But Crowder didn't get the point, did he?"

"Hell no, he's impervious; for him it was just another free pack. And then after the last meeting, when we finally got the report all typed, all one hundred and eleven pages, by God, we'd just broken up and there we were walking across the campus and Crowder suggests we should present ourselves to the Dean as his committee ready for another assignment. He actually says, 'We ought to keep it in his mind that after all we're his bright young men.'"

"Oh boy," she sighed.

"What can you say? Well, Silverman had it: 'Hell, Crowder, pretty soon I'm going to be a middle-aged bright young man!' And all Crowder could do was shrug that funny shrug he has when he can't figure out what's gone wrong. Well, all self-respecting committees ask to be discharged when the job is done, and Silverman explained that. Tersely, of course."

But too often his stories brought in the Dean, even when they began as wild accounts of Brendan Berrigan. She kept thinking that Dean Hastings' natural shyness—he was self-conscious with her, she thought—and his desire to do some really important things—all this Jack was twisting around to the Dean's detriment. For instance, the Critique of Culture program. Talking about how Berrigan had managed to report the Jensen disaster as a triumph for the Dean's principle that "town should profit from gown," he somehow reduced the Dean's plan, worthy enough, she thought, to cliché. He was always implying that Hastings' ideas were visionary grandeur arrived at as the result of ruthless desire for power. He would wonder about the Dean's friendliness to Berrigan. Berrigan became the Dean's fault because the Dean "couldn't see close up."

"You know, Ellen, Hastings likes Brendan because Brendan's such a flunky, and he likes me because I'm Princeton and Middleton and all that."

"And *so do I*," she'd reply.

"Go to hell."

But partly, she thought, it was Jason who kept Jack watching for the Dean to make the slightest move. That damned Jason, who was such a gentleman, so cool, so proper—and now so distant.

It was true that Jason compelled him to suspicions. "One has to watch one's step with that fellow," Jason had said to Emory one day early in the fall. And later, "You've seen the fellow with the sign 'The World Ends Tomorrow'? Well, I'm going to have one made that says, 'Prepare Thyself for the Battle of Hastings.' "

And Hastings kept doing little things—Jason had encouraged him to watch for little things: a reddening of the neck, a tap of the fingers. Jason held that Hastings accounted for Berrigan. Hastings could call on Berrigan for complete devotion through thick and thin. It was true: after the first few weeks, of all the so-called young men, Berrigan was the only one in whom the Dean seemed really to confide.

His own analyses became as minute and searching as Jason's. He tried to keep them from Ellen even as he wished to shout them at her. He could not escape the feeling that in some subtle way Hastings stood between them. He waited for Hastings to reveal some reservation about Berrigan. Then he waited for someone to tell Hastings what an ass Berrigan made of himself in front of visiting celebrities. That would have done it, for when he looked at the Critique of Culture Series, he concluded, at least in his cynical moments, that it was all Hastings' personal publicity venture. What would Hastings think if he knew that the eminent novelist whose manuscripts he wanted for the library had asked point-blank, "Who is the frenetic young man with the fat wife who has been steering me around and jabbing me in the side?" He also realized that anyone in Hastings' position was bound to publicize himself if he brought about any sort of educational reform. Either way, visionary or pragmatic, it made no sense to endure Berrigan.

"But that's the point, isn't it?" Jason would goad, "That's why he's a danger. He *does* tolerate him, he uses him, and that means in some awful way he has a blind spot. And that's why he'll break with you, Jack. Because he'll know you see through him, and he'll be embarrassed. Berrigan never does that. He's the faithful companion of his darkest hour. He'd howl in his sleep for Hastings' sugar, that old bear."

The closer he got the harder it was. Hastings' monologues began to tell upon him. He could feel his own face constricting to a scowl. Or Hastings would, in their occasional meetings, make some blatant effort at flattery, and he would have to look out the window, everything suddenly flat. But he knew that Hastings valued him, and he knew also that despite the clichés Hastings' push for the interdisciplinary was to be commended. Then, outrageous as it was, he found himself leaping mentally at the mention of Hastings' name, a veritable Brendan Bear. Nor would he avoid an excuse to discuss things with the great man when the opportunity arose.

Part of this was a little game he played with Crowder. At least this part of it he could tell to Ellen. He liked to demonstrate how Crowder brought out the worst in him. He had not read the book that had made Crowder a prize catch, but he reported Jason on it and Will's animal growls.

The game was telling Crowder that he had taken coffee with Hastings some morning and they had discussed a matter that would just possibly affect the bright young men's careers. He admitted freely, when Ellen smiled, that it was a sort of bitchiness worse than Crowder's own incapacity. Crowder infuriated him deep down; Crowder even got to Ellen.

Was that enough basis to start a love affair, he once jokingly asked her. She allowed it probably was.

But in respect to Hastings there was no meeting ground.

And with Hastings himself he would feign enthusiasms but remain silent when a word or two might have cleared things up about Berrigan. He would convince himself that the moment was not ripe, that the opportunity had only been an illusion, that it would not be graceful to bad-name a colleague, that it would certainly not be moral. Surely Hastings interpreted his silences as vague or even sullen disapproval or general unhappiness. Hastings would be self-conscious. Things were not going to improve, but he clung, or some distasteful part of him clung, to foolish optimism that he might use Hastings toward some vague glory for himself. Somehow he knew that Ellen knew this, but was Ellen also using Hastings in her own guileful way? Hastings liked her. He was going to support her application for a drama fellowship in the East. Jack didn't like this, didn't like her relationship to Hastings, whatever it was; but mostly he didn't want her to go away.

▶

Not long after the visit of Kit Jensen, Jack had to take stock. The Dean had called him to his office to discuss the Critique of Culture Series and the proposed new journal. The talk gravitated strangely toward Jensen. Hastings mused out loud about his hopes.

"You know, Jack, if I could just gracefully retire four or five of your colleagues, the English Department could get on its feet, and at the same time we could break through its parochialism. You young fellows provide a good nucleus, but then again at this point in time we may have to go around it, bypass it. That's why this Honors Program thing strikes me as important, really essential. It's beyond the departments in a sphere where we can really interact and implement." He turned in his chair and looked out the tall window down the mall toward the Medical College, perched on a slight rise a mile away. He was, indeed, Jack thought, a spyglass man. "The students here deserve it. They're good."

They were at least willing. They were rougher and often more ignorant than the New Yorkers and New Englanders of his former job, but they seemed somehow to profit from what a colleague pedantically called their "noble savagery." He liked their respectful attention, their pleasantness, even though he knew it was sometimes a different form of manners only.

"Yes, they are," he was glad he could agree, and he told Hastings why. But Hastings, as he went on, wasn't listening—only waiting for him to finish. The face took on a set smile halfway between smug contentment and embarrassed reserve. Was it that he didn't appreciate the candid analysis? Did it imply something about him? Jack felt for a moment the twinge of terror that in Berrigan probably vibrated every second from brain to the base of his spine. Jesus, he thought, how do you deal with this man? The idea that Hastings himself was a sort of noble savage crossed his mind. It hid. It peered from behind rocks.

"I had the idea," Hastings began, "that perhaps we could bring Jensen along with us on these plans. I thought he'd be a useful man to have here." It was impossible not to notice a newly opened envelope with Jensen's return address sitting on Hastings' desk.

"I wasn't too impressed with his talk."

Hastings seemed not to have heard. He was looking out the window. "I'm not sure he'd fit in."

"You mean Warner and Cassoway? The old guard?" Jack went for broke.

Hastings' staring at the Medical College ended abruptly. He removed his glasses. "What do you mean?" There was no smile.

"Well, I thought perhaps with Warner near his field." And so he tried to slither out by saying something that meant nothing. He knew that Hastings didn't worry about people's fields when he went hiring. All the bright young men were modernists.

"Oh yes, well that is it. A professorial appointment is difficult."

It had been a brush with the real Hastings. What had Hastings fished for? That Warner and Cassoway should not be allowed a veto? That Jensen wasn't worth the battle? Had he sought strength in Jack to go ahead? Or had he really desired to shut off talk? It was all very unsatisfactory, and it was difficult to say who was to blame. For a moment, from the year before, Doris Weinstock flashed through Jack's consciousness: "What can he do? He can speak with me and listen." Hell—he stooped to silent defensive recrimination—I'm not the clergyman in this setup.

Anyway, the Dean changed the subject, almost as if he had forgotten something or the previous words had never been uttered. The new subject was George Hungerford, who was to be, if Hastings could haul him in as a faculty member, the prize catch for 1957. Jack knew that Hastings had been after Hungerford for some time; the name was occasionally mentioned in monologues about the future. Hungerford was a young bibliographer finishing up a dissertation at Yale, an excellent addition because of the library's extensive manuscript holdings in the modern field. But Hungerford was proving, in spite of his youth, a tough negotiator. He had managed to keep Hastings on the string all year, probably waiting for other offers to turn up. As he listened, Jack did not fool himself: Walton University belonged to the new seam-bursting academia, not the ivied walls one used to associate inevitably with "college." Hungerford was probably holding out for a more prestigious spot.

Hastings mused out loud: He sought some way to convince Hungerford that Walton wasn't just a good place for him, but THE place. Oh, he had indicated what the library had to offer, and he had explained his plans for the magazine, and described the Honors Program, but somehow the personal touch that would make him see Walton as a place of intellectual excitement was lacking. They were west of the main centers of thought; Hungerford would naturally be coming to them with some misgivings about isolating himself. Could Jack perhaps write to him describing conditions here, the young colleagues he would be working with, the spirit of adventure, the rare opportunities? And they would have him down in the spring, if he couldn't come sooner.

By heaven, Jack thought, he had been dubbed Hastings' intellect salesman. Person was Hastings' poet, Ware his novelist, and Brendan Berrigan? His shadow. Suddenly there flashed before him an event that had occurred when he was a senior in prep school trying to decide on some fairly firm basis where to go to college. A few schools had offered him scholarships, and there had been the old-school-tie letters along with them. But the one he remembered best was something from a freshman at a small West Coast institution which tried to describe life there and tell him why he should definitely enroll. In the language of the time, it was corny. It told about sorority and fraternity life, cocoa in the evening with the faculty, and gee, some of them were really swell, they would talk to you about anything, just anything.

He had crossed that place off his list. Would Hungerford do the same after he described Walton's fun and games? How was he to know what Hungerford really desired? He caught himself thinking in a way that he had noticed in himself too often lately. He was now, it seemed, always trying to find out what other people wanted. He and Jason had begun to analyze possible reactions to Hastings' plans, and Jason had begun to discourse on "their situation." Brendan Berrigan was popping frequently into his office with some communiqué from Hastings' secretary to ask, "What does he mean by this? What does he want me to do?" Then they would read between the lines together. No. He'd have to do his best. As he put it to himself later, he saluted, about-faced, and left the Dean's office. He knew that his way of putting it reflected a resentment he was as yet unprepared to analyze. He mentioned the matter casually to Ellen.

"He's trying to confide in you, I think. You've impressed him."

"Yes, I'm useful to him," he remarked sarcastically.

"Well, my dear, he's useful to you. Friendships have been built from less."

He felt like throttling her, but it was impractical. First of all, she was probably right. More important, he was falling in love, and her rightness had something to do with that.

The letter to Hungerford went out after an excruciating day of composition in which he paced his office and went twice to the Beaver Room with Jason.

Jason had received a letter himself, that morning— from Kit Jensen, who was fishing, hanging in there, hoping for good news. So with that before him as an example, it was no surprise that Jason cautioned restraint. Jack's remarks to Hungerford should be on the level of feed bag reporting. So he did his best. He could not communicate all the ambiguities of a Walton existence, nor was it up to him to do so even if he was gradually learning that Jason and even Will experienced the same doubts and perhaps the same curious illusions. Subjectivity was not the thing here. He had seen too many colleagues subjectively damn everything from the moment they set foot on a campus. He would classify them according to type: the Easterner in the Midwest starved for culture; the antiadministration liberal who also happened to be completely naïve; the curriculum reformer; the critic of everything in terms of how it was done at HIS graduate school; the young ingroup Turk who sought student disciples and turned them against everyone else in order to build his own ego. No wonder administrators went mad. He had tried hard to avoid being labeled Group 1, and he hoped he was not naïve. He hadn't been particularly charmed by the program at his own school, and he certainly resented disciples. Anyway, he would try to be honest.

Then he discovered how difficult discretion was. Weighing each sentence as he knew Hungerford would weigh it, he discovered unspoken phrases nearly captured by the words he did use. After a revision, he thought, Oh hell, it will do. He had dwelt on Hastings' desire to bring good young faculty to Walton. He had offered as exhibits Jason, Will, and Ralph Ware. He had spoken of the Critique of Culture Series and future participants as well as he could, for Hastings had pulled the first one out of a hat, and Jensen as rabbit was strictly for the Alice world. He had described what he knew of the library's development plans. The department itself he had found most difficult to discuss. There the spell of Hastings could not make the facts disappear. Hastings might be able to pull rabbits from a hat, but could he stuff them back in again? So he had mentioned a few problems and tried to indicate hope for improvement. All in all, he would not want to write such a report very often. The letter had made him take stock of his own attitudes toward everything with which his professional life was now involved, and he could only conclude that the future depended upon Hastings, and that was the difficulty.

That night at a moment when he wanted most to forget Hastings and think only of her, she quipped, apparently apropos of nothing, "You play, I play, we all play the Hastings game!" She laughed. He looked at her curiously. Her face was cool, more ice than fire. He kissed her for a long time.

► 2

"Fight
onward
down
the field"

William Person

HOW TO FIND ROMANCE   [Once I give up to it, just for a moment, it keeps insisting, finding little crannies in my after-school afternoons. So I'm home again, solitary, the pressure off.] After that weekend in late October—the one he likes to recall—Jason knew, didn't he? If Kit Jensen ever came to Walton confusion would multiply. Already Hastings was vaguely musing, aesthetical hat on, how he'd "use" Emory and me on the magazine—relief from teaching, the works. He loved that word "use." But just try to "firm things up" or erect anything worth an asinine hope. Already I was waiting around to see what would happen, and Jack was sending Hastings memos by campus mail and ploying him up like mad. Funny, those two. Sniffing dogs. Already Freddy McCrea was leering down at me, saying oh he's terribly terribly excited about the idea, too. And I was beginning to see we'd have trouble coping with the literary talents combined in our Wild West show. Emory, Ware, and I could get along all right. And Jason? Harmless. And Dickie Mouse and Davis? Well okay—the old terror act. But McCrea? Nah. Literary taste of old-lady writers hot to print imitations of Firbank. Then Jensen, if he came, that exotic bird. Besides misreading a few poems, for which God knows I don't blame him, and missing the acrostic all these years, he hauled up a great stinking whale of foolish metaphysics and pranced like an idiot. Jack claimed he understood it and it was mostly wrong. Hell, he lost me in total ennui. But I don't hold things like that against professors. Actually Kit's for ahrt and all that and likes poets in his department. Live and let live, I say. The moral is: Line us up, each on his ass, we'd look like Blake's procession from the *Faerie Queene*.

It was Hastings and his "prolific disagreement" that got me: fighting and screwing at the same time. Oops, here comes that wonderful first year now, big black clouds of ideas and me trying to dance out of them or trying to dance Hastings' tune or Laura's tune or some pedantic departmental tune without being able to read the music or hear the band. Why? I had to learn what I was. I forgot even what I was trying to be, or maybe I didn't forget but let it loll around in my unconscious where it would rear up finally and strike out against the whole damned business. I believe I was trying to be a poet. Hastings wanted a goddamned characterless flunky, and Laura wanted a good, clean, Christian, go-to-work and home-at-night, moral-type husband. Old Willie the First knew that poets and artists are wild. Something had to give, and it was *this* old Will. [At least there's Ann to show for it. True to myself, we fight now and then, but at least she isn't proselytizing me all the time, and I can go out to the corner bar without being sent for at 11:00 P.M.] Too damned bad about Laura. Jason and Betty Lou probably think it's on my conscience. Jack has an opinion about it, too, maybe, but God knows what a brother-in-law really thinks. Even without the religion bit, where were Laura and I? Could I stand her always finding excuses for the Bears? Scene (repeated as the year goes on, like the eleven o'clock movie): I come home, and there is Laura all ready to tell me about Wilma's troubles, and I say why the hell doesn't she divorce him, and Laura frowns and disapproves of divorce and says they could be helped if Jack and I wouldn't be so terribly terribly critical of them and try to see their side. I say life is too short for that and stomp into the john and read *Time,* and then I'm really mad.

Laura even thought Henry Hastings a nice gentleman when she finally met him. [Remain calm please.] Why, she berated me through a couple of weeks afterward for all the misleading things I'd said about him, such as the college being run by his mother. Laura would say Hastings' mother died long ago, and I'd say so that's the cause of the snafu. Then maybe a week later we'd run the reel again. [Okay, Will, admit you're inclined to exaggerate.] All right. My style is hyperbole. But with Laura it was always the rose-colored glasses. So when I met Ann, who thought there was some truth as well as humor in what I said, and liked a beer now and then, and understood something about art, and didn't mind my swearing and general horsing around, well, I saw there was something else possible. And I guess people want to say the whole business began with her.

But she wasn't the cause. I was fed to the teeth—with Walton, not just with Laura and our happy home. Why, I'd been living in a world that couldn't be real. It wasn't just the Hastings hustle or even Brendan, but that marvelous, contextualist, organic totality—the unity of it!—like a poem that can't *mean* but does, as old Mac said, indeed *be.* Think: Walton's English Department as the mad tea party. Alvin Hatfield, straight from Carroll; the Mad Hatter, we called him. Twenty minutes in the department meeting just to tell us we should buy airwick for the phone booths: "Gentlemen, Ah simply cahn't unduh-stahnd why, WHY, we must tolehrate this abysmal stuffiness, this pestilential oduh and why some of my colleagues cannawt confine theah smoking to theah awffices."

And Dormouse Vanner explaining, puffing patience, explaining that there was, ahem, no line in the budget for it at this, ahem, time.

Then the curriculum committee! Of all departmental affairs it stomped me the most. Revise, revise, or apologize. Word came from somewhere above. Guess who? So we get together, but as usual Vanner builds a deadlock into the committee and all sides are heard—two sides mainly, a top side and then all the types who live on the underside of the rocks. Sneaky Cassoway's lieutenants, most of them, his presence hovering over us, name never mentioned. And bright boy Crowder. It got so when I saw Crowder in the hall I'd just growl and he'd scurry into his hole. I'd rather work with Hatfield. I couldn't figure out what Hatfield's position on curriculum was, but he thought he had one, and sometimes he even rushed in where Cassoway declared thou shalt not pass! Besides, we did know he was against stuffiness. Crowder? One of the hollow men, just a big old cornstalk. Cassoway puffed out his cheeks, blew; Crowder waved. Hold against all change, the cry. But the way Crowder talked outside our smoke-filled room to people like Berrigan he supported revision. Thought the word had come down from Hastings to prepare for fire and sword. Head at both ends. Knave, he.

Hadn't I come to Walton trained by observing the infighting? Wasn't I ready? Watch out for the pros, stand quiet, don't bitch about your courses or your hours, and keep some time for yourself and your own writing. But it wasn't that easy: attendance at freshman composition pep sessions with Dudley Warburton exhorting us all to think about method and point toward the machine-graded monster final. Hell, I didn't want to argue with

Deadly Dudley or anyone else about teaching composition. The trouble was I had to endure hearing the others run through all the arguments of Methuselah, and Dudley's querulous answers, and then . . .

But I'm reasonable. I can see how it's possible to want to resist change. Some time in late winter the curriculum committee interviews Klaus. He wants to enlarge the world-lit survey. Good idea, maybe. Spread the wealth. Let more peons escape from bonehead composition. Two terms of it, he wants. But he's an arrogant art-nanny and insults the intelligence of everyone there, and that's hard to do! Don't kill the goose that lays the golden egg, they say. Can't teach *Don Quixote;* it won't go with sophomores, they say. Horse shit, I want to say. But I vote against him to spoil his satisfaction. The way he talked it was like having a pastoral letter on art read out to us. The real trouble with Klaus was that he'd driven me to vote *with* the others.

After that meeting, I was shot. So: I stopped by the Green Lion for talk and a little shuffleboard with a couple of my writing students. Thank luck when you escape your colleagues and enjoy yourself. But time passes; dinner is over when I get home. There are searching questions from Laura. There are rhetorical questions. There are accusations. I was annoyed, but I told her calmly—quite calmly—that there had been this dreadful curriculum meeting with Klaus making the sign of the mandala over us (she didn't like that) and I had to wash out my insides with some beer. Well, it was all right; we were still speaking.

Too bad, though, because the next thing I know the old set is on and the same old situation tragedy floods the screen. Wilma has been by singing the blues. I like my blues by Peggy Lee, who is, I understand, a *real* Minnesota blonde. Is it really fair that a man who has sat with Crowder, popped back up out of Wonderland, and listened to Klaus's sermons on why we are all philistines, should late in the evening, hungry and tired, hear on his own hearth talk of bears and bags?

The gist: Wilma is distraught. Every evening Brendan Bear comes home and worries that Jack and Will don't like him, don't respect his judgment. Why, Wilma says, do they have to act like this? Why, Laura says, can't you be a bit more charitable? Why, I reply, quietly shouting, must Brendan Bear lumber through my life like this? Why, indeed, must Laura play peacemaker? If she wanted to be a sister of mercy why did she marry me? Tears. I rave. I am, I realize at the time, drunker than I had thought. I remonstrate. I follow her into the bedroom. She sobs quietly. This I cannot stand. It drives me to acts of daring. I believe I threw a shoe at the closet door. The children are wakened. It is all very sordid, and I have to get out of the house early the next day. Maybe it was a good thing I was drunk after all, or I would have been awake all night with my weird.

I had to keep saying to myself, turning a prayer wheel, Forget it, forget it, write poems. I'd understand why a guy like Fallon left academe and worked at Boeing, but then I'd think a little. Problems there, too, like dodging propellers and things.

Stoicism?

But I'm no stoic. Anyway, there was no time to practice it on the run from Hastings' hobby classes. I even went on a kick of reading Eastern philosophy: I have been a reed swaying in the wind, I have been a clod of clay under the cattle's hoof. Never could quite make it into full lotus. Jack, the bastard, telling me I had the stomach for it. No heart.

Guts?

Well, you can't slice your life in two. Finally you have to say to yourself, Why am I doing this? It's not true I was tossed onto Hastings' shit list after the great tribal wars.

No, indeed, and that was the trouble. There was Jack in fallen Luciferian gloriousness, while Hastings was still sending me poems to look over for the magazine. I was still writing little notes back, which he'd thank me for. No, when the blowup came, I just took a summer off and came back next fall for another try. Even a few days before I quit for good, Hastings and I walked across campus together, and he wanted a whole mess of my own, yes, my own poems to publish. Never sent them to him, though. Gone from town. Temptation maketh me jump. He was killing me with kindness because Jack was unfaithful and Jason suspect. All the time on my bedroom ceiling I saw Jack's scowling face or Jason's detached quizzical look. No, I couldn't do it. I'd take my chances with the fugitive presses, where at least they didn't wind vines and roses in and around your words.

It's even possible, though, that I could have kept up with Hastings and slid eventually into a professorship at Walton if that had been the only problem. But I'm not sure. Too many disarming moments: Hastings breaking out of a fairly decent conversation on the series to say, "Will, what do you think of McCrea? I'm hoping he'll work out on the magazine. I don't believe the department has made the right use of him."

I think, MY GOD, why me? I, pleasant Will, shovel forth a platitude. On top of that, the department worked me over. I'm still wondering how I was put on the curriculum committee, because in the department I was Poet, as against my role with Hastings, which was: Act like a junior executive with brains and lots of discretion and keep a pace to the rear. But in the department I was Poet. That absolved me from much sin even before guilt. Even *when guilty*. There's nothing like a bunch of English professors for thinking poets are an odd inferior race. Anyway, the mask of what the professor thinks a poet is allows plenty of freedom, since he has him confused with court jester, source in *Lear* or something. The poet: avoids the busy work committees because not suited, is never asked to make up freshman English examinations for fear of *what might happen,* remains far down the list of proctoring assignments, strives for the accolade "Good old Will, we can't ask him because *he's a poet."* Not because he'll mess it up, but because *he's a poet.* Different words, same thought. Worth the humiliation of being told by someone like Berrigan that he'll handle the details, if he didn't come sneaking back and assign them to you when the crisis hit. It may have even been worth it to let Berrigan *think* he was handling the details. But there's a limit. Hell, none of this explains the slip-up: me on the curriculum committee.

Well, generally the poet bit kept me clear.

Trouble in this, though. It isn't true about poets quite that way, and pretending it's true is a strain. You have to endure silliness, all the time muttering, "But I'll outscholar and outteach half of you. I'm really a competent-type individual. I'm normal, see!" It wasn't worth it making the assertion out loud. Look what I'd lose. Poetic license, call it. I was trapped.

Then at home, Laura: Why wasn't I normal teacher Will, and why didn't I diet and why did I have to play beatnik, and all the rest of it? I'd have to say, "But I'm a poet, damn it, and you should understand."

And then she'd say she didn't see any reason why poets should be big as oxen or any different from human beings generally, with the result that we'd really argue about who was champ of snide, and I'd go drinking with some of the literary kids [so forget it]. The truth was, I didn't mind the kids pasting signs like "Eat ice cream and DIE" on the fridge, but Laura comparing me to the beasts of the field . . . well!

End of term that first June: the summer session was

coming up; it was hot and dull. Jack was off in Seattle; Jason, Betty Lou, and the children were visiting the folks, and all the kids who saw me as their authentic Daddy Poet were out on the road or punching cattle in Texas or wherever the hell they were going that summer to find Life. After five weeks I told Laura I simply had to get away for a while—a couple of weeks maybe. She wasn't too receptive to that idea when it got through that I meant without her and the kids, without anybody. She saw dark plots, I suppose. But we had only one or two sullen discussions about it. Even got her to agree it might be a good thing.

I put out lines to a few people in the Northwest that I'd be coming through. That included Arthur Ryerson and, of course, Jack, up there writing. They said come along, so I trundled down to the station with my toothbrush and extra drawers. I was really anxious to see [Ann], no, Ryerson. Great man, he. I started to know him with correspondence on poetry for the magazine. He'd write gallantly back that he liked some of the things he'd seen by me. Did Hastings ever print one of his?

Anyway a real dialogue bloomed. Saved every one of those letters. They'll be worth something some day. Will mine?

Well, Ryerson was true Pops. Lessons there: Years in the fugitive journals, friends who owned printing presses. No other way through the rising fogs. Then that big stiff of a poet who made a page or two in *Kenyon Review* condescending to him, laughter his answer: "Most promising middle-aged poet in America," he called himself. He stoic? Who did more for my crowd than Ryerson? And he didn't just warm over the gospels according to Pound and Williams the way Olson did. "Okay, form is never more than an extension of content. What good is talk like this? Bring on the fiends!" He challenged us all, and

we'd think about our slogans, and I'd feel a little silly, all
that pontificating I did in the Green Lion—strutting in
front of my subjects.

Ryerson didn't even hate Richard Wilbur. He wasn't
Ryerson's favorite young modern, but just because he
came from Harvard or somewhere Arthur didn't sweep
him from the shelves. Funny, after I'd known Arthur a
while I could see why he hadn't founded a school or built
up a claque. Taste too eclectic, style, too. He was always
disappearing behind his poems.

I'd gone hook, line, and sinker for the New American
Poetry. [Why wasn't I in it?] Kinetic as hell, I. Take not
the name of Charles Olson in vain: Thou shalt believe in
Creeley, Duncan, Koch. But after those letters I loosened
up a bit, and then Arthur in person was to loosen me up
some more. Finally, I was eclectic as hell.

After stopping in Portland on the way up I was even
happier to see him, or Jack, or anyone. In fact, I was
desperate for *life*. Because in Portland I had a couple of
hours between trains that expanded into two doleful days.
The reason was that I called up Scooter Wells. He said to
meet him at the Manta Ray about ten and stay over if I
felt like it. So I stood there at the appointed hour, and he
appears with a great big tall Negro poet named Levi Mc-
Leod. I hadn't seen Scooter since the old days when he
printed up his own books in a basement in Fort Wayne.
At the Manta Ray that night was some local trumpeter
coming out of retirement—forty days in Bend, Oregon,
or thereabouts—at the age of twenty-six. The poster said,
"Wally Returns." We shook hands, this big Scotch Negro
and me. He said, if I recall the exact words, "Hello,
man," staring over me down the street, which wasn't hard
for him considering he was about Wilt the Stilt's height.
And those were his last words that evening. Scooter
hadn't seen me for a couple of years at least; but he
wasn't exactly bursting with the heat. I did get a few more

words from him. Ten or twelve in about two hours of hearing Wally blow endless variations on a lost original. He was, I must be honest with myself, very good.

I'd say something to Scooter about how was Margie or something, and he'd lower his lids, slide stiff in his chair, and sibilantly whisper, "Later, man, later." So I drank myself silly. I don't forget leaving the place, but I don't appreciate the details either. Levi McLeod, all seven feet, faded away into the night. Never saw him again [and he's not much of a poet even if he is a Negro, which is the poetic thing to be these days, I guess, if you can make it]. Next afternoon there is Scooter rushing me to the Seattle train, talking like mad, giving me a list of poets to look up in Seattle and cordial as hell.

"Look," I say, "why didn't you tell me some of this all those hours last night?"

He stared reproachfully at me, his eyes sad as a bloodhound's and almost as red. "Hell, man, I have my local reputation to look out for!" And then he laughed so damned hard he had a coughing, snorting spell, and ended admitting they weren't so cool up north and there'd be plenty of talk. So I was content to get on the train, hung as I was with life and letters.

[Honestly.] It wasn't until I got on that train and suffered the late-afternoon whirls that I thought of Ann. Hangover must have affected my libido. Then it came swelling into my consciousness that I'd see her again. I thought of her at Warner's party, and she stood there in a haze of idealization—young, pretty, and neat enough with a quip.

Inevitably, I suppose, we met almost at once [that's the way all good stories run]. Jack had rented a ramshackle downstairs floor of an incredibly dilapidated 1910 frame house. It was on the side of Capitol Hill looking west across Lake Union, and there I bunked for almost the whole time. I tried as best I could not to break into Jack's routine and even developed a bit of one on my own. Jack would work inside every morning on his critical book, and I'd go out on the porch that hung on the hillside and watch the boats and try to compose a few lines. Did that every morning, except the times I'd sleep off a party. Let's see, did Jack ever get up later than about 7:30? No, it didn't matter when he went to bed, he'd be reading or writing until about noon. He was a real monk about it. Yes, real discipline. He was a disciplined bastard, that Jack. And parties. Yes, the best was the one that brought me and Ann together—the first one.

So Jack collected Arthur Ryerson and his wife, a few people from the University, the man from Tacoma with all those jokes about outdoor privies, more than anyone since Chic Sale. Puget Sound bridge tender—time to compose. And maybe a dozen other people dropping in and out during the evening. Then a few neighbors who heard the noise and just came along in. Then, finally, of course, Ann and George Brocklin. Remembrance: that night the fall before when Warner entertained the Alf Landon of our little world, Kit Jensen. There I was standing talking to Jensen and Freddy McCrea, who was cracking jokes about Jensen's having forgotten to bring along his food-taster, when Jensen himself came up with Ann. Didn't really meet George, but I saw him talking with Sheffer and a couple of students most of the evening.

Ann: one of those women you notice right away; not really stacked, but a sort of willowy beauty and a classic nose. And lo, she could talk. I remember when she opened her mouth the illusion didn't vanish. She didn't chew up her sentences as if they were double bubble gum, and her nose, well, it wasn't to shout or whine through, the way they do it back here in Ahia. Besides she was eager to talk. All about the painting she was doing or trying to do when she had the time. She knew Ryerson. We talked and drank Warner's Sneaky Sam punch down to the maraschino cherries. In fact, by the end there, we were sharing that little settee, and I sliding farther and farther down into recumbence and she leaning over so I could hear her above the noise, her beautiful long brown hair framing her face—I imagined we were tented in. Maybe I'd just drunk too much of that fantastic, awful punch, but I had the impression that—well, I wasn't ready to suffer the consequences anyway. Besides, Truth in the Form of Laura was immovably present. Slunk I mentally to my lair. Nothing, nothing more to it than that. [And it's damned ridiculous to assume either of us was making plans to cohabit ten months later a thousand miles away. I suppose Laura was just fed up and frantic when she told Betty Lou that one.]

The party Jack threw enabled me to see him in the old element. His friends—just their existence—proved the eastern Ivy Leaguer bit was more or less a masquerade. In fact, that night we had a lot to drink, and, Christ, there I was broaching the subject of his double life. He even admitted to playing a game when it was useful.

"How the hell else do you get along? We all play games, don't we, Will?" he would say, leering at me, and I knew he was baiting me, accusing me for the hell of it of my own masks. This annoyed me. "Anyway, I'm not really sure I play games. It happens that I like that kind of clothes, fraud or not—yes, probably fraud—I. Have you ever really looked at Waltonites in the cafeteria for Sunday dinner? My God, Will, you don't have to play American Gothic just because you're folks, you know!"

I laughed, because I thought of old Jason's face. He was always joking about people being folks. "Sit up and act like folks, Emily," he would say. Or "My, Cassoway certainly wasn't folks today, was he?" Now I watched Jack picking it up. Personally I've never cared much about dress, but I suppose that's my fault. Still, Jack was a bit fastidious.

We were on the masks argument, and neither of us would let it go. It was Jack's opinion that I was the Masked Marvel of Walton. I'd be the last one destroyed by Hastings or squeezed to death in Berrigan's embrace. I'd be teaching the American-literature survey eventually, because Warner would say, "Good old Will," and Cassoway would say, "Good old Will," and I'd do my duty and need not fear harm. Jack was funny as hell, yeah, and it made me mad, even from Jack.

So why not argue back? "Okay, it's all well for you to take the high-and-mighty moral tone, with your book out and eastern degree. You don't *have* to kiss Hastings' ass. But I'm just a poor boy from Ohio ["Ahia," the bastard interposes] and a poor poet, to boot. I mean, I want to get along with my work in peace. I need some—"

Interruption: "Oh hell, come off it! I think you'd not describe yourself quite that way. You've complained enough about Berrigan's kissing Hastings' ass."

"Berrigan doesn't kiss Hastings' ass; he IS Hastings' ass."

Drunk and getting nowhere. Besides, Jack was saying he *wanted* to teach, he *liked* it, it wasn't just a living. If the mask was necessary sometimes to fool the snobs in the profession, well, he'd wear it. In fact, sometimes he thought it was an ideal he was seeking and not a mask he was putting on; and it was a damned sight better than pretending just in order to survive so you could keep a job that gave you some free time to write poetry. I was getting goddamned bored with this.

About now Ryerson turned up at Jack's elbow, letting on he'd heard. "Are you boys warming over Yeats?" Glad he'd interrupted. Jack was probably getting the best of me. A hell of an arguer, Jack. I'd have hated to be examined by him. Besides, it wasn't sporting. We were both getting a bit angry. Jack liked to think of himself as an independent soul—the basically self-made bit. Didn't know much about his background then. Always assumed his family was well off, but I was wrong. One day we hitched a ride out to Shoreham School, where Jack had gone. The Brocklins lived there. And we walked around. Big tank for Northwest socialites to immerse their kids, I guessed. But then Jack told me how he'd gone there. Sat on the headmaster's doorstep with a recommendation from his coach in Portland, got in by waiting on table and playing on the teams. A way to make it into the Ivy. They had good teams, he said. I'll be damned, I thought. Old slight Jack. Why he didn't even watch the Beavers play now. And by golly, there was Jack's name inscribed on a plaque. 1942–43 Basketball: John Emory, Jr., Captain.

"You were a big shot in these halls, dad."

"You bet I was," he laughed, "and I washed a lot of dishes, too!"

And then Jack worked his way at Princeton. Prided himself he'd taken on just enough of the veneer. [Damn braces, bless relaxes. What's enough ain't sufficient. I won't hone my life.]

Ryerson intervened just in time to prevent shouting. It wasn't really desperate, but there'd been enough probing, it tickled a bit. Everyone knows how goddamned honest everyone can get with a few drinks in them. Ryerson's line was simple enough. I was Person and Jack was Jack, and we had to find our own integrities. I wondered where to look. Probably all the way back in front of the drugstore on the corner of Main and High Streets, London, Ahia. That's when I started going bad, loafing around in a straw hat and terrorizing the girls with the old Model T. I thought: It all sounds good, but Berrigan's Berrigan, too, and he could hunt through the jungle of himself forever. Then I gave it another try. Ryerson's idea only works for real people, maybe. Berrigan was Jungstuff—projection of the Walton collective uncon-scious. Meanwhile, there was Jack insisting his idea was only a projection of something implicit in symbolist theory, ethics into aesthetics. [That aesthetics stuff bores me. Wrong end of telescope.] But Berrigan—I should ask someone sometime, someone outside our circle, whether he really existed.

As a matter of fact, Ryerson's attitude that we were judging each other by some standard we should apply only to ourselves made sense to me all the same, even after Jack got through tracing its history back to Kant or somewhere. It was damned difficult. Defend yourself in your mind against the bears of this world. Make yourself.

Well, we couldn't go on with this much longer. Jack was distracted to the porch by a buxom girl named Genevieve or Geraldine or something, and the last I saw he was looking at her like a mountaineer ready for a steep climb. Arthur Ryerson and I shared a bench of some sort and shoved off on a long meandering conversation about why some critics didn't write a good book on Williams or Rexroth instead of the umpteenth-hundredth book on Eliot. It was, I thought, a good discussion, ending with Ryerson, now I suppose well oiled, intoning Yeats's "Wild Swans at Coole" and then, all warmed up, "The Wild Old Wicked Man." By this time we had an audience, because Ryerson really *was* a Big Daddy and not just some Green Lion clown. They lay around on the floor.

Then I said a comic poem of mine about waiting outside the A & P for Laura and what I saw through the glass. That changed the tone a bit, and Ryerson added the part of "The Lemmings" where the theories about why the lemmings drown themselves are explored. That got us to beasts, and almost no one I know except a professor at Smith is more verbose than I am on beasts. So I composed something:

> I see him mutter bellerable words
> and cannot find the flower he deigns to eat.

No Ferdinand, my lectures at his feet
he'd trample like an elephant in turds.

Methinks perhaps he suffers constipation:
he hasn't fouled this pasture one whole hour
and wants, if I can estimate his glower,
upon my words to practice defecation.

Yet every day I see him pulled about,
a rope in ring. This beast can flout
my class, but likely cows tug at his snout.

Pavlovian bovine starts at hourly bell:
around the table this young bull
snorts for his brown-eyed heifer in the hall.

Drawn from life. The light verse me, but not really my style. I hope.

It was almost a regular old bardic competition, but no prizes and no seriousness allowed:

Baboons are dignified at play
until they turn and lope away.

Degeneration had set in. We were at the limerick level when George and Ann Brocklin arrived from another gala event. This startled me into a reasonable facsimile of pale sobriety. When I shook hands with George his palm was moist. Oddly elated, he. Back in his mind he remembered me vaguely.

"Oh yes, you are the Walton friend of Jack's." Neutral as water. It was pretty obvious he didn't know this party was for me. Besides, he was in a hurry to get to the kitchen, where the whiskey was. I could tell the next one was the one he really wanted. Also, it was the one downhill, for all-American boys at least. Later I saw him, only his head—it didn't come out of the kitchen for hours—shouting at one of the university people something about how his students, by God, didn't need to be told about the comma splice. The only reason I heard this was I'd quit drinking whiskey to keep sober and upright, and was thinking of rifling the refrigerator for beer.

When Ann came in she was a little loud, too. [Gawd, I am getting choosy.] Maybe she was just trying to reach the level the party had already attained. But she looked great; her hair was still long and down both sides of her face, and she was darkly tanned, so her blue eyes were vivid. And she wore—what do they call it?—a simple blue cotton dress with a big scoop in the front, and her legs were smooth, tan, and shiny. I excused myself the luxury of a stare and got over there as fast as I could. In the middle of one of Ryerson's sentences I took off.

"Oh, we missed the recitations," she said. "I knew we should have come earlier."

"No difference, not much high seriousness, I'm afraid. And we mouthed it a bit. Pastoral stuff. You've been at another party perhaps?" [Impertinent of me.]

"Oh you mean George. He's drunk, all right. All the way over I argued with him about driving. We had to talk him onto all the landing strips. Had dinner with the Wests. They were coming, but Janet got sick on the martinis, so Dick took her home. You'd like Janet. She's a real doll, and all herself, too."

"Aren't you? I mean I thought I was admiring all of you." Oh I was sly that night.

"Me? No." She laughed. "I left me outside when I climbed into the pit." I could not tell whether she meant this party or some larger aspect of her life. Then she glared. God knows what she meant by that, but what the hell. Maybe she's a bit nuts, I thought, or drunk along with George. That happens to the best of wives. [In the best of all worlds, my shoddy world.]

"Yeah, well, is this the pit? I'll admit, looking around, that there are some likely snakes." I was thinking, metaphor hopelessly mixed, of the mountain that had come to Jack.

No answer, but she sipped some beer and looked out the window toward Queen Anne Hill and the car lights coming around it. "Jack says you're a good poet [bless him]," she said. "Is Walton beating that out of you?"

I was a little surprised, but then I suppose Jack naturally bitched to his sister.

"Hell no." I tried to make it sound like a ridiculous question.

"It won't beat Jack either," she said, still watching the cars.

"No, we're Spartan types, but we'll both be bruised up a bit."

She turned to me. "You're really lucky, you know. At least your world is big enough that you can still get away, and there are people to talk to." [My, we were serious that night. And I thought that then.]

"Have you heard of the invention of the telephone? I believe the Russians have announced it. My Dean can get me night and day."

"Yes." She laughed again. "I've heard about your Dean. But I mean you don't have to *live* with *education* and our responsibilities to the students and—well, I wish we lived in a university environment. It's nice when Jack comes. It's as if they'd let us out of the stable or something, and we meet people." I thought of my colleagues. [Repress them here.]

"But you already know some of these people. The Ryersons?"

"Oh yes, but I only see them when Jack comes. I think they bother George. He doesn't seem to have much to say to them. I mean past the problem of grade eleven George just doesn't . . ." Didn't finish, just drank the beer and said, "I need some air."

So as natural as a stroll in broad daylight I went into

the night, with my proper emanation, my garden of delight. And it was a relief out. Mighty stuffy air inside. We walked and talked. No, she talked and I listened mostly, and we sort of supported each other along the way.

"I try to get out by painting," she said. "I'm not bad. I have a studio down the hill. That's how Jack got his place, same owner."

"Well, if this party keeps up, you'll be evicted tomorrow." There seemed to be a whale of a lot of noise coming from the house.

"Oh no. Did you see the tall character with the beard sitting in the front room there, sort of propped up?"

"Yeah."

"Well, he's the landlord. He paints, too, but brother it's terrible. I think I'd prop myself every night if I painted the way he does. Would you like to see my studio? It's not far."

Lord save us, I thought, I do believe I am being seduced. I gave way hopefully.

We started down the hill. "Does your husband paint, too?" I asked. I knew damned well he didn't.

"No. My husband should have been a missionary." That was gratuitous, but I took it as a simple gift.

"What church?" I asked. It was rhetorical, of course.

"Only God knows. That's the trouble."

[Monks in the age of Charlemagne, Deists in the age of Blake, Educationists now. Problems of the Football Helmet. Administration of the School Cafeteria. Pig Patrol, my sister Madge calls it at London High School.]

"The real trouble is he thinks everything can be worked out if we just sit down and talk. But when we sit down it's an analysis of *my* problems. You'd think he was advising a pubescent ninth-grader, and it's in those terms he gets out of education texts. Why, I could do better with the ladies' journals. If he'd read some real psychology! Of course, he doesn't have any problems himself."

We approached the old row of store fronts where her studio was. I could tell the drinks had freed her tongue. She was a bit plowed.

"My husband, my husband is a damned fool," she pronounced, pressing out the words. "Here, come up out of my pit." She unlocked the door. [Keys, locks, see, you goddamned Freudians!]

It was a big room with a tremendous window facing toward the lake. Served well enough for a skylight in the afternoons, I could tell, but there was also a small skylight in the roof. Same view as Jack's but much lower down and closer in. New sensation, beside the boats, not up above them. There were a couple of big canvases on the floor leaning against the wall. Too dark to make much of them, but I pretended to study.

"Come off it." She was laughing. "They're no good, just doodles. I don't finish them. Here's one over here that's not bad," and she held up a picture of a little girl. It wasn't bad, but I couldn't see it very well in the dim light. All we had was what came in from the waterfront and a candle she had lit. "Electricity's off," she said. I looked at some others. She didn't seem very self-conscious about them. I liked that. I liked her.

She went on. "I haven't been here long. It was a big argument with George before I did it. He wanted to fix up the garage out at school. But it wasn't just for my art, dear; it's escape." That was funny, I thought. Part of her anyway tells her what's true. She was at the window now, and we watched the boats.

"You know, in some ways I like the view from here better than Jack's. You're closer to the boats here, down on their level. It's the big panorama up there." She paused. "No, I've got this place because here is where I find myself again. I'm really nuts about it. All this time—Mothers' Club, cocoa for the boarders, dinners in the refectory, bridge with the J. Etherington Joneses. Maybe you can see." I could see all that. "I'm no good making talk. Besides, my life was disappearing. Do you know at night here you can see shooting stars if you watch the sky out this window? Millions of miles away, burning out over a long period of time, I suppose, but for us it's just a moment." That was a little incoherent, but I think I saw what her figure meant.

"Catch the joy as it flies," I said, standing there planted like some big silly bush. An old tug was docking across the lake.

"Something like that. I think Jack catches the joy."

He is tonight, I thought, God bless him.

But I was philosophic, to serve the mood she wanted. "No one catches it all—leaks everywhere." But I did know what she meant. Trouble was, the drinks were wearing off, and maybe it was just as well, because our souls were naked and our bodies grew there obscenely clothed. Ann was trying to dance out of her big black cloud. I wondered if I kissed her whether those angels of providence would flap away.

I kissed her, and she kissed me back, and then she extricated herself, whispering "Stay there," and walked into the darkness behind a divider in the back of the room. I turned back to the window and stared at a big blinking sign advertising a marina across the lake. It showed a man endlessly and with undiminished energy jumping in and out of a boat, in and out, jerk, jerk. I thought, We all have our own rhythms. Days, even years, have their rhythms. I'd jump back into Walton soon, or was that jumping *out* of the boat?

She was talking. "I think you have run off, too—don't turn around, please—I think you have run away like me."

I wasn't sure I wanted to discuss me, but for the sake of the situation I would not rock our poor little raft. She went on. "I could tell about you and your wife last fall."

"You hardly saw us."

"It's not hard to tell. That's why I'm not trying to hide my own problems. There's no use. Everyone except George knows. Anyway, that night she grasped at you all the way across the room."

"That was because you are a beautiful woman; anyone would—" I turned around, and she was just behind me in the darkness. I could see the whiteness of her breasts and stomach where the tan wasn't, because she was naked.

"You turned around too soon," she whispered. I held her, and somehow we got over to the daybed, and somehow I got some of my clothes off, and all at the same time—I was a cartwheel of activity, all right—I caressed her smooth body, her breasts and nipples, and she said, "Take me now."

"Yes, Lord, yes," I think I uttered, and so I took her— too fast, I guess, and we lay there under one blanket and no pillow and we watched the lights playing on the ceiling and the back wall, for a big boat of some kind was going out.

She said, "Sometimes I think I won't go back."

"Let's think it over. You really mean you don't know how to break away."

"I guess that's it. Conscience and what Mama would think. Do you—I mean—well, do you love your wife? Oh, I'm sorry, that's a rotten question."

"Why not ask it? I ask it, but I don't know. We live in two different ways now. I thought we reached each other, but now it's pretty rare. Sometimes when I crack a joke or something, it all lights up, but the basement windows are dark. I doubt we can make it any more. I'm a Hastings man now." I spoke that last sentence to myself.

"What?" she asked.

"Oh nothing."

"Jack told me you were having difficulties. I didn't just guess about your wife."

"Oh?" I was annoyed again. It didn't seem to be any of his business, and besides, I didn't like the idea of Ann's knowing that outright. It put her actions with me in a different light somehow.

She saw I was peeved. "I shouldn't have said that."

"If you knew it, I guess it was all right."

"No. We shouldn't say everything we know."

"I'd like to know all you know." I was getting corny and trying to get back to the kadoodling. But she wanted to talk now.

"If I tried to tell you, it would come out wrong. That's why we shouldn't try. That's what's wrong with George. He wants to discuss everything." For someone who didn't believe in telling very much, she was certainly ready to go now. But after a while I silently persuaded her to try something else, and it worked, and then I went to sleep for a bit.

About four o'clock I woke up with a start. Ann was dressed and smoking a cigarette.

"It's late. What about George?" I was agitated. "And your baby sitter?"

"Oh, don't worry. The kids are camped out, and never mind George. He'll know I'm here, if he knows anything."

"Good God, woman! That's what I mean."

"He won't come. Probably sleeping it off anyway. He aches, too, you know. Anyway, I don't care." She was cold and severe. "You go to Jack's."

I argued, I don't know what about really, but she pointed me up the hill with my jacket slung over my shoulders. When I found my way back, there was just a touch of sunlight suggested in the sky. George Brocklin was crapped out in the front-room daybed that I usually slept on. Jack's bedroom door was closed, and hanging from the doorknob was one of those "Quiet is requested for the benefit of those who have retired" signs that you steal from trains. I thought it was fair enough for George to have my bed, so I took a couple of coats out of the closet and lay down on an old army cot out on the porch and watched the morning creep across the lake. It was very quiet, and from the middle of the city I could hear the slightest sound across the water.

Geraldine or Genevieve or someone, who turned out in the morning to be Jennifer, if I remember, made breakfast. George slept on. Jack was soon flopping around in a pair of huge slippers, talking about Ryerson and some of the people at the party. Jennifer, on the other hand, would have made a good soulmate for Levi McLeod. The night before, I thought she was just made up in the deadpan style, but this morning I could see it was her real face. Like a mask, I thought, but neither the comic nor the tragic one. Straight absurd. No words from her. Pretty soon Jack and I took the coffee out to the porch. As far as I know, Jennifer cleaned up the kitchen and vanished up the chimney. I saw her again one night in the local pub. But Jack never mentioned her.

Out on the porch it was different. Jack, serious as hell: "I didn't want to say anything in front of Jennifer, but I think maybe you ought to disappear for an hour or so."

"Why Jennifer? Hell, she can't talk, can she?" I tried levity.

Jack laughed. "Her range of subject matter isn't very large, but she does have a small working vocabulary. No, listen. Ann's business is her own. If she wants to whore around it's all right with me, but I can hardly protect her or you. Now George was drunk, all right, but you don't forget things like that. Of course, he doesn't know how long you were gone."

"Christ," I said, "you don't have to call it whoring around. And I don't need the protection you can't give or don't want to give, or whatever it is that's eating you. [Who was saying all this?] Personally I don't think you care anyway. And you know I'm not the cause. She invited me. . . ."

Jack was mad, but he controlled himself. "I know that; God, I know it." Suddenly I felt sorry for him. I could see he was concerned but didn't want to be.

Then through the window we both saw George, bleary-eyed and hair ruffled, ready to make his entrance.

But he turned off, like Muggs following Hamlet's ghost, to the kitchen.

"Too late now," I said.

He was back with a cup of coffee in a minute. "Some party," he offered, with marked originality. We nodded.

"I suppose Ann went to her studio. Guess I'd better pick her up. Sorry I took your bed. Don't remember much about it. Whoof, it was those martinis before I came." He smiled sheepishly and held his head. "I was paralyzed when I got here."

I couldn't tell whether the poor bastard was lying or not. He wasn't going to say anything, I guess. We all sat there, and I watched a bus all the way across Aurora Bridge. George had not sat down. In fact, he decided to go right away. Jack saw him to the door.

As they went out I could hear George saying, "We've got to talk it out some time. I'd like to see you soon."

Back on the porch Jack growled, "The poor bastard's a perpetual student."

I didn't feel much in my conscience, but I allowed that I was probably to blame.

"What, for seducing my sister? For George being a poor bastard? Anyway, I've got to go down to the store." And for the first morning I could remember, Jack didn't hole up to work.

What do I do now, I thought, and I knew I wanted to do something about it. Ann had spoken of becoming herself. She'd probably been reading the educational jargon, too. Hell, you couldn't blame her; she lived with a talking textbook. I knew what she meant. But I didn't know which was my own self now, whether I had lost it long ago and was looking for it or whether I was trying to get out of this old hide of a self and find me a new life. I didn't like my state of mind very much. I realized suddenly that for a whole day I hadn't really thought of Laura and the children. Now they flooded back in. I was tossed up on the sands of my own conscience and lay there gasping. I thought of my little girl waking from a nightmare and crying out in the night. An immense ennui settled upon me, as if there were nothing worth doing. Was my Nausicaä dream of last night real? Would she come, running lightly in a filmy dress as they do in the cigarette ads, parting the tall grass and ferns on the shore's edge and, barefoot in the sand, revive me with Kools or Marlboros? I could not move. The great weight of the sky pressed down. A few birds wheeled. I thought, I must choose my life. But let me rest now, Lord.

Jason, Ellen, The Dean

CONVERSATIONS TO REMEMBER   There was a long letter from Jensen in his box, and he would read it before the Dean's meeting began; in fact he read it as he strolled over to the Administration Building. It was absorbing enough that he really didn't notice her beside him when he reached the entrance steps.

"You seem to be making the most of every minute, sir. Hello, Jason."

It was Ellen Fraser, and of course she thought he was avoiding speech with her.

"No, I'm just an old mail hound. You remember Mr. Jensen. It's a letter from him." They entered the elevator.

"How could I forget him? He's a great correspondent, isn't he?" Her sarcasm annoyed him. Her face said to him that the sarcasm was somehow for him, even though her words were about Jensen. Besides, it wasn't the most direct way of saying that the Dean had been hearing frequently from Jensen. He wondered whether the Dean was irritated. It was a bit of a bore to go on answering Jensen's letters. Betty Lou had warned him. The man would line everyone up against everyone else, she said.

They stood silently as the elevator ascended. Self-consciously he examined the letter again. He did not want her to intrude upon him. There was nothing he could say to her.

Jensen's letter was a diatribe against Hastings and Mrs. Bolyard for failing to answer his queries about the fate of the essay he had submitted to the *Review*. Look here, was its strident ring, how long is it going to be before Hastings will say whether he'll print my essay? All he does is talk eagerly about plans. And does he or doesn't he want to negotiate about a professorship at Walton? The question is, pal, what kind of a show is your pal running?

This Jason read twice, seeking some less obvious motive behind the words. He went over the potpourri of remarks about people Jensen had met at Walton, jibes at the president on his own campus, and finally some friendly words to be passed on to Fred McCrea. These were especially puzzling. It wasn't at all clear why Mc-Crea should be the recipient of Jensen's attention. Betty Lou would be disgusted with his meditation on the matter, wondering why he made such a big thing of it. There was Ellen standing next to him, but it was Betty Lou who kept talking in his mind. She was probably right about his trying to track every nuance down. Still . . .

The elevator stopped. He ushered her out. She smiled at him with extreme ingratiation. He discovered no way to avoid it. In the hall they parted company silently. Everything was unsatisfactory. At that moment McCrea himself emerged from the Dean's office.

He breezed past. "Must hurry off, Jason. Have a good meet." He blew a kiss into Ellen's office as he went by, crooking his head as if the door were too low for him. It almost was. Had McCrea become one of the Dean's crew? Obviously from his remark he knew why they were all meeting today. It was just possible to put this together with Jensen's message and conclude that McCrea figured in Hastings' plans, and that Kit Jensen somehow knew it or had intuited it. Jason sighed to himself. He really couldn't stand McCrea, and he disliked these meetings even if they did have their own strange fascination. He had come to Walton to teach, think, and write, and somehow these aims had been replaced by a vague nameless goal he was being driven toward, though he was sure he could not recognize it if it suddenly loomed up.

As he seated himself in the Dean's office, he remembered the first occasion after Jensen's visit when they had sat in the very same places, like robber barons in the gilded age, around the long, polished, carved-leg table in absurd high-backed leather chairs. The Dean, behind his own desk, had gone on at length. Today would follow the established pattern. Now came the dread familiar beginning—Hastings warming to his task.

And then: "Let me parenthesize for a moment"—it was the Dean's favorite expression and it drove Jason wild, almost made him smile foolishly when he heard it. Hastings' character was becoming before their ears the shape of the clichés that he mouthed. Jason imagined him vaguely as a great mass of verbiage, a whole hill of it, shimmering like Jell-O. As trifle was to dessert, so was Hastings to true rhetoric. But there was no stopping him, and Jason struggled to control himself; Hastings would go on embarrassing the men around the table, who were so sensitive to verbal nuance that they marked people's talk as they would a freshman's theme.

And Jason knew he ought not to look at Emory, because the slightest reply of the eyes might destroy all the self-composure he grasped so tightly and break him up into hideous laughter. But he chanced it. Emory was his own kind of show, tense and scowling, as if he were prepared for the pain of a dentist's drill. Luckily their eyes did not meet. He noticed Person next, engulfed in what seemed to be an immense ennui. Jowls sagging from his cragged cheekbones, he was slumping farther and farther back within the wings of his chair. Berrigan's eyes flickered at Will, catching his attitude. And there among the others was Crowder, pipe-smoking, trying to look donnish and unflappable. A look at Crowder caused Jason to recover at once from the threat of laughter. And with the laughter gone he was left seriously to study the two scientists from the lower campus. He eyed them, seeking somehow a message. There they sat—apparently good-natured, perhaps a bit puzzled, throughout the Dean's monologue. He recalled Person saying one day that he'd had a beer with Finch, the fellow studying elephants' blood, and tried to explain Hastings to him, but Finch didn't seem to care a damn. Why? Jason asked himself, when even he'd been driven into some sort of crazy competition, like shutting the door on Klaus that night in Jensen's hotel room. Was it their monster grants that left them free of desire for Hastings' vague gifts?

He had been listening with half an ear. As the digression neared some sort of conclusion, he watched the Dean peer off into the past to rediscover his subject. Hastings sighted it; there was a shuffle of feet, a rearrangement of buttocks, a planting of elbows, a propping of heads and necks. Jason tried to imagine how he looked to Jack; Jack was glaring at him, or at the world in general. He damn near laughed at Jack.

They had been called together "to review the success of, to firm up, the Critique Series, and to engage in a fruitful discussion of ends and means," an exchange of ideas illustrating "the dynamic interaction of study and classroom." The Dean had begun with certain oblique remarks about the visit of Jensen. Although another critic had since come and gone, the meetings tended to return to that first visitor, as if something were not settled. But Hastings skirted the matter even as he wished to divest himself of an opinion on it. Jason was used to his talk about firming things up; he knew well enough that Hastings was a fluidity man.

139

They were an audience.

"I'm sure every one of you recognizes the important contribution of this series. I'm most anxious to have your support and interaction in making our full commitment to the college interdisciplinary programs. So it's criticism in the largest sense we're concerned with. Yes, criticism of life. [Staring above them—a pause.] Now all of you have other duties, and you may feel prior commitments, and that's as it should be. Those of you on leave next year—research grants, Guggenheims, National Science, ACLS [nervous laughter]—I want to keep in touch with you. I hope you'll be scouting out new ideas and recommending plans and people, and then there's the magazine that must take shape for spring. And just to parenthesize again here, I don't want anyone so committed to these programs that you lose your potential in the departments you work in and don't get that book out or don't find your departmental situation anything but to your liking when promotions come around. You'll want to talk individually with me about your direction relevant to our programs and how you want to advance with them. You must keep your own interests. You are all scholars, and I hope gentlemen [laughter], and we want it that way, and I need your support. And just to put in this expression: we may have to enlarge this group or keep it changing from time to time [gazing at the chandelier]. By the way, Brendan, is the next Critique all set up?"

"Oh, ah, Mr., Dr. Hastings, it's all ready; the committee will meet Wellek at the plane, hotel reservation, I've reserved, er, ah, yes, at the Cumberland. We wanted a, a good, as you said, select audience. Then the seminar next day, and the luncheon. I hope you can make it for that, sir."

"Good, fine, Brendan."

The Dean was examining his notes. Berrigan was still talking. Hastings heard him but not, perhaps, what he said, shutting him off finally with a simple "yes." Certainly Berrigan's plans, which Person had made the day before, were far too minuscule for Hastings to be interested in. It was possible to imagine the state of Hastings' notes for this meeting, they were lying before him—very sparse, three or four major headings and lots of room for fancy footwork and forward momentum. It really was impossible not to enjoy the spectacle of Berrigan facing the onslaught of verbal vanity that the Dean was capable of mounting. Berrigan's visage underwent change after change as the Dean flitted from subject to subject. But suddenly this was no longer simply amusing or vapid. It had become tense. Emory, with the others silent, had chosen to draw the Dean out, steering him back to plans for the magazine. The Dean parried with rhetoric: Their aim was to hit a high standard and yet appeal to more than an academic audience. Then came alliteration: The magazine was to be literate but not literary, regional and reflective. It would bring the region to the world, and the world to the region. But it was clear that Emory would demand more than alliteration and balance.

Jason wished desperately for the meeting to end. This whole magazine bit: he hadn't cared a hoot for it, really. What was the point except to take time away from all the other jobs there were to do? And he really didn't like Emory's baiting Hastings with questions. It was unnecessary. He knew his uneasiness was apparent to Hastings, and the Dean's eyes were searching for its cause. He had to sit silently and stonily, even if it was only because he couldn't really think of anything appropriate to say. The Dean probably thought him somehow disapproving; it was funny how the Dean watched them all most intensely when Emory had him on the spot. What was the real function of the magazine? This meant: Was it really a university's business? And this, boiled down a little more, became "Is this your own publicity venture?" Yes, Emory was striking to the heart of Hastings' dreams of grandeur. Hastings countered with generalizations about educational vision, cross-disciplinary liaison, and culture. Emory pursued with questions about specific policy. Emory would ask them because no one knew just what his duties were, except to be present at these meetings.

But Jason couldn't decide whether he worried about Jack because he worried about himself and they were somehow tied together in this or whether he was simply embarrassed because the situation was awkward. He knew Betty Lou would say they were acting like the faculty wives. In any case, he supposed that there was reason to worry more about Will's psyche than Jack's. Will looked ready either to fall asleep, to be sick, or to bolt from the room. When Jack bored in, Will hid his eyes with his hand.

It went like this:

"Fine, Jack, fine, very good. You'd better write that up in a memo. We'll circulate it. Of course we want this magazine to grow. It's not an overnight process, but then we can't have a late bloomer either. The successful magazine makes it from the start. And now, gentlemen—by way of parenthesis—this magazine will need a heart, a literary heart, not regional, not lowbrow and not fake highbrow. Incisiveness is the word. I was just talking to Harold Telber the other day about his reminiscences of Lawrence. When those manuscripts come in . . ." It all faded into a discussion of the rare-book room.

Jack sought to edge back. "Henry [My God, Jason thought, that will get him, but Hastings never blinked, just stared blandly at his inquisitor], there are some mechanical matters of handling manuscripts that we ought to talk about." But somehow on this day the Dean was more abstracted than ever. He refused to spar, seemed hardly to be listening, and finally excused himself, which meant that he had dismissed them. The Jensen business remained unsettled, hovering over them. There was no talk of an editor, no talk of Jensen's essay.

Jason descended in the elevator with Berrigan and Jack, who was gruff to Crowder, openly and needlessly. As they left the building he hated the whole day he'd put in, seeing Ellen, hearing the spiel, watching everyone's inadequate defense. Now he saw that Berrigan was agitated. The explosion came suddenly. "What'd he mean saying he might change the committee? Is he gonna replace us next year? Does he think we're not doing the job?" He tried to interpret Hastings' every mood and tone.

"Christ, Brendan," Jack said. "Let's not speculate about that. Let's get through this year." Berrigan laughed nervously. He's not stupid, Jason thought to himself, as he had over and over again; and then, as he had not until then, I am being drawn too far into all this. I must keep my own counsel. But that was hard to do.

It was late in the day, back in his office, when he remembered he had left his briefcase somewhere on the Dean's floor. And so he was back there just in time to see Ellen Fraser ushered out of Hastings' office, hand held by the Dean.

Late that afternoon, Ellen had come around to believing that when the Dean asked her in after his meeting with the committee it had not been just to tell her about the possibilities of the drama fellowship. And curiously he had blushed, yes, he really had blushed when she thanked him profusely for writing the letter to help her out and for promising to talk personally to some people he knew. He had offered more than was necessary, even for a former student.

"Stay for tea," he said, hardly looking in her direction, fingering a small Mayan head on his desk. The Dean always had tea at this time in the afternoon—when he was free. Yes, he had blushed. She had been aware before that he liked her, but not that she was really in a position of some power. She did not know quite what to do with it, but she knew that something must be done. He had already done her a favor and was going to compound it, and without conscious exercise of power on her part. It struck her somehow as ironic. Things didn't usually take place that way.

"Will you pour?" He got up from his desk, walked to the window, and looked down at the Quad. She poured. There was a long silence that was unsatisfactory to her, but apparently not to him. There's a bit of the ham in him, of course, she thought. She watched him. There was something memorable about his pure white hair, his fair skin, the wiry tension of his body but something strange, too, as if he were made up for a part. He was an actor. He didn't dislike suspense. He played with his audiences; she knew that from having been in his classes. "Well," he said, "well."

She could not decide for or against speaking, but she knew suddenly and surely that he was greatly attracted to her in a way that had its sexual overtone perhaps, but was also somehow not quite sexual, or overtly so. He wanted to own her in some way, but be owned as well. It was the latter that somehow prevailed. Because of this passion when he half looked at her and treated her regally with flowers at her desk, never forgetting Mrs. Bolyard, too, he found it necessary to do something for her, something that would probably take her away from him in space, yet require her remembrance forever that *he* had done it when it needed doing.

Finally she spoke softly, knowing now that what he most desired was her confidence. "It's been a bad day?"

He looked at her for a moment, turned to his desk, then settled again at the window. He was very self-conscious, she thought, but the pose was really well done.

"Everything is difficult," he said. "Nothing is easy. This job, this job is a trouble-shooter job, a job for a fast gun. Oh, I've heard it, 'Henry Hastings, the fastest Dean in the West.' Slogans get back. I can even guess who made it up. They'll say you don't get into this job if you don't have a fast gun. But I didn't take it on for all that. It's for what you can build—educational policy, programs, people. . . . Now this man Jensen with his letters and demands about his paper on one side, and these young fellows on the other. We don't want Jensen bleating around the country. But the young fellows are against publication."

"I guess you'll just have to decide it on its merits," she said as softly as she could.

"Of course, of course." He frowned. "But these young men. And Jensen threatening, saying Walton will be lucky to hang on to them—Talbot and Emory." He did not look at her. Why had he mentioned only those two? For a moment she wondered just what he knew about her. "Well, I can't make them out. Sometimes I have the feeling there's really nothing that can please them. Here I've put them on committees, given them a lot of responsibility on this magazine venture and the series. And yet they're not, well, somehow not lined up with us. What do you think, Ellen? Is Jensen's thing so bad, and if we reject it—well, if we do, where do Emory and Talbot stand? Will they feel justified?"

Suddenly she sensed his real fear. He could not let Jason or Jack feel that *they* had accomplished something—as long as they made no overture of some sort to him. He went on, "Some people can't be pleased, some people are insatiable. You know them, Ellen."

She wondered how she was to take that, decided to ignore its deeper possibilities, and answered, "They can't be blamed too much, and they aren't as fierce as they look, I'm sure." But she wasn't really so sure, thinking of Jason watching and of Jack's intelligent eyes. She decided she was lying. She went on, and meant it, "We really do appreciate you, and I especially for all your help on my application. I'm really grateful." She knew she needed his help. "Some people have different styles, but they know you're doing a big job."

"And they talk about me. There's not any warmth, no real interaction. I'm cut off from them. Well, I suppose they can't understand what I have to deal with. You work with what you have." She supposed that meant the English Department, which Jack had such contempt for. He was no longer talking to her, she could tell. He was talking out loud to himself about himself.

"And the other thing is they don't seem to interact among themselves." She was beginning to wince at that word. It began to seem obscene. "Now when I was starting out as a young instructor here, we had a group that learned from each other." His voice trailed off into preoccupation. Then he came over to her and took her hand. This surprised her but she tried to smile.

"Ellen, you're a good influence around here, my dear. Why, in the office, you've . . ." The sentence was not completed. "Well, this hasn't been a good week. We haven't moved ahead, from what I can see. In fact, I had to terminate a contract yesterday, someone who's been here quite a while. Yes . . . Ellen, thanks for listening." He was maneuvering her to the door. She knew he was a master at ushering out. She'd seen him do it many times. Now it was happening to her. No difference. There was a set smile as he added, "We'll all miss you, because you're going to get that grant! Wait and see!"

She could be neither embarrassed nor amused. She could decide neither to accept his pleasant words nor to analyze coolly the means by which he cleared her from his office. She found herself for the moment overwhelmed by the inevitability of his isolation in the position he held, by his pathetic desire, by the inadequacy of his words. But standing in the doorway, her hand still in his, she faced Jason Talbot down the hall watching her. Hastings had seen him, too, frowned imperceptibly, and turned back into his office.

Jason, damn him, watched her gravely, one eyebrow perhaps slightly raised. She smiled hard at him and walked to her office door. He had seen the Dean's grandiloquent hand-holding manner. She hoped she had been cool. She was really furious with Jason, and even annoyed with Jack by proxy. Those two! She was putting them together the way Hastings had. She shrank from that, but she had done it.

▶

By that time Jason had learned something:

Well, yes, I had. The day before, John Temple, across the hall, had been quietly packing up his books. I hardly knew Temple, who had seemed to me only a small, ineffectual middle-aged pedant. He taught the Elizabethans when he could and filled in mainly with freshman and sophomore work. He was, in other words, one of the many associate professors permanently, or so it appeared, cut off from the Promised Land. Now the office was empty, but after our meeting with Hastings, Ralph Ware unlocked the door and began to put his books on the shelves.

On my way back to the Ad Building to get my briefcase, I looked in. "Trade with Temple?" I asked.

"You didn't hear? Temple is sacked."

"In mid-term? With tenure? Why?"

"You *are* new here, aren't you?" He was amused. I felt rather silly. "Well, you see, Temple's parties for selected students have long had a certain fame in these parts. Oh, they were secret enough for years. But suddenly the circle has widened. He's the efficient type. I don't think he's ever had a steady platonic boy friend like Sheffer."

Everett Sheffer was our top Victorian specialist and the director of the college Honors Program. He was a Californian, Stanford, I believe. Athletic in build, with a graying-blond, crew-cut head. He'd written a pretty fair book about Aubrey Beardsley. Several Beardsleys hung in his office.

"Yes, he's been sacked by the administration. Something last weekend, I think. Anyway, Hastings, or whoever it is, certainly isn't taking any chances of a scandal. So out he goes."

"I suppose it would have been a real embarrassment to the administration if it came out that Temple was involved with students."

"Embarrassment. Good heavens, there's nothing worse with the folk, not even Communists. Besides, Temple's been around here a long time, almost as long as Hastings and Sheffer. I think he came about the same time that Laurence Fenrow and Lila Warren did." Ralph was grinning again, broadly. "You know, the crowd that congregated here just before the war." Old Ralph, he always bombed you with that disarming, completely open smile.

That did it, of course. It didn't thump me over the head because it had already sunk in imperceptibly over the whole fall. I ticked off those names again. They were the people who steered the Honors Program in English—Ralph had neglected only McCrea. It was from running English Honors as a sort of pilot program for the College that Henry Hastings had advanced to Dean. They as a group constituted the advisers. They did a good amount of the teaching. They were all Hastings' old colleagues, and now he had sacked one of them—someone on the fringe, but, still, one of the group. And Hastings had Emory's committee revising the Honors Program.

I considered this while I got over to the Ad Building for my briefcase. Lo and behold, on my arrival, there was old Ellen holding hands with Hasty Hank. She knew she'd been had. So we were even. I couldn't help feeling that this was a good thing. But I didn't like the chummy bit much either. It said things about her that I guess I'd suspected. I wondered, for example, how much of what Jack said leaked back to Hastings. But a bigger question at the moment was whether or not Hastings was going to send the whole Honors crowd out of power. I was probably overstating the possibilities. But I decided to test my speculation on Emory.

Luckily, the next time I saw Jack he had just lunched with Sheffer. Now Sheffer wasn't my type, or should I say I wasn't his? There was always something curiously distant in his manner, almost as if he lived in another world and dropped in on the department occasionally to collect his mail. I guess Jack liked Sheffer. They had both written on the nineties, for one thing.

At lunch that day, Jack had casually mentioned the Honors Program revision his committee had been working on. The committee was *ad hoc,* straight from the Dean. Before he had gone very far, he knew he'd put his foot in it. Sheffer smiled, but the smile was ironic, perhaps long-suffering. He was polite and asked a few innocuous questions. Then suddenly Jack sensed something amiss.

"You mean you don't know about our committee and these proposals for revision?"

"No, nothing." And Sheffer added after a moment, "I don't know much about what goes on around here these days." The tone was more than ironic.

Now Jack was embarrassed. "Good heavens, why I thought you'd been involved in setting us up. Why, I just assumed . . ."

But there was little to say. Sheffer merely continued to

smile. I think he liked Jack. No. I mean I think he thought well of him, realized Jack wasn't plotting.

After reporting all this, Jack said to me, "Do you suppose Hastings is casting the old Honors people out, with us as the instrument? I know the teaching's a sort of adventure among the masterpieces, but just for the sake of politics he ought to consult the staff people."

Now that was silly and inconsistent. Jack usually complained that Hastings didn't ride over the old guard often enough. Now he wanted discretion. But I didn't take that line. There was another that would rock Jack more.

"Aren't a few things beginning to meet your eye?" I said, taking a bit of pleasure in teasing old hawkeye Jack with my clear Olympian insight. He always prided himself on knowing what was up and keeping a clear head.

"What do you mean?"

"Well, Temple was sacked."

"Yes, Ware told me about that, but what's that got to do with Sheffer and the program?"

"Temple did a little work in it."

"Yes."

"And Sheffer does, and McCrea, and Fenrow."

"Christ, don't go on. But Sheffer? Well I don't know. . . ."

"Of course it may be nothing at all, but he certainly does spend a lot of time with a certain, shall we say, protégé." I was a little nervous about this, because Jack didn't *want* to think about it.

But he *was* thinking. "I suppose sacking Temple was also a sort of warning. What's next?"

"Not out of the University, but perhaps out of power. It looks as if he's going to swing the Honors Program away from them and remove some of their importance. And don't you suppose this whole business is a strain on Hastings?"

Jack saw what I was implying. "You mean, the busi-

ness of his coming here about the same time and . . ."
He had been sprawled in my office visitor's chair, but now
he leaped up and strode to the window, peering through
the Venetian blinds. "Jeesus!" I must say I got a bit of a
kick watching old hawkeye Jack take it all in—slowly,
like sippin' bourbon. I guess I'd unconsciously planned it
that way.

"At least it looks as if he's running out on his old colleagues, running scared," I added.

"Yeah, that's what I thought, too, but look, what
difference should this make to the whole situation? Any
administrator would do the same; besides, he might really
think that the plan needed to be overhauled. He'd certainly have fired Temple under the conditions. The whole
thing is too pat the way you set it up. It doesn't allow the
man any objective judgments."

I was amused. It was like Jack to worry the whole
thing out and take Hastings' side just when Hastings
looked his worst. He often did that. I remember a couple
of times when he even defended Klaus to Person. Mainly
he wanted to put it out of his mind, the looming suspicion
that he was dealing with a personality, indeed a whole
situation, the dimensions of which he had not understood.

Person's reaction was worse. He feigned prior knowledge, but I could see that the complete picture shocked
him. He snorted and blustered about his fate being tied
up with a bunch of fairies. He didn't give a damn about
their Honors Program, but he wished to hell Hastings
would retire Freddy McCrea to pastures removed from
his own. He was referring, of course, to the magazine,
which looked as if it might take a lot of his time. I was
amused, because when it wasn't taking his time he complained about Hastings not giving them anything to do.

Well, it did begin to take up time, because in another
week we were meeting frequently. It soon became clear
that Person and Emory had a plan. It was to see that

Dickie Klaus and his sidekick Davis, whom Person detested and Emory had no confidence in, exerted little influence on editorial decisions. The whole thing was highhanded, a sure way to annoy them. But I remained silent. Davis and Klaus were no friends of mine, and I wasn't very deeply involved in the magazine bit, and didn't really want to be.

At meetings, usually something like this would happen:

We wait for Berrigan because two weeks ago Berrigan has taken some manuscripts home to read and hasn't returned them. Person exclaims, "Aw hell, he's not going to show. I'm damned if I'll track those manuscripts down this time. No more special trips over there for me." His meetings with Wilma have taken a lot out of him. He rolls his eyes up to the ceiling, then stares moodily into space. This amuses Jack, who smiles broadly, which influences Dick Klaus to chuckle discreetly, as if in on the joke, and Crowder to shift uncomfortably around in his chair, appearing for some unaccountable reason to shrug, shaking off an insult. Busily then, he lights his pipe.

"Say," says Crowder, puffing. "I think the article on Cozzens from that fellow in Michigan was pretty fair. Has that been around?"

"Oh Christ," comes forth in a low mutter from Person. He sighs and stares some more.

"Not very sound in his remarks on Céline," Klaus adds, "but I liked . . ."

Drowned out by Person shuffling back his chair and saying, "God, I will go find Brendan," and making to stalk out until Ralph Ware suggests he stay a little longer and perhaps they can wrap up the present business.

Klaus smiles sheepishly. Crowder slinks behind his pipe and puffs domestically for the rest of the meeting.

But Klaus is never quite put down. He implies that perhaps he and others—meaning Paul Davis—should be consulted about the poetry. Emory suggests with apparent sweet reason that after all he and Person are the ones getting part time off from teaching to do magazine work and naturally the bulk of responsibility should fall on them.

Davis, having screwed up his highly emotional being to the pitch of a few desperate words on this subject, is interrupted by Fred McCrea's sudden lanky appearance at the door.

"Heigh-ho, boys. Hard at it, I see. Never let it be said we don't do or die for old Walton. I bring a message from the chief. Oh say," draping himself over Davis's shoulder like an umbrella, "isn't *that* story a goody. We really *must* have it. A little in the mode of Eudora Welty, I'd say. Yes indeed, sheer Eudora."

The message itself proves innocuous, merely material for dramatic entrance.

McCrea is not with us long. Off to deal with more important matters. Meanwhile, Ralph Ware, our coolest head perhaps, brings peace and gets us adjourned. We each lay down the sword of words for a while. We are all experts at its bitter use.

Something bothers me as I leave. Why are Berrigan and McCrea off on the edge of this venture? Could they have foreseen the fate of the editorial committee? They both managed to skip any meeting at which Hastings wasn't present. Whatever their motives they hadn't wasted their time. The manuscripts that were eventually published had been either commissioned or somehow fished from the mail by Mrs. Bolyard and sent directly to Hastings himself. While we were meeting to choose material for the first issue, McCrea was editing stuff already decided upon. And he never told us.

Then came the day in March when we were called together and handed galley proof to read. Emory was a study. I don't think he would normally have complained about reading proof, but he put up a ferocious bluster about it when it came to him that reading proof was *all* that he was going to do for the cause. Person tried acceptance, but it didn't fit him at all. Well, he'd intone, we'd been bushwhacked and that was that. The only thing left was to retire from this goddamned frantic activity and merely do our duty until our enlistment came up.

No one likes to be sent to play games, but we were partly to blame, no doubt. I don't mean to criticize Jack, because deep down, after you took off their costumes, his motives were as pure as anyone's are when he thinks he is right. He did, however, overlook something in Hastings' character which was becoming plainer and plainer every day.

Hastings found it difficult to say no. He would rather offer vague agreement to some plan and then disregard it than offer a simple and final no. You could say that Hastings learned somewhere along the line that he couldn't control Jack and the others, so he set them to games. Or you could say that he meant the best at the time and really accepted suggestions only to be carried away and take in contributions indiscriminately. You could even say that he didn't have any plan and let things evolve. But the interpretation that I lean to is that his actions were a result of his emphasis on vague enthusiasm coupled with a sentimental desire to please. All that made "no" an obscene word. He was willing to be had if he could have the person who had him.

Well, Person and Emory were badly deflated, particularly in the eyes of some of their colleagues on the staff. I don't think Ralph Ware, who was content to write his novel and teach his classes, cared very much, but the other two really did want something to be done with the literary side of the magazine. So after calming down they went to Hastings, and they thought they had gotten him to let them find a piece of fiction at the last moment for the first issue. Just to show readers, and possibly contributors, their intentions, they said.

And that was what led to the blowup when George Hungerford arrived. Because Hastings didn't like the story they chose and let them know in no uncertain terms. Then, of course, Klaus and Davis played I-told-you-so.

Meanwhile, back at the ranch, Person would come by about once a week after spending two or three hours with eight colleagues trying to revise the curriculum and the program for English majors. His huge body would shuffle along the hall, his face that ashen gray I'd learned to expect when his patience had been sorely tried. It was after one of these meetings that, loaded with Hastings and curriculum, he went out to the local bar with a couple of his poetesses and didn't drop in at home until nearly midnight. Finally, when he came in pretty drunk he and Laura had the inevitable fight. Things were strained enough between them even before this. They had taken to making little insinuations about each other to their acquaintances. Laura just didn't have the experience or the style to handle sarcasm. It came out of her all wrong, seemed too deeply felt. What once had been charming was now astringent and bitter. Betty Lou and I tried to remain friendly with the Persons, and we wouldn't have been deeply involved with their problems at all if it hadn't been for the Berrigans.

In truth, Ellen was annoyed but tried not to show it when Jack put her on the spot this way. Since stepping from the Dean's office, the old thing with Jason had turned around, and now Jason was smiling at her, not avoiding her, even as he distanced himself from her by his smile. So when on the next day Jack said that he wanted to drop in on the Talbots, she was annoyed. But she was outraged at herself, because the annoyance was exactly what she knew Jason wanted. Damn Jason, as he watched you, because while he watched, you always did *something,* were caught *in* something. Like the Baptists dancing to "The Old Rugged Cross." Both ways they were taken—whether they stayed on the floor or walked off.

Besides, he had seen her again in the Beaver Room with Berrigan and the Dean, and the Dean had elaborately asked him to join them and he had agreed. She watched him quietly while Berrigan exuded over the *Walton Review* and the Dean's face became that embarrassed smug smile. Why, with Jason screwed up like a turnip and blaming the Dean with his eyes, how else could the Dean react? Hastings was embarrassed, but *that Jason,* he'd read it that Berrigan was stroking Hastings' back! She found herself scowling, and Jason caught her at it. His eyes twinkled; he puffed on his cigarette. Oh, he was something! And he did something, too.

"Mr. Hastings, I had a letter from Mr. Jensen today, and he's still wondering about his paper. Has there been some mix-up? I suppose it better get back to him."

Berrigan froze, alarmed. She could not look at anyone.

"Why, Jason, why, I believe we sent that back, didn't we, Ellen?" There was a pause. "Why, yes, I'm sure it went back long ago. Could the mails have lost it?"

Berrigan made strange embarrassed sounds. She answered, "I don't really know, Mr. Hastings. Mrs. Bolyard handles all that."

Hastings glanced at her with a slightly stricken expression. "That's right, of course," he said. "Well, we'll check on it." He had wanted support from her, and she had failed to provide it. Jason looked surprised. She enjoyed that, but she knew that if she had it to do again she would have supported Hastings and bugged Jason with a blank, blank face, even if a lie was involved.

If Hastings was testing her, Jason was testing him and

embarrassing Berrigan. Berrigan hadn't been happy about the fading away of the Jensen business. No professorship, no editorship, no new paper. It somehow soiled Berrigan's image.

And now, with the idea of taking her over to the Talbots', Jack was bugging her, innocently or not. Jason would be suspicious of her despite her momentary betrayal of the Dean. But there was some luck: when they arrived, the Berrigans, of all people, were there. Jack was furious. She felt oddly that it served him right.

▶

Well, we hadn't planned it that way. Jack had sort of invited himself, or we'd invited him, I don't really remember, and then he said he was going to bring Ellen, which was okay, I guess, though I wasn't doing nip-ups about it. Then, about eight, who should appear unannounced but Brendan and Wilma. Apparently on the morning after the spat Wilma had come around to see Laura. Person had cleared out early, and Laura was still down in the dumps and told enough for Wilma to get the picture. That was the thing about Laura; she just *said* too much too openly, and now, unfortunately, too desperately. Wilma couldn't keep off the subject. There were plenty of times, God knows, when Wilma had cried on Betty Lou's shoulder about Brendan and the antics of his behavior-day. She even went into detail about their sex life and how crude and unsatisfactory a lover he was because he was either a wild bear or so prepossessed inventing professional predicaments into which he could fall that he ignored her entirely. There's more, but I blush to tell it. Also, there were the fights. Often, after those, Wilma would come to Betty Lou looking like a wreck—that two-bit glamor that Brendan demanded running in strands around her ears and in streaks down her face.

What really got us, then, was the condescension in her

voice when she wondered solemnly just what *we* could do for the poor Persons, who were having such difficulties, and the darling children, and on and on. Brendan chimed in, "Yeah, Jason. Will's gonna deal himself right out of things. You can't go around getting drunk with the students and get away with it. We're supposed to set an example. I mean, they expect to look up to their professors. And anyway, the scandal—Will running around with coeds." He didn't get the idea that someone might *want* to deal himself out of things, which, of course, was what Person was doing.

About this time Jack and Ellen appeared. I intercepted them in the front hall and tried to indicate with hand signals that the Berrigans were uninvited, and I whispered that I hoped they would leave soon. Of course, I was wildly optimistic. The Berrigans stayed on and on. Nor did Wilma shut up about Will and Laura. This was particularly obnoxious to me because Wilma knew well enough that Jack was a close friend of Will's. Wilma was always nervous and talkative around Jack. When they first met she tried the device of wholesale flattery, and Jack retreated into his shell. When that didn't work she made efforts toward literary talk and again found that Jack would not communicate. He tended to ignore her, and if there was anything she couldn't stand or understand it was being ignored.

Only last year at MLA in Chicago, after Walton was all over for us and we were dispersed to the four winds, she was still trying. I met her in a bar at the Palmer House, and we had a drink together. In came Jack. I knew he saw us, but he pretended not to. Wilma trotted across the room and practically dragged him back to our table. We talked, or, that is, Wilma talked—and when Wilma talked she interviewed you.

"How do you like it where you are now, Jack?"

"Just fine, just fine."

"Do you see Ann and Will Person often?"

"Not too often, but we write."

"I guess you're glad to be away from Walton. Things are going well now though."

"Yes, I imagine so."

"Of course, you were one of the ones who didn't like Hastings, weren't you?"

"I don't give a damn one way or the other, Wilma."

It went like that.

Then he excused himself on the pretext of seeing a pre-Walton colleague. As he crossed to the bar, Wilma watched him go, a blank expression on her face, shaking her head as if with incredulity. I don't think she noticed that I saw her do it. She had not lost her composure; she was even a little melancholy, or at least puzzled, by what had happened to the happy group which by now she had convinced herself we once composed.

Sometimes I think poor Wilma's life was a series of such rebuffs. And yet she was smart enough to know why Jack was contemptuous. So I stayed on and had another drink while she took me all through the department and Hatfield's latest speech on airwick. But we were far apart. There were no confessions. Because I could no longer see it all at firsthand, she could now make her life anything she desired. I felt sorry for her, damn me, because I could read between the lines.

It was also outrageous of Wilma to go on about the Persons in front of Ellen, because of Ellen's working for Hastings. Why she should complain, I couldn't fathom. Well, yes I could. If you're competitive, you compete. Wilma was the type to arrange her shopping at the A & P to coincide with Mrs. Vanner's. And Ellen wasn't just working in Hastings' office. She was his protégée. I guess, from what others said, that she had a real dramatic talent. Well, she was cool and pretty and kept herself together.

Anyway, nothing stopped Wilma on the Persons. Ellen

didn't say much, except when Wilma directed some questions to her, testing her out, so to speak, to see what her real relation to Hastings was. That week she probably set loose a whole gaggle of rumors about Ellen and Hastings.

Brendan and Wilma bent our ears about how we all had to stand behind Hastings, with asides that Will's going out and drinking with the coeds was not, definitely not, the proper style. It developed into a real paean of praise for our leader—and all for Ellen to take back to Hastings. After a while, though, Jack simply had enough, or maybe Ellen signaled him in some way. They managed to beat a successful retreat. In the hall we saw them out, the traitors. Betty Lou even told them what they were. Jack laughed and said he'd be expecting us to get even. Ellen smiled ironically. She was tolerating me. Brendan and Wilma were on our necks until midnight, with Brendan all abristle about Jack's consorting with the secretarial staff.

Finally I couldn't resist it. "You're just jealous, Brendan." I let the ambiguity of it sink in. Either way I had them: Brendan thinking I was fingering him because he was jealous of Jack's pipeline to Hastings, or Wilma suspecting Brendan of a roving eye, a lecherous mind, and perhaps amorous efforts in Ellen's direction. Brendan chose to incur Wilma's wrath.

"Oh, she's a lovely girl, and bright, very bright. She was in my night class this fall. Trained by Hastings in Elizabethan drama."

And in what else? I wanted to ask, but I didn't. Wilma was bristling now, and Brendan caught it, slumped in his chair. The evening was not a success. Why hadn't they gone to the movies?

▶

It was cold, all the stars out. The car hummed. There was something hypnotic about the sound and the snow-covered starlit fields, but Jack had to bring them both out of it, back to what they had left.

"Are you beginning to see what I mean about the heavy bear that goes with us?"

She was silent, smoking. They'd decided to drive out through the country to a crossroads bar and play darts.

"Oh come on now, say something."

"Pretty please," she said finally, staring straight ahead at the road.

"Pretty please, what?"

"Close it off."

He laughed. It was a laugh of victory. She could not accept it.

That drove him to want to say more, but he didn't. Something in him was reticent, after all. He felt suddenly it was right.

She held back until they were out of the car and seated with the drinks before them. He got up to throw some darts.

"Okay," she began. "You've been waiting. Let me ask the questions, and don't bolt! Why is Jason so intimate with the Berrigans if he dislikes them so much? Masochism? Sadism? Do you know why? Because he can't resist them. They feed his ego. He can be superior to them. In spite of those soft manners. He gets ahead of them every time, just by taking them in. Every time. And there's something in you that enjoys it, too. Why did you want to go over there tonight? To dwell together on your common hatreds? What are you all after? What *difference* do the Berrigans make? You are drowning in a morass of analysis. If it's not Berrigan, it's Hastings. You are all running. The only difference is that Brendan puffs when he runs."

She had wanted to hurt him; no, just to get at him. To bring it out. But when it was over, she felt cold, naked, knew her own weakness. He was standing facing her. He looked at her, an insolent gleam in his eye. He turned carelessly and fired a dart near the bull's-eye. Still with that gleam, he leaned on the table, bending above her.

"You've got it, baby. It's glory, just like the great egg said. It's why you took the special reading course with Hastings after you'd fluttered those green eyes at him in the sophomore fiction class. It's why you ended up in his office. You knew he sat on the committee that gives out those fellowships. Why, you're going on to greater things, aren't you, young lady? And via our Dean. Why, you'll ride him all the way to New Haven or wherever it will be. It's glory. Come on, let's get out of here." On the way back they hated themselves, desired the comfort of each other, the detachment each of them in the right circumstance was able to muster.

▶

Jack Emory was at the center of the disaster that accompanied George Hungerford's visit to Walton. Jason supposed that his own position had been compromised as well. Hastings knew of his friendship with Jack, probably through Berrigan. But as much as he regretted the break, the manner of its occurrence, and his own likely implication, he did not have it in him to resent Jack's actions or to worry about himself. There was a certain inevitability working. It was possible, however, to resent Wilma Berrigan's action as she gloated evilly one night at their house. She called Jack arrogant and uncooperative. Nor did she refrain from pointing out the futility of getting ahead by dating the Dean's secretary. Berrigan's reaction was different. He was genuinely alarmed. But that also came clear with a little reflection. He wasn't the vindictive type; he didn't hate anybody. Jack's difficulties were potentially his own. If Hastings could act that way toward Jack, why not toward him?

Then there was Will. A look at Will was enough to

reveal that he just didn't have the nerves for what had transpired. The debacle of the Hungerford visit had left him agitated and depressed and looking for a Wailing Wall. Jason was it. Will came around complaining not only about Hastings but also about how he was innocently caught in the middle between the department and the Dean because he was on the curriculum committee.

There was perhaps something to it, Jason admitted. Teachers could get awfully worked up over curriculum revisions; and the Walton faculty was worse than most on the subject. Maybe Will was being watched to see what he would do; after all, everyone who wasn't somebody suspected that Hastings had ordered the committee into session, and Will was his boy on the job.

But maybe Will's style would carry him through. Jason was amused at him as he went over the issues: Walton's English faculty and the curriculum it offered were like some great sea sponge growing out of control toward chaos. Will allowed that he'd been chosen to squeeze it out. There were all those courses added over the years to placate teachers who had risen to tenure positions and never taught in their fields; and there were not enough students to fill such courses. But if anyone tried to erase a course from the books, long speeches on the virtues of minor prose writers would ensue. It was a mess. Try to do anything, Will argued, and everyone went to the closet, got his musket, and prepared to defend hearth and home. Well, Hastings probably *had* wanted the reorganization.

So after it all died down, the curriculum committee met and awarded the same old courses mainly to the same old people. After the final meeting Will reported:

"By God, we awarded me Blake and Keats, at least, but that's all we accomplished. I'm bushed. We've sat half a damned year and done nothing! You and Jack got those modern courses. But I can't figure out what's up. Old crew-cut isn't going to teach the Victorians; and one of the squatters gets to do it. The peons play musical chairs."

"I can't believe Sheffer would give up Swinburne," Jason said.

"He's not even down for graduate classes in the fall. Hell, maybe he's eloping with that Iranian or whatever he is."

The answer wasn't long in coming, but it was equivocal. The next morning as Jason passed Warner's open office he was beckoned in.

"Well, Jason, all that old committee work went down the drain, didn't it? Just the same, you and Will came off all right. We gave both you boys good courses." Jason could not smile. He made an effort at solemn friendly interest. Warner was indicating that he deserved some credit, but anyone could see that he wasn't really too disturbed by the report's being defeated. The unrevised curriculum was allowing him to dish out patronage as he saw fit. He would let the group that flocked around Cassoway take responsibility for defeating the revision. Warner didn't like Hastings worth a damn, but Hastings couldn't blame him. Unless, Jason thought, Hastings knew precisely how the thing had gone.

"When you've been around here as long as I have and dealt with Alex and watched Vanner sit on the fence, you are satisfied with little victories. Anyway, Caesar isn't going to take much pleasure in the vote." Jason was learning how he played the game. He'd have ruined the vote himself if it was really to his advantage. Warner was welcoming him into the club, and Warner expected allegiance. It was, after all, the old Walton way. But how responsible *was* Warner for the course, and what price would Jason have to pay?

"I hear that Jack got the modern poetry," Jason said, fishing.

"Yes. You know how?" He was leering, tilting in his chair.

"No, how?"

"Well, you remember our friend Temple? It just proves you have to be discreet."

"You mean that Sheffer is going?"

"For a semester."

"But is that the reason? What happened?"

Warner circled around the point; he was clearly trying to imply that Sheffer was being sent away to cool off. Staring out the window, he mused, "Yes, when we were first here in the old days, why Sylvia and I used to see a lot of the Sheffers. But not any more. Beautiful daughter, you know. Wellesley next year. He just doesn't seem to care. . . ." And the remark trailed off. Jason bit his tongue, did not pick it up, as Warner had obviously wanted him to, but he knew he had been tempted to muse with Warner about Hastings' next step. He guessed Warner knew little, would go on pumping him.

So they merely sparred, Jason sensing Warner's annoyance, knowing that if he remained distant, Warner would seek to draw him out only so far. He'd keep his head, old Warner. He knew that the departmental chairmanship would be up for grabs soon, and he needed all the votes he could get.

"You know"—he smiled like a devil—"we didn't think Berrigan was quite ready for upper-class work." He stretched and rocked. "That old boy may need to be told to spend more time in the department instead of running Hastings' errands. We count for something over here, too, you know."

Jason was determined to be his match; he would not be drawn in. He did not permit himself a smile, and he thought: Warner can take the lion-face bit because he expects every brush to be a real engagement, and maybe he's right.

"When Caesar gets through with his friends they just fade away. Berrigan better not wander too far from us."

There was no doubt that he was referring to Temple and maybe Sheffer. It was more likely that Hastings had merely given Sheffer a term off on some project or other. Warner bulked Berrigan with Hastings' "friends." Jason pondered this for a moment, sitting there. Then Alex Cassoway undulated by the door, pipe in mouth. He stopped long enough to glance in and observe Jason in session with Warner.

Oh oh, Jason thought.

"Hello, Jay boy," he said, and passed gracefully on.

With Jack Emory

HOW HE MANAGED   George Hungerford had not
been content with a single letter, mainly because there
had been hardly anything in it about the department.
Hungerford was a frank and penetrating questioner interested in the power structure, so it became necessary to
describe the departmental menagerie with as much detachment from the zoological metaphor as it was possible
to muster. In the beginning, of course, were Cassoway
and Warner. It was hard to find Cassoway because, despite his influence, he seemed to melt ectoplasmically into
the mass of Walton departmental life, a disembodied,
even spiritless, spirit of the place with no perceptible
shadow, elusive, vacant, present by his absence, his smoking pipe, his capacity to view with alarm. In another climate he might have faded totally away.

Then there was Warner, who sat on top of Hungerford's field at Walton, who ran modern American literature with a tight rein, tough, crude, whose actions were
transparent. Better, perhaps, than a transparent man, but
dangerous nonetheless. Warner had sensed, before Jack
knew it himself, his growing distaste for Hastings, and
gradually became more open and sarcastic, forcing him
to share some private joke. It was unpleasant. It implied

that Warner had him roped and was proceeding to tie him.

He found it impossible to say all this to Hungerford, much as Hungerford desired it. He buried his letter in generalizations. Hungerford replied, somewhat annoyed, with "Who is this Berrigan fellow who has begun to write to me? And is Jensen really going to move to Walton?" The academics could show Bell Telephone something, he thought.

But more important, he realized that Hastings had balanced Berrigan against him, and he was disgusted. It drove him to enigmatic and ironic reply. Hungerford would have to learn of Brendan for himself. After all, Brendan spoke eloquently and in his own style. As for Kit Jensen, that was back in the dark past of October, or was it November? Who knew now? By Jason's account, the correspondence file in Hastings' office continued to grow, but it was one-sided.

He realized that he should not let it get him that Berrigan had been put to writing Hungerford. He knew full well that there was no complaint against the principle, but why Brendan? Was it part of a pattern of estrangement? The Dean had clearly become less accessible. Mrs. Bolyard was protecting him with a vengeance. With the first issue of the magazine surely ready to be made up, there had been no answers to his and Will's suggestions, and some contributors were writing peevishly to ask what had become of their manuscripts. One afternoon he and Will tried to discuss magazine matters with Hastings and were turned away by Mrs. Bolyard, who did not regret informing them that the Dean was briefly out of town. He believed she lied. Hastings had made departmental news by lunching with Cassoway downtown that very day.

They went to McCrea, who, in the know, told them no fiction had been accepted for the first issue but wouldn't venture to say that Hastings was avoiding publishing sto-

ries. It had probably been foolish to bring it up with Mc-
Crea. It would surely make Hastings mad, and it would
get back.

Jack thought about a brief moment in one of the fall
meetings when Hastings mused over the possibility of
starting a "little magazine for literary art—apart, that is,
from the journal we are going to put out now." Was
someone supposed to have taken up the stick and run? Or
was Hastings testing them all to see who would be loyal to
his bigger, far grander idea? It was clear from that brief
speech that the little-magazine temperament or taste or
whatever one called it bothered Hastings. But one had
also to be charitable. Surely Hastings wanted his protégés
to take part in his programs, to have their names associated with his—for their mutual benefit, of course. But
down below the dreams and grandiose plans, the magazine was looking more and more like a personal chariot
for Hastings, who had all the time planned to be editor
himself. Even McCrea, though he rode the fence, alluded
sarcastically to this now. And Hastings was not going to
take any chances with his so-called staff. They would ex-
ist in name only, providing some modicum of publicity
for the magazine and for Hastings by their enthusiasm
and some for themselves. What could be more equitable
from the politician's point of view?

This was annoying. He had been made a hanger-on, a
scrambler, a goddamned ad man for his own ego; a part
of himself had been willing to go along.

So when Richard Fallon finally sent in the story he had
promised Will to submit, Jack knew without formulating
absolutely anything to himself that an opportunity had
somehow arisen. It was a story that Hastings, if he was
running upward, would hardly dare to print. On the other
hand, if the magazine was to publish fiction at all, the
problem must ultimately arise. A magazine touting Walton and its forward-looking Dean, its library collections,

its artistic press, its studies in education, its position as a center of culture for the whole region, its sensible use of substantial gifts—a magazine with these aims would have to avoid some things and settle for the insipid. Fallon's story was in some respects a study of insipidity. On its surface it even read as if it were straight out of *Cosmopolitan*. Then, strangely, things were done and attitudes adopted that turned everything inside out. The reader discovered or should have discovered that his leg was being pulled or that he himself was the villain. It was the story of a college romance, in which the sentimental clichés uttered by its protagonists constituted the half-serious style of the story and the whole of the characters. The characters were not unmasked in their own pathetic, because innocent, inanity. They had no masks. It was a segment of the student mind dispassionately on show. The tone was so close to the sentimental that it could easily be misread as belonging to the genre that was, indeed, being unmasked. Above that, it took the people it seemed to complain of seriously and as worth knowing, and yet none of the characters was able to articulate or perhaps even to own a profound thought.

He recognized not only all this in the story, but he saw the characters, with their fraternity-sorority love affair and their sordid seduction, as part of every college teacher's life. They were the people to whom he tried to speak, not the Doris Weinstocks necessarily, though there was probably something of Doris in the heroine, or of the heroine in Doris, but the ones who would not shoot themselves in Russian roulette or jump off bridges. Instead, they would somehow muddle through life. Their attitudes were the attitudes which he tried to polish up a bit. They were, he thought, those of the gentleman C student, the modern barbarian.

But something *was* wrong. The story, with all its unique and praiseworthy effort, was not quite up to what it attempted. It failed in crucial places, or went too far. Ralph Ware knew it and thought Hastings would reject it. Besides, he couldn't see Hastings publishing something with such a subject, let alone in the first issue, but he was willing to go along. He'd publish it in his own magazine, he said, and it was, he guessed, his function to recommend material honestly. Jack caught Will Person as he was entering his Green Lion phase. They had already discussed whether Hastings had any intention of doing something seriously with poetry and fiction or making it obnoxious decoration. It was easy enough to get Will going on editors who used poems for filler. So Will was agreeable, but he said, "It's ridiculous to try; he'll never take it."

So Jack pushed them into vague accord, and the story went "up." He appended a note saying that apparently it was the Fallon story or no story for this first issue. By that he meant that at this date they could expect nothing else to show up, but he knew, too, and didn't hide it from himself—but contemplated the ambiguity with savage glee—that Hastings might read the note as a sort of ultimatum with the implication that they doubted Hastings' motives. Mrs. Bolyard blocked their way into Hastings' cave, but could she prevent him from coming out when it filled with his own smoke?

By the time George Hungerford was to arrive for the finally scheduled visit, Jack knew that he was in Hastings' doghouse, and guessed that the story was the cause. He succumbed to a vague guilt. He was present when Mrs. Bolyard detailed Berrigan and Talbot to meet Hungerford at the airport. He knew that Mrs. Bolyard did not like him, and he could tell that she had deliberately told them their duties in his presence. It outraged and amused him at the same time. Hastings, of course, had no way of knowing that the letter he had been commissioned to write Hungerford had flowered into a lengthy exchange.

Hastings had probably forgotten all about the matter. Hungerford would surely wonder why he was not among the greeting party. It didn't make the best of sense. Berrigan, always a team man, turned to him and said, "We'll pick you up at your house." But Mrs. Bolyard was sharp with her correction.

"Dr. Hastings prefers a more intimate group. Just the two of you is enough, not a party." She glanced his way. With Berrigan, confused and distressed, mumbling acquiescence, he asked Mrs. Bolyard whether or not Dr. Hastings had any magazine business for him, and she cut him dead with a sharp no. As she turned and opened the door to the inner sanctum he saw, through the crack, Hastings sitting at a table surrounded by rare books and manuscripts, his face set, staring at the wall. He had undoubtedly heard everything, for the door had been slightly ajar.

It was with vague amusement now that Jack watched the jitters overcome Berrigan. The least suggestion of violence by Hastings was cause for alarm. Brendan was feeling sorry for him. He really was.

On the first day of the visit there was no opportunity for him to meet Hungerford. Hastings invited Berrigan, Talbot, and some of the departmental brass for drinks and dinner downtown. Jason's report that Hungerford had asked after him was little consolation, for Jason couldn't say what Hastings' reaction was. His back, he lamented, had been turned, his neck a neutral tan. The dinner had gone off well enough. Everyone got along, including Warner and Cassoway.

On the next day, quite suddenly, he was returned from Coventry to attend a luncheon. With Person and Ware he trudged over to the banquet room of the Union building. The magazine staff complete was to be present. Before they sat down to the canned grapefruit and single maraschino cherry half he had learned to expect, he did shake

Hungerford's hand, but Hungerford had only the opportunity to say he was glad they had met at last, that he had been introduced to the departmental powers, and when would they have a chance to talk? There was nothing to do but reply with his stoic voice that he'd be delighted to have a talk if Hastings could fit it in. No use pushing it farther, and if Hungerford took the message to Hastings the result would be neat. Hungerford was perhaps perplexed.

After Hastings' arrival, slightly late, everyone found a place around the long table, the Dean steering Hungerford to a position between McCrea and Crowder. Jack found himself, by everyone's default, at the foot, facing up a long row of faces toward Hastings at the head. He spent the meal cracking jokes with Will Person. There were so many people at these meetings that one rarely had much contact with the guest of honor. So it was easy to treat oneself as a stage prop.

Toward the end, Hastings spoke to the group.

"I've asked George to join us at one of these typical staff luncheons so that he can meet us all in this, ha ha, our habitat, and see how we carry on our business in this informal way of ours, how we let things evolve or bubble up from our discussions. Some hereabouts no doubt call it a witch's brew [laughter] . . ." It went on. What wolfsbane would boil over today? He looked at Jason; bug-watching, Will called it.

"We are about to go to press with the first issue. Most of you have seen it in galley. I think the designers have done a simply great, a swell, job. I think we've achieved a balance and maturity which will grow into something with the proper implementation. [Pause] But it's gotten back to me that there are some of you, that some of you are not happy with, well, with the way our interaction has gone. Please punctuate my remarks by remembering that this is our first issue. We don't, ahem, build it in a day, do we? [He paused again, as if looking for something.] Some of you have felt we are weak in fiction and you have pressed me to publish something. [He paused again, reaching for the water, but he did not drink. A curious expression came upon his face. He was frowning deeply. His complexion seemed to have reddened.] Well, I shall tell you now that *I* am editor of this magazine. *I* am responsible for what goes into it. *I* am responsible to the Board of Trustees and the sources of our endowment. And *I* must take the rap, and mind you, I am willing to do so for its failure. But I shall not be pushed. I shall not abdicate my, ah, my responsibility. Now when a couple of you submit a story to me, I must think about our readers, about its excellence, and its, its rightness, yes, its rightness for us. Because if something is not right for you, then, why, you must leave it. . . ."

"What readers?" Will whispered in Jack's ear. "Hell, who are they?"

"You know what readers," he replied. "The boys who will make Henry Hastings our next president, our next governor, our next . . ." But Hastings was continuing. A wave of insolence came upon him as he listened again.

". . . and I simply do not mean to print a story downright offensive to those readers, whether it be by William Faulkner or, who is he? Richard Fallon, whoever he is."

Jack watched the Dean pause, not yet finished, but the pause was a long one, and there was an opportunity to be risked. So from down the table he took it.

"Well, he *is* fairly well known, and he does have a good reputation. His short stories were up for the National Book Award, and he's been in New Directions stuff and *Evergreen* and *Accent*—places like that. People do know who he is."

"I cannot see, Jack, what difference that should make, but all right, I might have been wrong. Maybe the story should have passed. In my own opinion it was detestable trash." He was looking grim. "So I passed it to some other readers whose judgment I admire, whose judgment I *know* is good. And he, they, thought it juvenile and trivial, 'dismal collegiate growing pains, seeds for the daws to peck at.' "

"Like the *Prelude*," Will whispered, but the analogy didn't really fit. Ware choked a grin. Jason was red-faced, holding his head high, puffing a cigarette.

"Those were his very words, one of them, I mean. Yes, what did you say?" Will had perhaps been too loud. Hastings had thought the whisper a reply. His face flushed again. He knew now there had been a *sotto-voce* remark. "But what I don't like—the story was only a story, after all—is the impression some of you have that I'm not making the decisions around here. Because I am, and if that isn't satisfactory you should find areas of interest where you can work more happily."

"Hog Wallow A & M," Person whispered.

Jack sat there trying to suppress a smile, which was indeed at variance with his feelings, for as he avoided smiling he was also registering surprise and slight fright at Hastings' direct attack. His risk had been all too successful. But was this dirty linen aired in front of Hungerford really worth it? He watched Will stirring his coffee and wondered if Will was blaming him. But Hungerford was more interesting. Hungerford stared, chin level, at an old clock on the mantel opposite him, hardly an emotion visible. Periodically Jack saw the slightest twitch of a jaw muscle. Somehow Hungerford sensed that he was being watched, and slowly his gaze turned down the table, and their eyes met. Hungerford's were bland but direct. They seemed to require a reply, so he offered a nearly imperceptible, he hoped, wink. Hungerford's eyes turned back to the clock, just as Hastings was saying,

"Perhaps this fellow Fallon is a friend of someone's. I know you boys wrote to people personally, and I'm grateful for that help. . . . Incidentally . . . want you to continue the good work. And after that parenthesis, I'll say we can pay him off, if this is eating any of you, but we shall *not* publish him. And by the way, what we are running is *not* a little magazine, and that kind of mentality simply isn't big enough for what we have in mind. Now some of you may be happier in the context of that dimension. All right, then we'll see about starting one out, one that is a credit to Walton. But I'm not going to publish any minor journal myself." Then abruptly he shifted tone. "It's clear somehow that we just haven't opened up the right channels of interaction lately. Perhaps that's been my fault. Now maybe we can remedy that if we all pull together. . . ."

Those sinuous meanderings seemed to have left the group stunned into either meek acquiescence or wondering, silent observation. Jack knew himself undergoing some subtle self-torture. The rage was underneath; he was conscious of his heart beating. A reckless impertinence possessed him. And he did speak, for he knew there was really nothing any longer to be lost.

"Mr. Hastings, we tried to see you several times, but Mrs. Bolyard kept telling us you were out of town." He knew it was foolish, and he recognized that Hastings was suffering abysmally and probably knew that with every word he had driven the wedge deeper between himself and his protégés. He would let him suffer some more.

"Let's please leave Mrs. Bolyard out of this," Hastings interrupted, or meant to interrupt, but Jack had finished his remark. "And I have been meaning to say to this group assembled that Mrs. Bolyard is a fine lady and should be treated with deference due a lady. She is not this group's flunky."

He thought he had always showed the proper deference. Mrs. Bolyard was tough and not always very polite herself. But that didn't matter. Person's face hung trapped between a smile and a grimace.

"She has an immense job and cannot stop to explain to everyone what she's doing or why or where I happen to be. . . . And this leads me to a painful parenthesis. Some of our guests this year have not been very graceful either. I am sick and tired of being attacked daily in the mails by people unhappy with our editorial decisions, with people—whether in Kansas or elsewhere—telling us how to perform our job." Hastings was off and away. It was clearly Kit Jensen who had gotten to him. By the time he had come full circle, the subject would be generalized into pleas for interaction and team play. They would all have to wait it out. Jensen had certainly managed to get under Hastings' skin. He had done them no favor, but it was possible now to think there was some method in Jensen's madness. Jack could imagine Jason bear-sitting past midnight.

As for himself, he felt oddly relieved and free. There it was, the quarry had been flushed, but at an unexpected moment, in front of a prospective newcomer. Yes, the staff *had* been set to playing games. And yes, they were supposed to be content with the bone of recognition he gave them on the masthead. Finally, if they weren't satisfied, he'd make them, like an angel, another magazine. But that meant they were spoiled ungrateful children without the requisite vision.

Had George Hungerford figured it out now: why Jack had been given no chance to talk to him during the visit? It couldn't be very hard to put two and two together even in a place where they sometimes added up to five. If, that is, Hungerford had understood against whom Hastings' attack was primarily made.

They had risen from the table. Over his shoulder as he went for the door he saw Berrigan speaking rapidly into

Hastings' ear while poor Jason and silent impassive Hungerford waited nearby. He could guess that Berrigan was trying to clear himself. For a week or two Brendan would probably treat him as if he had the plague.

It was when he walked away from it all in the clear cold air that he realized that Hastings' performance had affected him more than he thought. Even in a two o'clock class he was reminded, when he forgot momentarily what he was talking about and fumbled foolishly. Nevertheless, it was only a surface anxiety, as if he had been there before, as if he were strangely gratified that it had all finally occurred.

During the whole past few months he had dreamed in premonition of some such debacle. Why? Because he had been witness for months to the gradual failure of his relationship with the Dean. In each successive meeting, from the first one in the fall, when he had been embarrassed by Hastings' curious parody of Madison Avenue jargon, to this last one, when he had simply been angered by it, the gulf had widened. Hastings, his feelers out—like Berrigan—surely could sense the embarrassment radiating. But what really was anyone capable of doing about it? Who was ever fully aware of the face he put forth? Who could afford that sort of containment without risking his sanity? Errors, mistakes, foolishness all the time. One had to keep making steps in spite of them. So Hastings had no longer really been looking him in the eye, except when it was as if he were saying, "Now I *am* going to look you in the eye," and then it was unbearably melodramatic. They might as well have been two dumb beasts; they might *better* have been dumb beasts. Speech destroyed their communications. It was pathetic that anger should have been the result. But surely he had taunted Hastings without mercy, perhaps seeking the inevitable denouement.

Later, in his office, he heard Ralph Ware say it all:

"Well, it worked. That's what they must have said at

Los Alamos. What will we discuss around the fires next winter?"

He had opened the door to the knock of an exhausted Person in time for Will to answer, "Our pasts," managing a grim smile. "Jesus save us, the monkeys really threw shit at the walls today!" He collapsed into a chair. "You seem to be bright boy of the week, don't you?"

Jack answered, "We shouldn't have done it, should we? That's the moral, isn't it?"

Ware was philosophical. "Oh, I don't know. It was going to happen." And then, with the image that had been haunting Jack, "Any dumb beast will defend himself."

"I suppose it's going to blow over," Will said, "but I think there's something more behind this."

"Well, there's Jensen. Lord knows how Jensen has used our names in all those letters. You heard Hastings lay into him," Jack said.

"Hell, it's more than old Kit." Will smiled in a pained way. "Someone around here has been complaining about us."

"Who's the candidate?"

"God knows, we're surrounded. There's Klaus and there's Crowder, and big-mouth bear. Hell, it could be any of them. Crowder has it in him, all right, but I bet it's Brendan."

"No, I think Berrigan's innocent. He doesn't know a thing about what's been going on in the magazine staff."

"He doesn't know what's going on anywhere. That's the trouble. He's rushing in where he doesn't know what's going on! Danny Kaye among the Rockettes. How'd you like that crack about Bolyard? Why I didn't know she was human, let alone female."

"Just an aside for good measure. Parenthesizing, it's called. The fact is he had me confused with that seventeenth-century fellow—Klegg. Had a fight with her over some library stuff. I guess he got pretty wild. Klaus told me about it."

Person grunted. "Yeah, but you know all that talk about certain people being dissatisfied? Where did he get that? Not just because we sent him some Boeing foreman's story. No, someone has tried to make us look bad."

Was it really, as Person insisted, the little people complaining? They tried to arrive at the finer points but failed, because Jason Talbot knocked and entered.

"Little Lord Hungerford's back in his hotel for nap time, thank heavens. Well, boys, get your bags packed. That was a streamer, wasn't it?"

"Best performance to date," Will said. "The acting showed verve, though somewhat in the romantic style. The question remains: Will it go in the big city?"

"If he gets friendly critics," Jack replied sourly.

"My, he is most certainly touchy these days, isn't he?" Jason offered. "And Brendan's old pal Kit Jensen hasn't helped any of us out this day. By the way, I have something to brighten the afternoon and hasten the cocktail hour. Do you know the reader whose judgment Hastings intoned to us?"

"Oh, Christ." Person sank into his chair and shaded his eyes.

"Laurence Fenrow, that's who."

There was some recompense for being present for Person's comments. "Hell, an expert on heterosexual relations. Why didn't he get Christine Jorgensen if he wanted a diversity of opinion? Do you know, that guy backs *Gone With the Wind* as the great American novel? No, this is it, this time this is it."

"Look," said Jason, "let's assume you were wrong about the story. I mean let's assume it for just a minute. Is there any excusing him then?"

"There is, there is." Jack had to admit it. "Particularly if we knew he would blow up and we were baiting him."

"Is that excusing him or condemning us?"

He didn't have to answer, because Person was on to it. "What is this crap, Jason? Why, for God's sake?"

"Because you can't ask a man to be more than he is, I think Jack means."

"Well, while you experts in psychology figure out how we all crawl down off our couches, I'm going home and beat the wife," and Person shuffled out. Watching Will go, then contemplating the door, speechless, Jack was one with Jason and Ralph.

After a while he said, "Will won't buy it."

"Well, you had a suspicion about Hastings and it turned out true. Think of it as knowledge gained," Ralph answered.

He shook his head. "I'm not the disinterested gatherer of knowledge, I guess. But you're right, we put him on the spot, and it was a nasty place to be."

"He's playing for big stakes," Jason said.

"Yes, it's just as well to know it now, but some time in the last few hours I thought to myself that I didn't care. Do you know, I'm just beginning to suspect that Kit Jensen doesn't care either, maybe never did. Why, he's the biggest Hastings baiter of us all! Maybe you have to be a bit berserk not finally to care."

Jason smiled at him. Jason knew he somehow cared, knew it was all twisted up in him. It made him feel miserable. He wanted Jason to think he was above that kind of fear.

But Hungerford did accept Walton's offer.

"Jeesus, after all that!" Will exclaimed.

"Yes, after all that," Jack affirmed. The word had been passed via Berrigan, but Jack had already known and kept his silence. Hungerford's letter had been somewhat coolly cordial, but friendly enough to have built into it a strong, indeed, in Hungerford's eyes, an overriding, reason for coming to Walton. Hastings had laid on a sort of curatorship of the modern-letters collection and a lightened teaching load. Hungerford wanted to work on something in Walton's collection. The luncheon had alarmed him, perhaps, but not enough to frustrate the pursuit of manuscripts.

"Who knows?" Jack said. "Maybe here's one fellow who can use Hastings so efficiently that there'll be no mess afterward." He didn't expect Hungerford to stay long at Walton after his research was completed.

Will snorted. "Yeah," he said, rolling his eyes.

Not long afterward the business of end of term closed in, and Jack rode out a month occupied with conferences, papers, and exams. The famous committee's work was over for the year. Little communication emanated from the Dean's office. The luncheon meeting had become well-known lore. He didn't really care, except that it had all gotten back to Ellen, and it somehow stood between them, though outwardly things were the same. He was in love with her; she passionate but independent. But their conversations had changed. They tried very hard not to mention Berrigan or the Dean. He decided to put the year behind him if he could as soon as his grades were in, and set out by car for Seattle and a summer in which he might possibly work uninterrupted on his book. Summer school where summer's cool; he remembered seeing the slogan on a U. of W. catalogue.

Even though he left Ellen with misgivings, he knew it was necessary to get away. The drive in a pleasant June turned out to be strangely agreeable. It was not merely release from the routine of university life and the sloughing off of his committeeman's skin (he liked the metaphor because there were snakes in those weedy places), nor was it merely the opportunity to read, write, and think. It was the thing itself, the release from appearances into sheer reality, or out of it even, depending on one's meta-physics. Once in his car and into the scrubby countryside west of Walton he became a traveler out of meaningful time, and the events and objects of his three-day trip were merely the heraldic figures of an Edwin Muir poem. It was a world of pure form in which time was measured in space and space in time—miles per hour; and all was reduced to abstraction. He felt the moments of this world as simple linear experience: In a small town somewhere in Utah, he emerged from his car to get a Coke at a gas station. The town was nothing special, hardly a town at all —a new loud gas station amid old dilapidated buildings. But the sun shouted at him and struck the pavement and lit up all the windows in the warehouse across the street so that they shone golden. There was the curious wheeling to a stop of the motor's humming, the release of the muscles of his knee and instep as he stretched and walked about. Suddenly simple movement was all the world he needed, and neither the destination nor what he had left behind seemed important.

To live for a day in pure abstraction was a luxury of the spirit. Since his first meeting with Hastings in Chicago and his acceptance of the job at Walton things had moved toward a climax he was as yet unprepared to imagine. He had early felt the tug of it, and it was as if he had been handed a script to memorize his part. But he had not yet read the script through to the end. Now he wanted to get outside the play for a while, only to find himself without makeup.

By the third day of his trip, instead of crossing the Columbia at Umatilla he took the road west to Portland, acting upon an impulse which, he decided, must have been lying quietly in his mind all along. Indeed, when he acknowledged it, he was dominated by it, and it permitted nothing but the passivity of listening to the radio. The morning thus moved quickly. Soon he was standing, with no clear consciousness of how the last few timeless hours had passed, in a Portland cemetery before a simple slab-marked grave. In the green field beyond, a horse was gliding into the blankness of his mind, moving with ambling angular symmetrical gait below its thick floating body. Reaching a fence, it stopped, stretched neck across, and stared ahead at him with a stare he had seen and marveled at in horses and some men. Did it communicate the animal's real feelings? It projected a momentous calm on the surface of a twitching expectancy.

The area where Jack was standing—past fence, newly sown grass, and two new graves, from the staring swan neck bridging from pasture—had not too long ago been pasture itself. Death was spreading from the highway, taking away the animal's field, forcing it back toward the fir woods beyond. Perhaps that same animal had grazed where he now stood, where the cemetery had recently sprawled in its own symmetrical boxlike pattern beyond its own shade trees toward the true pastoral.

The cemetery began with a four-lane blacktop highway which buried its own original layer of red brick as it ran west and out of town. The highway was important. He remembered that his father had once, not long before he died, complained: Now when he drove east into town, there was a funeral always coming west. He was getting sick of it, working at cross-purposes with death. And he had meant it; he was already a sick man, but no one knew. From the road the cemetery loomed up not as a cemetery at all but as a huge sphinx-shaped building heavy in the front like the false façades of the old post-Prohibition night clubs that lined the highway farther west out of town. It was a great white building with a row of tall poplars lining the highway before it. At night, lights flooded and yellowed its façade as if it were a world's-fair fountain, and the words LINDHURST CREMATORY AND COLUMBARIUM stood shallow-carved in the light above a high-columned door. All the U's were V's.

He had hated that building since, as a small child of eight or nine, fear had compelled him to make some excuse for hiding where neither he could see it nor it him as he went by in the car. Especially at night he had wished to avoid its great sphinx-thrust at the world and its fierce, austere shadows. It was a face in the dark with a flashlight held beneath it. He would sink down in the front seat of the car to examine what lay behind and below the dashboard, until, the great sphinx safely past, he could again observe driving ranges, nightclubs, and taverns farther up the road toward home.

Of all that stood behind the columns and the big iron double doors, ornately carved and ring-hung, that child could conjure only the vaguest of material images; and yet the existence of vagueness was itself real and terrifying enough in his dreams—a congeries of urns and darkness, of moving shades out of Homer and Egyptian mysteries. In that childish half-light which seemed located somewhere between memory and premonition he had created an exotic rich nothingness. At twenty, when his father died—twelve years ago now—he saw finally that strange interior, the unused but carefully polished and dusted oak chairs, the decorative urns, the heavy carpets. For the doors had opened to him so that he, the elder child, might choose the proper casket for his father's proper burial somewhere farther behind the great iron gates, which finally themselves did part, the driveway leading around behind the pompous array, skirting Babyland, with its small pink and blue neon sign, the hearse bearing the casket past the older monuments and private mausoleums to a newer, merely tufted area stolen from the horse.

Yes, it was twelve years since his father had gone underground. On the day of the burial the dirt had been trampled down, and in the ground around the grave only a little grass had begun to show through the eroded light-brown mud. Soon, he had thought, the grass would make it look like all the others. And he had been right. At any rate, the stone was plain. His decision there had been correct. For a moment now, as he contemplated the grave and the standing stupid serene animal across the fence, he imagined that the horse had solemnly nodded to him, was calling him. Had he, indeed, come back for some message, some hidden knowledge of himself?

Had he returned to watch himself watch his father slowly die again? For it had been a slow business, that dying. He had, he knew now, watched death enter the soul, move to the mind, and finally claim the body. The first dying was perhaps the most spectacular. His father had loved them all with a Victorian sort of tyrannical possessiveness. It was a love purged of intellectual content, of any restraint in the direction of either tenderness or rage. It ran its course aimlessly. He acted upon it when the spirit or the body moved him to. He did not think about it, and there was thus no clear-cut morality in it.

The weakness of the man himself, the triviality of feeling divorced from intellect, wrestled love down into ludicrous displays of temperament. He loved himself, or, rather, a wild romantic idea of himself which he tried to project into the reality of home and business. After his death the bills began to arrive: the flowers ordered delivered daily to his hospital room as if from friends, the useless box of chocolates, the new radio, the elaborate chess set. It was too easy to remember him surrounded in his hospital room like some Egyptian pharaoh in his tomb. They had all thought them gifts from business associates, and that illusion was only one of many, for he had made them incompetent. There was no provision for catastrophe in cash, plan, or even in preparation of the spirit. Jack in the war, or nearly in it, stateside; Ann innocent and decisionless; his mother incapable of action and nearly of thought. It was pathetic. His father, even dead, had them collared like Pavlovian dogs, but there was no longer anyone to ring the bell.

And so, reviling the dead, Jack had found himself explaining to his mother that it was the illness that made John Emory squander in the last few weeks even more than they possessed. But he could not then convince himself that it was the illness alone. He mused savagely that in fifty years perhaps it would all be remembered by great-grandchildren as eccentricity, recalled only in pictures. What a shame that there was no beard!

Standing before the grave now, twelve years later, he tormented himself as he had over and over again in the past with the tantalizing possibility that the sickness was simply a logical extension of his father's total moral being. Indeed, the whole question of where moral responsibility ended and sickness began was now bothering him again. That was probably why he had come back here. Sickness required one reaction, and moral weakness or simple turpitude another. The nature of his responsibility to himself, to his students, to his friends, and even to his enemies at Walton (if they were enemies) depended upon whether Walton harbored a sort of massive gnawing mental cancer or whether it merely contained something like good old-fashioned evil. He had begun to think himself infected by it, whatever it was. Recently he had discovered himself flailing out in all directions, taking joy in trivial snide victories. He did not believe it was like him to think and act in this way. Yes, the problem his father's dying life had posed for the family, had they known it, was presenting itself again before him. But there was nothing here except such random thoughts as these and the dumb beast, staring from what was left of his pasture, and many more graves. He contemplated the horse and walked toward it. It snorted, bobbed its head, and ambled away into the field, turned halfway to observe him quizzically, swished a fly from its flank. He turned back toward his car. Rest in peace, he thought.

He wasted no time in Portland.

The drive up to Seattle on the new highway was fast and free. As he drove he considered the horse. Capable of speech, what would it have said? He had begun to wonder whether the horse was not lucky. In the past spring he had been teaching *Faust* to his sophomores: Faust lamenting the uselessness of words; Faust sitting in his study where the cobwebs kept out the light, complaining because words failed to deliver to him ultimate knowledge; he really suffered over the limitations of language. But men had since refined their suffering. Now they knew that words were masks, and they knew the struggle of getting through on even the simplest levels. He thought how every day words betrayed Hastings to them, how Berrigan cowered behind his barricade of words, how easy it was to let words mask the things one can't quite say: with Doris Weinstock the words of the pedant, with George Hungerford the words of the diplomat, with Hastings the simple failure of the mask. The Faustian paradox, which all spring had sent him marveling sweetly before his classes, offended him now. He thought of perfect silence, the grunts of beasts.

The perfect silence was also an interior silence, a silence associated plainly with some pure abstract duration, but he had lost all that somewhere south of the Columbia, and now the flood of Walton pressed upon him again. First, Ellen. Silence had played a part in his relationship with her, but there had become a tense purposeful neglect about it. The silence was often what they refused to say to each other about Hastings. He could feel the tension of these silences more deeply as the school year came to an end, when Ellen must have known what he wanted to and could not utter. So the only silences that finally he could freely tolerate were those of their love-making. Our bestial life, he thought, and his mind cringed. He was compartmentalizing his world, shutting the words of his lives into their respective glossaries. Thou shalt not take the lord thy employer's name in vain before thy lady love. It was easy enough to agree wordlessly about the Berrigans that night after they left the Talbots. With Hastings it would have to be different. He wanted her to say she chose him, to deny in some little way her benefactor. As yet, silence was her answer, silence when she knew about the Hungerford luncheon.

Or was he asking too much? Perhaps she was right to keep erasing the past as she did—tear everything up every twenty years. Was it Jefferson who said that?

On the morning he was to leave they had breakfasted on the screened porch in bright, heavy, pungent spring weather with lilacs about them. In their passion of the night she had not, never, said she loved him but had moaned softly to him some wordless animal truth. It was enough then, but now he was not sure. In the light glinting off the mountains as he drove rapidly north he could not escape the suspicion that her silence was avoidance. But then he began to castigate himself for trying to judge her and for assuming that the whinnying pettiness of his politics ought to be of other than passing interest to her. Was he, as long as he stayed at Walton, going to judge everything by its relation to Hastings or some other abstraction (for Hastings had become a symbol), even his love affair? Or by its relation to the whole Walton balance of power? That was probably the way Crowder ran his career and his life, too. Well, he wouldn't do it. It was only a job. But he knew, even as he vowed it, that it wasn't simply a job. It was his life, and he had, without knowing it—because one slipped into life—dedicated himself to the Doris Weinstocks of the world. It sounded hackneyed enough, even to himself—false words again, purposely masked by sarcasm. But he knew it was true of the best of his breed, whether they were merely frustrated actors or not. And most were. No matter how heavily they swathed their hopes in irony. He thought himself among the best, or getting there.

And now driving, he brooded, as he had brooded in the last month during his odd hours, over the events of the year. This he hated as much as anything. It took up and wrung his soul dry. He suffered over the victory of academic trivia. How much time had they all spent deciding what Hastings meant by a sentence he may only casually have dropped? How much time cleaning up after Brendan Bear? How many classes unprepared or navigated through on last year's notes because some celebrity had to be entertained? And who was to be blamed? He didn't have to entertain anyone, or did he?

On a night after the Hungerford visit, Hastings did come up in a conversation with Ellen. He was still smarting, wanting to tell her what had happened, to defend his own position. But he tried too hard, and made a mess of it. By the time the whole story was turned into words it had seemed hopelessly trivial, a squabble among old maids. You had to live in it, perhaps be possessed by it. And Ellen seemed preoccupied, listening all right, but with nothing to say, until—"I could tell some time ago that you wouldn't get along with him. You are different types, but I think he admired you. Something he didn't have—and maybe even desired. If you understood that, it would help." But it had not been enough, either from him or from her, even if it was true. And then she succeeded in changing the subject. After he drove her home they played at love-making for a while, but now he was preoccupied, and gently she sent him away. He did not forget what she had said, though it had seemed little enough at the time.

And now it kept asserting itself as he drove through

Tacoma, where you had to cut right down the main street and stop for all the lights. Ellen's words charged him, and he would have swerved to avoid them had their streets been visible and the words metal and plastic. Was it really as easy as all that? Were there simply different isolated people and no meeting? Berrigan? Hastings? His own father? And no more, simply no more to say? Or to expect. He supposed that Jason took people that way, each one a separate study. People to look at. But did Jason simply turn their insides out and gently abstract their ticking parts? Exhibit A: a strange *Homo sapiens* native to administration offices of large universities. Thrives on sociological textbooks, multiplies rapidly, possibly hermaphroditic. He had sometimes thought that Jason's ceaseless analyses were obsessive. But was it possible that they actually prevented obsession from making its nest, that they simply masked a moral position which assumed that everyone was locked into himself, everyone a study? Jason was always being surprised by people, but he expected to be surprised, a lover of intrigue, who, as far as he could tell, never really intrigued. And through it all Jason was comparatively clean; he had nothing really against him except that expression of detached observation. His position seemed to work. But only for Jason, by Jason's laws, for he was not Jason. He and Will would go raging in the mad darkness because they were their own animals. They would rage in their own ways, and Hastings was *his* animal. And the lot of them, they did not speak across the low and little air.

He flipped on the radio and listened to Leo Lassen broadcast the Rainiers' game with Vancouver. He had lost touch; the names, except for one or two veterans down from the majors, were all strange. He should get the *Sporting News* again. The hell with it all; there was a summer ahead. He wondered idly whether he could still hit a curve.

It was after six when he approached Shoreham School, where George and Ann lived *in,* as they called it. *In* was a little brick campus cottage. Deliberately he drove around the south edge of the grounds past the baseball field, stopped the car and looked. The trees were bigger. He remembered how it looked in 1940, when he had come there. Then the trees were all sticks. Now there was an air of lushness, and part of the infield would be covered with shade even at three o'clock. The summer campus was quiet and cool, and he noticed a fancy new, possibly electric, scoreboard in center field, and a wooden fence. In his day, when you got a ball in between right and center it rolled into a ravine and maybe a mountain beaver hole. The infield was manicured, too, or had been; though it was a bit grown up since school had let out. Beneath, it was in good shape though. He remembered suddenly poor Frank Morris and his glasses and the sun, trying to field first base in the dirt and pebbles they used to play in. How he wished then that he could carry the ball over to Frank. And he himself had played shortstop a whole season on that pan and made but one error. Like a machine, someone called him once.

It was not the same place. In the spring there had been two hundred kids there and a mess of masters, none of whom he would know and who would not know him, even though his name graced the plaques in the main hall and there was probably a picture hung somewhere in the gym. The football coach had been Warburton. Where was he now? Sold cars for a while, he remembered. A son of a bitch, had centered the ball ten yards over a punter's head in some bowl game. He was a good coach if you could stand him. Some janitor was walking slowly beyond the fence, coming to turn on a big moving sprinkler. He'd worked one summer doing that, 1941. This place had helped him. But it was not, of course, the same, and now it was the world of his sister—odd thought—not his.

Living *in* would mean for George Brocklin a schedule of study-hall supervision on certain evenings and occasional weekend duty, riding herd on the dorm boys, but it was summer now and the whole place had that lazy quiet useless air of a private park or old estate. He remembered, anticipating what George would be doing, the routine of Shoreham. He could guess George's life. It was hard work, all right. He earned his money and then some. In fact it was a life. He mused now that it took also a particular sort of ambition, which one might very well miscalculate as no ambition at all. He knew he could never abide it himself. But that was he.

It was likely George would stay at Shoreham. There was perhaps something right about it for him, from the engagement to Ann in Portland when she was two years out of high school, through the Seattle public-school job, to the present. He was a rich boy, so he nurtured all those naïve illusions about democratic public education as the *only* thing. He didn't realize he was only resenting his parents, who kept him safely tucked in third-rate boarding schools all through his childhood. Where better to learn life, if realism was the seamy side? But George must have had some native insulation, because when he was surprised he didn't expect to be. Now, of course, he had gravitated back among his own, though probably Shoreham could now be called first-rate as such schools went. George wouldn't be blasted out of the womb again. His current passionate arguments for private education came with only a hint of guilt.

George met him at the door, with little Betsy peering, sticky-fingered and finger-faced, from behind her daddy's legs. In her hand she held a rubber dog. He knelt down and tried to find a safe spot to kiss, settled for a peck on the forehead. She smiled.

"You're Uncle Jack. I know you." He had recognized her, too, even in her commando disguise. George was wearing a soiled apron and held a dish towel more wet than dry. He was tanned and crew-cut. Lots of work in the garden.

"Oh my gosh, we didn't expect you till tomorrow. Ann's down at the studio. Come on in. Have you eaten?" Prospects for food did not look very promising, but he was hungry. "I think we can fix something up if you haven't." George led the way into the kitchen. There was a chance to stand for a moment or two contemplating the living room on the other side of the hall. It surely hadn't been picked up in days. Betsy's toys were strewn over the floor, and there was a huge spot on the rug in front of the fireplace, where old envelopes and letters lay heaped on the ashes. The remains of an orange graced the hearth. A curtain was missing from a window, apparently pulled down, for the hanger was bent. On the davenport were piles of books and newspapers. A pair of rubber pants and a child's blanket were tossed on a big wing chair. Tacked to the wall above the davenport was a still life. Not very good, he thought.

It was clear that in the kitchen George was trying to keep even with chaos. He had been washing dishes. "The beer is in the fridge; help yourself. There's the opener. Sit over there if you like." George was pointing to one of the chairs pulled back from the dinette table next to Betsy's high chair, which held what had not made its way to Betsy's face. Jack pulled out the chair. Its back felt sticky. Old shellac and food, he thought. But the seat was relatively clean. What wear will do. He cleared away a spot before him on the table and set down his beer. He could hear Betsy singing somewhere in the house. He imagined Gerber's peaches spreading like chicken pox over walls and furniture. He knew that Ann was not the best housekeeper. Grubby, his mother had said of her, but it had never been quite this bad.

George washed on. Jack stared at him. He looked tired underneath that healthy all-American tan.

"I didn't know Ann had a studio. She's painting again?"

"With a vengeance," was the reply. It was out of character. There was a touch of sarcasm unlike George. "It's near where she got you some rooms. They're all ready, incidentally. You can move in tonight if you like, or stay here." He opened a bottle for himself and sat at the table. "You might as well know it now. Ann and I just aren't hitting it off. I've wanted to talk to you. I thought maybe the studio would help. I mean, she's wanted to paint, said she couldn't do it here. Well, I understand that. She wants to express herself, she wants to develop her own character and her capacities. Heavens, as a teacher I appreciate that. And, well, she hasn't much chance, I guess. But somehow the studio has just driven a wedge between us. I try to discuss it with her and she says, 'George, all you want to do is discuss. I want my life.' And I try to tell her we take on responsibilities with husbands and children, and that *is* life. But she accuses me of dullness and having no respect for her as a creative individual. Oh, I don't know. She doesn't even seem to want to spend the time with Betsy and Tom. It's okay in the summer, when I'm around the house, keeping it such as I do." He laughed an embarrassed laugh. "Oh, I saw you take in the mess. She hasn't lifted a hand for a couple of weeks. But I don't know how she'll expect me to teach and do all the work around here in the fall. She's at the studio all the time, forgets to come home for dinner sometimes. For all I know, she's shacking up down there with some dead-beat painter. She seems to know enough of them now. Last time I was down there three or four of them were lying around the studio drinking beer, watching her paint. After that she made me—yes, she made me agree not to come down again. I don't know what's become of her, really, and you know what this will do to the kids." He would not look Jack in the face now. "Why all the studies say . . ."

"Yeah, it's hard on the kids," Jack intoned. He didn't want to get on George's theories of upbringing. The Gesell lectures last fall during their visit had been enough. He looked around. George cut a somewhat foolish figure. Did Ann? With all that money in the family a little bit— quite a bit by Ann's standard—might have been put to use to save this business, but George was on a white horse about money.

"Look, George, if you tell me where Ann is, I'll drive down, and then she can show me where the flat is. That might save a trip. We have time to talk later on."

It had not been what George wanted. He had wanted to say everything, and now he was crestfallen, but suddenly Jack wished to see Ann and to see her alone. So he made his exit, hoping to catch Ann before she drove back herself.

George thought he could make it in time. "She said she wouldn't be back until late. We planned you would come tomorrow."

"Yes, well I got away a day early." He hadn't, but there was no use arguing about the distance. George was probably embarrassed enough at seeing him, as it was. He had learned quite a lot about embarrassment recently.

He drove downtown over University Bridge along Eastlake following George's directions and then turned off to the shabby old curtained store front which was Ann's studio. He knocked, and Ann opened the door. She was surprised, too. He could see guests in the room behind her. She kissed him on the cheek and brought him in. Her face seemed a bit drawn. She was without make-up, and there was paint on her old sweater and slacks— all black. But even with her hair stringy and her lips gray he could see she was still the pretty model-type she might have made a career of being. And perhaps that was the matter.

"These are the Dorseys. They paint, too." The Dorseys turned out to be a thin, ascetic, horn-rimmed young man in a sweatshirt and jeans with cowboy boots and a stout young lady similarly attired, who, as far as he could tell, was only beginning her beard. They did not stay long. It was rough. Being "family" put him among the untouchables. These people, he knew, were always escaping family.

When they had padded softly out, passing him as one passes a museum statue hung over from an unfashionable era, Ann smiled at him, more herself. When she had introduced him he had hardly recognized her voice—high and artificial.

"I've so wanted to talk to you. I'm glad you've come." She came to kiss his cheek again and hug him.

"You didn't tell me you'd started painting again. You didn't tell me you'd taken a studio either. Very nice. How are the neighbors?"

She disregarded the question. "Yes, and I've found a place for you only a block up the hill. Jack?"

"Yes?"

"I suppose George has already gotten in the first word and discussed *us* with you."

"Well, he did sing the blues a bit. From what I could see, perhaps he had some good reasons. He looked pretty sad in that apron."

"Oh now, you aren't going to start in on me. I forbid it." She was washing out some brushes now. "It was bad enough when Mother was here for the first baby and I had to take all her advice. And the Brocklins! God, the Brocklins, with their Cadillac and those awful sport shirts."

"You married them; I didn't."

"I didn't have any life at all."

"This is living?" he muttered, looking around.

"Yes, damn it, it is, by the standards I've been used to."

"I suppose you'll expect me to say it. It's escape. Maybe you're right to try to escape. I don't know. I imagine George may be pretty hard to take, with all that education nonsense half the time, but he hasn't beaten you, has he? And you people have enough money. I don't see why it must lead to this. No, it's escape. Why not try to settle it? The kids are the losers, you know."

But he was a miserable salesman and he knew it. Furthermore, his remarks had been either avoidance or soap-operaeze. The money was George's, and there was George's guilt about it and his moral sense about it, and God knows what else, and they both knew it. That is, Ann knew that he knew. So she was scathing.

"Come off it. You sound like Dad on his high moral-instruction level. If I want the Guiding Light I can go back home and play the radio while I wash dishes. What about me? That is the question." She was drying the brushes, walking about, dripping on the floor. No harm there. By the look of the place, it had stood up to plenty of paint. "Besides, I just can't stand any more theories of life adjustment. He's read every damned book under E for education and M for marriage. Thinks we can adjust our sex life or something. Jack, look. I'm like you. I think I have some talent for living or doing something. I thought you would understand this. Don't be big steady older brother."

Our family, he thought, Jesus, our family. We think someone has locked something in us. Adjustment to life, creative capacities, self-expression. Advanced finger painting. We don't grow up in America. He was walking around the room looking at the canvases.

"They're no good," she said. "I haven't got anything

right yet. I just keep boiling inside." He thought of a bad popular song. "I want out, and he just moralizes at me with that big blank percentage of a stare. Do you know, he tells me that forty-five percent of all wives are . . ."

"Sorry, I don't want to know." At the window he could see boats on Lake Union. She was staring at a canvas. "I stopped at Dad's grave in Portland."

She was surprised, almost gaping. "Well, why did you do *that?*"

"Oh, I don't know. I thought there might be something there."

"Well, did you contact the spirits, heap big swami?" She laughed gaily for the first time, and her face was alive with the sort of charm he liked. It was as if for a moment they strode across the air. He smiled foolishly. It did sound silly, he admitted to himself. Like George Moore and AE going to Newgrange to rout out the Druids. He sensed now her desire to approach him in something like the old way, to follow along after him, her socks drooping, stopping to pull them up, and he calling, come on, Ann, come on (she had always praised him, perhaps only because he had never called her Annie), we'll be late for the game, and she sitting there, watching him when he came to bat and cheering and laughing when he made it, occasionally, to second. He never had any power. And then skipping back, telling him how everyone thought he was the best fielder on the team, her brother. She was proud he was her brother.

He gave her an answer. "I think I almost said it about myself, but I'll say it about both of us now. He's alive in us. We must not forget it. I hate the idea, but he's the force that drives us—he or some force back beyond him."

She did not answer. That was a seat too close to the field.

In the twilight she took him up the hill to the old house where she had rented a ground-floor flat for him. They were too late for the sunset, but he did watch the city lights above the lake and reflections in the water. Before Ann left to go back to Shoreham she arranged to return in the morning. They would talk then. He thought of George and the breakfast dishes. On the way out she could not contain a last sentence. "It's easier for you; you can be a wife to your work."

"Don't quote Yeats to me at this hour." But he smiled when he said it. Besides, he wondered how the poet's words had been maneuvered into *Home Journal* inanity. "Anyway, have you noticed my work lately?" She laughed. His letter in the spring had described some notable Walton characters. Whore, not wife, he thought.

As he watched her walk to the car, he first thought her high, solemn, and proud; then suddenly he saw a striving little girl, and finally, though he hated it, a suburban housewife in a slick short story. Maybe we all should get out, he thought. Then he sought the porch and watched a lake boat moving toward the canal. A phrase out of Thomas—"through the green fuse drives the flower"— pumped through his head. It had been, it now seemed, the tune of his motor all day. We have deluded ourselves, he thought. We have let our principles grow from a mess of inheritance. We want ourselves. Now for the first time in years he acknowledged his own blood. Now he remembered a walk with his father to a local ball field where the town amateurs collected. Among them was a one-legged man, who batted, hopped to first in great kangaroo strides, and struggled in right field with fly balls. They watched the game a long time. He was fascinated by the man's bizarre effort and his near success. After a while John Emory said, "Something must have got in that man's way once." Having made that analysis he watched a ball soar far to right field and the center fielder retrieve it, the one-legged man hopping furiously and almost fast enough toward the fence. "There's your ball game," his father remarked, and took out his watch. They walked home in tall July shadows. It was 1933, the year John Emory had quit his job in a huff because the office wanted to send him out on the road. Quit anything in 1933!

I shall not, I shall not become moral big brother. I shall not pontificate about responsibility. I shall avoid when possible making stubborn defenses of George Brocklin for the sake of defiance, and I shall try to keep my mouth shut when Ann talks about self-expression. But he knew the hopelessness of oaths, because to say nothing was to lock oneself up, and to say only a little was to speak the very same clichés and fake the tone of moral superiority he wished to avoid. He only wished she could see that they all had to give in sometime. Better to do so before the coma set in, when the tawdry souvenirs of ego were only flowers and expensive chocolates. He wished she could see that she was expecting something from, even worshiping, him just as she had always expected something from her father, who always brought home a surprise, who took four clubs out on the golf course and came in under eighty and stood the drinks, who walked them down to the corner drugstore and sat them on stools for the best soda in the house. For Ann there was always that bright world out beyond her, and when their father's world crashed down around all of them and they pawned the silver, she, charmed by a white dinner jacket and a convertible when none of them had a cent, married George. She doesn't know, he thought, that she is loving herself.

Through that summer her glorification of his life drove him to moods of disillusion, for he found his mind working back over the winter of the year and judging the reality rather than her dream, reconsidering the alternatives at every crisis. He found little he liked, gradually dismissed every action as filled up with his own egotistical pride, and cursed and recursed the force that he knew was flowing in him.

Once, drinking beer with the Ryersons, he told the tale of Fallon's story. Ann was with them, for they were at the tavern near her studio.

"But then really you were in the right. He rejected the story because he was afraid of the subject. It was puritanical." Ann's eyes flashed. "That's the whole trouble. If you're a real artist you have to speak the truth and see reality, and you can't avoid sex if that's part of it."

Ryerson laughed and said, "And it is, but I can write as badly about sex as about anything else. It's full of clichés, anyway. Why couldn't Fallon? I've not seen his story, but it doesn't *sound* top drawer, does it? The way you describe it, with all your own reservations, I mean."

"That's the trouble," he admitted. "It wasn't top drawer, it wasn't really suitable. Ann doesn't quite get the point. He was probably right to reject it on several counts. But we weren't arguing about the rejection, or at least I wasn't. The whole thing was a silly misunderstanding. That's what makes it so intolerable." He was lying to himself. He knew it was not a misunderstanding.

"But can't you straighten it out?" Ann asked, apparently ready to accept correction.

Ryerson was still smiling. "You usually can't, can you? Somehow these things get too deeply involved. All the personalities and the things that happened years ago, pride, honor, and all that—and it's the way it happened, not really what happened, that destroys our hopes. That's why science doesn't replace art. It's the way it happens that counts, that causes us to act as we do. According to formula it would certainly seem that any human argument could be settled, or, for that matter, left open in less than howling disagreement, but how many really are? Think of all the bruised egos."

"Well, can't you write him and state your case and agree he was right?" Ann asked.

Can you speak to George? he wanted to say. "No, that would be the sort of abasement I've seen too often there. And he'd interpret it that way. He wants protégés on his terms. I'm no Brendan Bear."

"Do you see what I mean?" Ryerson triumphed. "The story as story never was the issue. The real argument hasn't ever been stated, maybe never fully understood. It's a matter of personal art, personal styles. Jack doesn't like his style. But you can't get off free in this, Jack. I mean you did push him too far, and you admit you wouldn't go to the wall for that story. That might make him wish to go to the wall against it, and with reason."

"Yes, but we're talking about perfection. The story was no disgrace. He shouldn't have said the things he did about Fallon."

"Style again," Ryerson muttered, "it's all style."

"Hell, he doesn't know Fallon, and he'd never read any of Fallon's best stuff. There are lots of things I see in the situation now, all right. The story was fairly good, really an interesting experiment. Little-mag stuff, if you want to make a silly distinction. I think most people misread Fallon. He pushes the line on sentimentality very close. After all, that's his subject. Most college kids *are* sentimental; most people, for that matter. So he opens a couple of hearts. But all right, the story isn't up to his best. Ralph Ware knew it, Will Person knew it. But we had nothing else. I can see the subject wasn't suitable."

"Well, why not?" Ann insisted. "Can't he stand it?"

"We seem to have come around to the beginning again. No, that's not the point," Ryerson said. "He has to think of his readers, like any editor. He can't offend them. Jack knows that. And Jack also knows he was deliberately baiting him."

"Touché. I'm an ornery bastard. Let's say the story was there, and I allowed myself to forget Hastings' peculiar position. Or let's say I reminded myself of his position and then went right ahead. That's why he should never have been editor in the first place."

"Unless his aim isn't disinterested and he is using it to his own ends is what you were about to say; and you somehow knew this would flush out his motives and make him look bad. But if it had been your choice alone you would have printed it."

"I would."

"But then you have different ambitions."

"Yes. I wouldn't have thought of the same consequences. You're a tough prosecutor."

After the Ryersons left, Ann challenged him. "My God, you discuss like George. You'll squeeze a moral out of it either way."

It was probably true. Was the rest of the summer to go on like this? Oh, hell, let her stand for art and truth, he thought. She wouldn't be the first innocent those goddesses had tormented. Meanwhile, he was feeling all of his convictions melt, his whole year's existence flash by him like trembling circus clowns. He did not like their faces, which were gaudily painted.

Then Will Person descended upon him fresh from Walton with news of the poet's life. Things did not improve for Ann and George. Neither had things apparently improved at Walton. Although he was glad to see Will, he discovered that Will's presence forced disorganization upon his life. Walton came trooping to the Northwest in body as well as fanciful illusion. On the first night, Will regaled him with a long comico-sardonic story about Laurence Fenrow's summer party and McCrea falling into the swimming pool bearing gallantly down into the depths a plate of spaghetti and Caesar salad. Because he offered nothing about Laura, there was room to wonder whether something was deeply wrong. It had long been clear that Will ignored in his talk what he could not cope with. There were other questions, when at the party George got drunk and Will and Ann slipped off. Were they both escaping their intolerable marriages, or was Will merely an opportunist? Was Ann?

Then George began trying to engage him in discussions, and he had sometimes to listen. George's frankness about his sexual life with Ann embarrassed him into silence, and so did the analyses which George would make of his own soul. For Ann was right, George really did believe there was an abstract solution to each problem. It merely had to be isolated. Just then everything in life seemed to be saying there never was, and he could not explain his attitude to his student.

He knew that Ann and Will were spending the days together. And George was keeping Betsy at home. And the boy, Tommy, was still on some hiking trip or other. Once or twice he got up nerve to talk with Ann about responsibility, but Ann would not listen, or, if she did, forced herself to ignore him. Besides, he felt foolish and halfhearted about it and realized that he could not get past his own clichés until he committed himself fully, and he was not ready for that. He saw that mentioning the whole problem in this way he would only be driving her toward Will. With Will, too, there was little that could be said. Will seldom mentioned Ann when they were together alone. He was probably conscience-stricken about the affair.

Finally George came around with an appeal for intervention—once and for all. So he did try once more—with Ann.

Failure: "George asked you to bring this up, didn't he?" She was scornful. "You wouldn't have mentioned it otherwise. It's not you to do it." She meant it as a compliment, but he was sure it was, in any objective way, a frightful condemnation.

"I suppose I'm a bad moralist. But look, it isn't really a moral question maybe. You're escaping into a crazy ideal. There is no purity of the kind you want." He almost added, "Let alone with Will." But he knew that she would realize without his writing her a letter that he was pointing at her vision of Will the artist.

Then she accused him of conscious hypocrisy, of losing his ideals and giving in. Person was being held up to him as their unwobbling pivot. But he knew Will far too well for that; Will had trod lightly enough to have a clean bill of health all over Walton except in what was left of his home.

"Well, what are you going to do? You can't live in this limbo of yours forever." She did not answer. Poor Ann was still the family baby. He could feel her reaching out to him for an answer she could accept, for a solution. She was suddenly afraid. She had mustered the courage to break from George, but now she was like a bird released from a cage. She did not know where to fly next. The simplest answer would be to cage her up again.

"Will does have a wife, you know, and children. Or is Will only a convenience?" He shouldn't have said that. It was too sarcastic, too easy to misinterpret. Mainly it misled her about his attitude toward Will. When he said it, he was thinking Will could go to hell.

"What do you think I am, a whore or a nympho or something?" And they were off for a short gallop. No, he didn't mean that. Her eyes had hardened, and she said, "Give up speaking for George because it's the easy out. Besides, it fits you like a clown suit." Then very deliberately: "Let's understand that George and I really are finished up." Well, she was moved at last to say it. Till then she had wandered in a desert of discontent, but now she was ready to enter the lion's palace. He hoped it was a decision based on more than Will Person's central ton of presence, and that she was not merely fleeing into a dream. For a moment he had been pleased with himself for having evoked some positive statement from her, but now he decided that he was merely avoiding involvement and it had all been luck.

But after that bold assertion, Ann didn't act, and things dragged on: There was, after Person left, an apparent effort at reconciliation. Ann lived again with her husband. She would not mention Will in conversation, nor did she confide anything. The Brocklins went to the zoo with the kids and lay on the beach at Golden Gardens, Ann always with her brushes. He did not like this change. Now it was he who wished for action. But he said nothing, settled in on his book, and managed to finish a final draft.

Late in August he learned that he had been selected for a Thompson Fellowship, which meant he would be free of Walton for the whole spring semester. He was very pleased, and in September he drove the long road back, vowing to teach and otherwise keep his mouth, and when possible his ears, closed.

On the first night, he saw Ellen, and they celebrated their respective good fortunes with steaks and wine. She had told him that Hastings' efforts on her behalf had borne fruit. She would go east to study drama next summer. Hastings had written very strongly for her and had even stopped in New York in July to see the secretary of the committee.

He was just a little annoyed, uncertain whether she was glad to have him back or simply exhilarated over her good fortune. But he smiled grimly at himself for it. They drank some good whiskey at her apartment, and later in the evening they made love passionately and without any awkward preliminaries. After it was over she was quiet, looking at him contemplatively, propped on one elbow.

"You are like me," she said, leaning over him for a cigarette. He reached for and held her breast. "Don't. I'm trying to talk."

"I like your silences."

"They just give you time for maneuvers. We're talking beasts, after all. It's time we talked. I mean, you don't want to give yourself away. We're both holding out for bigger stakes."

"Is he going to give you yours?"

"Oh, he arranged the fellowship, if that's what you mean, and if you're suggesting anything more, I don't think it's funny."

"Well, you're the only person I know who's gotten anything from him for nothing. It's usually a piece of the soul, I believe."

"No, not that either. I gave him friendship. I was nice to Mrs. Bolyard. I laughed with him a few times. It wasn't hard."

"Maybe it isn't for a woman."

"Oh, come on now. You know, he really wants to be liked. I don't think he understands why he can't break through to you people."

"That sounds a little like Laura Person."

"That's Will's wife. What about her?"

"Oh, nothing. Do you really think it's our fault? My God, you can't get a direct answer from him that isn't so vague it's meaningless. You can't get to him, and here you say he's trying to get to us!"

"I think you know he is. Maybe he's trying too hard. Don't hold that against him. You might even find it's a likable quality."

"Look, Ellen, you know what happened all last year.

You know Berrigan and the Hungerford business. But you haven't sat in on our meetings, you . . ."

"Shh, you're getting excited. See? You're obsessed. I didn't want to talk about Hastings. I just wanted to talk about us, to say you are like me. You won't sell yourself cheap. I'll admit I got his help without paying much of anything out. I'll admit that the fact I'm a woman has something to do with it. And don't make a wisecrack! He's never been less than marvelous to me. I appreciate it."

"Even if he's a charlatan?"

"I don't know that he is. You tell me."

He didn't say anything.

"Do you know, I think *all* of you people are obsessed. You've made Hastings the original snake by sitting around railing at Berrigan and blaming him."

His answer began with the argument that there had to be some cause for a mass obsession, it didn't just grow, that this proved his case, and so on into the night it would go. But he stopped short of rant. It was too complicated, so finally he didn't say what he was thinking—that Hastings hadn't bargained for her soul, but had silently bartered for his, so it was easy enough for her to offer moral exhortation, and so forth, and so on.

Instead, he took her cigarette and before she could complain too much kissed her. "I still like your silences." He felt for a moment a terrible loneliness. He held her tightly and put his face to her hair, their bodies together.

"We are apart," he whispered. "Is it all my fault?"

"I've given myself to you."

"Not really."

"Yes I have, I really have, but you aren't free to have me. I am afraid for you. Now you are going to tell me that it's harder for a man to get out of himself."

"I won't now. It's hard for everyone, I suppose."

"No, you would be right. And the more responsibility you have, the harder it is to sort out the right and wrong, if there really is any. Maybe Hastings isn't big enough for it. I don't really know, but the point is, who knows until he takes it on?"

"You said forget Hastings, Ellie, so forget him." He turned from her and stared at the ceiling.

"Can I risk a fight to say don't call me Ellie?"

He smiled at her. "There's ego for you. I love you. I should say marry me. I want you."

"I would say no."

"Not ready, am I? I've got to finish all this off. I'm so preoccupied with Walton I can't grasp the moment. I'd like to say go east and give me time."

"Yes." He was not sure what it was yes to, and he didn't take the chance of asking.

"Yes, because you won't pine away for me as long as you're haunted this way. If I stayed here you might marry me by mistake, get me to say yes when I was coming or something. You beast." She giggled foolishly and kissed him softly.

"I'll stay here tonight," he whispered.

"Okay, but no elegies."

▶

On the next day he dropped down to the office to read the summer's second-class mail and pick up his teaching schedule. His impulse was to slip in and out without seeing anyone and then drop by the Talbots for a cup of coffee. But he met Jason in the hall.

"Just got my schedule, Jack—no surprises. Warner was right; I got that course." For Jason that would mean two composition sections: the sophomore fiction, and, as a plum, awarded by the curriculum committee, through the grace of Warner, a course on Yeats and Joyce.

"Your times okay?"

"Not bad, no eights. I notice Roper isn't around though. Someone must have been shafted, or he'd be grinning in his office."

"Don't be too sure. Around here you grin in your office if you *have* shafted someone."

He did not like Virgil Roper, who made up the schedules. Why? Because, he guessed, he hated pedagogical default, which had given Roper the modicum of departmental power he wielded so grandiloquently. Incompetent really, he thought; got the job because they tried to keep the poor man out of the classroom as much as possible. He was important now.

He walked in with Jason to find his summer mail, packed away somewhere in a cardboard box. In his cubbyhole was his fall schedule. He looked it over. Jesus, he thought.

"Take a look at this."

Jason read it. "Man, it's you they got."

"I knew Hastings would be through with me on the magazine, but three comp sections and 'Readings in English Literature'? Whew!" That was the course for nonmajors that mainly drew engineers and aggies looking for a spot of culture. Roper had moved modern poetry to spring term, when Jack would be on leave.

His first reaction was a sort of panic, and then he was angry. By the time they had walked up the stairs to his office he had become articulate and was playing to his audience. But he thought simultaneously, Poor Jason, he has to listen to this. Surprised at his own detachment, thinking it was all just and according to the plot, he wondered to himself whether or not he really cared to complain at all.

► 3

"Hail
to the
victors
valiant"

William Person

MAKING A PEACE   The trouble with me is I try to make everything art; but life always was poor material; art always has to improve on it, deliver a golden world, hero and heroine embraced in mutual orgasm on the last page, clowns and dancing girls, sadism, masochism, symbols, and subtle machinery. Keep the slobs reading. But I am reticent about myself. I can't drag myself and Ann into a novel. It would turn out like a movie with the main scene censor-cut. Couldn't make head or tail of how the people got where they are.

The result for me? Afternoons like this one. I long to blow off the past; there's no place to release it all. So I play literary politics. I ask other people how *their* books are coming along. Cal Harmon in Denver writes back, Why aren't you at it? Go ahead, he urges. He wants someone else in his pickle. He's writing this stupendous sex scene, see; but he can't get it right. Platonically there's only one real sex scene, he argues. So he traps me into a competition. We exchange orgies, but Cal can't appreciate my subtleties—imaginary gardens with real toads. Alex Cassoway and Love Dove, Hastings and Bolyard! They meant nothing to him.

For my own uplift, I completed my best effort with

suave round Klaus caught and suffocated to death in the embrace of monstrous Wilma. Scene: Dickie Mouse in her cabin on the *France* (a rough sea is blowing) come to read her his MLA paper on *Endgame.* She drugs him with champagne; they smash glasses, bottles. Wallow in squalor on the floor mid broken glass.

But Cal hadn't met Klaus, didn't think the characters real enough, and certainly not ideal. I tell him my memories are fantasies anyway. He thinks I need help.

Upshot: The Kal-Har-Mon Do-It-Yourself SEX SEEN. Supply the names and places in the blanks, and there it is. Needn't be heated in the oven. I had a lot of fun putting Brendan and Wilma into it as follows:

> "Aha, by Jaysus, baby, you have gone and done it this time, with the new black nightie I ordered for your own all the way from Neiman-Marcus in Dallas, that is," said he, the veins on his hand standing out as he clutched the doorknob.
>
> "Yes, Brendan, you big ugly lovable bear," she panted in her teeny-weeny voice, turning modestly from him and thus revealing under the fragile black lace her callipygian beauty. Indeed, one could well see that under the gown, which clung to all her different parts, she had an exotic and firm, but not too heavy, though luxuriant body.
>
> "I shall turn out the light," he said. The veins of his hand pulsated toward the light switch, but suddenly he remembered that he did not know where it was.
>
> "Besides, then you could not see me in my nice black lace things which feel so ummy on me because the lace is made out of real silk," she breathed. Besides, also, he was afraid of electricity, which had been installed in the old mansion so her father could, before his death at age one hundred and six, show dirty movies. "I shall ask him to inspect the lace more carefully," she said, in an aside, "and in this way he will be unable to avoid being overcome by passion. Then," she continued pensively, "I will

kiss him on the neck, and he will grasp me in his strong, handsome arms; I hope that tweed jacket does not scratch too much. It is not as nice as bearskin," thereby showing that she was cultured, having read such things as Huxley.

"That is true," he said pantingly. The blood was coursing through his veins, and also arteries.

"Look at the silk in this lace!" she cried haltingly, brushing back a strip of her blonde hair, which had fallen over her well-shaped, exotic, big-moon [my addition—ed.] face. "Feel the quality!" Inside, in her inner being, her stomach was churning with desire. She could feel electricity in the air, static and otherwise. "This is love," she cried to herself, pantingly. He was approaching.

"The hell with the electricity; full speed ahead," he muttered, garbling Dewey's famous words. "I adore silk lace," he breathed. There was a sort of craving in his eyes. This craving was equaled only by that in her own, as she was drawn to him like electric sparks from a Tesla coil, where the two little balls come together at the top, she thought. She could smell the masculine, strong odor of his tweeds.

"Yes," he cried, "it is silk!" Unbidden, his strong masculine hands ran themselves over her gorgeous, enchanting, exotic, and firm, though luxuriant body. She melted into his arms, hugging him passionately.

"Do you hear my heart beating?" she asked.

"Not very well," he replied. "Perhaps I should listen with greater proximity."

"Yes," she answered him, thinking, "His strong, masculine body has excited me to the point . . . what is it they say? . . . the point of no return!"

"Will she have me?" he was wondering.

Her delicate, yet strong arms entwined him all around. Her delicious curves revealed themselves to him somewhat further as his unbidden hands discovered the many catches holding her scanty garment together. Her flesh, firm yet soft, white as snow yet full of the color of life, entranced him altogether. With the strength of sixteen men he lifted her in his arms. He staggered. There was a sharp knock on the door.

"Yes, sir," he panted. "Yes, sir, Dr. Hastings, coming sir."

He came.

Cal had said it all. [Curious, it's the days I don't go up to the plant that I start back into that bushy past. Something keeps wanting me to write it out. But I'm reticent.] Ann and I didn't lose ourselves in each other's arms. In fact, it wasn't even very successful, and I thought at some point, I am a beast, I am a beast. I wasn't playing with a metaphor either. No, I meant that I, this man here, was indeed a beast. I lived in an old shaggy skin, and what I really wanted was out and past it all into Ann's world, because I sensed that in Ann's world there might be a sort of salvation waiting. I wanted whoever it was had me by the scruff of my ruff to ungather those dry goods, and soon.

[The hell with everybody. It wasn't a silly affair. And I wasn't falling for Ann because she'd treat me like a genius. Go to hell, gossips.]

I shouldn't have gone back to Walton, I should have stayed lit out. My reputation wouldn't have been any worse. Back at Walton in the fall all I felt like doing was knocking over people I met in the hall. Analogy: way back in 1938 my folks and I were vacationing up in Michigan, and we had Cubic with us. Cubic, our big collie, a real work dog. Brushed, he looked square, like a block. Cubic wanted to go everywhere. One day we were all going on a long bicycle trip and we thought he'd exhaust himself, so we left him there in the motel. And when he got back this big damned beast had hopped up on my parents' double bed and pissed a soaker through the blankets. Spite and violence. That's the way I felt at Walton—locked up. [Hours home from the plant are free now.] Some people do piss on the bed. For that one decisive act, I always admired Cubic more than any dog I ever had. Emory did it when he quit the magazine, and some people think he was wrong. Emory did it because piss is sometimes deserved. Anyway, we're all beasts when we're trapped. He did it consciously, and he must have known exactly what the results would be, because he was a sly-enough character. In fact, a real operator. He knew he'd have to leave Walton after that.

God, last December at MLA when he and I were in the lobby [yes, Jesus, I too] together. There emerging from a crowd was the brat face of Crowder. And it was sickening, Crowder affecting not to know where Jack was teaching now, as if he'd gone to Siberia or Nevada. Jack burned. But there were no words until Crowder went away, and then: "I wasn't wrong to blow that place." Hell, Crowder knew damned well where Jack was. He knew where everyone was. The first week at Walton he spent memorizing where all the faculty members got their degrees. Wanted to know who was important. He had a really deep mind.

I remember, too, my roommate at Indiana, 1945— Tim Walkup. Both of us were just out of the war, Tim a veteran of the Bulge. He'd talk about his old man, his entrepreneur father, who made three fortunes and lost two. A big-time investor up in Chicago. I never saw anyone read the way Tim did, history and politics. He studied diplomacy, and he knew plenty about the Near East, even began to learn Arabic. But there he was taking a full business course at IU, because, well, he'd developed his father's tastes and he simply had to have a lot of money. And he knew he could make it if he went in with big Dad. But he really wanted to go some place like Benghazi or Alexandria or Beirut.

One night I woke up and there he was pissing dead asleep in the closet we shared, all over my jeans and other pair of shoes. He did it again a couple weeks later in his own briefcase, and then he was off to Chicago for a long rest from studies and a psychiatrist. So now, married and with kids, he's an executive in some big restaurant chain. I doubt he's introduced any Near Eastern dishes. A few years ago the old man was scalped again by some West Coast Injuns. What does Tim's wife think when he somnambulates out of the sack and lifts his leg on the bedpost, because I bet his lost career is still the ghost who walks.

Yes sir, the pressure builds up. I wasn't dancing around in my sleep yet, but there I was back from Seattle for the fall term, and a couple of things happened that made me bring blasphemy into the house in the evenings and generally strain my relations with Laura. On those nights she might as well have been a Carmelite for all the talk I'd get out of her, and there I was with the old-fashioned idea that wives are supposed to help out the old man. She should uncork the beer and, when the old man pauses, punctuate with, "You're right, the blighters," or "You tell 'em, Will," or "Don't let them get away with it." Laura would read *Ladies' Home Journal* or the I Love Luce magazine in the kitchen and check her mind in the deep freeze.

Well, a new season was upon us, Emory at bat. Hastings' first pitch was low and inside, but there it goes off the scoreboard in deep left center. I don't know to this day exactly what kind of delivery it was, but the result was Ralph Branca stuff. There'll always be a dent with some paint chipped away near the strike box. Hastings blamed everyone in the ball park but himself. Let me figure it: Jack's resignation from the magazine staff and Hastings' invitation to the first hooey-boy meeting of our second fall must have crossed in the mails. When we turned up we watched Hastings get hopping mad. The back of his neck a Georgia farmer's. Poor Hungerford:

two meetings and two tantrums. [Hell, I won't lose any sympathy over him; that boy can take care of himself.] But he must have been stunned.

No more stunned than Davis. When we went over to Hastings' office, I thought to myself, Well, who's next? And for a while it looked like no one. There was Hastings setting out on one of his characteristic verbal rambles. A little early-season wildness, the innocent rookies would think. First the cultural series: Berrigan was good for a few sentences of enthusiastic newspeak. Warmed up, then, Hastings fires a couple of dusters at Davis: What had Davis done for the magazine to deserve time off? Had he recruited any articles worth a hill of beans? Questions and more questions. Davis sprawled in the dirt. A palpable hit, yes, a palpable hit. But why? What had he done to deserve this, except to be what he was?

Slowly truth comes: A couple of days before, Jack had unwittingly snookered Davis and demonstrated that it's hopeless to help a fool. All spring Klaus burned because Hastings gave Jack and me some time off from teaching for the magazine. So when fall rolls around he talks Davis into approaching Emory on just how this coup was accomplished. Klaus naturally saw everything achieved by pull or stealth. That Hastings simply thought we were useful didn't dawn on him. Emory is frank with Davis. He tells Davis he merely asked Hastings for the time off, true, and that was that. Flushed with courage and charmed by the simplicity of things, little Paul toddles over to Mrs. Bolyard, gets an appointment, and has one word from Hastings—NO. Then he moans around the department that Emory has led him into a trap. In fact, he even says this to Jack.

Admirable restraint, Jack's. Did he know Hastings would dust Davis off? From then on Hasty Hank had a new whipping boy, maybe because he didn't talk back to that initial no. But behind it all, Hastings was really mad at Emory, who had just up and quit. He topped off the meeting with puff and huff about people pulling their oars, loyalty, even friendship. I was almost sick. And then, after the we're-all-in-this-thing-together-around-the-table bit, he fires one just on the knees: vague talk about promotions and raises. Not the wild sky's-the-limit hooey we used to get, but ominous suggestions. It was an effective three-inning stint for early season. Knowing what I know now, I could have understood his revenge would stick old Jack in rank, then boost the loyalty of Berrigan and Crowder and their ilk. But I wonder. Who would have taken it like Jack? No bench splinters for him!

For a while after all that, Hungerford would drop in to the office with a tall, courtly northeastern-gentleman-type oiliness and, between compliments, try to work the count around to Hastings. But I didn't want to play. I had enough worries of my own without acting confessor to newcomers, particularly someone who could ride out the storms snug in the rare-book room. So I'd mimic with my lovable old St. Bernard face the foxy leer of Warner and offer cryptic statements like "Hang around and you'll see more" or "That one was midseason form, and it's only October." Hell, anyone who signs up to play for Walton needs a few weeks of panic just to ease in properly. Hungerford was shrewd enough to get the picture. He dropped a few remarks about inexcusable bad manners to one's subordinates, which meant he'd better watch his step, hadn't he? I couldn't have agreed more, nodding sagely, stroking my imaginary Longfellow.

Besides, just about now my mind was dancing over hot coals, because I was carrying around in my pocket Ann's latest letter. She was writing short notes to me at my private postbox, where I picked up my rejection slips, and I was replying with long semipassionate creations or wild verse letters in the style of Dryden. Some of the better ones I didn't actually send; I have them around still. [Literary remains for Old Kindly to plow through. Cash for the descendants.] The more anatomical ones, they are. [You bet, Will, the Walter Benton money-makers.] This latest letter was brief as usual, but with that expansive meaning the academic critics like these days: in short, she is indeed pregnant, and it's I surely. She hesitates to tell me, but then she thinks how would she, if she were a man, like it not to know she was someone's father. I can see that.

It was all matter-of-fact. I notice, old philosopher me, that in situations like this it's the woman who takes the practical dispassionate view, while the men go to pieces proposing wild adventurous solutions. All to the good, really; because sometimes one needs wild adventurous solutions to slice through the fog of reason. And that is my style, so I went around inventing. I even forgot to growl at Davis, or to drop around and butter up Warner or make my jovial complaints about the incumbent governor to Vanner when we loomed up ghostlike before each other in the intellectual fogways of our hallowed halls. Let's see now. It was around this time my dream about missing classes began to recur. I hadn't seen it since the first few months of the year, and now it was definitely wide-screen stuff. Something like this: I would be drinking in a Walton tavern or in Farmer John's in London when the phone would ring, and it would be Vanner's secretary. I'd know at once what it was all about. I'd grab my coat, leaving a pitcher of beer on the table, and run all out of breath through town to the campus, except that it would take me hours because I'd be getting lost and coming to the same canal over and over again, and no bridge. Finally I'd get there, and Vanner would say only, "This is the last time," smiling behind his pipe and handing me, again, my schedule. Suddenly I'd realize that I'd failed to meet my classes for a whole month and they were waiting for me now.

Variation: I'd be a student, and Vanner would tell me I was failing and I'd apologize and run off to class. Sometimes Berrigan would be in the dream. When I got to the room he'd be shouting, "No, this is *my* class. Next room! Next room!" I'd go, and the room would be empty. Once Ann was sort of there, but Berrigan came rushing in saying, "That's not your class, that's not your class!" I'd never find the students.

Then, a couple of days after Ann's letter, one of those three-day sprawlers took place—the visit of prima-bibliographer Thomas P. Halloran, better known among textual scholars as The Halloran, our lord of printers' errors from the Florida swamps north to the Catskills and west past the Mississippi. By luck of the draw, he was Jason's responsibility, but I wasn't out of it. There had to be the inevitable seminars, the lecture, the party, with attendance required. By that time Laura and I didn't bother to show ourselves together even at official functions. She'd gone back to doing part-time nursing. We were living together separately. No fooling her. We hardly talked. If I mentioned horrendous divorce, she'd just walk away from our conversation back into the business of what remained of our household.

Call the Halloran visit a climax? Why not? I rush off to an eight o'clock dribbling egg from chin to tie, see students from nine to ten, teach again, and then sit solemn in the bibliography seminar, where Halloran tells us all about pinpricks in the A, B, and C manuscripts of Carlyle. Then a big-circle luncheon at the Faculty Club with Hastings presiding as best he can at an oval and expecting us all to be very bright. [Mr. Clean, I.] Great sport, because Emory and Hastings avoid speaking now. And Crowder droning on about Faulkner texts, with that absurd pipe drooping out of his mouth and he lighting it and puffing and still droning all the major irrelevances. Utter collapse without those props, I bet.

After that we have a long lecture on the bibliographical stupidity of most and maybe all critics. It's one of the few times I've wanted to take a critic's side. Apparently they're all at fault because they use a text where a few words and commas may be in doubt. The upshot is that the only right text of, say, *Hamlet* is the gospel according to Halloran. Hell, we all know an editor *makes* a text. Maybe I should destroy all my manuscripts, print fifteen variant readings of each poem, and falsify the records in Madison County Court House. Aunt Sara would arrange an inside job for a bottle of vodka. Think of the notoriety. Maybe someone will eventually write a book saying the Duke of Argyll wrote my stuff. Imagine the books, then, about *that* one. And letters to *TLS*. If you are a poet, create some puzzles and gain undying fame.

[Whoa, there's all that to remember about Halloran and the party that night, second year of the beasts.] Beyond attending all these functions and shaking the limp salmon hand of our guest, I stayed deep in the dungeon of my worry about Ann and what I could do to get Laura to consider divorce. The party was given by our own venerable textual scholar, Dr. Pyles (what you get bending too low and long over old folios). Pyles, in his dotage, had little part in the politics except occasional pronouncements on the obvious superiority of *how we used to do it* and the decline in morals. Even so, he'd get off an occasional left jab at Cassoway's legions. It probably helped a bit. Cassoway was intimidated by venerability. There was a hitch: Pyles was a snob, discovered his own opinions by whim. There were lots of reasons to dislike Klaus, but, hell, Pyles didn't know anything about them. He disliked Klaus because he was a Jew. Jews, fairies, and FDR. Also, oh yes, the uncultuhed—most of the department, the University, the town.

Well, in spite of culture Pyles liked to get people roaring drunk. His punch far surpassed anything Cassoway or

Warner produced. His greatest success: a few years before I arrived, some young instructor passed out from eating a dozen cherries from the bottom of the punch bowl. An exaggeration maybe [ha, ha, who me?], but those cherries could marinate an ulcer. On Halloran night Pyles had spooked up quite a bit of vodka in fruit juice, everyone was thirsty, and there was Berrigan at the ready after a day of recruiting colleagues to attend Halloran's fascinating lecture. He slobbered up about four or five cups right off. By the time Jason and Betty Lou and the hangers-on pulled up with the guest of honor—late, as usual, after dinner out—Brendan had his old fidgety self juiced up like a new torpedo, ready to blast. Because that fall he had been put in full charge of the cultural-series arrangements, with time off from classwork. Klaus and Davis rankled in the wings.

It was a big bash: fifty or sixty academic strong, decent weather, and possible to get outside for a breath of cool air. That's what I did off and on until Jason rolled up with the royalty. Emory came in about the same time. We stood, then, in a corner and discussed the recent issue of *Poetry*—something about Zukofsky's poem on a dog, Jack remarking it was funny how most poets preferred cats to dogs, unless the dogs were dead, and Zukofsky seemed to be an exception. I said I was a live-dog man, and the shaggier, droolier, stronger the better. I restrained myself from saying my live-sheepdog poem.

Jason was standing nearby talking to Halloran, and past them there was Berrigan. He was loudly explaining how he taught the introductory fiction course. I could imagine the details. The handbooks hadn't hit the market yet, so Berrigan still had to go rifle the library for articles to crib from. We all noticed he was well along with the drink; Wilma did, too, and she was trying to get away from Sylvia Warner across the room, probably to stick the cork back in Brendan. Suddenly everyone in the vicinity turned in Berrigan's direction: Davis's voice piping out, high register, "You're nothing but a goddamned salesman." Striking idea. Truth from the mouths of babes.

For a moment Berrigan was stunned. "Watch this," said Jack, nudging me, and there was Berrigan pushing Davis up against a wall, all ready to squash him, holding him by the shoulders, shaking him, his great paunch formidable, and all of him outraged.

"Don't say that, whaddya mean saying that?"

But Jason, beside him now, had Berrigan by the arm, managing to relieve the pressure—poor Davis, nearly flattened on the wall like Tom and Jerry. Meanwhile, there was Klaus, mosquito-buzzing all around them. Calm old Jason's idea was to take Brendan for a walk. Wilma, escaped from Mrs. Warner, helped steer, but Brendan was not about to go peaceably. His ego had been bruised by the truth, and he would struggle free to stomach-bump again.

Then enter old Pyles from the kitchen with an armful of bottles. What he apparently saw: the tail end of a mannerless scuffle. Davis, safe away and back to the wall, was receiving accolades from various associate professors. Old Hemorrhoids could only be deeply pained. "What goes on here?" He spoke loudly, turning to me, who was nearest him. "See that those gentlemen [meaning, we came to realize, Brendan and Jason] make up their differences elsewhere!" I hopped the way I used to for old Colonel Stoneface Calderwood. Between us, Jason and I recaged Brendan in the garden, with Wilma fussing along at our side.

Plenty of dark looks when we returned, and Wilma always between Berrigan and Davis, Brendan still mumbling and past discretion. But now, his drunkenness turned inward and, his eyes glassy dull and narrowed, he kept sullenly to himself.

I wonder what Halloran thought of it all. He may not have noticed anything, locked leering and ehehehing and aheming with Ellen Fraser, old lecher. When Jason and I got back we joined them, but only after Clarissa and her Love Dove ostentatiously snubbed us, noses high, as we entered stage rear through dining room and French doors. There was Pyles in hideous combustion. None of us thought all that much about it at the time. Pyles was really sort of out of it. But the old boy wasn't that far out, just confused. The way I later figured it, Pyles complained lustily to Hastings and Cassoway about the deportment of certain bright young men. Me? No, I was clean. [Ha ha ha. Still am. Cleaned out. Walton washed through the old guts. Operate by absence here and keep an eight-hour day.]

But there's more to shovel up to keep the record straight, because that same evening George Hungerford and Jack had one of those cordial conversations that somehow found their way back to Hastings or Cassoway or someone, and I think I know how. That night Hungerford had spent a lot of time talking bibliography with Halloran, his old professor in the days past. Jason says Hungerford had asked Halloran's advice about a job offer, eastern school, small and tony. They'd discussed it in the back seat of Jason's car on the way out to the party.

When Jason and I brought Brendan back from the garden tour, Hungerford and Jack—and Ellen and Halloran nearby—were discussing the offer, and—Jack tells it—Hungerford has all this guilt about the ethics of accepting an offer when he's only been at Walton three months. I bet it was ethics! Hungerford: a gentlemanly type, but wheeler and dealer on his own level. The point: someone must have taken Jack's spoken advice back to Hastings, which, considering Jack's state of mind about then, must have been swift and sure. Why, he must have told Hungerford to agree to ride dust-eater on the nearest stage just to free himself of the place.

Now one thing about my pal Brendan Bear, silent during all of this in his corner nearby, is that Pyles can fill him up with vodka and let him go a short round with Paul Davis, but he'll bounce back with ears pricked up, and he'll be lucky. I don't know who told Hastings, but it wasn't Halloran, and I'd be surprised if it was Ellen—why should she? But someone let Hastings know Hungerford was thinking of leaving and that Jack had shouted run, run.

All told, that party blew the lid off things for a few days. After viewing Brendan Bear with that professional eye of his and watching Hastings claw Davis and then the wall (and vent his spleen on Emory), no little old advice from Jack was going to drag him away from Walton. He *was* going to run, run on his own steam. Well, he got away clean, didn't he? Damned if Hastings didn't send him off with cordial best wishes. Written off. Best forgotten.

The disaster was Jack's, but he didn't care because he'd probably get that offer from Emerson. Play out his hand.

But poor Jason—single to center, advance to third, caught in a rundown near home. Hastings' suspicions fired. From that night at the Bear-Davis match Pyles had no truck with Jason. I can see it: Hastings receiving high moral criticisms from Pyles and snide commentary from Cassoway. Then there was Jason's friendship with Jack, because Jason didn't treat Jack like a leper. Hastings saw Jason and Jack conspiring in the Beaver Room more than once after that.

Finally, there was Jason's face. It looked deep into Hastings the way it looked deep into me. Vipers down there, too. And maybe Hastings had little heart-to-hearts with his dancing bear, in which certain names came up for review.

I didn't expect him to have heart-to-hearts with me. But surprise! A few days after this, lo, Mrs. Bolyard has me sprinting at a rapid lumber across the old Quad to Hastings' secret hideaway in the library, from which he directed that sprawling network of intrigue known as the *Walton Review* editorial board. Hastings wanted to talk to me, it was important to come right over, he was flying to New York later in the day. I didn't think I had to *run* over, but even so I kept up a steady pace and took the left-hand walk instead of the right to avoid in the distance Professor E. Malinowski, who had confused me early in my career at Walton with someone he thought he knew. Always collared me, if I got too close, for a long talk about Russian novels, including his own, and the awful "quarrelink" which ruined Tolstoy's married life. Oo vas I supposed to be? Never found out. Clearly my opinion was highly regarded from the way he saluted me in the German style. I: bent on promptness and loyalty.

Mrs. Bolyard danced the usual, which is to say she cautioned me not to take up too much of the great man's time, and I refrained from reminding her that he'd asked for *my* time, not I for his. It would have been a hopeless gesture; besides, we were all supposed to be nice to Old Mama Bolyard. Hastings was walking around under his bibliographical hat, dodging the various tables of his hideaway, reading from a sheaf of papers. "Look at these manuscripts, Will. I'm choosing one for the cover of the winter issue. Just in from Dublin, and we had to pay well for them, but they're worth it. Puts us ahead of Texas in the modern field, and we bid against them, too!"

I mumbled words which vaguely sounded like a bibliophilous sis boom ah, and then I waited. Hastings hadn't called me over to look at his toys.

"I liked those poems you chose in the last batch, Will. You got my note, didn't you? [I hadn't.] Don't know when we'll use them. Perhaps a poetry issue for you to put together or a supplementary section with the young moderns chosen by you." I neglected to say that "modern" was a word meaning about 1914 or post-Georgian, but what the hell.

Mrs. Bolyard peeked in at the door. "Dr. Hastings, your plane leaves at two-thirty." She glared at me. I smiled weakly and waited. Finally he replied to her, "Oh yes, thank you, my dear." She hesitated, glancing at my toes, my fly, my tie, my head, and shut the door behind her.

It hadn't come yet, but it would.

"Will, I'm worried. You young men have perhaps the greatest opportunity in the country here. This is the place of the future. Why, in ten years our library—well in five years, boy!—we'll be way ahead with the moderns. For a bibliographer or a critic there's a nest here; why there's a field of clover." He paused, metaphor-bound. Then in a lower register: "I suppose you've heard about Hungerford."

Dumb old I. It wasn't very convincing, though. "No, what, sir?"

"He's leaving us, Will. He's going east. Why? Do you know? I think he got the wrong idea about us out here, because this was the place for him. Too late to do anything now. I think he's been misled, and I think we ourselves have done it. Fact is, there are some people you just can't please. Crybabies. You give them opportunities, and all they want is more, going around causing dissension and giving bad advice. And their manners, Will. Why, when these visitors come—and in parenthesis let me say these people are brought here for you young men —why, when they come they don't want to see a consarned hog-tying match. We have to put our best foot forward." He was walking as he delivered this speech, but now he turned and faced me across the table. "Will, I want you to know how much I appreciate the way you've worked on this magazine and helped with the firming up, getting it under way, setting out." His voice was trailing off.

But it came back strong. "Tell me, what do they want?"

I took the question as rhetorical and not requiring an answer. To marry your daughter? Because if it was a question, it was also a challenge. Old Jason wasn't the only interpreter. I was learning how, too. He went on.

"I guess they just don't want to play on the team. Well, they can stay in their offices." He was leaning over a large map of Dublin, spread on a table. "I'll not bother with them." Then he looked up, came around the table, took my arm, and slapped me on the back, steering me at the same time to the door. Real warrior, in his way. Collecting battle stripes all the time.

"We'll talk some more about the poetry business when I get back from New York. You keep after it, and maybe by spring there'll be a whole issue there. Good-bye now, thanks for dropping in. Wish you folks would come by like this more often." I thought: So it was I dropping in after all. Rewrite history. And the poetry stuff; that only meant he was putting off publishing any poems indefinitely. I got so I could read that language.

I was out. Mrs. Bolyard was in. "Your taxi arrives in five minutes," she said loudly enough so that I, down the corridor, could hear.

After that, Joe Btfsplk had nothing on me in the way of black clouds. In addition to all Hastings' innuendo against friends, my work collecting poems (some from friends) was slipping down the drain. But, more important, here I was clean as a whistle outside and dirty all over inside. It was easy enough to conclude that Emory was going and Hungerford gone and that spies were everywhere. But there was old faithful and noble Will, no crybaby he, no complainer. Why, I was right up there in the galaxy with the passive who obey reason—Crowder, Klaus, and the flutter boys. Jesus, I was depressed with my own hypocrisy. In the years ahead I would continue to send poems to Hastings that he would probably never print. I would meet in somber high court to hear endless orations by Hastings and watch with ennui sagacious pipe-sucking nods of agreement from Crowder and the new Crowders to come. I would continue to shoot needles full of tranquilizers into stomping, wailing bears, to witness faculty discourses on body odor in the phone booths. And I'd be alone in the hall with the mice. Jack and Jason would be far away, and one of these days Ralph Ware would finish that big novel, toss it all over, and snort toward somewhere in Arizona or California. I? Sheepish camp follower, male whore to the muse of Henry Hastings' policies.

It was bad enough thinking these thoughts on a bright sunny October day with winter in the offing. It was worse to go back to the office and find Berrigan lying in wait. He was in his restrained mood: his manias and phobias sugarcoated by Miltown. So when he entered all of the Person domain that I still controlled he walked with solemn deliberation. Minister. Funeral director.

"I see you're back," he said, looking straight at me with glassy eye and blank brow.

"Yes," I said. Self-evident. The question translated was the following:

"What'd he say?"

"Hell, what d'ya mean, Brendan?" I was annoyed. How did he know I'd been to Hastings? What business of his was it anyway?

"Well, I thought maybe he'd said something about the program of the *Review*," which, translated, asked what was he going to do to Emory and, perhaps, Berrigan, since those little setting-up exercises at Pyles'.

"Nah, we just talked about poems for the magazine,

that's all. He wants me to get together some more stuff. Nothing else, Brendan."

He didn't believe me for a minute, because his world didn't work that way, and, come to think of it, Walton didn't either and *was* his world. Besides, Brendan's question really was: What was Hastings' mood, and what was his blood pressure, and did he look worried? I'd known what he meant, but I wasn't playing.

"Gee whiz, Will, Dick Klaus says Hastings is mad about Hungerford and blames us. And you know? He said something about Jason insulting Pyles. Do you know anything about it? I mean, golly, that's terrible, really terrible."

I didn't answer a thing. About then my stomach wasn't sitting too well, and I just wanted him to go, go, go. Anyway, he was only fishing to find out if he'd been implicated.

But he wasn't going to go.

"Will, I don't understand Jason getting involved like that. You can't go around insulting the profs. Why, if I were in their shoes, I'd be mad, too. And Emory, he doesn't seem to care what Hastings thinks of him, does he? Why can't he straighten out?" Which meant that if we weren't careful Emory would drag us all down with him. "I think you and I ought to give him some advice. Maybe if he apologized or got together with Dr. Hastings it would be okay. I mean, we do need to stick together."

He was pacing now, just as he had the first time I ever saw him.

"Anyway, let me give you some advice, Will. Stay cool, and play on Hastings' team, and keep a hand in with Cassoway. He'll help you out when it comes to the promotions. And then we'll have this old department by the balls. Yeeeeeh [off the ground, he], but you've got to keep calm. And just between you and me, I'd stay away from the student-poet crowd. You'll get the wrong kind of reputation with the professors. I mean, I understand and all that, but some people are more conservative."

Then suddenly the frayed old ropes that held down our hallowed hall were slashed and we were floating off into space together, Brendan and I, and who knows who else in his own little cell. The whole room seemed lightened, and I was held to my chair by an unknown force. If I looked out the window I expected to see Mars flash past. I couldn't stand it any longer.

"I'm tired, Brendan. Leave me alone."

He stopped in his tracks and looked at me; his eyes narrowed.

"Yeah . . . okay . . . yeah, fella, I will."

On the way home I tried to recite all the things I should have said, but I didn't have the profanity for it, and besides, what would have been the use? Never got home, as a matter of fact. Stopped off at the Green Lion, and they tell me that on top of a table there I said all of "The Lemmings," which is my drunk poem ever since Ryerson said it in Seattle, offered to lead a procession to Pyles' house, and then, when that didn't go over, to fill up a pitcher with piss. Next noon, when I woke up, it was awfully quiet around the house, and then I realized that it wasn't the house at all but the bedroom of a nice sweet serious little graduate student. Trudy Wells, I think it was. Let it be Trudy. But where was she? I lay there alone and looked at her B.A. diploma, stuck in her mirror, and her open wardrobe. I counted her shoes, which she kept on the hat shelf, and tried to keep my mind off yesterday. It was odd. I felt pretty good. No hangover. I noticed now noise from the kitchen.

She had always, to this moment, as far as I could remember, been Miss Wells. Poetry-writing class the year before. And that was that. Well, I dressed and smoked a fag or two, and she called breakfast from her little kitchen. Embarrassing. I didn't remember much of anything, and none of the important parts. Also, I couldn't stand the way she was watching me.

I started with, "Thanks for the breakfast."

"You're welcome. Hungry?"

"Yes."

Silence. She was smiling. Had I or had I not completely disgraced myself? Probably had. It was my pattern.

"You needn't be embarrassed," she said. "You were a perfect drunk. All the songs you sang were quite off key."

"God, what was I saying?"

"Well, from what I could gather, you have a pregnant wife somewhere and one that isn't pregnant here, and another girl friend named Ann, who is just about the best lay in the West." She lit a cigarette. "And that isn't the best way to compliment the girl of the moment." I thought to myself that she might make a poet yet. "And on top of that, you're going to blow this place for another galaxy."

A bit garbled, but the ring of truth.

"And boy! You certainly hate Berrigan!"

Hate, I thought. I am sick.

"This is my life. Where are the prizes?" I asked.

No answer. She was a pretty girl in a shy sort of way. I thought to myself maybe we could get on with it now, and I tried an oblique approach. But it wasn't right.

"No. I'm sobered up, too, now. Besides, you're just trying to be a gentleman." That endeared her to me. She was being very decent about the whole thing, and I was glad.

"Well, I *don't* have two wives."

"I supposed not."

I hadn't really any wife, the way I looked at it. And Laura decided the same the next day, because after a long cool discussion she allowed that even Father Dunn hadn't pierced my pagan heart, and past trading in my old frayed soul or limbering up my psyche I was a hopeless bet. So she agreed we couldn't make it any longer. I moved out.

Which meant she'd take the kids, and when after a few days we had lawyers involved, we tried to talk about it. But it still wasn't the time, and I just agreed to whatever her lawyer said. The kids were hurt and bewildered, and I think they were even a little afraid of me, and I went away nearly bawling. But it was past redeeming, and Laura knew it, and I knew it, and I think even Father Dunn was ready to admit it, though he did his best to the end, and he was always decent to me, deserving or not.

Poor Laura, the day after I toddled back from Trudy's she finally cried and told me it was Walton's fault and mine, and I'd changed after Hastings took me up, and what did I think I wanted to become, chairman or dean? And why was I bucking so hard?

Why were we all bucking so hard? Me smiling and murmuring "yes, yes" to Crowder and cracking jokes to Cassoway and shining my shoes to go over and eat Love Dove's faculty menu No. 2. Me, me, me, I thought, until my head seemed to blow up like a balloon, and by the mad logic of nightmare hold in its trembling membrane all the gas of Walton. I could not stand it.

For about a month I wandered around Walton, slept with a poetess or two, presided in the taverns, and made myself the big daddy of everybody who hated life and letters. I was waiting for Ann to say come ahead.

Berrigan began to avoid me. There were, I mused, merits in decadence. Warner took me aside and whispered fatherly advice. I thanked him and drank myself blotto that afternoon. I didn't see much of Jack or Jason either. Jack holed up in his little house banging out a book. Jason was around, but I floated out of his orbit. Then Jack up and resigned to take the Emerson job. He'd pull out on his grant at the end of the term and not come back. Warner blamed Hastings. Cassoway smiled like a cat. People in the old guard rejoiced, but there was lamentation here and there, mainly because others were jealous. Berrigan was nice about it. He worded it around that Jack just didn't measure up to Hastings' standards.

But I was really out of it, covered with a black cloud, which wasn't just up above me any more but descended to the ground. I was a real William Bond. I'd just barely meet my classes. Once or twice Jason, I know, covered up for me at meetings when a couple of critics came out from the East. Hastings still sent me poems to read, or, rather, Mrs. Bolyard did. And lo, some of my own stuff that I'd forgotten completely about sending in appeared in the fall issue.

That brought Berrigan around, or I thought that's what it was. He caught me coming back from class and waved the *Review* in my face. I had to listen to his opinion that I was the new Whitman or somebody. I thought for a moment of bearded Whitman at Walton. The Walton Walt, I. But I dismissed the thought as beyond credibility before I fell cackling on the floor. Of course, Berrigan didn't really want to talk about the *Review*. What he did want was to tell me he'd been offered a job. The world *is* mad, I thought. [It is.]

Amazing: When Kit Jensen's efforts to catch on at Walton failed or just faded away, he went to work on some other unsuspecting administrator and landed the chairmanship at Sciota. What was he doing now but calling on Brendan to join him? That didn't really surprise me, but it did surprise Jason, who thought Jensen was berserk but didn't think he was *that* berserk. Of course, Brendan was splitting his skin. Going through his mind was the thought that now he was in a league with Hungerford and Emory. He was wanted. Everyone wants his own personal stooge, and I hear help is hard to get since the war. Brendan's problem was whether to let Hastings know, whether to tell the department, whether to take the job—considering always Hastings' feelings.

Admit. Confess. For one glorious moment I saw the sun shining through a great big hole in the clouds as Brendan trod on over the horizon to his new paradise. And I thought maybe I could just make it at Walton after all. But I forgot, like the Japanese who rushed back into the burning building to rescue the Emperor's picture, that Brendan was really just a symbol. I was still up around Mars. Of course it was all illusion—there were still all the others, and Hastings, and Laura making the best of it in our old home. No.

Two days Berrigan worried me over whether to tell Hastings. I said, sure, go ahead, nothing to lose. But Brendan, poor bastard, was afraid Hastings would say good luck and so long. So he waited. Finally he went to Vanner, and that's just about what he got. Why not? No one ever got anything else from Vanner. Old Pappy sat behind his desk and puffed his pipe, allowed that Brendan would just have to make the decision for himself. Dejection. Because he didn't realize Vanner couldn't do much else, even for his good men. Not a breath of promotion or salary, and now the cat was out. So Berrigan had to go to Hastings.

I don't know what really happened; he came back like Alice's cat, wreathed in smiles at one end and probably at the other. Full of the old opportunity song. Go to Hastings and it's the old petrol pump. So Brendan was filled up and didn't take Jensen's job. [And so I sit here on these odd afternoons when I don't have to teach wondering when I'll get a new stripe, hearing now and then from a straggler. Brendan got a raise and a promotion, Dean-decreed, and now he has some kind of special job. Probably working for Mrs. Bolyard. What a lift-off. I can see him every day swaggering after his stomach through those halls.]

It was my own stupidity. It was that ray of light through the clouds. I knew my emotions were playing me false. Brendan's going away wasn't going to do me a thing. His star would ascend now without me, or stay fixed in the firmament (which was more likely, knowing his talents). He could find someone else for the shit-and-shovel detail. He was only the catalyst that sent the Walton elements churning—or whatever they do. I'm no Erasmus Darwin sort of poet.

For a while I thought, How in God's name can Jensen hate Hastings so and still want Berrigan? Because Jensen really did bug Hastings with his poison-pen notes after Hastings delayed and finally rejected his paper for the *Review*. [Straggler report: major American poet still trying to get his money for a poem in the first issue and theatening to publish a Druidic curse against the whole University.] Then Hastings must have chickened and said why not send another article. Well, that's asking for the deluge, because if there's anything Jensen has, it's another article. But he must have felt he was dropping them in the ash can for all he got in reply. I suppose they're reposing in an out bin somewhere right now in that nest of Old Mother Hoorah Bolyard.

Of course, there were thirty reasons why Jensen wanted Berrigan, all clearly expounded to me by Jason one cool afternoon. They probably weren't all true, but somewhere he had the right one. I pick the idea that Jensen needed a butler as much as the next administrator.

But I, for one, had buttled my last. After Brendan let it be known all over creation that he'd reluctantly turned down his old friend, who thought so much of him, for the grander opportunities of Walton, I even wrote a zinger to Jensen showing him how lucky he was. This was not lost on old Kit. From what he said about Berrigan in reply I could have supposed he had fired, not tried to hire, him! Ah, what loyalty!

The term dragged itself to a close. I felt as if Big Daddy Lipscomb had caught me on the bootleg play. But then Ann finally convinced George that they couldn't live together. It didn't take long for me to pack my belongings, because I didn't own anything any more.

[There are times in your life, I guess, when you know events are moving fast and you want to gather them all up into a ball, as the great one says you should, but it turns out to be impossible. So you float into limbo, and you put them off. Put them off at arm's length. And then soon you are avoiding them entirely like old dull acquaintances from the club.] So I made it out to Seattle, all right, ready to gather events, but just as I thought I had them all in a big armful, the way Big Daddy picks up the opposing backfield, I tripped like the clown with the billiard balls, sprawled, and life went in all directions.

Which meant, indeed, we waited a while. Or I thought we were waiting. For George, for Ann, and, okay, for myself; because George didn't want it to happen, Ann was pregnant and detached, and I was recuperating from my little operation. They had taken out ten years, and with that some of one's stomach is bound to go as well. It was unsatisfactory, but everyone cared so much that we couldn't do anything or even show anything.

Except Jack, and he had the heebie-jeebies, could never stand anything that wasn't going to be settled. So it was a strain between him and Ann, and I knew George was pestering him. And through it all Jack was trying to finish his book. [We grew apart over this, and we have to grow closer again if we can—new people now, different perspectives.]

Ryerson was as nice as anyone to me—to Ann, too. He seemed to accept our situation cheerfully. I suppose he chalked it all up to life and poetic experience. At any rate he put us in touch with Dick Fallon, whose story had triggered Tantrum A35—HH Ref. Walton in my file.

I began to think Jack was maybe right about that story. Fallon really did study sentiment, lived with it, told me one night he'd chucked things after the M.A. and gone to Boeing; in academe, as he saw it, pure feeling on every level was perverted and no one any longer could have a good cry. It wasn't that he indulged in sentimentality himself, but he understood its pathos, saw there was something relative about it. The sentimental depended upon the perceiver sometimes. That's what his story said. Those kids were sentimental, but it was pathetic. [Hastings was sentimental. I see that now. We really did hurt him when we packed our toothbrushes, combs, and trusses and headed out.]

I liked Fallon, liked his talk. His own sentimentality was in the direction of fishing and fish, rocks and trees and moss, and even the flies that lived along with those things. One weekend he took us up to his cabin near Snoqualmie, and then he gave it over to us for almost a month after the baby came. It wasn't an idyll, but we did have a good time doing nothing, going native, the kids almost naked running off into the forest and their hideouts, and Ann padding about barefooted. Fallon would come up with his wife, Nancy, on some weekends, and we'd loll around from siesta to fiesta with things like California wine and spaghetti in between. I could relax with Dick Fallon. He wasn't pushing anyone around, and he didn't give one damn about the world I'd left.

Even Jack, the one time he came up, was nearly convinced it was going to work. He was a horse that didn't want to be ridden, though, eying us, ready to break for it.

It sounds funny to some people that I went back, and to Kit Jensen's department, for God's sake, they say. The gossips around would be better off with their own business. I had mouths to feed, damn it, and I wasn't going to get much free time in the building laborer's trade and only a little money tending drawbridges. Those seemed to be the choices, considering my talents. So when Jensen wanted me as chief bard [well, he is his own jester, it turns out, since Brendan Bear turned down the position] I made the best deal I could for courses and hours, and we hit the trail for the flatlands.

Ann doesn't like the climate much or the way everyone says "don't" for "doesn't" or the brown two-pant suits all the men wear, and God we aren't in any intellectual or artistic capital. But I grew up in these plains and don't get the claustrophobia some people suffer from when the hills aren't there to catch them. I don't have much to show except a few more poems for all this time, but I do get printed here and there.

And I guess as a chairman Kit isn't so bad really. He has the virtue of his defects: honesty. Oh yes, it gets him into difficulties, but it's the plotters you've got to watch out for. I suppose it was foolish, but the other day I finally did it. I told him I thought he was wrong about the Mortimer poem, and pointed out the acrostic. Because he was going to class with it, and I knew someday someone would lay it on the line.

He took it all right. Even made a show of it.

"My God, good God!" He stretched to the ceiling. "What a shock of recognition!" He shouted, groaned, and paced, but the last I saw of him he was gaily off to his students steamed up over the new complexities he'd uncovered with an interpretation to match and all the fun of a dirty joke.

Now that's eternal optimism.

Not all here are like Kit. Hell, it's the same all over— whinnies in the hall, the Cassoways and the Warners, the Dickie Mice and Crowders. Eternal vigilance is my answer. I go home, and when I get there I can swear and rant and blaspheme the Dean, and Ann won't go tch, tch or purse her lips or take the local bear's side (because he's ubiquitous, too—the bear goes always with us). In fact, she'll laugh and sometimes run me one better in invective, and she has a fine eye for absurdity, without half the tolerance. She was really under wraps with George. Had everybody fooled. And that father of hers. She gets on him sometimes—the scoundrel. What an egotist!

That's how I stand it. Not hearing at my back the moral wheel turning and that gray feeling reaching to my scalp. Now what was it old Kit Jensen did yesterday when the Dean of Education called him up? There'll be hell to pay. But I don't bother, because I'm home from the plant, where only my private demons egg me on.

Jason Talbot

I TELL MY OWN TALE   Will is embarrassed
about what he's done, particularly taking a job with Kit
Jensen. But come to think of it, one doesn't often hold
actions against people. You decide somehow on what they
are. Then, of course, you *expect* them to act accordingly.

But sometimes they conform too well to their arche-
type, and that strains tolerance. Take Ann. She makes me
uneasy. She's the art-appreciation type, complete with
starry eyes. When she and Will came through Pierpont on
the way to Will's reading at the Poetry Center last spring
I realized that there must be a lot of politics among poets,
and if you got them all together, you'd eventually find out
who the Cassoways, Warners, and Berrigans were. The
whole evening they were with us Ann sounded like a conductor in the literary underground. I don't really mind
when Will exercises his own pet peeves and loves. He may
not even be a very good poet in the long run, but he's
worked at it, and he knows which poets have meant
something to him. He's earned his prejudices, I guess
you'd say. But Ann's prejudices are plastered to her like
decals, and the corners don't always lie down. What is the
point, really, of resenting the fact that Frost is invited to
the White House and the President has probably never

245

heard of Charles Olson? Oh, I admit she'd had some highballs by then (Laura could drink her under the table), but still, I can't see where she gets off resenting Frost. I'll even admit I don't dig Olson—I've tried, and I can read Williams and Stevens, but the Gloucester bit eludes me. Perhaps it's my loss, but I'll just guess that Ann can't understand much of it either. She simply picked up the jargon from the poet crowd Will corresponds with and goes to visit.

Now that's the sort of thing that draws me away from Ann, that and the fact that as I grow older, well damn it, I just don't go jumping and slobbering on people like an Irish setter. Will senses this, and he thinks it's over the divorce and Laura. But he's wrong. Will was a bit silly the way he carried on, but who can really judge someone else's demonic life? Better to judge oneself.

So be it. It was a long time before I really understood what had happened to me at Walton. Crowder provided the crucial clue on a fine clear spring day sometime after Cassoway's ascension to the chairmanship was announced. Will had taken off, Jack had resigned and gone away on his research grant, and Hastings had dissolved the magazine staff into thin air. I was sitting alone with some muddy coffee and the *Chronicle* in the Beaver Room when Crowder strolled in. Sure enough, he sidled up and dropped into a chair beside me.

"Got a cigarette?" he asked. I swore to myself then and there that the *next* time he bummed a cigarette from me I'd toss him the coins and point to the cigarette machine in the corner. Trouble was, Crowder would probably offer bland thanks. He was a notorious moocher. Once, I saw him actually steal a cigarette from Davis. Five or six of us were sitting in the Beaver Room at a table, and Crowder sneaked a fag out of Davis's pack while he wasn't looking. Oh it was sly, but I saw it. That was really Crowder's trouble, not sly *enough*.

Crowder always said the kind of thing you never say to someone who isn't a close friend. This time it was, "Well, Jay, I guess the developments haven't pleased you very much."

I suppose he knew I hadn't supported Cassoway for the chairmanship. All the same, his presumption annoyed me. I led him on.

"Oh, I don't know. What do you mean?"

"Well, er, ah, ever since the party and all that."

"What party?" I hadn't any idea what he was talking about.

"For Halloran. When you had the argument with Berrigan."

That really annoyed me.

"I didn't have any argument with anyone. What made you think that?" He smiled a smile designed to suggest immense irony. But I knew what made him think it, because I was thinking about Berrigan and Davis, and I myself pulling Berrigan away and taking him to the garden, and how Jack and Will and I laughed about it later, saying I was probably going to be sacked for roughhousing. We had underestimated Pyles's power, had written him off as old and unimportant. Well, who would have guessed that Hastings would play for his support, too? Not us; we were naïve, and we didn't have the vote. But Pyles did.

Crowder went on with it. "Well, of course I wasn't there, but I heard that you and Berrigan had a fight. Alex [I caught the chummy first name, all right] said it was unfortunate that the two of you had to settle your differences in Pyles's house." There was no use discussing all this with Crowder. I just let him go on.

"You know," he said, "personally I was glad you did it. Berrigan deserves it, the way he snubs some of the senior men here."

I knew of whom he was thinking—the Cassoway people Crowder lunched with and sucked up to. I could imagine what they had to say about Berrigan in their klatches.

But Crowder wasn't interesting me any longer. I had suddenly remembered Hastings' speech to the committee about good manners sometime in November, and I had sat blithely thinking it was directed against a couple of young berserks who made life miserable for Mrs. Bolyard over Hastings' vague promises of research money. Of course, Pyles hadn't passed a word with me since the party, but he'd never passed words with me anyway. And Warner made digs at Berrigan, and allowed that it was good someone had boxed his ears. I never really caught on that he was complimenting *me*. I realized better than ever now that to have scuffled with Brendan Bear was to have descended to the bear's level. I knew, indeed, that he walked with me and he talked with me. In my imagination he told me I was his own. I stayed on for another cup. I outlasted Crowder.

When I went back to dwell on the night of the skirmish, Davis and Berrigan receded and the great grinning skull head of Halloran filled my vision. Halloran, the professional. He would have broken up no fights, but, like a jackal, taken the field to pick up the spoils. He was a real people-user. From the moment he came off the plane, his teeth leering and his short forearm pointed toward me, elbow held in at his side so that somehow I came to him to shake hands, I was in the presence of the complete academic warrior. I wondered at once what kind of a match Henry Hastings would be for him. Halloran would approach Hastings skull-grinning, for Halloran knew that Hastings had invited him because they had been at school together and he wanted to show off his prowess.

"And you gentlemen, ahem, I believe, are one of the exhibits. But if you're any good—" he frowned evilly— "Hank won't be able to hold you very long here." I had

never thought of that very seriously. Showing us off to big
shots like himself, Halloran thought, meant the good
among us would be lured away. I noticed after Halloran's
visit that Hastings himself took this line in a self-congrat-
ulatory way when he periodically launched forth on his
great-opportunity spiel.

And I remembered as well Halloran on the ride to his
hotel that night after Pyles' party, laying out his own
Baedecker to Walton with the uncanny ability of the professional intrigue ferret.

"I talked to Hastings today. He's changed. My, what
jib."

I remained silent.

"Oh." He laughed now. "I know I won't get any of you
boys to say anything, and there's no use me telling you to
watch your step." I knew he knew I knew. "But I can't
understand this Berrigan fellow, the one with the wife.
What use is he? Certainly, ahem, certainly gives a bad
impression. Streetcar conductor." He leered, giggling.

Then he startled me. "Should have let him disgrace
himself—tactical error on your part, Talbot. Probably
regret it."

He'd seen it all and calculated how it would fit into
academic politics. He was shrewd, and he was a realist.

"Still mum?" He leered again, and then I had to laugh.

"No," I said, "you have us all nailed down, all right.
Berrigan's just the spear in our side."

He liked that and giggled some more, even though the
metaphor was a bit confused. He continued to mangle it.
"Henry and his disciples. Say, what do you do, Talbot? I
mean, you teach the modern stuff? We have some call for
that. Of course, you'd have to go back to the Victorians,
ahem, ha ha, some of the time."

"Yes, well, I can manage pretty well back to Tenny-
son. I try to keep up."

"Hah." He stared out the car window as he said it and

then changed the subject. I had the impression of drawbridges raised, of mountains moved. I had noticed he liked Betty Lou.

The new subject was not far off. "So Vanner's stepping down?" he asked.

"Oh, he's been talking about it off and on for a couple of years."

"Well, he is. Hank's after a new one. Wouldn't have it myself. Too much shoveling out for the old heart, ha ha, and plenty of that at home yet. Ours wants out, too. I, ahem, I'm in line, of course. You watch who comes down here from now on. But it'll be a fight with the rednecks. Law of the Medes and Persians, ha ha, you know. Personally, I think he'll compromise. Needs support when he pushes for the presidency."

There it was, and in a month Hastings was vice-president of Walton and on his way. I kept thinking to myself all fall and winter, before I knew that Berrigan had gotten off clean again, that he couldn't afford to keep bears any longer. But I knew it wasn't right. I remember one night before Will left his saying that nowadays when Hastings looked into a mirror Berrigan smiled back, shouting "Hooey, hooey, hooray." There was something to it. Hastings' dialogues with Berrigan when he paced his office and Berrigan stood at wriggling attention were a sort of do-it-yourself psychiatry. Hastings really needed him.

What I still didn't understand was that Cassoway and Pyles expected Brendan to act like a bear and were only shocked when they saw someone other than Brendan— namely me—apparently growling and pawing around. I hadn't applied my own rule. Besides, there was something about the relationship between Hastings and Berrigan that made people decline to broach the subject of Brendan outright. Perhaps it was fear, never articulated, that Berrigan was, really was, Hastings' darkened self.

And to heave that being up into light would release an unknown menacing panic in our leader.

But I doubt that Brendan was the tattletale villain Will made him out to be; Will was looking for an all-purpose scapegoat. Brendan may have overheard Jack advising Hungerford, but he wouldn't have told. Indeed, Brendan's sense of tribal loyalty prevented him from doing anything so rash, and he was never sure of Hastings.

No, I'm pretty sure it was Ellen Fraser who spoke too much to Hastings, and I think Jack knew it. I remember having a beer one day with Jack while he waited for Ellen after work. We were discussing Sheffer and how Hastings had sent him off on leave and then replaced him as administrator of the Honors Program while he was gone. Jack was telling me that Sheffer was playing it cool. But he was bitter. When Ellen showed up, Jack whispered, "Let's not discuss it any longer."

But the real reason I suspect her is something Berrigan himself let fall. When Brendan received his job offer from Jensen, he had a real heart-to-heart with Hastings, and Hastings convinced him he should stay. It was bad, because when Brendan told me about it he kept punctuating the speech with wasn't it too bad I'd leagued myself with Emory, and it was important to have Hastings' trust to get along, and look what Hastings would do for loyalty. Look at Brendan—promotion next year, salary, courses, and research opportunities, administrative jobs. Look, even Ellen Fraser, why she was hardly important at all, was she? Just a kid, but she'd helped Hastings out, and she had really been enthusiastic when she worked on his projects. Why he could even remember hearing her telling Hastings just why Hungerford should stay on, with all the wonderful materials she had been seeing safely into the rare-book room. She was even ready to admit to Hastings that Jack was wrong there.

But Brendan didn't go on. He seemed to think he had
let something slip, and quickly he changed the subject.
Then I had to listen to him on how to handle the department. I could tell, though, that his advice was really a
form of gloating. He knew and I knew that my grade in
the department's book was descending.

And finally he ended in a sweat, saying that, by God,
when he made associate professor next year the department wouldn't be pushing *him* around any more, and
there'd be no more waiting helplessly for the right
courses. He'd have *power*. At about that instant a new
instructor named Dan Leary dropped by my office. He
was in time to witness this mild bear barrage, standing
openmouthed while Berrigan recounted where Emory
had gone off the track and ruined himself and how Will
would surely go off if he kept up the beatnik role much
longer. I felt sorry for Dan, just starting out.

Another time, with Ellen, I saw Jack get off on the
general untrustworthiness of administrators, and I could
tell that Ellen didn't like the subject. Jack's line was that
the successful administrator must be deceitful at times because he has to be an improviser and work with people
from day to day. All that was well and good, but he
added, "Nevertheless, they ought to tell the truth when it
can be told. Some get to the point where they can't give a
straight answer to anyone about anything." During this
lecture Ellen was stiff and unhappy. She knew who the
real subject of the discourse was.

And Ellen was unhappy because I was there to hear,
but there's no point in going into all that. Jack and Ellen
had some sort of thing going on that involved Hastings,
and I never was quite sure what it added up to, except
that it had something to do with personal independence.
Well, they were both their own people. Strange, after the
competition and all, after Jack left I used to see Ellen
alone having coffee or walking alone, never with a man

all that spring. I guess Jack would overlook Ellen talking
to Hastings because Hastings didn't ever manage to use
her, while he was always using people like Berrigan.

But the question was no longer "What about Hastings?," for by now Hastings had become not the variable
but the known quantity in our world. He had no more
surprises for us. Our problem was to face the enigma of
ourselves. Could we muster more than sycophantic passivity or stony-faced ferocious resistance? There was,
after all, that curious demon of energy and enthusiasm in
Hastings, and somehow we couldn't nurture it for whatever good it was capable of bringing forth. We so avoided
the temptation to extract personal gain after a while that
no good of the general sort came out at all. Our very
strength of resistance proved to be a weakness.

Will flew from the whole business because he was
frightened by the specter of his own sycophancy. He flew
from the temptation to want the world of hooey that Berrigan produced so grossly from under the rocks of our
own consciousness. Perhaps in hating Berrigan we were
simply hating our own temptations. But we should have
looked skeptically at our own resistance.

Will's last flight is said in the legends that survived him
to have been in the classic style of the day—spread eagle
into the pond. But from my point of vantage it wasn't
really spectacular at all; he just faded away. Betty Lou
and I saw less and less of him. One day late in the fall
Warner called me into his den and ambled slowly up to
his real subject, which was Will. Warner seemed to like
Will—if affection was an emotion he really possessed. At
any rate, he believed that in a secret ballot Will would
oppose Cassoway, so he took the serious fatherly tone.
He'd heard tell, so he said, that Will was having troubles.
I nodded, but not knowingly. It was my intellectual
basket-case look. Well, he went on, lots of people have
their troubles and some jeopardize their careers. "Like

our friend down the hall, getting reckless." That was Sheffer. But Will had a good future here, nobody to bother him, tolerance of poets in the department. The question was, Warner said, how much beatnikism would Hastings tolerate?

"You know, Jason, Hastings is a conservative gentleman." His lip curled slightly as he said this. "And all those goings-on I hear about, well, they'll get back."

"Hell, what's the difference?" It was Jack Emory's voice. He stood in the door. "All Hastings wants is loyalty. Look at Berrigan." Jack had overheard. Recently he had been on fairly cordial terms with Warner.

Warner motioned him in. "You may think so, but there are certain kinds of scandal that will terrify him, especially when he gets to be president."

"Ha," said Jack. "How soon?"

"Not long, not long," and Warner doodled contemplatively on his desk blotter. "Not as long as you think."

"You make it sound like days."

"No, months—vice-president in days."

And Warner called it. Hastings' elevation to v.p. came two weeks after our meaningless talk about Will. There was not, however, any immediate change in things. Now we were trooping to another, more leather-bound office for our recognizably fewer communal duties. Will's decline continued. I began to measure it in proportion to the number of times I would see him. When we met I noticed an embarrassed reserve. Rather than become more hyperbolic in his denunciations, he chose silence, and I realized that when Will was most verbal in his assaults against the world he was also happy. Will might really have slid slowly into the pond like a silent crocodile if a couple of things hadn't happened.

The first had to do with Jack. When Jack interrupted Warner and me, he had something to say to us. At the first blank moment he brandished a letter.

"What do you think of this?"

Warner, his glasses off, held the letter at arm's length, and studied it. "A good offer," he said. "You going to take it?"

"What would you do?" Jack said. "Show it to Jason."

"Well, I'd surely have some fun." Warner handed me the letter.

It was a good offer, an associate professorship, a big raise in salary, a reasonably good institution. I knew Jack was as good as gone. But he was restraining himself. Warner must have known this, too, but he didn't let on and treated the whole thing as if it were a difficult decision. Jack and he still kept up between them the fiction of his commitment to Walton.

"If I have anything to say about it, the department will meet the offer. Then it will be up to Caesar."

Jack laughed, but it was an ironic laugh. "Well, I'll take it to Vanner."

But Jack was playing, and Warner was playing, and we knew that Vanner would merely call a meeting. After it was over I heard that they couldn't get any kind of answer out of Hastings. Jack resigned the next week. When Will heard all about it he was fit to be tied. It may not be a coincidence that he moved out on Laura a few days later, and for a while he just bunked around where there was an extra bed. He made it to most of his classes— enough at least to keep everyone except Warner and perhaps a few others in the dark. I took a couple of sessions at the last minute for him when he rang up and gave some thin excuse. These requests apparently made him feel guilty, because after the second time we saw almost nothing of each other. He was embarrassed or ashamed.

The second thing was the business with the police. Will and a young visiting poet named Hugh Richard were on the town. They had parked a car late at night about two feet into a bus stop near the Green Lion, and a cop ticketed them just as Richard was emerging from the bar. He went over to discuss matters with the officer. From there on the stories conflict. Richard said in court that the officer used abusive language. The officer said Richard was drunk and disorderly. Will left the Green Lion a few minutes after Richard. Apparently he saw Richard and the officer arguing and went in their direction to make peace. He'd had some beers. When the wagon came he was hauled away, too, and the first charge was assaulting an officer.

I don't believe it. I don't think Will would assault anyone, drunk or sober. His weapon is the blade between his teeth, alack. But he may have made some fancy oratorical thrusts of the stiletto, four-letter variety. The whole business was unimportant, but the Walton newspaper is always happy to discover professors cutting up, and it took some quick action by Vanner, who had friends on the *Chronicle* and in city hall, to get Will away clear without a trial. Warner told me that as soon as the call came from the police station Vanner was in his car and down to the station, talking to the police and then putting pressure on the reporters. Didn't call a meeting.

Nevertheless, the bug was out. A sort of ground swell of rumor began to form, and it got mixed up unfortunately with the Temple business of the year before. Scandal in the English Department! I would hear things now and then about Will tossed off irrelevantly in people's conversations. The kids were calling him "the Pope," and it was well known that he corrected his papers in a far corner of the Green Lion. Clearly if he was going to be fired it wouldn't be for the reason that Temple was let go. The poetesses seemed to be taking care of him.

By now everyone knew that Jack wouldn't be back after his leave. Suddenly everyone who had a gripe or a piece of gossip came to him to unload. Hatfield took him to dinner; Warner closeted with him; Klaus and Davis dropped by to see whether he could go to lunch. People who had studiously ignored him now recognized his presence in the halls. He was a celebrity even among the legions of Cassoway, for those discontented ones had never dreamed that he was anything but on the way up at Walton. His differences with Hastings were magnified out of all proportion to fact. Crowder, I hear, worded it around that Jack had wanted to be editor of the magazine, that he was jealous of Berrigan. But others saw him as a sort of hero; they had "misjudged" him. He stood for sanity, after all. In the midst of this Jack held his peace. It must have taken a good deal of restraint.

When the semester ended, Will just disappeared, didn't even tell us he was leaving—shoved off. This surprised and saddened me. We had been good-enough friends. I wondered now how good. Warner simply shook his head as if to chalk up another casualty in a long war.

When the word got through to the multitudes, Klaus called on me. He affected perplexity, but you could see he was tickled by the intrigue. Why was good old Will quitting? What would he DO? No new job, no security, a pretty good deal with Hastings tossed high in the air. And Jack, too, what about Jack? By the time I had patiently explained the truth about the Fallon episode, Hungerford, and other more ephemeral matters, Klaus was aflutter with the enormity of his own danger. Klaus in his own way respected Emory and wondered how such a person could have so surrounded himself with booby traps. I began to think that boobies were made, not trapped, and then I castigated myself for wasting my time with Klaus and relaxing my mind with such puns.

But, Will was a mystery. I didn't think Will had it in him. I didn't think he had the guts. I had become accustomed to Will's exaggerated exasperation and discounted it plentifully in order to arrive at reality. One way I rationalized it was that Will was really running out on his marriage, not spitting in Walton's eye. But I wasn't convinced. Maybe there was some hidden reservoir of strength in Will that I missed. Maybe his cowardice was really only surface embarrassment, a sort of egotism, and it was this that made him, not even by choice, fade away from Betty Lou and me without even a good-bye.

I said that we all have our troubles, and I started out to tell about mine. But mine didn't mature until the second semester, when Jack Emory and Will Person were gone. I missed Jack. The last week he was in Walton he gave what he called a true party—that meant his real friends. I was a bit surprised that Warner was there, but I knew now that Warner amused Jack and could no longer really touch him with his involvement in campus politics. Ralph Ware was along, and Will was there, too, but he ended up asleep in a neighbor's car on the street, and I believe Jack finally bunked him on a davenport. I hardly had a word with him. What I remember best was that he sang lustily in Jack's front yard, "I am a poor slob, a poor Walton slob," off key and loudly, to annoy the neighbors, for whom he had some odd hatred.

Jack was playing the stoic experienced warrior. Perhaps he was unconsciously aping Warner. I don't know, but it didn't quite fit him, because he was really a mental fidgeter. He said to me, as he watched Ralph Ware undo a bourbon bottle in the kitchen, "We come and go, but Ralph stays, endures, and publishes." It was a remark meant to be overheard, and Ralph did hear it and laugh.

"That's the way I feel tonight. I'm the land itself."

"How do you survive, Ralph?" Jack asked, grinning. "Don't you register, or is it some newfangled academic thermostat?"

"Don't think I don't care, boy; but you'd be surprised how many poems you can write and scenes you can sketch out during faculty meetings. I listen only with this ear. Besides, Walton's been good enough to me—lots of

summer here, the kids like it, Margaret has friends among
the townies. Hell, I may even end up regional."

To me the town of Walton hardly existed except to sat-
isfy material needs. I had been there two years and knew
hardly anyone outside the University. I think Jack was in
the same position. It wasn't that I avoided people; the opportunity never seemed to arise. I suppose I'm socially
passive. Betty Lou knew some of the neighbor wives, but
I merely nodded to the husbands and they to me. I don't
bowl or play ping-pong, my golf is horrible, and the yard
is my hell. They are suspicious of us, I thought. It isn't
just the old business about radicals on the campus and all
that. They really don't know what we do. And I had
come to the point where I only imagined what they did.

"Mow their lawns and cook their steaks," Jack said.

"No, there are some darned interesting people around
here, besides the executive class," Ralph said. "Anyway,
that's been done."

"Then you admit that you see these people for the sake
of your novels."

"Not quite, Jack—for the sake of my own experience.
But you don't go out ruthlessly and build your experience. You just do it, you let it happen. You don't fight it,
at least. The point is that I find myself doing things. It's a
drag sometimes." He was pouring drinks.

Ralph got more kick from talking about anchovies to
the Italian on the corner than he would from a whole series of academic victories. I remember one day when
Jack was madder than hell about something Klaus had
said or done, and Ralph stopped him.

"And what did you expect from Klaus?"

Nothing more. Jack ceased, cocked his eyebrow. He
knew he'd been had. "Just that, just that," he shouted, but
it was histrionic now, not from the soul. I admired Ralph's
seaworthiness, but I had a real affection for Jack's shouting smile.

Anyway, I missed him.

And so I was disheartened when the second semester began, in February. There was the awful indignity of Brendan Bear thumping his chest over the offer from Jensen. But then he was thrust into a dungeon of solemn worry by Hastings' next act, which was to inform us all by curt letter that the *Walton Review* staff was no more, that "in the future the *Review* will operate with an editorial board at large, which will, in fact, comprise the entire faculty of this university in a single ongoing interactive endeavor." Hastings had taken all he could and perhaps dished out all he had. Anyway, no one could say that Hastings was not still thinking big.

I did have to endure one more romp with Berrigan, who came around and laid the blame partly on me with a homily about loyalty and cooperation. He saw me obviously as the leftover particle of Emory spirit. I didn't quite exude confidence in the chief.

You know, I think perhaps Brendan was right. Maybe Hastings was a bit frightened of me. Shaving in the mirror one day after Brendan's visit, I thought to myself, There's something about that face. The moment passed quickly, like a shower in spring, but I keep recalling it. It wasn't so much resistance, after all. No, it was—well, no one wants to be watched as if he were behind bars. But you must live with yourself. Too late to change those creases by then. Besides, Brendan and Wilma didn't bother us much any more. I had the sense of an order passing. It was funny, too, how after Hastings told Brendan he'd be promoted Brendan stopped pushing criticism and new modern-literature courses and knocking the old guard. Once, in May, I saw him at lunch with Crowder and Hatfield. Later on, I suppose, he was at Cassoway's table.

Because about March Vanner resigned the chairmanship. I didn't hear about it until one day Hatfield came barging into my office with a big sheet of paper.

"Heah, heah, you'll sign this, won't you, Talbot? Need to get some decent administration, some leadership for once. Put some life back in the old place." It was a petition in behalf of Cassoway. I decided not to explain, just told him I wasn't backing anyone as yet. I hoped he'd understand. Oh yes, he understood. Said he didn't much like people shoving things under his nose either. I could think it over, but don't sign it if I didn't want to, no, damn it, don't sign under duress! I almost liked him for those moments. An odd one in his own pack.

The petition, I'm told, eventually had over half the department on it, and Warner was licked before the whistle blew. It was either Cassoway or someone from the outside. I must say that old Alex ran a clean campaign. He sat on his porch like McKinley and let the opposition wear itself out in protests. He did not change. He gathered in those who came to him—the great departmental septic tank, Will once said—but he never sought votes. He was neither more nor less friendly to me when we met in the hall. It was still the execrable "Jay boy," with the blank smile, which signified nothing and certainly nothing good.

The only hope was that Hastings would not want him; but I guessed that Cassoway might just turn out to be Hastings' candidate. Our once formidable committee no longer met or even acted except through Berrigan, who was now apparently in charge of the critical series. We had no influence. It was a lull before the storm, or so it appeared.

Meanwhile, I had received a letter from Halloran at Pierpont. It raised the question whether I might be interested in making a move. If I was, he would take it up with the chairman, and something might be arranged. Nothing was simple, I would have to remember. I studied the letter. It was brief. Was this one of those roundabout ways that a department sometimes has of feeling you out un-

officially before the official powers have to commit themselves to paper? Or was this Halloran's private business? I
could not tell. I did not really want to become involved in
the politics of Pierpont, but it was possible, too, that I
would need to discover an escape hatch fairly soon. So I
wrote back marshaling my interest. Finally the chairman,
name of Groat, sent me a curious letter which suggested
that his department really needed a Victorian man for the
next year but in a year's time the modernist post would
come open. I sensed that the letter was a reluctant one,
and I pondered further commitment. Besides, I wasn't all
that enthusiastic about Pierpont. It was a long way off, in
Pennsylvania, and the move would take us even farther
than we now were from Oklahoma and the folks. But I
suppose smart old Halloran had sensed the tone of things
at Walton and knew if he dangled a little bait I would
probably bite. I said I'd come along to be looked over.

It was not an auspicious visit. I arrived in town rather
late in the evening, and Groat hadn't, for some reason,
been able to meet me at the airport. Halloran had hinted
that he would remain discreetly in the background, so
there was no one around when I came in. I began to
think, on the dark ride from the airport in a gas-leaking
limousine, that some of the hoopla we put on for visitors
was not so bad after all. I tumbled into my hotel room
nervous and tired, slightly annoyed. I wasn't anybody, I
knew; but, just the same, I was their guest.

No one was to pick me up in the morning. I found my
way through town to the campus, situated on a hill
among immense trees. It was very, very impressive, with
its old Georgian colonial architecture and its air of gentil-
ity retrieved from another age. It was not the new academic world. But where were the people? At 10:00 A.M.
it was as if summer vacation had set in. Then finally I saw
one or two tied, jacketed, and white-bucked young men
ambling along; but no masses of students in the various

states of undress we called "collegiate" at Walton, no policemen directing traffic, and, above all, no coeds. Pierpont had never admitted women.

In the English Department's office, a large sweating secretary with a deep whiskey baritone confronted me as if I were from another planet. She looked fierce, but I was glad by that time to see another speaking, living being. She sent me into Groat's office without more than the usual ado—after I was able to certify my birth record, my fingerprints, my rank. The last left her unimpressed, probably confirmed her first reaction to me.

Groat was a short, balding gentleman with a lugubrious, tired air about him; but he did not delay in setting up for me an itinerary of interviews with significant departmental powers. I had the distinct feeling that he wished others to perform these distasteful duties involved in my presence. Eventually he mumbled something about Halloran's coming by later. That was, I suppose, to lay the blame where it belonged.

My first encounter was with a man named Bryan. I had heard of him, and I knew he was the person I was to replace. Groat pointed me to his office, and I was on my own. I knocked, and Bryan opened his door, offered a hand while examining the chandelier, and retreated at once behind his desk, which he had situated in executive fashion, facing the door. There he rummaged in a file. I sat down.

"Let's see, hmm, now, you are—you're Mr., ah, Talbot." Long pause. "From where?"

I decided to let him play out his little game. He knew damned well who I was and where I came from. He had been waiting for me.

Finally he produced some papers and laid them neatly before him on his desk.

"Oh yes, Walton—yes. And you're in the modern field?"

"To a certain extent." I did not like this man. Why should he be interviewing me as if I were a master's candidate he had never seen?

Then it came clear. He was practicing.

"Well, you realize that the job for which you are applying is the one I am leaving. I am taking the chairmanship at Suffolk, as you may know."

I didn't know, I wasn't strictly an applicant, and I was getting mad.

So I told him.

Curiously enough he did not trample up his lair or even bare his fangs. In fact, his whole attitude changed, and he became slyly confidential. Face down the barbarians, I thought, and it worked. If you are going to look like a lion, you might as well roar a little.

"This isn't a bad job, Talbot, not a bad job. I'm not leaving because I'm fed up, you know. There are, of course, problems. Halloran and Groat don't get along, but Halloran has power, and Groat listens to him. If he holds the vote, Halloran probably has the chairmanship in the bag for next year. Groat wants to step down anyway."

It's the same all over, I thought. Only the names are changed, to fool the innocent.

"But politics aside, life is pleasant here. If anything, it's too pleasant."

What he meant was the usual. There were some people who were dead, but their bodies had somehow never been claimed; consequently they had to be tolerated. They wouldn't go away.

"What about the administration?"

"The Dean, the President? Oh, they're all right. The Dean's a chemist who leaves us alone most of the time. The President, well, he's a lawyer really. Conservative, traditionalist. The administration doesn't move much here. Frankly, it's a source of dismay to me. There's a lot to be done." Hastingsism.

Whew, I thought. Let them stay where they are. This sounded like a good-enough post-Walton rest camp, if nothing more.

Bryan hadn't turned out to be too bad after all. A bit pompous perhaps. He'd begun with a neat piece of white paper and a well-sharpened pencil to make notes on my answers, but he ended up letting me conduct the interview. I should have had the pencil and pad.

Then Halloran burst in, breathing hard. He had meant to stay away until noon, but I sensed that he couldn't restrain himself.

"Getting along all right? Just wanted to say hello; I believe Groat will want to show you around." That was my signal, but Bryan didn't respond, so I got up to take my leave. Bryan remained vague and preoccupied. I noticed that Halloran had barely acknowledged his presence. No vote there any longer.

In the hall he said sharply, "Bryan's out of it." And that was that. I was returned to Groat. Pierpont's system of faculty selection was grinding its gears, perhaps skidding on wet pavement, like Spenser scholarship. Out in the spring air, heavy with blossoms, Groat began a curious monologue. He would want me to be sure I liked it here. There were problems. He'd learned, himself, to adjust to the slower pace, and there were a good many traditions which seemed silly to outsiders but meant a lot to the old-timers. Could I, by the way, take the Victorians just for one year? He was really worried about that. Besides the modern lit there would be other teaching I'd have to prepare for. I could not tell whether he was regretting that he himself had come to Pierpont and was waving me away or trying to remove me from the picture by systematic discouragement.

I never really found out. He went off the record now, asking about people at Walton—Alex Cassoway, whom he'd known years ago in graduate school. "Poor old Alex," he mused, and then laughed. "Poor old Alex. They finally gave him his Ph.D. though." The "though" he left hanging. In spite of what? But I could guess what he meant. I told him Cassoway was an important man at Walton. He offered a short smile and asked me if I was really interested in this job. I said, finishing the sentence he had interrupted, that Cassoway might be the next chairman. He grinned, repeating his question. I said I was. Somehow I had broken the ice.

That night, Halloran had me around for drinks and to meet people. It was the usual slow, pointless 9:30 party that we all somehow keep putting ourselves through. After everyone had stayed the necessary length of time, we were alone.

"Well, what do you think?" he said. "Will you take it?"

"I've had no offer." No trump leader I. Were they that afraid to be turned down?

He didn't like that, but he knew the score. "Well, that's shrewd, but let me tell you, there's no use hiding it. Groat will quit the chairmanship next year, and I'm the only possible choice. You can include that in your calculations. You'll hear from us." Yes, I supposed that Bryan hadn't been in Halloran's bag, and that I'd be the crucial vote. Halloran would try to bull me through, and then he'd simply waltz into the job he wanted.

I went back to Walton with all that very definitely in my thoughts. I was greeted, almost as if it had been planned as part of the plot, with the announcement that Alex Cassoway had been appointed chairman of English. A *fait accompli,* Warner, red-faced and stony in his office, called it. Hastings, I now knew, had retired to his inner sanctum. The hobby boys were no more. Those who had not dispersed to the four winds would really have to scramble for Cassoway's favor. And for some it would not be easy. I wondered what this would do to Brendan Berrigan. I suspected what it would do to me.

Another day, and a letter came from Groat. It said little. They were glad to have seen me, grateful for having received my bibliography (there were perhaps a few too many reviews compared to articles), and no doubt I would hear from them again shortly. Then a curious negative sort of letter, which began by not offering me an associate professorship and asking me whether I would accept my present rank.

I had prepared myself for this eventuality. The job had not attracted me *that* much, so I declined the lower rank. I thought that Groat was trying to shake me off his back, probably because of Halloran. As an assistant professor I would not have a vote.

Then for a few days I was convinced that luck had deserted me for good. Because Cassoway began to have little heart-to-heart talks with his staff. I would never have declined even Groat's reluctant offer after my own interview. It was a disaster of its own unique kind. Alex puffed his pipe, and I sat with nothing to say.

"Jay boy, let's get to the point," he said. "Just what is the future for you here? Warner is comparatively young still and sits on your field. I won't deny either that there are people opposed to your promotion. They have at times resented your manner. Take Dr. Pyles, for instance. I don't think he will see reason. And you have not been deeply engaged in department affairs, but those instead of the, ahem, College."

Revenge works itself out, I thought. With Pyles I am a boor, and Cassoway is still relishing his new power.

"I hear you have been approached by Pierpont."

"Well, yes." I didn't say that I had already posted my reply.

Cassoway leaned forward to fill his pipe. "I doubt that your offer will help you with promotion here. You should know that."

So there it was. For a wild moment, I felt like rushing out to phone Halloran to say I'd reconsidered. But I knew that would be a mistake. I was getting cleverer. I knew I was stuck.

Later on I learned, and, sadly, from Berrigan, that in the meeting of the Critique of Culture Committee, now composed of Henry Hastings and his trained bear alone, Hastings had said he knew of my trip to Pierpont. He was writing me off. "No young man around here is going to force his promotion that way." He even intimated that Emory had tried it. Anyway, Cassoway must have known of Hastings' displeasure. By a simple stroke Hastings could have seen me through. Instead, he had given up on us as a group, gained the alliance of the whole Cassoway troupe, and thus trapped probably a majority of the department in his camp. The balance of power had wheeled around the still minority of Warner. I was thinking dark thoughts, but they remained deep inside. There was no one for them to talk to.

But then Groat pushed the old chair up to the typewriter again. It must have taken all his energy. They had reconsidered and would offer me an associate professorship. I wondered if they had refigured the ratio between my essays and reviews or had made some simple comparisons with their own bibliographies. In the next mail came a jovial note from Halloran.

"Good boy!" his typewriter chortled. "You held out, and he had to come through."

I could see that he considered me a potentially worthy ally, because by awful chance I had appeared to play in behalf of my career with cunning or dignity or both. I had not sold myself cheaply.

►

It was a hot summer down at the folks' place in Ardmore, and I was just as lazy as I could be for the month we were there. Chuck and I did some fishing in Lake Texoma, and I was tickled pink when he caught some cats on the first day. I suppose you know what a gar looks like. They were my luck. But I wasn't complaining, not after my escape. Anyway, they don't look bland, like Cassoway. You know what they are. All that month I'd try to sleep late, but it wasn't easy in the heat, and the evaporative coolers the folks had just wheezed and whined in my head. I'd finally breakfast and walk downtown for coffee at the counter in what you couldn't really any longer call a drugstore, and then I'd drop into Dad's store, where he'd probably be sitting in a rocker talking to a couple of old gentlemen friends in from the country. Not much business really, except Saturdays, and then I'd go down and help weigh out the nails and sell pots and pans and sometimes a big item of hardware. Betty Lou lazed around, too, but she also took some of the load off Mother, for whom washing and general housework were getting to be a big chore. Just nothing, in other words, happened. Yeats be damned. I was drained of academic effort.

This is why, perhaps, Will's letter sticks in my mind. It became an event in an otherwise eventless period. It was the first direct word from him since before he had left Walton in January.

> Jay boy (Hah),
>
> I suppose you'll be kicking out soon to work for that old sidewinder Halloran. Remember what I told you about his inshoot, and wait him out. He's fast, but wild. You will be delighted, by the way, to see the enclosed, sent to me direct from you know where. [In the letter

was a newspaper picture of Henry Hastings apparently receiving a check from or offering a check to three large gentlemen, a set Cheshire grin on his face. Will had captioned it: "Okay, boys, here's the cash, now go get Person." I took this as a good sign, but the rest of the letter was not up to it.]

We are [I was supposed to know who "we" were, I guess] holed up in the mountains till our cash runs out. And that won't be long. Nothing to move but an easel, my typewriter, and voluminous files. [Will kept carbons of all his correspondence. "Money in it for someone, maybe," he'd say.] It gets down near freezing in the morning here, and when it's clear I mean to tell you I feel invigorated. Like old Frederic Henry himself. [He didn't, you notice, say anything about Ann's pregnancy, but she would have had the baby by now. Of course, I didn't know about it then.]

I suppose I'll have to find something to keep life and soul together—like teaching, maybe, but I dread the thought. Jack says that it's all a matter of simple physiological reaction. We couldn't take the pace. But I wish it was. No sir, it is a moral question. What was shit to Jack and you and myself was Shinola to twerps like Klaus and Crowder. Someone is wrong. It is, after all, a moral question. It *was* either shit or Shinola. Anyway, I feel cleaner inside here. [He *had* been rereading *Farewell to Arms,* the old sentimentalist.] So if you hear of anything, let me know.

The letter cracked a few jokes later on about Walton people. Apparently Will's spies were still out, but the characters he mentioned were graduate students and poets, people I didn't know. So the jokes may have been better than I thought. It was funny in a way that Will didn't seem to realize I hadn't known all those people.

Will's appeal wasn't lost on me. I sensed the embarrassed reserve that had grown up between us, but I knew also that he was appealing, as directly as his pride would allow, for help. I suspected he really was on his uppers, and though at the time I didn't know they had a new baby, I could tell by the odd reference to "we" and the easel that Ann was indeed with him.

But I had no pull anywhere. Not much hope in mid-summer anyway. Then suddenly I thought of my old pen pal. It would be the irony of ironies, but it was worth a try. I must pride myself, for a change, on my cleverness. I was very straightforward and simply told Kit Jensen that if he had a temporary appointment open at Sciota he might be able to get Will Person, the poet, back into academe, from which he had retreated in disgust because —well, because of certain events and people. I was a manager of people, a success at last. I thought of Jack scowling, of Jensen hooked to my line like a gar. It was Jensen's opportunity to show the world—namely Hastings. And besides, old Kit liked me and somehow wanted me to like him, perhaps even to overlook the idiocy of his offering Berrigan a job.

Whether Will knew what I had done or not, I don't know. When he and Ann came through, they never mentioned it. And Will's occasional letters that first year didn't let on a thing. I'll admit I was a bit miffed at them when they were here, because they were both playing hard at the antiacademic game, even though they were eating from the same trough as I was. Besides, Will is on permanently now, and he's getting fat on the slops. Will says that Jensen isn't a bad fellow and treats his poets, of which he has a nest of chirpers, with due consideration. Oh, Jensen is eccentric, all right, but he seems to work his aggressions off in the direction of the Dean, not downward. I hope this is true.

Somehow, as Will went on about his new boss, my mind went back to a cocktail party a few nights before Betty Lou, Emily, Chuck, and I got in the old Plymouth and headed out of Walton. Crowder sidled up to wish me good luck. I mean, he didn't just stride up, but came obliquely, as if to make it appear an afterthought.

". . . but I can't understand why you fellows wanted to ruin a good thing," he ended. I shall always pride myself on having kept my silence at that moment. And I've learned since then to vary my silences, ease the expression around the mouth and eyes, and occasionally to roar. This has helped me at Pierpont and earned the grudging respect or toleration of Groat and, I think, his opposites on the staff as well. Groat even takes me fishing now and then.

Of course, Halloran is a little disappointed in me for not agreeing with him one hundred percent of the time, but his system allows that only he can be right that often anyway.

Because, after all, I was a Hastings man at Walton, and one should profit from one's experience.

With Jack Emory

THE WAY HE WENT   Hastings was not to blame for assigning him three freshman sections at impossible hours and plunking him down for the fourth among engineers reading *Hamlet*. Schedules were worked out by Roper in the English office. Only as a symbol of the PLACE was Hastings really involved, and only as a sort of irrational revenge against the PLACE and against Hastings for having asked him to Walton could he use a bad teaching schedule as reason to resign from the *Walton Review* staff. Nevertheless, he permitted himself the irrationality. That was the way the game seemed to be played at Walton anyway. He wondered how his conscience would sort out his actions, for he knew he would wrestle with himself later on.

Well, he would probably not be at Walton much longer, no matter what he did. The grapevine of academic gossip had told him he was being considered for a good job elsewhere. The news came in the usual sinuous way—from a friend at his old school, who had heard from a friend at the school in question. He was awaiting with some confidence a direct approach. He admitted to himself that this knowledge made his contemplated resignation perhaps only theatrical.

But he did it. The reply from Hastings was brief and full of pique. He thanked him for his earlier interest in the magazine, regretted his inability to work with the team, commented on his well-advertised dislike of Walton, suggested perhaps he might be happier in more congenial surroundings, and wished him well on his research. A postscript announced that Roper had been instructed to look into his schedule. In spite of everything, Hastings managed a high note at the end, but the lines had been, once and for all, severed. Roper made some schedule changes, and Jack surrounded himself with his teaching.

The semester moved on toward Christmas. In mid-December he received in his office a surprise visit from Sheffer, who was back, tanned and heavier in the face, from summer and the fall leave, which he had spent in southern Europe. It was a surprise because Sheffer had just returned, and doubly so since there seemed to be a convention at Walton that professors seldom if ever visited the offices of instructors and assistant professors. As soon as Sheffer came in and sat down it was clear that there was something new in his attitude, an air of experienced resignation which he was offering to share. It was that of the cashiered general who, with no thought of leading a revolt, accepts with just less than equanimity his acre of grass and the time to write his memoirs. The pleasantries over, their talk moved to Hastings.

"Jack, when you first came here to be interviewed, things looked very different indeed, didn't they?" His eyes flashed, and he smiled faintly. "But you should know one thing. He really has changed. I used to be able to talk to him, but now he's thinking, always thinking, about something else. Yes, he has changed. I used to know him well."

"I don't believe it. It must have been in him all the time. You just don't change like that."

"Maybe the potentiality was there, but he *has* changed. You could get through then."

Sheffer, whatever he did or didn't do, was a decent fellow. But then, there was Jason's appraisal, and the whole argument Sheffer proposed vanished in a poof. In fact, the words themselves even became ambiguous. "He's changed." What did Sheffer really *mean?* After all, there might have been some good reason for Hastings to desert Sheffer.

"Did you know when you left that he was replacing you?"

"No, not right away. It came to me finally, but only after I was on the boat and had time to think. I was confidence-tricked." Sheffer grinned.

"Well, I can't complain. He's never said anything to me that he didn't mean at the time."

Sheffer laughed outright now. "I hope that gives you solace. Actually, I just dropped by to say I hope you'll stay on here, but you probably won't."

"No, I probably won't, but Hastings won't be the real reason."

"Oh?" Sheffer did not seem to like that answer. There was distance in his eyes.

"The reason will be that this place is sick—the department, I mean. Hastings grew out of it." He knew he had gone too far, but he was not hesitant now, because nothing was really at stake. He had rushed well past the outrageous desire for career and cause, which had jangled his nerves for a year. Nevertheless, he regretted for a moment that he had put his friendship with Sheffer in the balance. Was it worth the purgation his words had allowed him?

Sheffer declined to answer directly. "I've been here a long time." He was looking down at his shoes, two-toned, well shined.

"Yes, I know that."

"I suppose I'm part of it."

"Well, you're in it, but I didn't say that. I'm in it, too." He weaseled out. There was nothing more to say. It was difficult to meet Sheffer's eyes. Because they were friendly.

Later on, when the news was out that he was indeed leaving for good, old Pyles called him into his office. It seemed to be one of the old man's momentary impulses, but one couldn't ever be sure about Pyles. Jack seated himself gingerly. He had never spoken with Pyles in private before, their acquaintance being limited to departmental meetings and large social events. He had sensed early enough that they shared little.

"Mistuh Emory, you are leaving us, I heah."

"Yes, at the end of the term."

"I understand that you did not offer us the opportunity to, ah, engage the enemy, ha ha, and perhaps meet your offer." That was Pyles—out of the departmental swim, though he probably protected his domain. So Pyles could know little at first hand of the relationship between the young men and Hastings. Pyles would believe that things were done in the old way, that the department somehow controlled its own destiny, made its own appointments.

"What you are getting at, sir, is that I should have the professional manners to speak with Vanner about it and let the policy committee meet." He knew that Pyles would not like this frontal approach, but he harbored in his mind the thought that there was an opportunity before him if he drew the old man out and established the tone of their intercourse.

"Yes, I am saying that." Frowning, he fumbled with some papers on his desk. He had not expected this turn of the conversation. "Mr. Emory, I have, as you know, opposed the appointment of modernists and the watering down of our curriculum, but I recognize I am in the minority. That means I must accept the development. The

276

fessed to being a poor helpless man, collapsed into the same hapless Walton-made discontent that ravaged poor Hatfield when he thundered for airwick. She must, he urged, realize that it was childishness reaching out against childishness, because that was the way they played it in the local style. Then, she voiced a suspicion that it was all an act on his part, and he confessed again that recently he had found himself acting a part and that this was the way it should be, because acts—like his act before Pyles—were conscious efforts. And he used for illustration her own acts with him, which were finally better acts than her smiling girlish performances with Hastings—her impassioned, loving, laughing acts when she wanted, really wanted, Jack to be pleased with her.

"You are a damned intellectual," she observed, making it sound vaguely illicit.

"Aha, that's it. When you buttered him up, he never suspected it might be margarine, never looked closely enough. So you extract from him no sperm, but letters and documents and people he knows. And now you are off to the big cities, and he is pleased at having made his Daddy badge. Everyone is happy. It is a success."

"You are a beast."

"An intellectual beast. I have swallowed Doctor Millmoss."

"A Houyhnhnm."

"No, a poor horse of instruction."

She smiled, then became serious, detached.

He said, "Let's promise to meet before too long. I'll be coming east."

"Yes, and, yes . . ."

"What?"

"Nothing."

"You were going to say something."

She couldn't go on. So he said it.

"Perhaps you were going to say that this wasn't the time or place for us to have met. But perhaps I'll soon be ready."

She nodded, her lips tense, holding back something, perhaps tears. She was beautiful. He knew she had probably said too much to Hastings, maybe even in a way betrayed him, but he did not care and did not want to hear of it. He knew she did not mean to betray him. "I want, I want" lay ironically on his mind's tongue. The words of a child reaching for the moon. It had not been the right time. He left her, knowing that she, too, felt a deep sadness in the throat. He would do her the honor of not playing to or seeking the advantage of her sentimental feelings at the moment. Another time and place, he hoped.

At term end there were good-byes to make, but fewer really than he had imagined. There was an evening with the Talbots over a huge bottle of brandy, which sent them off together the next day on a Sunday hangover trip, mainly to clear the inner air, but also to symbolize some enduring bond.

After that he was not long in Walton.

There was rain in Seattle, the long winter rain that one could walk into and almost through without getting wet, the rain that came with the incessant low-rolling clouds funneled from the south between the mountain ranges, hanging along the Cascades and over the Sound. He was cut adrift in that sea of mist, and he prowled the town for a week before he could settle in to his work and the book he had tried to finish all fall but which wouldn't end itself without a contest of will.

In-between days, he faced in the quiet of his own darkness the face of himself and the face of Ann.

"I am pregnant, and he will come," she seemed to be

saying to him, and she was right, because she had now begun to see herself differently.

"Maybe not because you're pregnant, but he'll come. You might as well not underestimate yourself. Do you want him, though?"

"I want something." That was honest at least.

They did not make it closer. Ann had changed; it was not nearly so imperative that they should.

She was, he thought, like a dog entering a carpetless room, gingerly testing the footing, slipping slightly, looking tentatively back, forward, and around for a bit of rug. She came daily up the hill from her studio, sometimes in the car, always while the children were in school, to the same flat he had taken the summer before. His bearded landlord with the luckless brush and insipid canvases prized him as his critic-tenant and had kept the rooms vacant except for occasional transients all during the fall. She came and made more coffee than he could possibly drink and faced his few breakfast dishes, which in his own sort of monkery he would have left until evening. He could not tell what had really occurred during the autumn between her and George. That they were unwinding a small string was clear enough, but it unwound slowly, until one evening George came to see him, and they could not help talking outright.

Ann had said little except that George wanted to come. It was "about us," and Jack had braced himself for her confession or diatribe or whatever was pressing down from above to make her watch the floor as she said it. But it did not come, and she left that morning as quietly, the breakfast dishes done and coffee served with a single scone, as ever before. No ominous grimace accompanied her departure, no hint of a portentous event. He did not forget that she was pregnant and vegetating, but he knew also she was dead to her past and living in her own womb, waiting for the child or for Will, but mostly, he thought, for herself to come crying into some, if not brave, at least new world.

In this detached preincarnation she had so puzzled George that he had consulted his conscience even more of late, and he had, he now announced, thought to come for talk. He was tired and older.

"To the family head." Jack smiled ironically at his own words.

"Well, yes, I guess you are right. She isn't herself. Oh, I don't mean her feeling for me. I can see that's hopelessly damaged. I have tried to accept that, I think. But she isn't concerned. We just go on day to day. We unravel a little more, but nothing is settled."

He had himself felt detachment: the academic world was suddenly swept from him, and he was mistress to his work. A letter from Walton no longer meant anything.

George went on. "The point is that we must *do* something."

He was silent.

"Oh I know the child is not mine." He was up and pacing. Silence made him spell it out. "I just can't abandon her, even if she wants it. Besides, well, I don't think she's in good health—mentally, I mean."

Was it easy to be noble if you had money? No, that was not fair. He was simply trying to be decent, and he couldn't get through to Ann, because she wasn't talking, wasn't born yet, waiting for the miracle. "Is, er, the, ah, father going to do anything? I mean, I really don't know what she wants. I can give her money, the children, a divorce, naturally. I suppose she's ready for that. But if I bring it up, she's blank as a wall. It's eerie. Frankly, Jack, it's driving me nuts, too."

Often at night, in the droning conversations that seeped half audible through the floor boards from the flat above, he had heard Mr. Flaherty saying with seriostupid pomposity to his big, thick son, Hughie, or his Amazonian wife, Lena, "I do not know, I do not *know.*" As if that were really a considered opinion.

He found himself echoing those words and could not suppress a smile. George was disconcerted, did not know what the smile said, had not been used, lately, to smiles, so, seeing this, he tried to right it. "I *really* don't know." But it was no good. George interpreted it as betrayal.

So he ended with a soft promise. "I'll try to do what I can. I'll find out what I can."

One thing, George was more knowledgeable about dismissals now. He had been inclined in the past to stay on and on. But this time it wasn't really a dismissal. Everything was upside down.

It is true that once or twice in those silent mornings he had tried to suggest plans, divorce, establishment of the children's future; but Ann was hardly listening. He would try again. But there was no luck and nothing to report.

Then Will Person did appear, preceded by the first letter, nearly the first word, that had passed between them since well before the term had closed at Walton. The letter was not one of Will's extravaganzas, but merely a note saying that he was coming to the coast, could he bunk in for a few days. There was, in fact, no time to answer. Soon Will was at the door, with a single suitcase and a trunk down at the station.

"Full of papers," he said. "That's all I own now. Laura's cleaned me out. Even pawned my truss." Only the last was the Will he had known. The rest was a Will some of whose characteristics were stretched taut into parody—evasive, sheepish, tired. They fumbled with conversation for days, Jack working when he could, but less and less, Will pacing, visiting the tavern, seeing Ann when he could—and, as far as it was possible to tell, nothing, absolutely nothing, happening.

Until suddenly he realized, because George would

drop by and sit morosely over coffee or beer—always by design, when Ann was not around—that he was, by the drifting of time and events and by his own inaction, becoming George's ally, if not in spirit, at least by default. It was, however, a silent alliance.

George had probably never really been forced by events to act on anything that mattered. Spoiled, spoiled for the imagination. And Ann was, too, but in a different way, by remaining a child, so that each event—their father's death, her own marriage, the babies—had merely happened in the same world as her own. Or at the most, simply happened *to* her. And now she seemed still to be waiting for someone to carry her off. Her first George had turned out to be no fierce horseman, no saint, though naïve enough, perhaps, for a sort of sainthood, and it was uncertain just how Will sat to saddle. Besides, might it not as easily have been someone else happening along that night at the studio when it must have first occurred? No, not just *anyone.*

And he decided that George thought this, too, whenever George wanted to make some fair, even fine and gentle, gesture toward them. George would be thinking that Will was as he had been—a phantom of her desire, a vehicle for some subjective dream. No real existence. But that made it worse. The dream reaching out and capturing the first body riding by.

In those slow wet evenings with the clouds rolling north up around the mountains, Will's being became, however, more inescapable. George was making ready, gingerly testing the cold salt wave, to act. He could not quite bring himself to take the plunge, so he went in hesitantly, first splashing himself tentatively, laving his arms, walking slowly into the tide.

Because George really expected Will to confront him. That was the school solution. One day it became possible to remark that Will was probably suffering, too, for

George in his own self-immolation had, if he had ever held on very strongly to the real world, forgotten that there was a share of grief and desperation in everyone.

Was Will afraid of the confrontation? Was that sheepish avoidance, the eyes flickering away to the shadows, merely a sort of social cowardice which Jason had suspected in him, or was he caught in a walking dream, not yet emerged from his months of blankness?

Let us assume the latter, he decided coldly, and try to explain it to George. All these people sick with experience. And so he approached the citadel of George's naïveté, ready to say, "He really isn't the traditional home-breaker of the pulps. He is in shock himself from the destruction of his own house. He is, really now, a sort of casual traveler whom we have surrounded. Don't think too badly of him if he does not come to you and ask her hand."

Too ironic.

"I must do something?"

"Yes, I think it amounts to that." But he was not, even as he spoke, absolutely sure that he was right about Will.

So finally George gave them what he had been given, passing on in a generous but fanciful, because uncreative, act some of his income. Along with the children, of course. The income was for the children. Because George, true to all the books, knew that in marital difficulties the mother should have the children.

On the night before they gathered around the big old oak dining-room table, now cut down to coffee height in Jack's place, three of them—Ann, Will, and Jack—drove to West Seattle to see Richard Fallon.

He would never tell Fallon what curious part his story had played in the little drama of Walton, still going on, because Jason had just written, "Well, another snorter, namely me, has done busted out of the corral." He did not know Fallon well, and he would say nothing anyway.

Fallon would only be puzzled about how his little story of desperation among youngsters had brought to a boil desperation among men.

The story had recently appeared in a little magazine, and, by a quirk of fate, Dave Eriksen, silent for months in the East, but ever a friend, wrote mentioning casually a story by Fallon he had read the other day that somehow almost got to it, to the Doris Weinstocks and to the children.

He had, he realized, never consciously made the connection. It would take someone like Dave to touch at once the analogy. He thought of them, at that moment, emptying the mouse.

In West Seattle they talked, as a matter of fact, mostly about baseball, until Ann and Nancy (she was all right, a lovely girl) retreated from living room to kitchen, perhaps even out of doors. They didn't know where, for he, Dick, and Will were arguing inconclusively about whether indeed Twitchy Dick Porter was or was not the Cleveland right fielder in 1933.

"All this is slipping from me," he complained. "I knew it all once." Meaning, of course, the *Spalding Baseball Guide,* by heart.

But Will made it a mountain. "Hell," he said, "we all knew it, every bit of it, once, or at least too damned much," and drank his beer straight down. Did Fallon wonder what that was for? But they came no closer to Walton's truth that night, because Will was making art of what Walton got into their conversation, and Fallon was laughing.

". . . And so at the last one here was old Love Dove with Miss Elvira in the act of. Well, I can only describe it as feeling her UP; and Clarissa on skates, saying Mr. Person will, will you please please take me ulp home, and sinking to the floor. I felt, holding her there, like Dracula in an old Grade B."

"It's a subject for study," Fallon admitted.

"Yes, but the radiation, the radiation sickness!" Will was burying his head. "Well, you missed that party at least, Jack."

"That's okay. It was worse hearing about it." He sensed that Will, with his comic invective, was back in stride. Maybe something could happen. Besides, it was clear that he hit it off with Fallon. So did the women. Two married, well almost married, couples. He was growing outside of it already. He felt either too young or too old, and then just deeply inside himself. He yearned for Ellen. He would take advantage of the sentiment next time. He hoped for a next time.

Later, in his flat, with the five of them for dinner, it worked well enough again, but he was himself lonely in the laughter and prepossessed, thinking of Ellen and then of George and the children. After a while he found himself telling, blurting out, the story of the Weinstock girl's death, blurting it out because there were now a couple of dead soldiers, but also because it wouldn't come out any other way between irony and tears. Finished, he could not really remember the point that had brought it up, so he said, "It was your story in a way, Dick."

"Jeesus," said Will, and Ann looked pensive. Will (no, probably not) and Ann (maybe) saw themselves youngsters, but for the grace of each other, trapped. He had made or destroyed the evening, and he had, as had they all, drunk more than he thought.

▶

The book of rules called for solemnity and practicality, so eventually around the oak table they would sit thrashing it all out in a way that was completely unreal—the protagonists and Jack, counsel for whose side? So unreal that most of the time he tested truth by rising, walking to the porch or to the kitchen, just to see if from some other

287

angle the lights still shone, the world turned. For George, having convened his committee, which was to plan the curriculum for a few lives, presided as he knew how, despite emotion. Jack felt for him, stammering, his hand tracing the wood's tough grain on table and chair arm. And Ann secretive and almost coy, self-satisfied (damn her, he thought), pristine in her maternity dress (for it was March now), and waiting, waiting, simply waiting. And Will, tired, an air of deep, even sanctified, experience his aim, which expressed itself rather in labored resigned movements of shoulders, of neck, of eyes rolled to the ceiling.

The chairman's offer was hardly debated. The lawyers would in time be called forth and the matter of the children sweetly settled with all the satisfaction and security that legality brings. He observed rather wryly that a bit of money to employ in the event of such a crisis in one's life seemed to be useful. But what did it do to you? He knew that the very existence of the money, flowing through the bank account of George Brocklin, might have to be blamed in part for the state of affairs that it now figured to improve. How much had knowledge of that apparently unending stream from Mom and Pop influenced the marriage? Indeed, was it not part of the shape of George's mind? The spectacles he could not remove?

He had, he supposed, allied himself with George, because he had begun to understand some of all this, and because it was foreign and hateful to him and a ghost he somehow felt he must confront. If he could not forgive, or not love, he might understand. And when that occurred, forgiveness seemed irrelevant and, if not love, at least some curious abstract (perverse, he thought sometimes) affection flowed in to engulf him. He would try no longer to say that George was a poor fool without remembering that we were all fools, the Yoricks of our own mirroring minds.

Ann had sensed his change, surmised perhaps that he disapproved of her, because, of all things, it was she who drove them toward what must have been the traditional way. There was suddenly in her a hint of recrimination, the refusal to talk, and some sarcasm. Too schoolgirlish, he thought. We are not playing puppy games. George's mind was simple, and he saw it through, through quip and needle, to the decisive, money-and-marriage-divvied end.

Then he regretted Ann's feelings, because he had not meant to take sides against her, and in a way he really hadn't. He had only found himself ready to give George the right to his own poor self, to admit that George could, after all, be George. Had he acted treasonously? Or had he overestimated his own importance? Ann spoke little to him. He faded. No doubt she and Will had made plans.

About them he was afraid to ask. George's known munificence would not really support them. Will merely alluded to that problem and passed on to events. They were going up to Fallon's shack near Snoqualmie and spend out the summer. As soon as the baby came.

"What then?" sang the economic ghost, but there was no answer. Perhaps Will had not heard. But Jack heard, and remembered that his mother must have awakened often at night to the same question.

And in May the baby came, a boy; and anyone who had seen Will would know there had been no cheating against *him* at least. Plans were now afoot. The Brocklin children would finish school with George. A housekeeper would be fully employed. Then they would join Ann, Will, and the baby for the summer. Was Fallon prepared? Was everything tied down and the good crockery put up on the top shelf? It would be like an Indian raid, for the children were nervous and undisciplined from the year's hopeless impasse.

But it seemed to work out, though he heard almost

nothing from Ann except that he was to remember the little easel behind the divan and send it with Tommy. Art-nannies all, he thought. She was free to develop herself, but it was really an emotional, not even an intellectual, Charles Atlasism. He wondered if they were terribly broke, and consequently he expected almost any day the touching letter full of self-examination. It never came; only the supreme relief of Will's letter about his job:

> Well, Jack, my lad, you won't believe this, but, like you and Jason, I'm going to put on my rubber suit and oxygen tanks and plunge back into those deep sea caves. There are creatures down there we haven't even seen yet! Ann says we should go to Santa Fe—one of the stops on the road, you know—but how can I turn down a noble rider like Kit Carson Jensen? Why the sound of his words alone makes the experiment worth it! It seems, in short, that he wants a live poet to grace the ladies'-clubs roundabout. I am growing a beard so they'll get their money's worth, and in a month or two I'll have it properly spattered with egg yellow and snuff. Besides, Laura reminds me that I must pay and pay.

Jack went up for a weekend. Ann was domestic. The children ran about in the woods. They all painted a bit. His still life, Ann insisted, wasn't bad. It was wretched. What did she mean? Where did she get off praising such tripe? It was an affront, but he really knew that she was not meaning the words as they seemed to mean. Will lounged around, drank beer, kidded the children, practiced on a big guitar of Fallon's. All serene.

He crept away on Sunday and that night wrote a long letter to Ellen, the first in weeks, full of amazed and sentimental respect for Ann. Then he tore it up and wrote another with respect and irony, which he almost mailed, but then he decided that irony was too much in the fashion. So he finished by beginning a letter which warned her that he would be in New York for the MLA and to do nothing drastic until Christmas. (Two weeks later the reply asked him what he meant by drastic. September would be better. Why not come in September? She would like for it to be September.)

Then one night in August he took a look at George standing in his doorway and decided they had better sit in some, if not clean, at least well-lighted place, where there were other people to break whatever might have to be broken. But first, together they finished the dregs of a bottle of Scotch Will and Ann had bought weeks before out of some chance ten-dollar bill.

Then he remembered that Scotch day had been allowance day, that poor George had shelled out. It was right that he should finish the bottle and throw it away, which he did later that night with a long arching plop into the lake.

They sat for a while and stared at the row of big pickle jars and the bowl of hard-boiled eggs along the bar.

"Want one?" George asked. He had the habit of generosity when it moved him or he thought about it.

"Guess so."

So they peeled eggs carefully and neatly with immense concentration, making neat piles in their ashtrays and, finally, washing the eggs down with beer. Then they drank some more, until George's rare silent self had fled. Essentially he was a talker, the silent self a boarder, no better than a hanger-on. A little more or a little less naïve, or maybe simply in another age he would have been a successful evangelist, and a sincere one. It could not be helped. He hoped that tonight would not be a bad one like the last time when George was tearing himself from the children and shrieking down under. It had been bad, nearly with tears. And momentarily he had hated Ann, chiefly for what seemed to be oblivious smugness but was really, he supposed or hoped, self-protection and the firm decisiveness he had been seeking from her for months. Nothing satisfactory, and he dragged himself to judgment.

Always George had worried questions to the ground. Now, his analytics defeated by months of confusion during which Ann, refusing to talk, had totally disarmed him, he was quiet, sunk in some wondering passive acceptance of life as it came to him—straight through the eyes. Only slowly did the drinks drag him loose and willing back to his old habit of relentless pedagogical pursuit, but now it was not an urgent chase, only the shouting and barking after everything had been decided. He was curiously calm. Soon Jack recognized that he himself was becoming the subject of George's talk. He was not sure that he liked this turn of events. It was enough for him alone to dwell upon himself, upon that moody malingering egocentricity which seemed to have been strangling him throughout the last couple of years.

"I wonder," George said, his face striving for and nearly succeeding in achieving an expression of ironic humor, "if it wasn't some romantic vision of your freedom that made her do it—regret her position, I mean. She always thought you were leading an interesting life. She used to speak about you in graduate school. And then, with children . . ." He gazed toward a pickle jar, his chin propped in the tripod of neck and forearms. He looked a head, lolling there. Lopped off.

"She used to talk about how awful it had been with your father, especially at the end. He must have been quite something. Up and down the economic ladder. And then the whole year after he died."

God knows it had been bad, because Ann at eighteen would give up college after a year, when they all tossed the week's wages on the dining-room table. And their mother would be frantic for days with insomnia, wondering if she could hold on to the house, grieving that poor

Ann might marry below their *proper* station. It was pathetic: their mother had thought at least *that* had been avoided when she found George.

"She used to talk about your father and how she admired him so, until the shock of the debts. Then she hated him, I guess. And just about that time you were emancipated, leading what looked like an exciting life in the war, and then Princeton." It was when Princeton came up like this that he wished devoutly for everything to stop. George was too self-satisfied, and too silly. He felt like throwing glasses. "And then that intellectual life, teaching in the East and no big responsibilities and knowing poets and publishing your book, and . . ." But his voice trailed off, until he stopped entirely and then said, "I want a pickle. Pregnant, I guess." His laugh was just below a sort of hysterical giggle. But he picked up the line again: "And so there you were, her new shining example, her new but unapproachable father-figure."

"Well, I'd never thought of my profession or my life in quite that way."

"But she did; never finished college, never got to be a senior, when you can't wait to get out and some of the professors begin to look pretty silly. And don't tell me you didn't like the worship." He was a teacher, himself, waving a finger. "Because, as I see it [his words were thicker now], there's a bit of the old man in you, too." He tried to smile and shrug off his own statement, but it was easy enough to see he was glad he had said it.

"Oedipus, do I hear?" Because Arthur Ryerson had appeared suddenly at their booth, through the smoke and beer smell and the noise that had raised everyone's voice to a shout. "All Oedipus, I suppose." He sat down, for George had moved over a bit for him. "Speaking of symbols, I hear Will has gone to the mountains. He'll make a bad poem of that, poor man. But where can you go? Too much nature around here, can't get it all inside you. Besides, shouldn't mix it with high emotion. Look what it did to Shelley." He was changing the subject, seeking the abstract because he suddenly realized it was George beside him. But he was botching it, and soon Jack was trying not to listen—a good man, too, Ryerson; we all stick our foot in it some time.

George's words had been no revelation to him, only that George would say them; for months now he had known it all to be true. Even in his most bitter periods of resentment and disillusion he had been partially awake to it. Had Ryerson not appeared, what would he have found to say? He did feel a kind of identity, after all, with his father. He loved himself enough to think it love. But would he have protested had not Ryerson parted the smoke?

The beer had made him feel unwilling to argue with himself. He would admit to loving Ann, and she must admit to loving that wild image that remained in him, only the third or fourth carbon of some old gentleman who rode out from Massachusetts willfully to escape sin and told the Indians to move over.

That loving careless romanticism—because there was no frontier now out where all the savages were white, protestant, and republican—had ruined Ann's barely civilized marriage with an insured income and, in the parlance, a "nice guy." And all that had made her actively seek her own frontier. Had it, too, created her proper destiny? He thought, And perhaps she is free of me, after all.

George had been talking to Ryerson. The words filtered back in. "Well, they're doing it on my money, but what the hell. Who cares? Who cares?"

But suddenly Jack did not wish Ann to be completely free of him or he of her, only of reason.

Later, in the efflorescence of two whiskeys, a few beers, and a walk to the lake and back up the hill, Jack propped himself up in bed and watched lights playing on the ceiling and wall. He could not sleep for thinking. Of daddies big and small—fear, hatred, power, dependence, love, the grave plot in Portland, of himself and Ann and how she had lost a father twice, once in death and again when she began to think what his life had been to his children. And she had, by lack and pining desire, because she really was a young, romantic, and somewhat intelligent girl, constructed, from the silly outward grace of his own partly Princeton-patched and wholly insular but not insulated surfaces, the image of a gay, intense, meaningful life. He had been a big daddy and had not known what to do about it. Does anyone know how to be a big daddy? Some, he supposed, slowly learned, when they ceased to seek like children for its secret.

It was in its way awful, he thought. People searching, like Ann or even Brendan Berrigan, each in his own kind of pathos, and all the daddies searching, too. And all the children, for who was more a child than George, who had done at the last the gentlemanly, even, he supposed, the fatherly, thing (after studying like a schoolboy in all the books the way to make a home)? And what really was Hastings but a child seeking children to call him Pops? To lead and tyrannize and gather from them their thanks and appreciation and their debt. Someday he would throw away whatever book, mythical or not, he read at night and indulge in one simple act.

> Dear Child, I also by pleasant Streams
> Have wander'd all Night in the Land of Dreams;
> But tho' calm and warm the waters wide,
> I could not get to the other side.

He still could not stop thinking, thinking back now, back to Walton.

▶

295

He forced himself to make the appointment well in advance, and it had dominated his mind ever since, taking precedence over his last few Walton classes and his thoughts of Ann's troubles and even Ellen. For a long time after the famous spring meeting, every thought of Hastings had sent his nerves reeling. He had discovered himself groping back down the dark alley of his own past stupidities to relive them in a better way, to capture them for his own. He anticipated the meeting with no great hope, but he did foresee himself ritualistically blotting out the two whole years in the act, as one erases with a flourish the diagrams and scribbles from a blackboard after a not very successful lecture.

Miss Lamb, no more than a corporal, ushered him into Hastings' new domain. He had not seen it before. It was smaller than his Dean's office, but in terms of leather and general opulence it went far beyond. In the old office there was always a table or two piled carelessly with books, magazines, letters, the contents of filing cabinets. And the shelves were stacked with books, so that their every cranny was filled. Here all was neat. Perhaps in the old office the impression was too calculated to suggest the administrator-scholar; but now even the illusion was no longer apparent. He began to value the illusion. It was possibly a sincere effort. Now, in the single large bookshelf each book sat in its pristine dust jacket. He saw that the library comprised, arranged by date, the publications of the university press. Except for the top row: Dickens, the Victorian novels, *Who's Who in America,* sharing space. On a sherry table top sat a large Webster's. Everything in place, even the desk clear except for a single file folder placed for consultation. Hastings himself stood behind the desk, staring out his tall wide window toward the observatory and the old chemistry building. Jack thought capriciously of Thurber facing his ROTC officer. Completely irrelevant, except for the absurdity.

After a moment Hastings turned around, talking before the pivot had been completely executed. "You know, Jack, for ten years Masters has been trying to get someone to take seriously the fact that we need a new chemistry building. It's downright dangerous to have all those kids in that firetrap. By God, now that I'm here I'm going to do something about it! Sit down, sit down!" He came around the desk, pulled up a chair, sat smartly, crossed legs. They faced one another as on an old-fashioned railway coach. "You've come to tell me you are leaving us. Dr. Vanner sent on your resignation, of course. Couched, incidentally, in excellent language." He was comparing unfavorably the previous letter about the magazine. "I wish you luck."

Jack could not answer. He looked out the window. A student he recognized as one of his desperate repeaters was dashing madly across campus. The tower bell was sounding the beginning of class. He saw him at that instant drop his notebook, papers spreading across the brown winter lawn. He ran about trying to retrieve them. Two coeds on the path nearby watched him as they passed. It was easy to imagine them giggling at the figure he cut. He wished somehow to rush out to him. Borgman was his name. Henry Clay Borgman, chasing the last sheet of paper out of Jack's range of vision.

"Of course, I think, I'm convinced, that the opportunity is really here. I can't help feeling that where you are going is perfectly all right. A piratical institution as far as getting faculty, I must say. But we are looking ahead more rapidly, particularly with the state's expanding economy. But you haven't been happy here, so you should go. Yes, you should go."

"I just wanted, before I took off, to come over and . . ."

But Hastings was not really listening. He was on his feet and at the window. "Yes, I think we can do it. Now that Honors Program plan, that was, in my opinion, your best work here. Now we can go ahead. It's no secret that my predecessor was skeptical of it. He didn't like some of the implications—intellectual elite and all that. But now the situation's different." He still watched something across campus. "But you haven't been happy here. I've had several reports. Dr. Cassoway expressed some worry about you even last spring. You didn't seem to take part or want to know your colleagues. He said he'd never even had lunch with you . . ."

"He never asked me."

". . . or seemed able to communicate with you."

Jack decided he might as well say it.

"If I'd had any doubts, the rumor that Cassoway may become chairman would have been enough to send me looking. He represents what's wrong with the department!"

Hastings whirled around. But his expression was entirely bland, and Jack saw that the remark had not dented him, had not really been the cause of his pirouetting so quickly. He was thinking far ahead of Jack's voice. "But what I regret most is that some of you couldn't find it in you to have more affection for me personally. One wants to work among friends, one needs to feel that there is more than just a sort of tacit cooperation. That's what we haven't had, isn't it?" But he was at the window again with the question.

Jack wanted to say to him, "But when have you given us the chance?" Even as Hastings appealed to break down the wall between them he was building it higher by choosing to ignore the remark about Cassoway. Prolific disagreement? You just couldn't be frank with him. When you were, he turned you off before your argument made sense even to yourself, and you were a fool. Even as Hastings evaded replying, since this was a ritual situation and it no longer mattered what was really said or done, he was reaching out for aid—drowning in politics. He can't reply to me about Cassoway. He can't trust me not to repeat it. He can't afford to lose Cassoway's vote.

So Hastings thrashed around, while there he stood, immobile, leaning carelessly on the deck rail, neglecting to toss even a rope. Things had gone too far. But as he felt this coldness, this fact of their separateness, almost this sadistic delight, he was oddly moved. He wondered how he would have felt a year before had this moment then occurred between them. Could he have exerted his influence for good, and could he—inexperienced as he was—have helped? Finally, were there such moments he had overlooked? No, he thought not. Furthermore, the moments would have to have been of a different quality then, because he was different. If Sheffer was right, Hastings was different, too.

Even now, with Hastings retreating behind his vice-presidential desk, the moment was lost, but in it he knew more of the terror of Hastings' mind than he had imagined before. Hastings had dragged himself up out of the pit that was Walton's English Department. He had married well, acted correctly, done some scholarship, hoped, and in a case or two, perhaps, betrayed old friends. But he had probably saved a few as well—Sheffer, though in a sense betrayed, may well have been saved. And he had tried to find a place for McCrea. The risks probably haunted him. Scandal would ruin his administration. But with the younger men, where he most desired to succeed, he had failed. Did administrative paranoia claim him early and motivate him wholly? Did he really lack courage? Was he too jealous of his own position? Was it a vein of pomposity which made him occasionally play the bitch? Did he need Berrigan as a butler? Must he glory in Crowder's obsequies? And beat the poor puppy Davis? Was he the fake Person thought him, the dangerous mon-

omaniac of Jason? Or, saddest of all, was he overly conscious of his own limitations and seeking to hide a pov-
erty of intellect behind a façade of enthusiasm, always
trying to figure out what the intelligent act might be on
the basis of watching others whose minds he knew surpassed his own? Terror: Was he, after all, what one
simply must expect of the new academia?

Suddenly he really saw Hastings before him. He wished
to reach out, to say something that would strike away
their antagonism and a part, at least, of the past; but
nothing real came—only trite rejoinder to the formal
words of farewell that Hastings was speaking. He discovered himself forced back into a state of mind that now
seemed its own cell. He did not like it there.

As he walked out of the office he couldn't recall precisely now what impulse had made him come to Walton
in the first place and what hopes and fears had guided
him or led him into dark forests once he arrived. But, too,
he thought of Hastings no longer as the simple immense
academic operator, watching with Cheshire-cat cunning
his own every move in the business of his career. He knew
that Hastings would have liked to be such a man, but he
could not be. Could anyone really? Should he have liked
Hastings more or less for this obvious flaw in his mechanical brutality? And as he questioned he was overcome
with a curious sadness, not as if something had passed
away, but as if something had never come to birth or was
a monster stillborn.

In the quadrangle outside, a squeaking January sun il-
luminated the gold ball on top of the flagpole. There
flashed before him from twelve years before, as they had
lowered his father's casket into the ground, the same sun
lighting up the white gravestones in the soldiers' cemetery
off on the hill.

What, he wondered (old symbolist that he was), could
be the point of that?

▶

Now it had been three long days since Ann, Will, and the kids had come down from their mountain; after a single night of talk and beer he had made no effort to communicate with them. As far as he knew, they would leave tonight on schedule for her so-called new life, unmarried. But that would be settled in time, and no one need know. It had been four days since, sitting in a chair facing the front screen door in early dusk, he had suddenly become aware of a shaggy, dirty collie staring expectantly through the screen across the dark air of the outer room into the circle of light where he sat. The suddenness of his awareness joggled his memory. The collie stood on all fours with head no higher than the crown of its back, perhaps slightly lower, its neck thickened by a heavy ruff, no doubt uncombed from winter, arching sinuously and tapering to a long pointed nose. He had not seen the collie come up, but he knew that it had mounted slowly, head down, with nose and neck almost swanlike to the tip of each stair. Its eyes glittered slightly in the light, but not like a cat's, and its face told him exactly what it wanted, though doglike it kept the secret of its why.

The dog wanted in, with a patience and intensity that suggested there was only futility in ignoring or even actively discouraging its silent demands. He remembered a strange little dog that had appeared at a cottage his parents had once rented for some summer weeks. It had insisted on its right to the front porch. Several days passed before a neighbor told them the cottage had been the dog's home until the present owners had bought it for rent property six months before.

The collie barked. Only a squeaking yip, ridiculous for such a large dog; it sat on its haunches now, swung its left paw up and down, scratching the screen. Jack made a

point of ignoring it and went on reading, turning obliquely in his chair, the collie still visible out of the corner
of his eye. It stood again, walked in a circle, then another,
flopped on the porch floor. Jack's attention held now, it
groaned deeply. He could see above the frame of the
screen the fur of the collie's back humped like some old
rug over which a door could never swing open.

Two hours later, after hearing the collie's intermittent
groans and yips, and watching it move through the same
cycle of action—standing, sitting, pawing, and circling—
he walked to the door and pushed against the fur bundle.
The collie sprang to its feet, and in its haste to enter, head
low to the door corner, made it impossible for him to
open the door more than a crack. Blocked in the brief
confusion from the immediate completion of what was to
be a philanthropic effort, he allowed the door to close
with the confused collie's weight, strode to the kitchen,
and took some food from the refrigerator, leftover stew
and milk.

In the past four days the collie had made itself at home.
It had come with lice about the neck, and he had sheep-
dipped it in his bathtub and nearly sheep-dipped himself.
Since then he had allowed it the run of the place. The
collie had no license, no identification tag, no clue to its
ownership. In those four days the dog dominated his domestic existence—he fed it, washed it, brushed it, walked
it. It had by its own volition become his charge, and he
had become involved in ownership without quite realizing what had occurred. But eventually his ad, placed in a
Seattle paper, brought results. The phone announced that
there was indeed an owner. He was not really pleased.

In an old Dodge sedan complete with children calling
for Lassie (the simplicity of the name had evaded him),
the owners appeared. The father was embarrassed, the
collie friendly and sniffing, but not exuberant. The children seemed to have confused him with a pony. All was

shortly accomplished. He turned down the gesture of a reward and sent the rest of the sheep dip along, hoping it might be used. Collie and family were in the car, the dog blasé, the children hanging about it as it braced itself on the back-seat cushion with nose out of the window waiting for the wind.

By the time that this living property had been exchanged for thanks, the rightful owners newly returned to their responsibility, the finder relieved of it, it was dusk. He had re-entered the house and walked to the back porch alone. Sitting there looking due west toward Queen Anne hill, where the new street lights patterned the hill in an arc like a motionless Ferris wheel, he saw in a fit of capricious musing everything in a sudden single configuration of air, earth, fire, and water. The whole scene was a wild dreamlike allegory. Below the carnival's trade mark, which were those lights, and encompassed by them like the ancient anthropomorphic picture of earth and sky, were the lineaments of some profane comedy. The houseboats moored together in strings out into the lake below him were caught burning with reflected lights. The long hill and the bridge hung in the sky to the right. The bridge arched over the canal leading to the Sound and finally the ocean; and behind the hill, completely shut off from his view by that massive hill-wheel of lights and houses, were the mountains he could not see. If he leaned out over the back-porch rail and looked down, he could see the shore where Ann's studio stood, now deserted even of canvas.

Looking at this arch of carnival lights for a moment he felt it suddenly drained, like so much allegory, of essential life, of real people. It was a curious illusion, for the lights moved, the city was not exactly quiet. Walton had driven him solitary from the world. He wanted Ellen to be with him, and he thought for a moment of Jason sitting quietly watching from a chair in the Beaver Room, of Ralph Ware working, working and taking the politics as it came, as perhaps it had to come, and of Henry Hastings, his wheeling-and-dealing rhetoric, his awesome dreams of Walton grandeur. For a moment, Crowder, yes, even Crowder, shuffled into the picture, as on a campus walk—getting along, just getting by, to class. The poor bastard, he thought, but he did not wish to pity him. Where was Berrigan? He could not quite get Berrigan in. Like Professor Godbole in the novel he had worried down with a bunch of sophomores in the fall, he conceded that he could not manage everything, but he was willing to recognize that awful terror and imagined with some other eye the sweating Brendan blustering along the hall and rapping at his door. Would he open some day for bears? The world flooded back, and he thought of all the people who indeed were below him in the houseboats and how those catwalks must shake like tightropes when one ventured out on them, and how the least waves made them bob and jostle, and how dirty the water was. How many people would come down the walks later that night not much drunker than he had been when he came back from the tavern with George the night before? They would try not to steer off into the water, and if they were with a friend they would try to steady him and both might end up dunked. But it didn't matter that much. There were things to hang on to—old pipes, frayed rope ends, log pilings—and only the neighbors would hear the yelling.

It was nearly dark now: 8:30. Ann, Will, and the kids would leave on the train in a half hour or so. He stood for a moment and watched the car headlights move in counterpoint to the blue lights of Aurora Bridge. Below it in the dark a lighted tug was pulling something out to the Sound. He heard Mrs. Flaherty upstairs shout something at Hughie, and Mr. Flaherty's voice droned "I do not know, I do *not* know." Hughie was at it again, asking questions. Jack went to the closet for his jacket—the night air was chilly. He had just enough time to get to the station to kiss Ann and the children good-bye, to wish Will good luck, to urge them to write. He was worn out with, nearly destroyed by, real and final farewells.